INTRODUCING MRS COLLINS

INTRODUCING MRS COLLINS

RACHEL PARRIS

CORONET

First published in Great Britain in 2025 by Coronet
An imprint of Hodder & Stoughton Limited
An Hachette UK company

The authorised representative in the EEA is Hachette Ireland,
8 Castlecourt Centre, Dublin 15, D15 XTP3, Ireland (email: info@hbgi.ie)

5

Copyright © Rachel Parris 2025

The right of Rachel Parris to be identified as the Author of the Work has been asserted by her in accordance with the Copyright, Designs and Patents Act 1988.

All rights reserved. No part of this publication may be reproduced, stored in a retrieval system, or transmitted, in any form or by any means without the prior written permission of the publisher, nor be otherwise circulated in any form of binding or cover other than that in which it is published and without a similar condition being imposed on the subsequent purchaser.

All characters in this publication are fictitious and any resemblance
to real persons, living or dead, is purely coincidental.

A CIP catalogue record for this title is available from the British Library

Hardback ISBN 9781399751612
Trade Paperback ISBN 9781399751629
ebook ISBN 9781399751643

Typeset in Bembo MT by seagulls.net

Printed and bound in Great Britain by Clays Ltd, Elcograf S.p.A.

Hodder & Stoughton policy is to use papers that are natural, renewable and recyclable products and made from wood grown in sustainable forests. The logging and manufacturing processes are expected to conform to environmental regulations of the country of origin.

Hodder & Stoughton Limited
Carmelite House
50 Victoria Embankment
London EC4Y 0DZ

www.hodder.co.uk

For my Mum

who, like Charlotte, is highly practical,

quietly capable, occasionally opinionated and

with a tremendous capacity for love.

VOLUME
ONE

CHAPTER I

Charlotte Lucas made a choice.

Am I doing the right thing? she wondered briefly.

But Charlotte had lived for twenty-seven years doing the right thing. She had been, at varying times, dutiful, obedient, prudent and polite – at least in public. Whether or not this was the right thing was yet to be determined, but it was her choice, and hers alone, and that in itself gave it merit.

'Yes,' she answered. 'I accept.'

She and Mr Collins stood in the lane, soggy leaves and wet gravel beneath their feet. She shivered; she had not had time to find a shawl. Mere minutes earlier, she had seen him approaching her house, walking with some purpose and, keen for a private moment without her family listening, she had run outside into the cold to greet him.

In truth, she had guessed in the last few days that the prospect of his asking her was a possibility, and she had prepared herself for it. Knowing that today was his last day in the neighbourhood, she had stayed near a window, ready, waiting, thinking about her answer, wearing a pretty but modest dress. No shawl though; it really was just the cold that she hadn't planned for.

Now, Mr Collins was approaching her too quickly, closing the few feet of space between them, gravel crunching underfoot with a wide smile on his face. 'Miss Lucas, your answer delights me more than you can know!'

He reached out to grab her hands, and she instinctively withdrew them, then realised her mistake and offered them out for him to hold. His clammy fingers found hers, and she trained her eyes on his face.

His face. A placid smile was fixed on her own but, as she studied his, she thought what an odd face it was: not ugly, but somehow almost without feature. If she were asked to describe him to a stranger, she would not know what to say. For some reason, she was briefly fixated on this obstacle.

His eyes are blue, she could safely observe, but beyond that she would be at a loss. *He has cheeks and a mouth* she might continue. Neither sharp not rounded, neither merry nor serious. His nose was a nose such as a man might feasibly have; his eyebrows were where they should be, more or less. She thought she might be having a turn.

Tall, she thought. *He's tall; that much I can be sure of.* She was relieved.

He was still holding her hands and seemed quite content. She had never looked another human in the face for this long before. It was almost meditative. *And he has dark hair! There!* thought Charlotte. *Not featureless after all – he is tall, dark and ... pious.*

He was still holding her hands, and she believed even he didn't know what to do with them. His grip was gentle. She would try to put that down as a positive.

After an awkward two minutes of clasping, he placed one of her hands on the other and patted the top one before finally releasing her. 'I should not keep you out in this weather, Miss Lucas. I shall talk with your excellent parents, and then I shall take my leave. We shall start making arrangements immediately, I think?'

'Yes,' said Charlotte, rather dazed, and then, rallying herself, 'Yes, we should indeed!'

And with such assurances, Mr Collins walked towards the house and found the front door opened for him before he could knock.

Introducing Mrs Collins

So much for privacy, thought Charlotte; someone had certainly been watching. He looked round at her and waved continually as he took small backward steps into the house, as if Charlotte were the Prince Regent.

Once he seemed safely inside, presumably in the library with her father, Charlotte crept into the house through a side door, found her way to the parlour and leant against a wall.

At that moment Charlotte found herself alone, with leisure to really consider the step she had just taken. She looked about the room; it had a cold light in the mornings, being north-facing, and the effect was enhanced by its pale-blue walls. And yet it felt warm, inviting, because it was filled with items she knew so well: the mahogany cabinet bursting with books; the old, worn globe that sat in the corner, moved there because it had kept getting scorched by the fire; the figurines on the mantelpiece, always treated with such care by her mother; the portrait of her grandparents, gold-framed, above the fireplace. She looked closely at that picture. Even in a formal stance, her grandparents succeeded in looking happy with one another.

Charlotte pondered whether she would find such happiness in years to come, for she did not feel it yet. She had not expected to feel a rush of love or a giddy excitement following her engagement – and she didn't, so her expectations were met. Good. Such feelings were reserved for younger or more romantic people – people like her sister Maria or her friend Elizabeth. She also did not expect to feel those things because this was, after all, Mr Collins, not a commanding naval captain or a rakish duke, nor even a particularly burly farmer. This was a financially stable clergyman with a large vocabulary, an even temper and the prospect of a generous inheritance.

She sat down. She drank the remains of her tea, which had long gone cold. She could tolerate cold tea. She could tolerate a great deal. Mr Collins had taken six full minutes to propose, during which time he had not required any response from her. He had listed every reason he had for marriage and for marrying *her*. If there were one word to describe the proposal, it was *thorough*. But in fact, this had given her ample time to compose herself, and once he had finished, she was able to greet him with a firm answer. His style of proposal suited her rather well.

And now, having given him the answer, she half-wondered whether she might panic; she put down the cup just in case. This had been, after all, quite a morning. Her life would now change completely; she would marry, move away, leave her friends and family. She had just attached herself, forever, to someone she did not know and who, judging from this short acquaintance, seemed to have half her intellect and a great many opinions about chimneys. She had reason to panic. But such a response would have been a first for her – and it did not come.

Her mother entered the room, shutting the door behind her, and looked at her daughter quizzically.

'I said yes,' said Charlotte, as if in answer.

'I know, darling. Your father has given his permission.' Lady Lucas searched Charlotte's eyes and did not see what she had hoped to. She wanted nothing more than to see Charlotte settled, but she was also a sensible woman and knew the compromise this was for her clever, cherished daughter. Charlotte's acceptance had surprised her greatly. 'Charlotte, are you absolutely sure?'

Charlotte was irritated by this. She knew she would likely have to endure disapprobation from other quarters, but she resented having to defend her decision to her own mother, who, of all people, should understand her circumstances. 'I am not given to rashness, Mother, as you know. Yes, I am sure. In truth, as soon as he arrived in the neighbourhood, I saw what a strong prospect Mr Collins was for marriage.'

'Materially.'

'Not just materially,' snapped Charlotte. 'He seems calm, well-educated, and with good connections.'

'He proposed to Elizabeth only days ago! You must understand my misgivings?'

'I do not relish that history either, Mother!' replied Charlotte hotly. 'I'm not delighted that he was interested in my friend before he noticed me; I do realise it is not the romantic ideal. Nobody will be writing about this union in novels or committing it to poetry. I shall not recount these details to my grandchildren as a touching story. But I will not allow my pride at being second choice to stop me from taking up what I believe to be a good opportunity.'

Her mother nodded rather sadly.

This irritated Charlotte more. 'Mother – I am engaged! This is *happy* news.' Charlotte didn't look happy; she looked livid. 'I do not wish to console you on my choice of husband. *You* should be *congratulating* me. It is a good offer—' Charlotte started to say, then added more bitterly, 'It is an offer.'

Her mother did not answer immediately. She occasionally regretted the extent to which her daughter had inherited her practicality. She sometimes wished she had raised Charlotte to have more whimsy, more naivety. Lady Lucas herself had married for love and, while not regretting it, had known enough financial constraint to want security for her daughter. But she also wanted love for her. And she knew this was not it – she didn't even need to ask.

Charlotte now had tears in her eyes and a reddened cheek. Mothers can have this effect on daughters, at any age and in any situation. No matter the fierce and independent women they grow into, daughters still long for their mother's approval, and Charlotte was still waiting for hers, frustrated and a little hurt.

Lady Lucas looked closely at her eldest daughter, her firstborn – her favourite, in truth. She moved closer to her, holding out her hands, and Charlotte instinctively reached out and took them. They stood together, eye to eye, as her mother tenderly moved a stray hair off her face.

Lady Lucas sighed. 'You deserve the world, Charlotte. But we do not always get what we deserve. Our task in this life to is to find happiness in what we are afforded and to improve what we find.'

Charlotte's mother had a great many idioms and proverbs at hand for every occasion, many of which she had rendered in embroidery and hung over the mantelpiece. They were mostly lessons in stoicism and had certainly had an impact on Charlotte's outlook, even if they made for rather drab decoration.

Charlotte nodded. 'I *know*. That is why I—'

'I know, I know. It is a good offer,' said Lady Lucas more encouragingly. 'I understand. You will have your own household, your own society and, God willing, children. The gift of children is worth putting up with a great deal. I will only ask you once more, and then will never repeat it, I promise: *are you sure?*'

Charlotte's eyes were dry now, and her heart had calmed. She came back to herself, rather harder and more resolved. 'It is a good match. I knew my mind when I accepted, and I shall remain firm on it. I shall have a home of my own. I shall start a life of my own. I have made my choice.'

CHAPTER II

Charlotte Lucas had not been offered many choices in her life. As the eldest of seven siblings, living still in her parent's busy home – which had more good standing than it did income – she had been shaped into a woman who was above all rational. And like many rational women, she was somewhat undervalued.

Her family's circumstances *appeared* rather elevated, but while her father was now a knight, his background had been in trade. He had risen first to mayor, from the influence accorded to him through his success in business, and from there, he had managed to propel himself to his current status. He was very gracious in his new position, displaying the confidence and merriness that had helped get him there, and even his appearance suited it: red-faced, rotund and tall, he was the picture of a beneficent gentleman. But once knighted, he had found a disgust for the business that made his fortune, and he had turned his back on it altogether, thinking those days behind him and beneath him. This had not been a wise or timely decision, as his wife had warned him, but his optimism trumped her caution, and Lady Lucas had not felt secure in their fortune since that time. If her husband could be elevated, he could as easily fall again, and she had readied herself and her children for such an event.

Charlotte had been raised in this careful, watchful spirit. She was diligent in her studies, not just to give off the air of being accomplished but because her future might yet require the ability to teach. She was helpful in the kitchen, not only to have a well-rounded knowledge of food and flavours, but because extra help was necessary. She was patient, not only with her siblings and with her friends but with her own prospects.

Love suffereth long ...

Not only was this another of her mother's embroidered moral decorations, but it was a phrase Charlotte had heard in church on countless occasions.

Love suffereth long and is kind. Love vaunteth not itself, is not puffed up. The passage from Corinthians made its way into almost every marriage service.

'The bride looks like she suffereth long and is a little puffed up,' Charlotte had once whispered to Elizabeth at a friend's wedding. Elizabeth had snorted, attracting disapproving looks across the pews. Charlotte had kept a straight face – always the good girl to all appearances.

So, Charlotte knew that she, too, must suffer long. Over many years, she had watched friends and cousins find their partner and marry and move away from her and make a life of their own. Sometimes, they stayed within the neighbourhood; sometimes, they moved to another part of the country entirely or, in one case, to Woking, which was worse. She had found herself looking upon these partnerships and departures with a detached air, enough that she had almost made a study of it: the art of securing a proposal. She enjoyed espousing her theories of courtship to friends, in part to mask the fact that she'd had no experience of it herself. She had many views on romantic love and yet had never felt it. She was, in truth, sceptical that it existed, which made it much easier for her to be logical about it.

Charlotte had never been courted. She had read about love in literature (and even, occasionally, in the scandal sheets) and had wondered when it would come for her, but it never did. Neither from her nor towards her. And so, she had decided she was an unromantic person, a woman for whom love held no interest.

But she *was* interested in marriage. Marriage had the potential to offer her more freedoms and more security – an attractive combination – and it was one of the few choices afforded to a young woman of her standing. But Charlotte, at twenty-seven, having been *out* for ten years, had begun to realise that she was unlikely to receive even that choice. No option had ever been presented to her.

Until today.

The next morning, Charlotte set off for Longbourn, wrapped up warm, steeling herself for the winter winds and for Elizabeth's reaction, uncertain which would be colder.

She had been determined that the news of her engagement would not reach Elizabeth's ears unless it was from herself. The greatest threat to this was Mr Collins himself; he had been residing at Longbourn, Elizabeth's family home, for the past fortnight, but Charlotte had entreated him to keep their engagement quiet until his departure, and he had set off this very morning.

Charlotte Lucas and Elizabeth Bennet had first met five years earlier and in spite of the seven years that separated them in age, had taken a liking to one another almost instantaneously. While Jane, the eldest Bennet sister, was the more natural companion for Charlotte; closer to her in age, and in temperament, it was Elizabeth who proved to be the right match. While it was obvious to all of Meryton society that the pair shared a sense of humour, their friendship had deeper roots. In Charlotte, Elizabeth found a patience and steadiness that was a welcome contrast to the Bennet home, a house held hostage by the chaos and caprice of Elizabeth's mother and her younger sisters. As for Charlotte, she found in Elizabeth a boldness and spontaneity she often felt she herself lacked.

That said, she knew her friend well enough to know she was a romantic and somewhat judgemental. Of course she was: being judgemental together was one of their favourite pastimes. How unhappy a circumstance to now be the subject of that censure, when ordinarily they would share in it.

As Charlotte was a just a few steps from the doors of Longbourn, Elizabeth herself opened them and welcomed her with a wide smile. 'Oh, Charlotte! Come in! Oh, I feel like I could sing!'

'Please don't!' Charlotte replied teasingly, pleased to find her friend in high spirits. 'What has brought on such drastic behaviour?'

'Why, you will join us in it when you hear – we may all breathe a little easier. He has gone! At last! Farewell Mr Collins!' cried Elizabeth.

Two of the other Bennet sisters stood behind Elizabeth in the hall: Jane, the eldest, and Lydia, the youngest. There was a giddy relief among them all – even Jane, who was usually tolerant to a fault.

Charlotte smiled awkwardly.

'Although,' continued Elizabeth, 'he threatens us with another visit, so while he is gone for now, we must be ever ready for his unfortunate return.'

'Like ringworm,' added Lydia gleefully, earning a look of disgust from Jane and a chuckle from Elizabeth.

Charlotte spoke before more was said that pained her. 'I have news, Eliza. Could we speak alone?'

Elizabeth's face fell serious. She showed her friend into the parlour and ushered out yet another sister.

Charlotte sat and looked her friend in the eye.

Like a cold bath, it was better to just get into it directly without delay; Charlotte knew trepidation would only make things worse. 'Mr Collins called on me yesterday, and he asked me to marry him.'

Elizabeth gasped, and her hands covered her mouth. She, again almost laughing, uttered, 'Oh! Charlotte! I am shocked … so soon after he asked … but anyway, I am sorry for you! Was it very awkward? Did he take—'

'And I accepted him. We are engaged.'

Elizabeth let out the remaining half-laugh she had been holding in. But seeing the seriousness on Charlotte's face, she stopped. 'Engaged to Mr Collins! My dear Charlotte, impossible!'

Charlotte had expected this indignation and kept her reserve. She cooly defended her position, and Elizabeth, with some effort, held back her natural incredulity long enough to offer mealy-mouthed congratulations. Both unable to speak further, they joined the Bennets in the next room, relieved for a while by alternative company.

But as Charlotte was preparing to take her leave, Elizabeth drew her back into the parlour.

Evidently her feelings had been bubbling away, and she now allowed them to burst forth, saying vehemently, '*Why?* Why did you say yes Charlotte? He is dreadful.'

'He is not to your taste.'

'He is not to *your* taste, Charlotte. We have laughed at him *together*. How can you make this decision? It makes no sense!'

'It makes perfect sense, Eliza. I am unmarried and older than you, and unlike you, I am not inundated with interest from all quarters.' Charlotte's patience was now wearing thin.

'Better to be alone than tied to a man like that.'

'Is it? Are you so sure? What experience have you of being alone? And living on what? You would have me be a spinster into my dotage, while you are married with children and a home of your own, and I, a lonely friend you have to visit occasionally. Is that what you would wish?'

'*What* is this fantasy you've concocted? Charlotte, I do not know from where these thoughts have come—'

'I have thought about this for *years*, Eliza! Do you not imagine that every season, each as fruitless as the last, I have wondered what my future will look like, wondered how I will secure my happiness, a home, a family. Have you, as my dearest friend, never considered that question *for* me? Or have you thought only about your own prospects, which are so much happier? Did you not think, in turning down such a man as Mr Collins so easily, what a lucky position you were in – to feel so certain of what you have to offer, of your looks and your advantages, that you need not even *consider* it? What a luxury that is, to be so sure. I do not have that luxury.'

Elizabeth was quiet but not calm, and she could not look her friend in the eye. After a minute, she said, 'I hear what you are telling me, and I do understand your fears … but I cannot believe you will find solace for them in *that man.*'

'I had hoped for support from you …' Charlotte's voice was low and warning now.

Elizabeth crossed towards the fire and began furiously poking it.

Charlotte continued, 'I knew you would not have done the same thing, but I am trying to do the right thing for myself—'

'You are not doing the right thing!' cried Elizabeth, rounding on her.

There had never before been a scene like this between them. For a moment, they each raged silently. Elizabeth was more openly agitated, whereas Charlotte, cursing the tears in her eyes, slowed her breath and found her stillness, which was a power of hers.

'You have made your feelings clear. Perhaps I will see you before I leave. Good day.'

Her cool grey eyes could have chipped ice into Elizabeth's, as she rose and exited the room.

Charlotte walked quickly out of the house, avoiding any other Bennet, and made her way towards home.

Once out of sight, she bent in two, stumbling and sobbing. She thought the sorrow would overwhelm her. She felt more let down by Elizabeth than her heart could endure; she felt tangible sharp pains in her chest. She had never been subjected to such an outpouring of disdain. And from the person she esteemed most in the world! She had read pity and disgust on her friend's face and had been made to feel foolish and small. Of the faults she knew others levelled at her, *foolish* had never been one. Plain, certainly, a little stiff, but not foolish. Foolish like Mr Collins ... And now, she had to start a new life with him, without a friend.

All morning, she had stood firm, but now she felt the ground go from beneath her. She stumbled home unsteadily and ran upstairs. She pulled her shoes off and threw them in the corner, tore off her jacket, loosened her stays and got into bed. So much had changed in so short a time.

'Was that you, Charlotte?' she heard her mother call from downstairs. 'Is all well?'

'Yes, Mother,' she called back in a reassuring tone, while pulling the covers up to her chin. 'All is well.'

2nd December 1811

My dearest and most precious lady, the keeper of my heart, Charlotte,

The very name now makes my heart sing – I know not what hymn, my dearest, perhaps even a Wesleyan anthem, but certainly a song of praise and of thanks, and one approved by God and by your father. I knew in my heart (though not immediately in my head) as soon as I met you that you must be intended for the place in which you have found yourself – by my side. I believe it is not only God's intention for us to wed but also mine.

Your first thoughts upon reading this must surely be to wonder how the news of our forthcoming nuptials has landed upon the auspicious ears of my esteemed patron Lady Catherine de Bourgh. Allow me to put you out of suspense, my dearest one, without even a momentary hesitation – without even the suggestion of delay.

Before I impart her reaction, let me tell you that she was eager to know my choice and indeed asked about the subject even before I had raised it myself; such is her generosity of spirit. When I first described you, the conversation went thusly:

'Who is her father?' was her first excellent question, to which I replied simply, 'Sir William Lucas of Lucas Lodge, my lady.'

'Ah. Very well then,' she replied.

Such vivacity of response is a great honour to you, my dear Charlotte, and when she heard that we were to marry forthwith, returning to Hunsford immediately, her delight was hard to surpass: 'You may both visit me within the month of your return' – an utterance that brings me only slightly less joy than your acceptance to be mine. Lady Catherine has such flair when it comes to her calendar.

To think of you at the altar before long is beyond delightful, but I am perhaps even more enthused to imagine that which must come next.

I refer not to the necessary act that must take place within a marriage, which I should not draw your attention to so soon, but which I have now already put to ink upon the page, so I shall let it be. But I should be at pains to mention that the prospect of that act brings me no fear or foreboding. I am happy, and indeed willing, to fulfil the role bestowed upon me as your husband. However, the future thoughts I referred to above are not of that act, which I now regret the repeated mention of – but in fact, they are of you in my home – our home – settled and happy.

To think of you at Hunsford Parsonage brings me great joy. I have wanted little in life but the peace and security of a life of duty, a pleasant enough position in society, friendship enough to be visited from time to time, and most importantly perhaps, the love of a wife and a family. (The patronage of Lady Catherine is an addition to my joy I never even knew to wish for.) You are the key to my happiness, Charlotte; I hope I can be the key to yours. I shall endeavour to be – until death parts us.

I do so wish us joy, Charlotte. I feel sure we must deserve it – two fine, goodly, modest people, embarking on a life in Christ, and in Kent.

Your humble servant,
William Collins

3rd December 1811

Dear Mr Bennet,

I could not settle until writing to thank you most humbly for your hospitality in these past weeks. So much has happened in a very short time that I would think it had been a year! (Had I not the dates written down in front of me, which I have.) In fact, as I left, I overheard your youngest daughter remarking that it felt like a year since I had arrived! That shows how in accord I have been with your family.

Your kindness in permitting me to stay and in allowing me to partake in a variety of social occasions with you and your daughters shows a great generosity of spirit. While I admit that there were advantages for you in having a man of my position join you in such company, I assure you that it was I who felt fortunate, even more than you may have.

As for myself, I am delighted to tell you that I have recently found the very greatest felicity – and only a mile from your own door! I am engaged to Miss Lucas of Lucas Lodge. She has made me the happiest of men, and I hope that she will name the day as soon as possible. We shall be married from Meryton, and it is my wish, as well as hers, that you and your family might attend.

I must touch briefly on the subject of the entail. I will not be ponderous. There is no reason for me to be explicit about something that is already well known – that being the fact that, upon your death, I shall inherit the estate of Longbourn in its entirety, and your wife and daughters will be left with nothing, perhaps destitute. I have no wish to speak of it. And yet I must, only to explain that my sole purpose in proposing marriage to one of your daughters was in kindness and selfless Christian charity – an attempt to rescue them from the future that was before them. I now believe that Elizabeth did me a great service by refusing me. She saw very well that I was making too large a sacrifice in asking for her hand. I hope that, in the future, she may receive a proposal from a more willing gentleman — as distant a hope as that may seem to you and certainly does to me.

However, I hope that your wife and your daughters will feel compensated for their future loss in the knowledge that their home will now fall to such a dear family friend as Miss Lucas. It must give your wife great comfort to know that such an intimate acquaintance, who has known the house so well for many years — and is, after all, local — will have the honour of being its mistress. That thought — of your comfort — guided me in my choice of wife, and be assured I mentioned it in my proposal to her.

I need not tell you, sir, how happy my current circumstance makes me. You married for love, one presumes, and so you must know how much joy springs forth from such a union. You have only known Miss Lucas as a life-long friend of your daughter, whereas I, in a week, have the measure of her completely. She is the perfect match for me: her temperament is calm, her voice is melodic, and her words are easy to understand. I have found myself a diamond in the rough of Hertfordshire.

I am grateful indeed to you for the invitation of a further visit, and I will gladly oblige. I will return in a fortnight to stay at Longbourn. I will spend the chief of my days at Lucas Lodge, becoming better acquainted with my excellent new relations, but I will happily honour the Bennet family with my company in the early mornings.

Until then, I wish you and your family every happiness that can justly be afforded to them.

Your humble servant,
William Collins

CHAPTER III

'The arrangement of the dinner service shows a fine taste, Lady Lucas, and may I admire your tablecloth? Is it cotton?'

Lady Lucas looked at her future son-in-law and fixed a smile on her face. 'It is linen, sir. But I thank you for your attentions. It is a fine design.'

'Fine indeed. I have always thought that simple floral patterns suit a house best, unless it is a very large, grand house, which may support a more complex aesthetic.'

Lady Lucas looked down at her meal, hiding a raised eyebrow. Attempting not to sound pointed, she asked, 'You have a particular interest in the decorations of a house, sir? You speak about it often.'

'I do, madam. I confess, I was something of an artist in my youth, and while I was never allowed to pursue it as a pastime, I retain a certain vigour of opinion about artistic matters, and I do believe one's house is a canvas, if one so chooses it to be.'

Lady Lucas, who was a naturally generous and diplomatic host, tired of Collins's conversations. He had called on her daughter most days this past week, for tea or dinner or a walk in the grounds. She consoled herself with the thought that those visits would soon cease, but then, remembering that the conclusion of them would bring about the loss of her daughter's company, she frowned and glanced at Charlotte. Her cool, calm expression, the patience in her eyes – she had learnt that from her mother. Charlotte would have this man, this conversation, every day for the rest of her life.

Introducing Mrs Collins

No, only for the rest of his life, Lady Lucas reminded herself, this rather dark thought giving her hope.

After dinner, Charlotte and Mr Collins sat close to one another in a corner of the drawing room, while the rest of the Lucas family occupied themselves nearer the fire. Mr Collins wore the black suit he always wore, constantly a little crumpled, the white neckcloth always tied too loosely and dropping at the neck, Charlotte observed. She wore a pretty but simple cream dress, with long sleeves and a surplice neckline. It looked well on her, suited her frame, and she felt it was a choice which must suit the present company, being modest but not drab.

Mr Collins, Charlotte noted, was quieter when they were alone than when in company.

He opened his mouth as if to say something, then thought better of it. Then, a moment later: 'I hope I did not offend your mother by mentioning larger houses earlier.'

'I assure you, you did not. She is not so easily wounded, and she is proud enough of Lucas Lodge to welcome any comparison.'

Mr Collins smiled tightly, and another pause ensued. After a time, he continued, 'I sometimes find that in my attempts to keep conversation flowing, I speak more words than I intend to, and they wander farther off from my object than I wish. My intention is to appear confident, and I hope I achieve it. I would not be much of a prospective husband if I were to show nerves in the face of a simple dinner party.'

Charlotte looked at him, but his eyes were cast down. 'You feel nervous in company?'

'Well, I do, a little. But I have learnt to fight against that. I work hard at self-improvement.'

'You need not fight against your nature with me, sir. I would rather you were as you wish to be, or rather, as you need to be?'

'I am thankful, Charlotte, for those kind words, but I cannot give in to it. I believe nervousness – shyness even – is not a welcome trait in a man. And is certainly not suited to my profession. My father, God rest his soul, was not a man who approved of weakness, in body or mind; he thought it rather self-indulgent, and I half-agree with him. I do not believe that God intends us to navigate through life with the bare bones we are born with, but to use the tools he has given us to learn new things, new behaviours. I have learnt to talk even when I do not know what to say. But I am not always … completely happy with what I say.'

Charlotte considered this, reeling slightly at how much he had revealed about himself. 'Was your father … a kind man?'

'No,' Mr Collins replied instantly. Then, as if to soften his response, 'Not kind in his manner, day to day, but he meant to do well by me. He was godly, albeit with a preference for the teachings of the Old Testament than the Gospels.' Collins glanced at her, to see if she understood his meaning. She did.

'Punishment for wrongdoing? Rather than turning the other cheek?'

He hesitated. 'Y-yes.'

Charlotte reached over and put her hand on his. He was shocked and looked up at her. 'I offer an alternative view: I have always believed that strength can be shown quietly. A commanding presence can be one who says less but understands more. When I feel nervous in company, I find strength in watching and listening to others. It arms me with information, and it calms me. And it offers the opportunity to examine the needs of others rather than focusing on oneself – which is the Christian way, is it not?'

Mr Collins was looking at her, enraptured. 'You are wise, Charlotte. I knew this from the start, but you prove it further every time we meet. I am grateful for you.'

Charlotte gently squeezed his hand and smiled. Had he been misjudged? Or judged on only his worst behaviour? She felt a little hope seep in, for the future life they might have together. She was enlivened and said boldly, 'I know you invited me to name the day for our wedding, Mr Collins, and I have tarried. I will do so now: 9th January, if it pleases you. Let us begin our married life as soon as we may.'

'A fine date, Miss Lucas – Past the duties of Christmas and the frivolities of Twelfth Night. I approve it heartily.' He looked around the room contentedly, his eyes resting on the Lucas family, seemingly having a merry time playing a card game. 'Charlotte, may I ask you a question?'

Charlotte realised that he had not asked her anything about herself yet during his visits and welcomed this correction. He was certainly improving.

'By all means.'

'Do you think your family would like me to offer them a reading from Ephesians? They appear to have run out of activity and I know Maria in particular enjoys to hear the scripture.'

Charlotte looked down to hide her expression, which betrayed her. 'That is thoughtful of you, Mr Collins, but I think their minds are in no state to receive it. I believe they will be preoccupied with whist until they retire.'

Mr Collins considered this, not entirely convinced by the response. 'It is no trouble, if that is your concern, if you think I would be nervous performing, given what I was saying a moment ago. Reading the word of God is no chore for me; I do not choose the words, and its goal is not to entertain but to guide.'

'It may be no trouble for you to read, sir, but it can be a trouble for some to hear. A few moralising passages from the Bible may put a sour taste in the mouth of someone torn from their gambling.' Charlotte said this lightly, with a grin, relaxing enough in Mr Collins's company to be more herself in conversation.

But his face had darkened. 'I am sorry to hear of this malady in your family, Miss Lucas. You may well imagine that I do not approve of cards taking precedence over piety. If this is true, I will hope to be a much-needed influence on your family while I can.

I try not to be evangelical in my beliefs, but where there is need, I will rise to the task.'

He looked truly aggrieved. Her face fell sombre, and she looked over at her family, laughing around the card table. Her father was mock-outraged at his wife's mode of play, and Maria was in hysterics at the face he was making. Charlotte felt a physical pull to be with them, to be in that circle, merry and light-hearted.

She looked at Mr Collins, who was also observing her family. He viewed them with interest and concern and a little puzzlement. If one came across a set of badgers in the wild, one might watch them in a similar way. He was very unfamiliar with their behaviour; he did not understand it, and somehow, he felt it potentially posed something of a threat to him.

He was right. His wife-to-be was thinking of what she might miss in her future with him. Would she, in her family life, get the pleasure of a light-hearted game of cards? Would the opportunity to laugh be very frequent? She thought not, for in his response she realised that, while he might have moments of reason, Collins had absolutely no humour at all; and that was a severe limit on one's personality, she had always found. He would never be in on the joke.

'I am sure that, at the right time, you will be an excellent influence on them, Mr Collins.'

Mr Collins warmed to this. 'Please, call me William.'

Charlotte immediately and instinctively felt that she didn't want to. *Not a good sign,* she thought, smiling at him.

CHAPTER IV

*Hannah
Wife of Charles Twyford
Born 7th July 1745
Died 9th January 1791*

Charlotte was clutching her bouquet and staring at the headstone. It had caught her eye as she left the church. This woman had died on this very day, twenty-one years before. Who had she been, Charlotte wondered? Just *wife* – that was the most she had been remembered as. Her husband had been allocated both of his names, and he had not even died. Well, he might have done by now, but this was not his headstone. It was hers, Hannah's, and she had not even been given her whole name. And no word of who she was: no *beloved* or *kind* or *gentle* or any of the insipid things that were writ on the stones of some dead women. They only ever list the gentle traits, thought Charlotte. They never say *outspoken and nearly always correct* or *fiercely loyal* or *physically very strong* or *excellent with horses*. No, always *tender* and *mild*, like the Virgin herself. And this woman had not been given anything except *wife*.

And now, as of a few moments ago, Charlotte was *wife*, too.

The ceremony had run smoothly. Charlotte felt comfortable and well-presented in her pale-blue dress and pelisse; she did not feel beautiful, but then she had not expected to. Everyone had sung well, and she and Mr Collins had spoken their vows as well as one could. At his request, they had heard about how long love suffereth, as if they did not know by now, and at Charlotte's request, they had sung 'Glorious Things of Thee Are Spoken'. Mr Collins was dressed in his ordinary garb, though better turned out than usual.

In attendance were the Lucas family, Mr and Mrs Bennet, Elizabeth Bennet, and two of Lady Lucas's friends. Charlotte's sister Maria looked angelic as her bridesmaid, eighteen years old with blonde curls and a breathless excitement about the event that was not widely shared.

Mr Collins clutched his hat now as he stood in the doorway, speaking earnestly to the vicar of Meryton. The Bennets had taken their leave, giving Charlotte an array of differing congratulations; Mr Bennet had wished her 'the best of luck' with a wry smile. Mrs Bennet had hardly looked at her and had said, 'Well, we all know you will have a comfortable life. I wish you well,' while visibly wishing Charlotte ill. Elizabeth had failed to hold her gaze for more than a moment, managing to make the phrase, 'I wish you joy,' sound like a death knell.

Sir William and Lady Lucas were wandering with Maria out of the churchyard, towards the gate. Charlotte stood unobserved, pondering what her own headstone might say, aside from:

Charlotte
Wife of the Revd William Collins

Frugal, perhaps. *Neat and tidy. Thin hair.* She was being rather hard on herself and was determined to rally before she left the churchyard, but she took this moment to be unmasked, at least to herself.

Low spirits had struck her as she walked back down the aisle after the service. She felt unrooted and anxious. The second she left this place, she would get into a carriage and depart for a home she had never seen, a place she was unfamiliar with and a man she did not entirely like. She reasoned that her feelings were to be expected and were, in fact, reassuringly rational. But the rationality of her feelings did not change the difficulty in experiencing them; she felt mad.

'My dear Mrs Collins, there you are!' Mr Collins appeared from around the corner. 'The carriage is ready. Shall we take our leave?'

And with that, she left her old life, and all that was familiar to her, to start anew in Kent. She braced herself.

As they arrived into the village of Hunsford, the winter skies were already darkening. Mr Collins had fallen asleep on the journey and was snoring beside her, his head fallen back against a cushion. She leant right out of the window and spied, not half a mile ahead, a pretty white house, with tall trees either side. As it came into view, she noted how the windows glowed against the drizzling murk of the afternoon; the candles and fires must be lit, and she saw a figure on the doorstep.

The rattling of the carriage on the drive woke Mr Collins with a start, and he hastily arranged himself, before realising with delight that they had arrived. He was rosy with eagerness to show Charlotte his home – *their* home, as she must think of it now. He helped her down from the carriage and, walking towards the house, began his introductions.

'Hunsford Parsonage is one of the oldest rectories in this part of the country, my dear – you will be mistress of a significant piece of history. And here – good afternoon, Mrs Brooke!'

'Welcome back, Mr Collins, and good afternoon, Mrs Collins – what a pleasure. You must be cold; we have the fires lit.'

The housekeeper smiled warmly, and Charlotte liked the look of her immediately. Mrs Brooke was a diminutive woman in her fifties, with a kind, lined face, wearing a smart brown dress and a bright-yellow kerchief tied about her shoulders. She indicated the front door, inviting her new mistress to enter, and a moment later,

Charlotte stood in the flagstoned hall, inspecting all around her, with Mrs Brooke helping her remove her coat and gloves.

Mr Collins showed her around the downstairs: his reading room, the drawing room, the dining room, and then a charming sitting room with bookshelves lining all of one wall and a comfortable-looking chair in one corner.

'I had thought this could be yours, Charlotte, for your own pursuits. I am not a voracious reader, but you see I have had shelves installed recently for the accommodation of your own books, of which I supposed you might have many and like to collect more in the future.' He paused, looking around the room, checking it was as he had left it. Then he looked at her for approval.

Charlotte felt the thoughtfulness of this gesture and, as occasionally happened, saw again a glimpse of the more thoughtful, agreeable side of her husband. Turning to him with real happiness, she said, 'I think it is perfectly suited to me. I like it very much. Thank you.' And she meant it.

Mr Collins's face transformed with the joy of a scheme done well, and he gave a quiet grunt of satisfaction.

Shortly after this, Mrs Brooke showed her around the upper floors and, at Charlotte's request, promised to save any explanation of the more intricate aspects of household management until tomorrow. The house was not large compared to Lucas Lodge or Longbourn, but, for a country parsonage, it was ample, and it seemed to have a wealth of land around it. There was much to explore, and Charlotte felt the excitement of it.

Once she had changed her clothes, she retired to her sitting room for the hour before dinner and started to set out her books on the shelves, choosing exactly the order and placement she would like, taking the time to examine each one, considering when she had last read it and when she might again.

Charlotte's chief interest in reading had always been to learn. Growing up, her father's house did not have the vast inherited library of an old estate (as Elizabeth had enjoyed at Longbourn), so as a family, they had built their collection from scratch. Because of this, Charlotte was not complacent about having good books to read; they still held delight for her. She had always encouraged her father to invest in heavy tomes that could stay in the family for generations – multiple volumes in gilded binding, from Smollett's *History of England* and Gibbon's *Decline and Fall of the Roman Empire* to the complete works of Shakespeare. But these choices were not only for display and prestige – they added to her and her siblings' education, and moreover, historical works genuinely interested her more than the sensationalist novels her friends seemed to enjoy.

Upon leaving her family home, she had not been able, of course, to bring with her all those books that were the backbone of the Lucas Lodge library, but she had amassed a collection that was squarely her own, including a dictionary, an atlas, a few smaller history books, a couple of the publications of Dr Johnson and – the only softening in her reading tastes – a wide variety of poetry. She had collections by Cowper and Scott, Blake and Burns, Donne, Milton and, her favourite, Wordsworth, whose *Poems, in two volumes* looked scruffier than their neighbours on her poetry shelf, ragged from use.

Her small library arranged, she stood back and admired it.

Tea had been brought for her and left on a small side table, steaming away. A fire was burning, casting shapes on the wall opposite, and Charlotte sat in the large cosy chair that she already thought of as hers, looking at the drizzle outside and enjoying the contrast of her own warm contented state set against it. She wore her grandmother's shawl around her shoulders.

There were challenges to come, she knew – she was not blind to them. The imminent wedding night held a good deal of disquiet for her. But here, now, she felt content. She felt, for the first time since Elizabeth's scolding, that her decision to marry had not been a stupid one. There was sense in it; there was comfort in it, and it was laid out before her in the pleasure of seeing her own books, in her own room, in her own house.

Mrs Collins sat back, pulled her legs up under her skirt, and took a sip of tea.

15th February 1812

Dear Elizabeth,

I hope you and your family are in good health. I am, and so is Mr Collins. I have not heard from you since leaving Hertfordshire, ~~which has been a great disappointment~~. I will now impart my news to you, ~~though you have not solicited it~~. My new home is comfortable, and I am growing fond of the village and the countryside around. While the house is peacefully situated, the landscape around it is pleasingly diverse.

My duties keep me busy during the week, as too does the upkeep of the house and of my garden and the occasional social event, though there are not as many as I have been used to. ~~This letter would be longer but I tell you nothing of my marriage because I fear you do not want to hear about it and will scorn not just it but me.~~

I write to ask you again to please come with Maria and my father when they visit me next month. ~~If we were ever friends, then you will offer me this service, if only in commemoration of a friendship lost~~

15th February 1812

Dear Eliza,

I hope you and your family are in good health. I am, and so is Mr Collins. I have not heard from you since leaving Hertfordshire, so I will now impart my news. My new home is comfortable and peacefully situated, and I am growing fond of the village and the countryside around; woodland, streams, thorny bushed lanes and treks across muddy fields abound. It offers the kind of walks you enjoy almost more than I.

My duties as the rector's wife involve making visits across the parish to see those in need: in need of food, solace, company or help. You might think I sound as if I am applying for sainthood, but the work makes me feel the opposite – rather pampered and naive next to some who truly suffer. I visit all kinds of people: a mother of eight who has just given birth and is of meagre means, a young widower who is grieving badly, a retired colonel who lost a leg in battle, and an elderly lady who is dying from God knows what and who remains extremely forthright and domineering, even while her colour is pallid and her body too weak to move. I think being near the end has made her more outrageous. I like her.

So, I see a great many people during the week. But I have not yet found a friend. I miss your company more than anything else I miss in Hertfordshire.

I write to ask you again to please come with Maria and my father when they visit me next month. I would very much welcome your company.

Your friend,
Charlotte

CHAPTER V

Charlotte rose from her bed in a panic and in an illogical stupor, having overslept. She rushed to the window, from where she could see anyone approaching the house. There was no one yet, thank heavens. She opened her curtains more fully and realised from the sun that it was no more than ten o'clock in the morning. The party would arrive no earlier than noon. She had plenty of time to ready herself.

The night before had been something of a trial. She had wanted a peaceful evening, in readiness for welcoming her father, Maria and Elizabeth the next day, but her husband – excited by the prospect of company and perhaps enlivened in a particular way by the thought of showing Elizabeth all that she had missed out on – had made it clear he wished to be intimate with his wife. As those occasions had been so infrequent in their marriage so far, she had not felt justified in demurring.

Their wedding night back in January had been an odd one. Charlotte had had taken a drop of brandy and steeled herself mentally for what was to come. She'd even pinched her cheeks a little and arranged her bosom; while she might not have been attracted to Collins, she still wanted to be attractive to him. He had come into the bedroom in his nightgown, carrying a cup of tea and a candle, looking for all the world like Wee Willy Winkie, and Charlotte could hardly countenance having carnal knowledge of a figure so comical.

He put down his tea on the mantelpiece, the candle on the table, and got under the covers with her. He took a moment and then, turning his face to hers, said, 'My dearest one, I am honoured to be the first to unearth the pleasures of—'

'My dear, if I may make a request, I am a little nervous—'

'Oh, my dear, but of course you are, I—'

'And as such, I ask that we might not speak during this time, so that our minds might be ... filled with the joy of what we are doing.'

'Ah.' He put his finger to his lips, and did a small nod, and an understanding smile, acquiescing, as he so often did (she counted her blessings), to her request.

He leant in and kissed her tenderly, nervously. His kisses, she found, were not overbearing – they were not too much. They were, rather, too little. While she did not want to be swallowed whole, this level of diffidence rendered any persuasion towards passion impossible. His hands hovered near her but did not yet touch. Finally, he had put a hand on her waist, still over the top of her nightgown, and she heard him murmur. His kisses became a little more fervent and his hand moved now up, to her breasts, still over her gown.

This tipped him over the edge. He gave a grunt, and his body was in torsion for a moment, and then he fell on his back, gasping. After a moment or two, he looked down, removed the bedcovers and, holding his gown rather carefully, left the room.

Charlotte did not know what to make of it. She was utterly confused. She could not be relieved, because she knew enough to be sure that whatever had just happened could not have been *it*. Her mother had not told her all, but she knew that bodies should actually touch and that it would last at least ten minutes and most likely be a little painful the first time. This had been painful but not physically.

After a long while, Collins quietly re-entered the room, in a different gown. He did not look Charlotte in the eye but lay next to her and, after a few minutes, said, 'That is all my energy can muster for tonight, my dear, but I give you my assurances that in the future, my appetites will be great indeed. I thank you.'

No woman wishes to be thanked after relations of any kind, but Charlotte was grateful for his good manners. If a marriage lacks passion, it is to be hoped that it will make up for it in etiquette.

But the promise of his future great appetite proved to be overly optimistic. While they had eventually succeeded in doing the deed, they had done so but twice in three months, which, so early in marriage, had been much less than Charlotte expected. Both times he had been prodigiously proud, and Charlotte was relieved that they were at least able to function as a couple, in this regard. But any other pleasure on her part was not forthcoming.

She suspected that Mr Collins, with a genuine wish to delight his wife, *would* have performed what was required with great alacrity, had he only known how. But he did not. And so, the nights they spent having any relations were very few, and those relations were very brief.

Last night had been the third time, and the memory of it was an irritant – a flat note to disturb her natural harmony. She wanted to be poised and in control when Elizabeth arrived, so she hastily washed, dressed in a new gown and went downstairs to check the house was all arranged – and tried to block out the thought of her husband's shockingly gentle embrace.

A couple of hours later, a carriage was heard on the drive. Charlotte, determined to be her usual self and ignore the reserve she felt towards Elizabeth, walked briskly out to greet the party. Her sister jumped out first, giddily excited, followed by Sir William, who then helped Elizabeth down.

Charlotte embraced her sister tightly and then her father. He went to pull away, but she delayed, clinging to his rounded, sturdy figure for another minute or so, to his surprise.

As she disengaged from him, she faced Elizabeth, and they both smiled tentatively.

Charlotte said, 'Thank you for coming.'

She couldn't quite read Elizabeth's expression. It might be the same hostility of their last encounter or something else – worry, regret? Charlotte realised she had started to forget her friend – forget her behaviours and her ways. She needed to relearn Elizabeth from this new place in her life – and soon, before she forgot entirely how to keep a friend.

Later that afternoon, after Charlotte and her husband had shown their guests the house and garden, Mr Collins took Maria and Sir William out for a walk, keen to show them the glories of Kent. 'I believe the beauties of our part of the county are beyond anything Hertfordshire might have to offer. I have heard it described by some as "God's Garden", though on reflection, I might have named it thusly myself, in a sermon or some such.'

Charlotte and Elizabeth stayed behind. If either party had hoped for an instant apology or appeal for reconciliation, they were disappointed. Between Charlotte's ability for cold reserve and Elizabeth's stubborn nature, their breach would not be quickly healed.

But some softening began in the sitting room that day as Charlotte described how she encouraged Mr Collins to work a good deal out of the house or in the garden, while she retained some solitude within her household. In this, she seemed to be acknowledging to Elizabeth that there was some truth in her judgement: that his company was not to be desired. Commentary on the house and its prospects was offered, and small talk about the health of their families took them across the hour's threshold without too much discomfort.

But they did not yet feel like friends again.

In those first few days, which were occupied with country walks and gardening and trips to the village, Charlotte endeavoured to show Elizabeth the comfort of the house, the independence she had within it, and the real joy she took in her duties as the rector's wife. Elizabeth followed, taking in all activities with a keen eye and willingly applying herself to any diversion that was suggested. Her actions, if not her countenance, showed eagerness.

On the third day of the visit, Elizabeth and Charlotte were gardening together, tending to the plants in the greenhouse. Both had a rosy sheen – flushed with the heat of the enclosure, with sweat on their faces – and being hot and bothered engendered an urge for frankness.

While staring intently at a tomato plant, Elizabeth said, 'I am sorry for what I said and how I behaved.'

Charlotte said nothing. She was waiting for more.

'You did nothing wrong,' continued Elizabeth. 'You did nothing but defend your own interests and in a way which did no harm to me, beyond taking my dearest friend away. I could not congratulate you, but I should not have admonished you for it. I should have understood. I am sorry.'

Oftentimes, when there is an apology between two people, there is a pause which feels pregnant with the expectation of a mirrored response. But Charlotte would not allow even her most polite instincts to give in to this: she truly had done nothing wrong, acting only in the natural hopes for her happiness, which any woman would – or should – understand.

'It is all well, Eliza.' She turned to smile at her friend, but Elizabeth could not yet return it.

Elizabeth's eyes were watering. 'Please say you forgive me.'

Charlotte immediately went to her and hugged her, her watering can dangling over Elizabeth's shoulder. 'I forgive you, you goose.'

Charlotte was more naturally the comforter in their friendship, being a little older and more steady, and Elizabeth felt such gratitude to be brought in again, out from the cold.

After a fine dinner that evening, when the ladies retired to the drawing room, Elizabeth felt bolder in questioning her friend on a topic that had long been on her mind. Maria was playing the pianoforte, providing a convenient mask for the conversation.

'Charlotte,' Elizabeth whispered into her friend's ear, 'how are you finding – having relations? Is it ... bearable?'

Charlotte was sensitive to the subject, not wishing to brook her friend's judgement or concern, but she felt more secure in confessing the difficulties of her marriage now that they were growing closer again.

'It is tolerable. And it has only happened a few times. In truth, I find the day-to-day affections harder, because they are expected so frequently and expected to flow naturally: a kiss on the cheek, a hold of the hand, a fond look. I have said it to you before, but I feel surer now than ever that I am not romantic. I feel like an actor, guessing at what a rush of love must look like or when a spontaneous embrace might happen. I do have kind feelings for my husband – he has many virtues which are only apparent on regular acquaintance, but I do not feel ... *that*. No rush of feeling, no flutters. You know this: I am not drawn to him. I've never been drawn to anyone. I can act the part for now, but it is very tiring. And I am only two months in.'

Elizabeth paused before replying, keen to check herself these days. 'You act it well, then, and your natural fondness for him helps – anyone can see that you are good with him, and more patient than most. Perhaps it will get easier, and perhaps affection will grow. They do say, do they not, that in marriage, sometimes love is wont to grow as time passes? Years give life to love.'

'Sometimes,' said Charlotte quietly, eyes fixed on the fire.

'Sometimes,' agreed her friend.

She would not say it, but Elizabeth felt quite worried by the crack shown in her friend's resolve. This situation – a loveless but comfortable match in a happily situated house – made sense as long as her sensible friend was *sure* that it did. But this was the first moment she had seen worry, weariness, even regret in Charlotte, and for her to show it suggested that there was a good deal more below the surface.

They sat in silence, until Maria finished playing and demanded a game of whist, a welcome distraction to them all.

CHAPTER VI

'You look well, Mrs Collins; the spring air must be agreeing with you. Though you do seem a little thin. You are walking too much, which I have warned you about before. I will ask Cook to bring you some biscuits.'

Lady Catherine de Bourgh occupied her seat like a throne and was demonstrating her unique ability to convey concern for and judgement of a fellow creature in equal measure. While the seats in the drawing room at Rosings were not arranged in a particular formation, Lady Catherine was somehow still sitting at the head. Draped in a thick ruby fabric, she – presumably deliberately – stood out from the rest of the company in their pale spring colours and light dresses. She was a naturally commanding presence, tall, strong-featured, and when she spoke, her voice was deep and powerful. Her words were ponderous enough to confirm her superior status, belying the fact that what she said was, more often than not, rather trivial.

'I assure you I am well enough and need not—' attempted Charlotte.

'Figgis! FIGGIS!' erupted Lady Catherine.

A weary older man appeared at the door.

'Bring some biscuits for poor Mrs Collins or she will faint.' She dramatically stirred her tea, then tapped her teaspoon on the side of her cup, which rang out like a bell, exactly timed to make her request seem like a divine commandment.

Introducing Mrs Collins

Charlotte knew Lady Catherine well enough now to make no further protest. She was feeling proud and happy to share the experience of visiting Lady Catherine with her family, and more particularly with Eliza, with whom she could reflect upon it afterwards in a way she had not yet been able to. Post-visit analysis with Mr Collins was always full of praise and self-deprecation and admiration of household décor, but with Eliza, it would be much more fun and far less complimentary.

As Mr Collins's new wife, Charlotte seemed to be an object of interest to Lady Catherine, and as her guest on many previous occasions, she felt that she had been met with approval. Charlotte had an ability to know exactly how to behave with different kinds of people and to enact it without much effort. Since becoming a regular visitor at Rosings, she had employed this skill often; finding the correct mode to suit the situation and behaving this way. As it made her own life easier to have smooth relations with her husband's patron, why should she not?

Bringing Elizabeth as her particular friend was, she knew, a risk to this finely tuned balance, but one Charlotte was willing to take. And, if a quarrel did occur, it would at least be a moment of diversion, which would make a change.

Lady Catherine seemed to sniff out the potential for discord early on. She seemed vexed by Elizabeth's prettiness, even though this was hardly the fault of Elizabeth. She proceeded to interrogate her new guest about her upbringing, her education and that of her sisters. Elizabeth answered for her family's slightly unusual manner of raising five daughters without reservation. Mr Collins, across the table, looked rather worried and at points dismayed by Elizabeth's lack of reverence. Charlotte, for her part, listened and rather enjoyed the exchange.

If only Lady Catherine were to meet Lydia and Kitty, thought Charlotte, *she would be truly shaken.*

When Elizabeth remarked upon the unfairness of younger sisters having to wait until their elder sisters were married before they might enjoy society, Charlotte positively grinned. Unlike her sister, her father or her husband, she had no fear of Lady Catherine, and she could see that Elizabeth did not either. Therefore, she offered no assistance to her friend or excuse to Lady Catherine. She was watching two strong, opinionated women find their match, and she enjoyed the sport. The conversation would not benefit from an umpire.

The next day held the opportunity for reflection, and Elizabeth did not disappoint. The two friends sat in the sitting room at Hunsford after luncheon, in loosened stays, the sewing they had intended to do discarded by their seats. Elizabeth had never been much of a seamstress and only ever did a quarter of whatever she started. Charlotte had a mind suited to it. She was currently working on an elaborate embroidery, a design of her own, formed of repeating patterns in bold colours: purples and golds – miles away from her mother's muted samplers. But she enjoyed it most when she could concentrate on it, and she did not want to squander the good company she had in this moment. It lay on her lap.

Elizabeth declared, 'She is extraordinary, and I do not mean that as a compliment. She has a martial quality to her. She would have made a very good governess.'

Charlotte chuckled, thinking of how such a comparison would be met by Lady Catherine.

'I do not think I gained her approval.'

'Oh, mere conjecture,' said Charlotte sarcastically.

'You are right. My conjecture is based only on what she said and how she acted.'

'Exactly,' replied Charlotte, smiling wryly. 'No, I agree, I do not think you will be a favourite with her, but you baited her!'

'I did no such thing. I answered her questions clearly and honestly.'

'But, Eliza, you also gave a lot of *opinions* ...'

Elizabeth gasped dramatically. 'Forgive me!'

'Only God can forgive you. Lady Catherine will likely not.'

About a fortnight after this, by which time Charlotte's father had returned to Meryton, news reached the parsonage that there was to be a visitor to Rosings: namely, Mr Darcy. Darcy was Lady Catherine's nephew, and Charlotte knew a little of him already.

She had first set eyes on Darcy at an assembly in Meryton, at which he refused to dance with anyone beyond his own party and was heard declaring Elizabeth only 'tolerable'. This had naturally set Charlotte against him; she had her own reasons to dislike men who scorned women at dances. But since then, she had suspected he had only made a particularly bad first impression. Charlotte had heard the list of accusations against Darcy, laid out by one Mr Wickham, another member in Elizabeth's circle of intrigue. Wickham, an officer in the local militia whose rugged good looks had clearly made an impression on Elizabeth, had painted Darcy as the worst kind of villain, and Elizabeth had been inclined to believe him. Charlotte had not been entirely convinced; she had not warmed to Wickham and therefore kept a more open mind about Darcy. She generally had good instincts for people's character, and while Elizabeth leapt to condemnation, Charlotte kept her counsel.

It had been many months since such matters last occupied her, and in truth, she was glad to have such intrigues reignited. Darcy's arrival would certainly bring a pinch of spice to the party. He would bring with him his cousin, Colonel Fitzwilliam, about whom no one knew a thing.

It was known that the pair would be in the neighbourhood but not when they might be seen, and so it was with a little perturbation that Charlotte, one morning, spotted her husband walking back across the park towards home, flanked by two tall gentlemen, one in a navy-blue coat and the other in the red uniform of the military.

'Eliza, Mr Darcy is approaching!' she called up the stairs.

'What?!' cried Elizabeth, running down them a few seconds later.

'Mr Darcy and his cousin are a minute or so away. I may thank you, Eliza, for this piece of civility. Mr Darcy would never have come so soon to wait upon me.'

'Nonsense. It is basic etiquette for him to visit Hunsford.'

'You know that is not true; it is not at all expected. Anyway, if you wish to fix your hair, now is the time.'

Elizabeth raised a derisive eyebrow at her, and yet she did set about making herself look decent. Charlotte even caught her pinching her cheeks and smothered a grin.

The doorbell rang just as the ladies reached the bottom of the stairs, and Mr Collins ushered in Mr Darcy – a dark-haired, imposing figure who towered over the company, commanding immediate attention. Next to him was a genial-looking man in uniform, a few years older than his cousin, smiling easily and looking round admiringly.

The bustle of introductions, taking of coats, moving into the drawing room and ordering tea, provided a minute or two to inspect the visitors. Charlotte, already knowing Darcy, took more of an interest in examining the newcomer. Colonel Fitzwilliam had mousy-brown hair, thick and rather unkempt for a soldier, and a weather-worn face. He was not entirely handsome, yet his manners made him seem the most appealing person in the room. Charlotte noticed with interest that he addressed every new acquaintance with equal courtesy, whether it was Mrs Brooke or Mr Collins. He was not as tall as Darcy, but then Darcy was taller than necessary. Colonel Fitzwilliam was broad across the chest, and his eyes were keen and ready to meet—

Oh! His eyes met Charlotte's directly, just as she realised she had been staring at him. He raised both eyebrows and nodded slightly, warmly.

She quicky averted her gaze.

'Do you find your aunt easy company?' Elizabeth asked, bold as ever, and Mr Collins's eyes bulged out of his head.

She addressed the question to Darcy, though it applied to both the gentlemen. Pleasantries had already been exchanged, but Elizabeth was evidently keen to delve into more challenging territory. Darcy took such a long time to reply that it wasn't clear if he was considering his answer or ignoring the question.

Colonel Fitzwilliam, to smooth over the silence, replied, 'Our aunt is formidable, Miss Bennet, as I'm sure you have found yourself. She has been very good to us, however, and with only Anne for her immediate family, her house is less populated than she would like. So, while her company may not be easy, we are glad to be in it.'

Charlotte warmed to his reply, while Elizabeth was clearly irritated not to have had hers from Darcy.

But a moment later, that gentleman stirred and said, 'I think you know by now, Miss Bennet, that I do not find much company easy, beyond my own household and most intimate friends. I will admit I find my aunt to be rather demanding at times and certainly very proud – a trait I think you deplore. But she is my aunt, and I am glad to see her when I can. And, may I say, I am glad for you to meet a member of my family.'

Elizabeth appeared baffled by the final statement, whereas Charlotte was not so puzzled; she had suspected a partiality for Elizabeth on Darcy's part for some time, and this quietly spoken communication seemed to suggest his intentions were serious.

Elizabeth was silent, apparently extremely absorbed by her tea. Charlotte watched her – and so did Colonel Fitzwilliam, she noted.

'Will you stay long in the neighbourhood?' Charlotte asked the gentlemen, returning the conversation to its track.

'I am staying at Rosings for a few weeks, Mrs Collins, but I will return to Spain thereafter,' replied the colonel amicably. 'My regiment is barracked on the other side of Kent, and we have been there for some months now, attempting to rebuild the ranks.'

'Can you tell us something of the war, Colonel? Have you killed any Frenchman yourself?' asked Maria breathlessly.

The colonel's face hardened, changing from its easy demeanour. 'What can I tell you … ?' He looked at Maria's face – so young and eager for a story. He chose his words carefully. 'I can tell you that it is starting to feel like the tide is turning – we prevailed against the French at the start of the year. And yes, I have killed many Frenchmen and lost many men of my own. None of it is as thrilling as one might hope.'

Maria looked deflated and quietly said, 'Oh.'

Seeing her disappointment, he added, 'But Wellington is everything you might have heard – very impressive.'

'You have met Wellington!' Maria rallied quickly with this titbit, as he had hoped.

'Indeed. A fine man.'

Maria satisfied, Charlotte spoke up partly in defence of her sister. 'I hope you will forgive our curiosity, Colonel. The war seems so far away to us here – partly because we have not known anyone in the standing army. We have met a few of the local militia who have been eager to discuss the war, albeit in theory, having no direct experience of it, but I think perhaps it is not easy to talk about battle once you have seen it?'

'No indeed, madam. Our last battle, Albuera, was particularly …' He searched for a word to suit the company he was in. 'Difficult,' he said, smiling grimly.

Charlotte smiled back, guessing that the understatement must be absurd.

She had never had a reason to think particularly about the war, though it had always been a constant in the background. She had occasionally read items in newspapers about it and heard stories from acquaintances with brothers in the navy, but none of her friends or family had such a connection, and so she had enjoyed the luxury of being removed from its orbit. She quietly prided herself on being well-educated and well-read, but as she thought about her ignorance on this subject, and as she looked into the face of this earnest man who had clearly had experiences far beyond her imaginings, she felt rather stupid.

Darcy was looking at his cousin earnestly, almost protectively. He put a hand roughly on his shoulder.

Colonel Fitzwilliam looked as if he might say more, but Mr Collins piped up at this point, unable to stand a moment of seriousness in which he was not involved. 'I apologise for the ladies' line of enquiry, and I dispute the idea that we are all curious about the war. I am sure we simply trust in God that we will be victorious, and I consider it none of our business how it is done.'

'I hope that you will trust in us, sir, more than God,' replied Fitzwilliam firmly, his face a little heated. 'As for it being none of your business, quite the contrary: I wish that our army's exploits abroad were more widely known by members of the very households for which we are fighting. And these things can only become known by asking questions when the opportunity arises.' Here Colonel Fitzwilliam glanced at Charlotte and bowed his head slightly.

The topic was left there however, and after a few minutes of more polite conversation, the gentlemen moved to take their leave. Darcy made his exit swiftly, saying 'Good day,' to all, and stood just outside the door, waiting for his cousin.

'Thank you for your hospitality, Mrs Collins,' said Colonel Fitzwilliam, making a small bow.

Charlotte curtsied, smiling.

'And a pleasure to meet you, Miss Bennet,' he added, craning around to meet Elizabeth's eye, eagerly.

'Indeed,' came back Elizabeth hesitantly. 'And you.'

Charlotte noted the attention. It looked as if her friend might be contending with more than one suitor during her stay in Kent.

While no one could have predicted two eligible men staying in the vicinity, their apparent interest in Elizabeth was not a surprise to Charlotte. Her friend had always had the looks and vivacity to catch the eye of interesting men, and Charlotte was well used to dealing with her various admirers. Colonel Fitzwilliam seemed like a good option, on first viewing. Charlotte could not help but notice his appeal.

'You are welcome to visit again while you are staying at Rosings,' said Charlotte to Colonel Fitzwilliam genially. 'We do not get many visitors, and we would be glad of it.'

'Yes! Indeed, my wife speaks truly,' took over Mr Collins. 'Any relation of Lady Catherine is welcome at any time in our home; your presence would be a *credit* to us—'

Charlotte interrupted him, saying briskly, 'Farewell then, Colonel Fitzwilliam.'

After he was gone, she turned to face Elizabeth, raising her eyebrows.

'He is only *just* a colonel,' Mr Collins pronounced over dinner.

To his disappointment, no one asked him to elaborate; Charlotte diligently sipped her soup, acting as if nothing had been said.

He continued regardless, 'I heard from Lady Catherine that his promotion is but two weeks old – so it is presumptuous of him to style himself thus on his first visit.'

'If he is now a colonel, then what else should he introduce himself as?' asked Elizabeth. 'There is no trial period on the position, as far as I understand it?'

'He must have been very brave to have been promoted to colonel so young,' observed Maria keenly, now an expert of military matters.

'Or wealthy and well connected. Let us not forget he is the younger son of an earl. It is lucky for those who have the money to purchase their next commission whensoever they please,' replied Mr Collins snidely and spuriously.

'It does not sound as if he has been especially lucky,' said Charlotte. 'I'm sure we will find out in due course.'

'Well, I thought him rather scruffy for a colonel.'

'My dear, he was in military dress!' said Charlotte, passing the gravy.

Mr Collins's petty remarks had perhaps been provoked by Maria, who, since the exit of the two men, had not stopped singing their praises, from their manners to their voices, their height (Maria really seemed to have a preoccupation with tall men) to their handsome faces. Mr Collins, who had never heard such thoughts about himself uttered by any woman, was quite allergic to it. He suspected that Elizabeth, too, was impressed by the two gentlemen, and having failed to secure her approval himself, he felt the stark difference between himself and them.

Unfortunately, his attempt to undermine the colonel had the opposite effect to the one he wished, making him appear worse in comparison. But Charlotte knew his foibles and his insecurities. She reassured him in quiet ways – asking him to read the Bible to her, remarking on how glad she was of a warm house in this weather, and putting her arms around him in bed – which, luckily, did not lead to anything more intimate. He was, at heart, a man of simple needs, and Charlotte understood them. She was good at the task of being his wife, and she took some pleasure in that. Not a great deal, but enough, for now.

Two days later, Charlotte was alone in the house– a rarity, with even Mrs Brooke gone to town, and she was sitting enjoying her solitude when she heard the crunch of gravel. Peering out the window, she saw Colonel Fitzwilliam striding up the drive. She was struck, oddly, by an urge to change into a nicer dress and tidy her hair, but his knock came quickly, and she had to answer it herself.

'Colonel Fitzwilliam, you accepted our offer!'

'I did, ma'am, but I did not expect such a personal welcome. Is your housekeeper not in?'

'She is not, sir, and neither is my husband nor our guests. You may therefore wish to postpone your visit.'

'Well, I leave it to you, Mrs Collins. If you do not object, I could stay a few minutes at least – I have walked far this morning, and your company is as welcome as that of anyone else I could have hoped to see. But I am certain you are busy, and your time is more valuable than my own. What would you wish?'

Charlotte blinked. She should probably send him away.

And yet, 'Come in!', she found herself saying.

'Your house is very welcoming, Mrs Collins,' said Fitzwilliam, holding a cup of tea. 'After spending time in the draughty halls of Rosings, a feeling of homeliness is appreciated.'

'Thank you. The bones of the house are already very beautiful, but I will set modesty aside and say I have worked hard on making it pleasant.'

They sat in the drawing room – a bright, cheerful room, which Charlotte had made alterations to since she moved into the house. She took the opportunity to glance around the room now, which gave her some relief. It was very unusual for her to be alone with a gentleman other than her husband; she felt the tension and, if she were honest, the excitement of it, and she worried it might show in her face.

'The garden, in particular, is a joy to work on,' she continued.

'It is splendid, and I only saw part of it.'

'It is finally coming to life; I've been looking forward to spring, and the daffodils have finally arrived just in time for visitors – they're a favourite of mine.'

'I saw them all along the drive; they make a fine greeting for us. How long have you lived here?'

'But three months or so. We married in January.'

'Ah. Is your new life to your liking?'

Charlotte felt it was expected of her to give an easy affirmation here, but there was something in his enquiry and how genuinely interested he seemed that gave her pause. 'I am adjusting to it, Colonel. I married with my eyes open to all that it might be – the joys and the difficulties – and if I may congratulate myself on one thing, it is that I was mostly correct.'

'Then I should congratulate you, too. Such foresight – we could use you in the army.'

'Do not mock me, sir,' chided Charlotte.

'I assure you I do not. I have seen just enough of society to understand that a woman's plan for her future – considering her own economic security, the diplomatic situations she might navigate, the compromises she is and is not willing to make, and calculating her best bet at victory, or indeed, at peace – is to be respected. Such thinking could rival any strategy put forward by a general of the highest order.'

'I hope you do not propose that women are schemers.'

'I do not propose that women are mercenary but that they are intelligent and aware and act accordingly. My position is such that I will have to make similar considerations when – if – I marry. There is no judgement on me for choosing carefully, and I would never judge a woman for doing the same.'

Charlotte listened and paused. She nodded, then gently smiled and asked, 'And what if one falls in love and security is cast aside?'

'Then you are one of the lucky ones,' replied the colonel, grinning.

What should have been a short visit turned into a lengthy one, and the afternoon sun was weakening by the time he stood to take his leave.

At the door, the colonel turned towards Charlotte, and they faced each other for a moment before he said, a little awkwardly, 'I had wondered if I might see Miss Elizabeth Bennet on my visit; perhaps you would pass on my regards to her?'

As it happened, Charlotte had been wondering about his apparent lack of urgency, how generous (or unguarded) he had been with his time and his conversation. She had even thought that there was something of a rapport between them. Now, it all made sense: it seemed as if her company had been endured in the hopes of once again meeting with her pretty friend. How tiresome, and how predictable.

She said politely but wearily, 'Of course I shall, Colonel. I am sorry you missed her.'

He caught her tone and halted his departure, saying earnestly, 'I am very glad I stayed, Mrs Collins. It is a pleasure to make a new friend.'

'Indeed, Colonel. Good day'.

He left, and she shut the door gently, standing pensively in the hall a few moments, before being interrupted by the sound of Mrs Brooke coming in the back door.

A moment later, the housekeeper appeared in the hall, saying, 'Oh, madam, I saw a gentleman leaving – did I miss a visit? I'm sorry if so—'

'Please do not make yourself uneasy, Brooke. It was Colonel Fitzwilliam, come to call on Miss Elizabeth, and she is out. He did not stay long.'

CHAPTER VII

It was on Easter day – or rather, that evening – that they were next to dine at Rosings. It was apparent that Lady Catherine had no other options, for she invited the Hunsford party only that morning, to fill up her table.

It being Rosings, and Easter, Charlotte felt justified in wearing one of her best dresses and doing her hair finely. She sat at her dressing table in the late afternoon light, looking in the mirror – a rare activity for her – scrutinising her face and her body. She wore a blue-grey gown that matched her eyes, cut low and tightly laced. It suited her well. She had a tall, slim figure, a thin waist, strong shoulders, slender arms, and she could afford a low neckline without, as her mother would say, *putting on an exhibition*. She looked at her face: not much changed in the last few years. Not many lines around her eyes and mouth. Perhaps she had not laughed much lately, she pondered. Her hair was prettily arranged, with a few heat-curled strands hanging down that softened her features.

Her pale face was not pretty, she knew. She knew this from evidence – from the lack of interest in it. As a child, of course, her mother and her aunt had made the usual cooing remarks, 'adorable', 'delightful', 'sweet', but from the age a girl starts to care about her looks, the word 'beautiful' was never once ascribed to her and she noticed the omission. She was never called *pretty*, nor *handsome*, and had more than once overheard herself described as *plain*. More often than that, her appearance had solicited no remark at all. But her face *should* have garnered interest, because it *was* interesting: eyes that wandered from blue to grey depending on the light, a long narrow nose, a mouth too wide for the fashion, a smile too broad when it was employed. She sat awkwardly between men's fantasies: a face neither plump nor delicate, a body neither luxurious nor petite.

Charlotte looked down at her flat stomach. It was early in her marriage but she still wondered when she might expect a change. She did not know how often the act must be performed to make a child, but she supposed it was more often than the three or four times they had managed. She must remember to ask her mother.

Part of her longed to be with child, to feel absolutely sure of her purpose – to be the most important person in someone's life and to feel a pull, an undeniable tie, to someone else – that would be something.

Still, she thought, there was plenty of time. And until such time, she could wear this dress, pulled tight. And she felt good in it. Special.

The smooth, translucent skin of her décolletage was striking. She touched her pale neck and her collarbone, imagined feeling somebody else touching them. It brought a flush to her cheeks, which she caught in the mirror. She had a pretty white ribbon threaded through her hair, which made her feel like a débutante. She smiled broadly, at herself. In that moment, she felt she should be desirable. She pictured herself in a moment of passion, envisioned a life in which someone might crave her. She imagined being kissed by someone who knew how and who could not wait to kiss her. She pressed two fingers hard onto her lips, leaving them ruddy and pink. She tasted for a moment what it was like to feel womanly, to feel attractive.

'My dear, make haste – the carriage is here!' called Mr Collins up the stairs.

She let her lips fall straight. 'Foolish,' she said out loud, shaking herself out of the pretence. She tucked the strands of hair tightly behind her ears, pinning them in place, with more vigour than was necessary. She looked again at herself in the low blue dress, sighed, and hastily began to make alterations. She added a white chemisette underneath the dress, rendering its deep neckline redundant. Before she left her bedroom for Rosings, she was transformed. Now fully covered from the top of her blue dress to the middle of her neck, her entire front was safely concealed in white lace. She placed an embroidered cap over her dark hair. She pulled the frilled collar tight around her neck. She would be the very picture of a vicar's wife. She would be seen as modest. She would hardly be seen.

That evening, she was placed between Lady Catherine's daughter, Anne, and her companion, Mrs Jenkinson, whose conversation was limited, requiring great effort on Charlotte's part. Meanwhile, Mr Darcy and Colonel Fitzwilliam vied over the attentions of Elizabeth, who was resplendent in peach satin and looked prettier than ever. Elizabeth was dared to play the piano and did so faux-reluctantly and, in Charlotte's opinion, poorly. It did not diminish her in the eyes of both gentlemen – it seemed to add to her charms somehow.

Charlotte longed to be asked to play. She was a good pianist and could roll out some Clementi that would stun them all as easily as she could butter her bread. But she was not asked, and she was not a part of that lively gathering. She watched Elizabeth and Darcy and Fitzwilliam and Maria even, chatting loudly and moving about the room, doing what they pleased, and she felt more detached from that world than ever.

She had wanted a settled life, hadn't she? But how she longed to throw off her cap, drink too much wine, smash out a sonata and laugh and laugh with Eliza and be flirted with by a soldier and shock the lady of the house and be looked at, and be *looked at*.

*

The day after the Rosings dinner was Easter Monday and Charlotte was to make her duty-bound visits to parishioners in need. On this occasion, she took her sister with her. Maria had always been light-hearted, a good foil for Charlotte as a sibling. She had none of Charlotte's seriousness, and she did not overthink. At eighteen, she was pretty: not just with a clear, rosy complexion, wide eyes and golden hair that curled naturally, but also with good health and openness and a ready smile and a near-constant amazement with what she saw. It had occasionally irritated Charlotte how she seemed to dance through life without a single vexation. But on this trip, she saw how her sister glowed. She seemed to shine on the people they visited; her positivity, her smiles and her light step were infectious. And this generous cheering of spirits was not an accident but applied deliberately.

Charlotte knew this only after leaving the last house. This had been that of Colonel Raeworth, who had lost a leg in the battles in Spain and lived alone. He said Maria reminded him of his daughter and had let her open his dusty curtains to the spring sun, something he had not allowed anyone else to do.

As the sisters left, Charlotte saw the moment Maria's seemingly boundless smile fell, her step gain a little weight and her chatter cease.

'Are you well?' asked Charlotte.

'Oh, yes!' Maria tried to reinvigorate herself. 'I am a little tired. I do not know why, though; I did not do anything, not like you.'

Charlotte smiled and linked arms with her sister, pulling her close. 'You did. You must know you did. You gave them all the smiles you have to give today. You beamed your sunshine on them until it dimmed. I think it is a wonderful gift to have, but it is tiring to maintain such a light. You need not smile with me, sister; be at peace.'

The pair ambled home, a journey of a mile or so, in step with each other. As they entered the parsonage, ready to flop into chairs, they were both shocked to discover Mr Darcy there, talking to Elizabeth alone. He was embarrassed and explained that when he set out, he had assumed a full party would be in the house.

Did you indeed? thought Charlotte, looking at his flustered face. They were all now standing, and Elizabeth was making eyes at Charlotte – raised eyebrows and a slight head shake to convey that she was as baffled by the visit as anyone.

Darcy made no eye contact, hastily made his excuses and left, leaving the three ladies to ruthlessly pick over every word and gesture of the visit. It was so very unlike him, Elizabeth ventured, to make a visit purely out of politeness and with no object.

Charlotte suggested that he must indeed have an object and that it was clear what it was. 'My dear Eliza, he must be in love with you, or he would never have called on us in this familiar way.'

Elizabeth shook her head. 'I know you think that, but it cannot be. He has no compliments for me; he is not gentle in his words and remains as awkward and unrelenting as ever.'

'I think he does not know how to make his suit. Just because he is a handsome, wealthy gentleman—'

'And tall!' added Maria breathlessly.

'And tall,' agreed Charlotte, 'it does not follow that he is practised at wooing. Why else would he pay you such attention?'

'He did not come to pay *me* attention; he came to visit all of us. It was bad luck for him that you were out.'

'Yes, I'm sure Mr Fitzwilliam Darcy was desperate to talk to the vicar's wife about the weather or discuss a passage of scripture with Maria here.'

'Indeed!' Maria began indignantly.

'Sorry, Maria. But he did not come for us.'

Eliza sighed. 'Well, you will not be persuaded otherwise, but in any case, his overtures would be of no use while I think so ill of him. I should do much better with Colonel Fitzwilliam!' She said this with a laugh, but Charlotte did not join her.

'You would.' She had turned very serious suddenly. 'He is a fine match. I am not sure he has much money to keep a household, but he is a very good man, I think. Will you return his interest? He certainly likes you.'

Eliza caught her friend's odd tone and looked at her appraisingly. 'I was only joking, really.'

'Why would it be a joke to you? He is a good match and worthy of your serious consideration.'

In the pause after Charlotte spoke, Elizabeth was trying to read her – the conversation felt suddenly precarious, and she was not sure why.

'Has he mentioned something to you, about me? Last night?' asked Elizabeth, trying in vain to piece together her friend's sudden investment in this scheme.

'When might he have done that? He did not speak three words to me all evening, and neither did you.'

Maria wordlessly slipped out of the parlour at this point, but only to listen to the exchange more comfortably from outside the door.

'You seem angry,' said Elizabeth warily. 'Is it something I have done?'

'No, I am not angry,' said Charlotte, angrily. 'I just hope that your eyes are open, Eliza, to the opportunities before you. As I see it, Darcy's cards are almost laid on the table. And the colonel is very obviously interested in you, and yet you laugh at the idea of him as a suitor. If he is a joke to you, you should not have acted as you did with him last night. You encouraged him. Either that or you used him to spark interest in Darcy, which, if that was your goal, worked very well. I congratulate you on the scheme.'

This was shot with a cold venom at Elizabeth, who was hurt but, moreover, dumbfounded. She was not used to such cool hostility from her friend – or such judgement.

Charlotte felt a flush in her face and realised her fists were clenched. Yes, she was angry. Why? She began hurriedly unfastening the lace around her neck.

Elizabeth did not match her friend's anger with a fire of her own; she was too occupied in trying to understand her friend, trying to solve her reaction like a puzzle.

'I think,' she began haltingly, 'that you want me to be more grateful for the attentions I receive.'

Charlotte thought about that for a minute. Her first instinct was, *Yes, precisely!* but upon further reflection, she did not like its implications. Why should her friend be grateful for something she had not asked for? Lady Catherine had seemed irked by Elizabeth's prettiness, which was absurd. Was Charlotte not behaving similarly in blaming her friend for being charming? Yes, she returned the lively conversation she received, but so would Charlotte if she were single and being pursued. She imagined she would, anyway – for her, it would always be a hypothetical.

Elizabeth had had interest in the past from many quarters, all of them unworthy, and Charlotte had never examined her response to them or thought she should behave differently. Why did she feel so now?

Her breathing had slowed. She removed her cap from her head and found herself able to meet Elizabeth's eyes. 'I am sorry. I do not think that. I did not enjoy last night. I suppose I am getting used to being just a wife – and an unimportant one – in a gathering such as that.'

Instead of instantly contradicting her, Elizabeth took a moment to consider what she was saying and took her hand. 'I am sorry I was so distracted. For what it is worth, you are the most important person in my life. You and Jane.'

Charlotte smiled at the sentiment but said knowingly, 'But I think not for long, Eliza. Let us see.'

Elizabeth, relieved that the storm seemed to be over, laughed and said, 'You sound like a fortune-teller.'

Charlotte sat, relaxing a little. 'Cross my palm with silver then, I would take it.'

'No. You would only give it to the poor.'

'Eliza! You are godless. And I would not, actually. I would buy a new apron.'

'Such indulgence! She is as hedonistic as Prinny!' cried Elizabeth, and Charlotte cackled at her and at herself.

Deeming it safe, Maria entered the room again, with biscuits – medicine for the former tension. Charlotte pulled her sister to her side and squeezed her. She must appreciate her time with them both, in such close company. It would not last much longer.

10th April 1812

Dear Lizzy,

I am forced to write to you as I see you have no intention of writing to me, your own mother, even though you are away for what seems like a year. Things are very bad here – Hill is away visiting her sister who is dying, so you can imagine how we suffer! Your father, as you know, can hardly butter his own toast. Yes, he can read Latin, but can he fold his own nightshirt? Can he make a pot of tea? No, he cannot. I honestly do not think the timing could be worse. With Jane in London and you gallivanting around Kent, it is the worst time in the world for Hill to be away – I cannot imagine how her sister has chosen now to be so very ill, ~~if indeed she is so very ill~~. I have been informed she is very ill.

I have had two letters from Jane; she is such a good girl. She has told me that she has seen the Bingley sisters – such nice, well-dressed ladies – and has been to several parties. She must catch some attention in London with a face like hers. I hope she remembers to show herself off. Modesty will be her downfall, mark me. It will not be yours, I shouldn't think.

Mrs Timpson, whom I am sure you will remember, is lately with child, which is her tenth. Her tenth! You will have your own thoughts on that, I am sure.

I have seen Lady Lucas, as she styles herself, and she tells me that all is well with Charlotte and her new, very fortunate situation. I have had to hear it from her, Lizzy – as you have not written me any news! Have you met Lady Catherine De Borgia? How large is the Collinses' house? Does Charlotte make it nice? Have you met any gentlemen on your stay? Have you worn your peach dress?

Why must I list these questions, Lizzy? Why have you not already offered the answers yourself? The least you can do, as consolation for *your rejection of Collins, is bring me news from Kent – a story, a little gossip. Is Charlotte with child? Has she gained weight? Do they talk about inheriting our house? I am sure they do.*

I think you are coming home soon, and in truth, I will be glad of it, particularly while Hill is away. My great fear is that when she returns, she may be grieving – and, while I pity her, she will likely be at half capacity.

Your father is not well, but it is always hard to tell with him. He has a cough, which as you can imagine is a strain on my nerves, and he has gotten a little thinner – but that may be simply because Hill is not around to bring him cheese constantly. But I think he is not very ill. I think he enjoys the attention – something I cannot understand.

Write soon, Lizzy, and come home. You are missed.

Your mother

CHAPTER VIII

'My dear, it will not be acceptable to Lady Catherine for Elizabeth to be absent without good reason.' Mr Collins was frantically dusting the top of his hat as Charlotte fixed her bonnet in the hall, readying to leave.

'There is a good reason, William. She is unwell. She has been confined to her bed with a headache all afternoon and is clearly in a great deal of pain.'

'Being in pain is no good reason not to attend tea, my dear, when the tea is offered by so high an acquaintance. A headache may be concealed, with good skill and a willing heart—'

'William. Elizabeth is not attending, and that is an end to it. Lady Catherine may glower, but I can withstand that, and so can you.'

Mr Collins knew when he was defeated but was grudging indeed to set off to Rosings without a full party and with a dusty hat.

It was therefore a smaller gathering at tea than they had been used to these last few weeks. Lady Catherine, of course, was at the helm, but in absentia were Elizabeth, Anne de Bourgh (who was also feeling unwell) and, surprisingly, Mr Darcy whose non-appearance was the subject of some speculation.

Mr Collins sat himself next to Lady Catherine, attending her closely, while Maria sat with Anne's companion, Mrs Jenkinson. As Figgis was pouring tea for them all, Colonel Fitzwilliam opened the doors and entered. Spying a seat next to Charlotte, he sat himself next to her.

'Ah, *one* of my nephews has deigned to attend, I see. Pray, where is Darcy? I am sure you must know,' inquired Lady Catherine, with a frown.

'I'm sorry to disappoint you, but I do not know. Perhaps some urgent business came up, or he has been set upon by the local beasts in the woods,' replied Fitzwilliam, walking to the drinks table and pouring himself something.

Charlotte grinned, but Lady Catherine did not laugh. 'I do not find the possibility of serious injury to be an opportunity for humour, Fitzwilliam. I enjoy a joke more than anyone, but there is a time and a place for levity, and it is not over oolong.' She took a sip and added, 'And there are no beasts in my woods – my keeper is fastidious about such things.'

'You are quite right.' The colonel smiled tolerantly. 'I am sure Darcy will return soon.'

This satisfied Lady Catherine enough for her to turn back to Mr Collins, and Colonel Fitzwilliam sat down, holding his brandy, then shifted in his seat so that he could look at Charlotte more easily.

The invitation to tea had come at rather the last minute, and Charlotte had not had time to arrange herself as fully as she usually did when going to Rosings. She wore the only suitable dress she had that was clean, which was very simply made, sage green with short sleeves. Instead of a chemisette, she had worn a cream shawl – which, in the warmth of the room, now lay folded beside her. Her hair was simple – it was naturally straight, and she hadn't had time to curl it, so it was pulled loosely back into a tuft with a few front strands falling loose. Before they left, Mr Collins had not thought she looked ready for the occasion, but she had maintained that her appearance was adequate.

Now, Charlotte felt she had made the right decision – Lady Catherine had not taken any notice of her, and she felt comforted by that.

Introducing Mrs Collins

'What has your day held, Colonel?' she asked, facing Fitzwilliam. She felt reassured to be sitting with him: they talked easily with one another, with no agenda or pretence. She had never found such company with a man before and appreciated it.

'Nothing of special note,' replied Fitzwilliam. 'I spent the morning corresponding with my officers and trying to learn how things fare in Spain. I have a good friend in London who kindly writes with any relevant news he finds in *The Times*. It is delayed, of course, but sometimes quicker than the direct correspondence I might receive from the front.'

'And how do things fare? If you can explain in a way I might understand.'

'From our acquaintance thus far, Mrs Collins, I know I need not simplify. But, for the sake of a pleasant conversation, I will say only that things are improving, and we have reason to be hopeful.' He had plastered a tight grin on his face.

'You need not be brief, sir. I would like to understand more, if you are willing to tell me. You can be explicit.'

The colonel took a deep breath. 'Why then – it is true that things are better. The deadlock we have had for so long has been broken, thanks to Wellington. In January, he laid siege to a very important city that opened up the route from Portugal. This already makes all future endeavours easier – or, possible – to attempt. My men say, "When Wellington fights, he wins," and so far, it is true. In battle, in action, he is a marvel.'

'Were you led by him, in – at the battle you mentioned when we first met?'

'No.' Fitzwilliam took a sip of his drink and paused for a moment. 'I wish we had been. We were led by Beresford, who … He was immensely brave, but the whole thing was – a shocking mess. The worst the army has seen since the start of it all. We lost thousands, *thousands* of men. It was – I will not be explicit, Mrs Collins. I would not wish it on you.' He pushed his hair away from his face roughly.

'And *you* ... you lost many – friends?' Charlotte asked delicately.

Fitzwilliam's face was hardened, very different from his usual easy countenance. 'Yes. Many.' He took another large sip. 'One in particular. But also, many. I must – find a place to put it. I cannot have them at the forefront of my thoughts while I am' – he gave a bitter smile – 'sipping tea with my aunt or making morning visits. I would be rough company indeed.'

'It is easier when you are sipping brandy, perhaps?' Charlotte said. She had not meant it as a jibe, but it had an effect on him.

'Yes, I – excuse me.' He rose and walked away.

She thought she had truly offended him and that he would leave the room. But just as she was panicking, he returned, having left his glass on the table in the corner.

'You observe me well, Mrs Collins.'

'I did not mean—'

'No, I know, but it is a concern of mine. I used to drink a good deal more, and in the months after our – after Albuera, I leant on it very heavily indeed. I was not in good shape and not fit for company. I should be more careful now and not slip back into ...'

Charlotte looked at his downcast eyes, how his hand twitched a little with nothing to occupy it.

'I cannot know what you have endured, sir. But from the little you have said, it is only natural that you would need something in the way of comfort.'

He looked up and met her eyes, which looked on him with compassion.

'Thank you,' he said. 'But that comfort, in the end, has not been good for me; until recently, under its influence, I was not a pleasure to others or to myself.'

'I see. What brought on a change?'

'Darcy.' Fitzwilliam raised a smile and straightened himself subconsciously. 'He has known me since infancy and recognised the poor state I was in. He had seen that path trodden by another member of his family and knew it could not be tolerated. He was strict with me, even brutal, and it was the best thing anyone has ever done for me.'

Charlotte nodded. 'It is a very good thing, to have such friends – friends who care enough to be harsh.'

'It is. Have you such a friend? Is Miss Bennet such a one?'

Charlotte thought for a moment of how Elizabeth had railed at her for her accepting Mr Collins. Was that Elizabeth showing care for her character, protection of her future? She supposed it was. 'Yes. She is.'

'Then we are both blessed. I walked with Miss Bennet this afternoon in fact.'

Charlotte sensed that he wished to change the subject and also noted an odd pang of jealousy within her. 'Oh. Was she well?' asked Charlotte. 'She has had a headache since she returned.'

The colonel looked concerned. 'Well, yes, she seemed a little out of sorts when I left her. I am sorry it is worse.'

Charlotte waited for him to ask more about Elizabeth, but he did not.

A moment later, the front door was heard opening and shutting, and loud footsteps clattered in the hall

'Is that you, Darcy?' called out Lady Catherine. 'Pray, come and join us; you are very late indeed.'

There was no immediate response to this; the footsteps had quietened.

'*DARCY!*' repeated Lady Catherine, and then to the room, 'I am sure it is him.'

The door to the drawing room opened, and Mr Darcy walked just two steps in and stopped. His face was a little red and his mouth drawn into a hard line. His fidgeting body ached to leave – that was clear. One of his legs was hardly in the room. 'Good evening to you all. Please forgive me, but I cannot stay. I have pressing business to attend to.'

'In the evening?' enquired his aunt, sceptical.

'*Yes*,' Darcy replied tersely, before leaving the room and slamming the door.

Lady Catherine was shocked, and Mr Collins was directly on hand to mollify and comfort her – a job he had been born to do.

Charlotte turned to Fitzwilliam enquiringly. 'Have you any notion as to why he is in such an ill humour?'

He looked as surprised as she. 'I truly do not. My cousin is rather secretive at times – or, I should say, he enjoys his privacy, and so it has been on this visit. I will try to get the truth of it later tonight.'

The pair were now sitting very comfortably together. It was fortunate that all other parties in the room were so well settled in their pairings that there was, for once, no other demand on their time, no one pulling them away.

'I know nothing of your family, besides Mr Darcy and Lady Catherine. Would you tell me about them?'

'I will not,' replied Fitzwilliam playfully, kindly. 'I have talked enough of myself. I would like to know more of you. I have heard about you from Miss Bennet, who has said very fond things about you but few specifics.'

'Well, I hardly have a career to regale you with, sir! I have not travelled or written a thesis or committed a crime. What would you have me tell you?'

Fitzwilliam laughed a little but then thought for a moment. 'If your time were completely your own, and money no object, what would you spend your life doing?'

'You mean, if I were not ...' She glanced at Mr Collins briefly.

'Yes,' said Fitzwilliam. 'If you were free to do as you wished, unencumbered.'

Charlotte took his question seriously and gave it her consideration. 'I fear my answer will disappoint you. With so much freedom, I think I ought to say I would travel the world, discovering new lands and having grand adventures, or that I would ride an elephant or be an actress on the stage or ... swim the ocean!'

'You don't want to ride an elephant?' asked Colonel Fitzwilliam, his face a mask of seriousness. 'You shock me.'

Charlotte laughed. 'Perhaps I do not know enough of the world, to make such a choice, in an informed way.'

'I have seen a little of the world and of new lands, Mrs Collins, and I assure you, I feel no better informed.'

'Well then, I will tell you. I would read as many new books as could be found. I would have the most splendid garden and spend hours cultivating more flowers and fewer vegetables. I would ... I would wear looser dresses, and I would not curl my hair, even for a ball. I would see my friends whenever I wished, and carriage journeys would cost me nothing and take no time at all. I would walk for hours. I would talk freely, but only when I wanted to, with a companion who loved to walk and read and laugh, and who matched me in temperament and taste and humour. I would run more and dance less!'

She was alight as she spoke, her eyes bright and animated, looking here and there, picturing what she described.

Then she turned her eyes on him squarely and said, 'I would choose a peaceful life, sir. That would be freedom to me.'

He was staring at her intensely. 'And what of passion?'

She frowned at him rather sharply. 'Why, that is part of it all,' she said, as if it should be obvious. 'To find passion in all those things, and passion with another. I have never agreed with the stories that say you can have either true love or calm waters, that real love must be turbulent. I do not want to believe that is true. And I *know* that the other side is certainly not true. A life *without* passion is not a peaceful one.'

'Your life is not ... peaceful now?'

She looked away from him, to her hands that she clutched together on her lap. 'No, sir. I am not at peace.'

'What are you both talking of?' Lady Catherine's voice came shrill from across the room. 'It appears you are having a lively conversation, and I must have some part in it.'

Sighing, Colonel Fitzwilliam replied, 'We are talking of riding elephants, Aunt. Have you the inclination?'

'Oh. No. I have seen one, you know, last year, at Covent Garden. It was not as large as I had been led to believe.'

She continued, and the whole party was expected to listen. The evening drew to a close not long after, and Colonel Fitzwilliam accompanied the Hunsford group to the carriage.

Mr Collins was first to say farewell, while Maria and Charlotte settled themselves in their seats. 'Please convey once again to your aunt our *deepest* gratitude for yet another wonderful evening in her company.'

'I shall, sir, and you are most welcome,' said Fitzwilliam. 'I hope I will see you again before I leave; I will endeavour to.'

'Oh! Your absence will be felt greatly by all, Colonel,' replied Mr Collins, dripping in sycophancy.

He would have gone on further if Charlotte, seated next to the carriage door, had not interrupted with, 'Well then, we hope to see you, and if we do not, we wish you well.'

'Indeed, Mrs Collins.' His gaze swept over the group just before their departure, and landed on Charlotte. His eyes remained there as the horses began to move, and as he uttered, over the sound of the wheels turning, 'I wish you peace.'

CHAPTER IX

The church of St Thomas the Apostle stood on a hill on the west side of the village of Hunsford. It was a rather squat Norman building, with a large number of stained-glass windows that were the envy of vicars across the county of Kent, if Mr Collins were to be believed, which he ought not to be. It was maintained by the church warden, a verger, a gardener and gravedigger – and Mrs Collins.

It ran the risk of being gloomy inside, its celebrated stained-glass windows rather dimming the natural light in the nave, and so Charlotte made it her regular duty to brighten the interior by adding extra candles (in winter or for evensong), hanging draperies and bringing and arranging flowers. This was already done by ladies of the parish, but she thought their efforts were rather meagre, verging on Quakerish.

On this bright April day, she had made the church ready for the next day's morning service, with a generous spread of white blooms all over – around every window, down the aisle, across the altar – until it seemed as though all was covered with a blanket of snow. The light was now beginning to dim slightly as she contrived to hang further greenery from the pillars, and she was perched atop a ladder, adding these touches with no small degree of precariousness, when she heard the church door open. From her view behind a pillar, she could not see who it was; nor navigate her way down, in all her layers, very quickly.

'Hallo?' she called.

'Hallo?' came back a man's voice, sounding bewildered. She did not immediately recognise it, echoing as it did around the empty stone church.

'Who is there?'

'Is that you, Mrs Collins?'

'Indeed.'

'Where are you? I cannot see you. I feel as if I am speaking to a celestial being; it is unnerving.'

Charlotte laughed, recognising the voice. 'I am behind the pillar, Colonel.'

She waved a hand to her right, which extended out far enough to be seen, and he spotted it and walked to her hiding place. She was up a good six feet in the air on a wooden ladder, which Colonel Fitzwilliam thought risky – he held the lower rungs to secure it while she tied the bouquet up. They didn't speak until she had finished.

She made her way down the ladder, minding her skirts, and he offered his hand for the final two steps. She smiled and shook her head – it is not helpful to take your hand off a ladder when descending with care – but she appreciated the gesture.

As she reached the bottom and turned around to face him, she realised they had accidentally ended up very close to each other, and she took a step back to remedy it. In doing so, she stepped against the edge of the ladder and knocked it sideways.

Instinctively, Fitzwilliam lunged forward to steady the ladder before it toppled, grabbing at it with his outstretched arm – only to unbalance himself. It was rather farcical, and in an attempt to steady himself, he clamped his other hand down on Charlotte's waist and unwittingly trapped her against the pillar with the full length of his body. (The ladder, crucially, was saved.)

This all took a matter of a few seconds, and once their composure and equilibrium had been regained, he looked horrified, while Charlotte was laughing heartily.

Once he saw this, he joined her. 'I am so sorry, Mrs Collins; I should not have tried to be a hero. Are you unharmed?'

'I am very well, sir; pray do not concern yourself. And your instinct to rescue ladders in distress must surely be praised.'

Her tone was serious, but he caught the glimpse of sarcasm in her and laughed again. 'I suppose not every gentleman can live up to such gallantry.'

'Indeed not, and a good job, too – women would be swooning throughout the day.'

They chuckled as they made their way towards the back of the church, where she had left her coat and basket. She removed her apron as she walked, her hands untying the strings from around her waist.

She had reacted casually to his touch, but she felt it now, as if his hand had been as hot as a branding iron. How tightly he had gripped her waist, how instinctively, pressing down on her hip bone to steady her, while her face was scratched by the stubble on his cheek as he leant over her. His grip was so different from the mild touch of her husband. She would not forget the feeling quickly and was grateful for the chance to walk it off.

'What brings you to St Thomas's on a Saturday, Colonel?' she said lightly.

'I come to take my leave. After such a pleasurable stay, I am called back to Spain.'

'Ah, of course.' She had known it must be soon. 'You leave tomorrow?'

'Early in the morning, yes. '

'It is generous of you to make the time, sir, in your haste. You came here expecting to see the rector, I presume?'

He hesitated. 'Not especially, no. I called at the parsonage already and said farewell to your husband and sister but found yourself and Miss Bennet were out. Mrs Brooke told me you would likely be here at the church, so …' He tailed off, a little bashful.

Charlotte grinned in spite of herself. 'Well, thank you Colonel. I shall be very sorry to see you go. Lady Catherine must be desolate.'

'Indeed, she would have me stay there forever, but then she also boasts of having a colonel for a nephew, so she cannot have it both ways.'

He was in his regimentals today, in readiness to rejoin his barracks. The gleaming red and white of his uniform became him. *How odd,* thought Charlotte, *that soldiers should always look so pristine when that uniform is destined for dirt and blood.* She tried to shake the morose thought from her head.

He adjusted his cross-belt distractedly as he continued, 'I called here to see you, but in truth, I had harboured some hope of seeing Miss Bennet. Do you know where she is?'

'Oh, yes, of course.' Charlotte had been expecting this. 'She is on one of her long walks; I am sorry you missed her. I could take a message to her, or – a token?'

Colonel Fitzwilliam looked unsure, pulled out his watch, and determined something. 'Yes. I would be so grateful if you would.'

Charlotte readied herself for some kind of embarrassing romantic item to be passed to her: a crushed rose, a torn-out page of poetry, a locket or some such. He produced nothing like that but invited her to sit down with him.

He hardly fitted in the pew; it was not a comfortable setting for sharing confidences.

'What I would ask you to convey to Miss Bennet is my heartfelt apology.'

'Oh! For what, sir?'

'Yesterday, I told her something about Darcy and how he had saved his friend from a marriage which … I do not know whether—' He was uncharacteristically hesitant at every word and said, 'Forgive me. My apology is about my indiscretion, and I do not wish to compound that by being even more indiscreet in involving you.'

'Sir, be at ease – Eliza is sure to tell me eventually, and you may rely on me keeping any secret.'

'Thank you.' He shifted in his seat, tilting his knees towards hers, to stop them pressing against the pew in front. 'Well then, here is my crime: I told Miss Bennet the story of how Darcy had saved his friend Bingley from a poor match, and I relayed all the objections to the lady and her family, which I had heard from Darcy. Miss Bennet listened and did not say anything, but I know now that the lady in question was Miss Jane Bennet and therefore I had been carelessly defaming Miss Elizabeth's own sister and her family.'

Charlotte took in this information. So Darcy *had* wilfully kept Bingley from Jane, after all. This would be heavy news indeed for Eliza. Charlotte wondered why she had not shared it, but then she realised this was probably the reason Eliza had kept to her own room this last day or so, with so much to concern herself.

The colonel continued, 'The terms with which I freely spoke of them, never knowing of whom I was speaking, were unthinkably rude. I only found out last night, in talking with Darcy, that this was the case. I would never have … I feel like an oaf, Mrs Collins, and I fear I may have really hurt Miss Bennet's feelings. I let my discretion fall away, all because—'

'Because you were enjoying her company so much and you wanted to retain her attention?'

The colonel looked embarrassed. 'Yes. You read me well, again, Mrs Collins. I have not been used to women's company this last year and, I must confess, I was carried away by it.'

'Well, I will pass on your apology, sir, and your concern for her – it speaks well of you.' Charlotte thought she would try to keep all options open for Elizabeth, brokering a future in this match, though there was a small pull in her gut as she did so. 'My friend is the best of women. I am sorry you must leave and suspend any feelings you may have for her, but perhaps on your return—'

'I thank you, but,' began the colonel, looking suddenly uncomfortable, 'while I have greatly enjoyed her company, Mrs Collins, I am in no position to make an offer and am not likely to be so.'

Charlotte was taken aback by his bluntness and said so to him, though kindly.

'Forgive my being forthright, Mrs Collins, but I think it must be helpful in matters such as this. And I feel I can be frank with you.'

Charlotte nodded, glad of what he said. She remembered the truth of his situation now. He had made mention of his position on one of their first meetings, suggesting he would have to make a wealthy match, if he did ever find the right time to marry. They were both of them reliant on the fortunes of their spouses, so she held nothing against him for the admission. It was probably rather humbling for him.

'Perhaps you will forgive my boldness now if I remark that it seems unfair that a colonel, fighting for his country who has endured so much, is not paid enough to pick a wife of his choosing.'

'Perhaps it is unfair, but it is as I always knew it would be. I am the younger son, and my brother has inherited all my father had, which was not so much as one might think. And I have always known my living would not suit a wife, even a rich one, if truth be told.'

'What a waste,' said Charlotte quietly, and then caught her own meaning and flushed. She hurried on, 'Does it make you very sad, not to have that choice?' she asked, thinking of Eliza.

'I hope you will forgive me if I say I am not heartbroken. I trust I have not raised Miss Bennet's hopes – I believe neither of us have been entirely invested, and I have been as open with her about my situation as I am with you now.'

'Ah, I am glad of it,' replied Charlotte, relieved.

He went on, with some hesitation, 'I have been... remarkably lucky to find the company I have these last few weeks.'

'Yes. Elizabeth has enjoyed your company, too, and she will rally soon enough – she has other ... she will rally.'

'I do not doubt it. But I did not only mean Miss Bennet.' He paused, looking at her more intensely. 'I have greatly enjoyed our talks, Mrs Collins. It is a pleasure to be – understood by another, and that is what I have felt with you. I thank you for it. It has been a privilege to become better acquainted with you.' His eyes seared into her own. He continued, 'In fact, I have never felt as—'

'That is enough,' said Charlotte, in an urgent tone.

The colonel was taken aback. 'I am sorry. I only—'

'I do not really know you, and you do not know me.' Charlotte would not meet his eyes. She went on hotly, 'I am glad our talks have been a solace to you, which must surely be because, as a clergyman's wife, I am a safe harbour for confidences—'

'I do not think of you in that way,' interrupted the colonel, too quickly.

She finally looked at him. His silence spoke more than his previous words had.

Taking a sharp breath, she stood suddenly, expecting it to break their conversation. He did not join her but stayed seated exactly where he was, his head at her waist, his body still, as if contemplating what he would do next.

She waited quietly, hardly breathing, as he slowly rose, until he stood over her, looking down. His eyes roamed her face, her hair, her mouth, and finally he said, 'I thank you for hearing me, Mrs Collins, and until we meet again, I wish you well.'

He took a step back out of the pew and, standing in the aisle, took her bare hand, which was rough and soiled from vines and leaves and tying string, and kissed it.

He walked out of the church, and Charlotte stayed standing there in the dim light of the church, looking at the open door, holding one hand over the one he had kissed, as if she could preserve it like a pressed flower.

When she arrived home a short while later, she found a full but quiet house; its residents and guests all scattered around in different rooms. Elizabeth had returned from her excursion, but was keeping her own company. Mrs Brooke told Charlotte that Colonel Fitzwilliam had called on them earlier and waited for an hour. Charlotte simply nodded and said, 'Yes, he found me – that is to say, he passed by the church – in the village, and he said farewell.'

As she entered her sitting room, she saw a small bunch of daffodils arranged in a vase on the side. 'Thank you for these, Brooke,' she called out, admiring them.

Brooke popped her head around the door. 'Not me, madam; the colonel left them for you.'

'For me?' said Charlotte.

'Yes, madam. Said they're your favourites?'

✤ 1801
MERYTON

'That will do!' Charlotte exclaimed in merriment, wafting away her maid, both of them giggling. Alice was still trying to fix a curl to Charlotte's temple, but it would not stay, and Charlotte insisted they give up. 'Who will mind a stray hair?'

'No one worth your attention, miss.'

'Quite,' answered Charlotte.

Looking at her full-length reflection in the mirror, she was pleased with what she saw: a very pretty green dress, not overly ornamented. It was not the most fashionable colour among Meryton society, but she wanted to stand out a little. Her hair was styled in a tuck, with the front tightly curled and pinned to fall softly around her face.

'Thank you, Alice,' she said, and the maid departed.

Maria came running in, a golden haired seven-year-old, full of admiration for her elder sister. She climbed onto the bed and asked again if she could come with her.

Charlotte sat next to her and hugged her tightly. 'I wish you could. Shall I fold you up and hide you up my sleeve?'

Maria giggled, her eyes widening in glee as Charlotte pinned her down, tickling her until she was bent in two and caused a cacophony that reverberated around the house.

Their mother entered the room, frowning. 'Charlotte, stop! You will spoil your hair!'

Charlotte released her sister, who ran off laughing and squealing. She stood, flushed, and faced her mother, pushing a curl off her face.

Lady Lucas looked her up and down and felt a rush of emotion. 'Oh! You look lovely!'

'Thank you, Mother. I will not disgrace you?'

'Silly!' Her mother laughed and, reaching into her reticule, pulled out something small. She held it in her hand as if it were a secret. 'May I add something?'

'I do not know,' replied her daughter suspiciously. 'What is it?'

'My goodness, have you so little trust in my taste?'

'No! You may dress yourself, but you do not know what *I* like.'

'Then let me show you. Would you like to borrow this for tonight? When I knew you would wear green, I thought it would suit.'

Lady Lucas held out a gold ring with markings on the band, beset with a small emerald, but there was something a little strange about it. Charlotte took it and examined it more closely.

'Oh …' she murmured, as she noticed that the cross-hatching was a nod towards scales and that the clasp of the stone was shaped like the head of a snake; as it joined the other side, the snake ate its own tail. It was rendered discreetly – one could not notice the peculiarities of the design at a glance.

'It does not seem very like you!' said Charlotte, impressed. 'Did father buy it for you?'

'No! I chose it for myself. Some years ago. It is an ooro … ooris …'

'Ouroboros,' Charlotte finished for her, still staring at the ring, engrossed.

'Yes! That's it.'

'It is a symbol of the cycle of life, I think – destruction and renewal,' said Charlotte, falling into her scholastic mode. 'Eternity.'

'Is it?' said her mother, grinning at her daughter. 'I just liked the snake.'

Charlotte smiled back at her.

'You and your books!' said Lady Lucas, as she rose and started checking Charlotte's hair.

'I promise not to speak too much of antiquity or the classics to potential suitors, Mother,' Charlotte said wryly, fiddling with the ring.

'Well, but do you wish to wear it? That was my object!'

'I do,' said Charlotte. 'I really do.' She slipped it on and danced her fingers around in a little flourish, enjoying the sight. 'Thank you. Oh, it complements my dress!' she exclaimed with pleasure.

'Yes, I know!' replied Lady Lucas. 'That was my rather my intention in offering it! Honestly, Charlotte, have some faith in your old mother.'

They both looked into the mirror, her mother standing behind her, proud and nervous. 'New beginnings, you say?' said Lady Lucas, lost in a moment of deep reflection.

'Not quite, no; it's more of a cyclical—'

'Oh, heavens!' Lady Lucas laughed, exasperated. 'Never mind! Come, let us go downstairs – your father is waiting.'

'So, Lady Lucas, this is your eldest, and what a pleasure to see her! Has she been out long?'

'I thank you, sir,' replied Charlotte's mother. 'Tonight is her first formal occasion.'

'She is a credit to you. What a well-presented young lady.'

'She is fond of dancing, sir, if your legs grow restless.'

Mr Weatherby laughed and nodded but made no reply.

The evening had started off well – Charlotte was asked to dance immediately, by the handsome son of a family friend. They did justice to a cotillion, but he did not request a second. She was asked after that by an older gentleman, a widower, who said during the dance that she reminded him of his daughter, which Charlotte did not feel entirely comfortable with. She was not approached for the next, or the next. She felt a little embarrassed – she had come very ready to dance every dance, as most of her friends had during their first evenings out.

It was ten o'clock before Charlotte was asked to dance again and that was by her cousin, Frederick, who was fourteen and had not yet learnt his limbs. He was not tall enough to perform some of the required steps with her and kept staring at her bosom. It was a chance, however, to be seen on the floor, and she took it.

After that, she danced with a very elegant gentleman called Mr Bailey. There was some chatter from her mother after this, but Charlotte had gleaned enough from his manner and conversation that he was not entertaining romantic thoughts at present – not towards women, at any rate. She then waited out three dances until there was a chance to play the piano instead. She started making her way to the unoccupied pianoforte, ignoring the disapproving looks of her mother. Once seated, she began to play a sprightly country reel, a piece to allow others to dance and allow her to fade into the wallpaper, to be a fixture and not an ornament. She played for the next few dances, until it was very late. She started to wish she were wearing white or pink or another more ordinary colour, to blend in with the other young women. She felt rather exposed.

By the time she rose from the piano, half the room had emptied, and hardly any gentlemen remained. Her mother looked rather sad. Charlotte, taking her cue, felt rather sad also.

When they got home, Charlotte dallied in the hall a moment to ask her mother if there had been many eligible men there tonight.

'Not – not many,' was the reply, but her mother had hesitated, and unluckily for her, Charlotte was not easy to fool. She nodded slowly, understanding.

'I am not so much a prize as some ladies in the neighbourhood,' she said, which made her mother's eyes flood with indignant tears.

It is one thing to understand that you have not been picked out for special attention by anyone, but it is another to watch your daughter experience such a marked lack of any attention and realise its implications. It is, perhaps, a heavier burden for a mother to bear than for the daughter herself.

'You, Charlotte, are worth more than any of them. You looked wonderful tonight, you showed them your skills, and I am sure you will dance more in future. You have more to offer a husband than any young woman I know. You are not a prize to be won, but upon my word, the man who does win you will be lucky indeed.'

Charlotte smiled softly. 'You are biased, Mother.'

'Of course I am, and I will always be. But I am still right.'

Upstairs, Alice helped her undress. Charlotte took off her emerald ring and asked Alice to return it to her mother. Once the maid had gone, Charlotte laid out her green dress on the bed and looked at it, admiring its beauty, and she felt that it had been rather wasted tonight. Determinedly, she steered her mind towards the practical.

'Well, at least I may wear it again soon – after all, it will not be well remembered.'

CHAPTER X

Life became much quieter following the removal of so many visitors. Elizabeth and Maria had left shortly after Darcy and Fitzwilliam, so the reduction in society was sudden, though not unwelcome at first. Between settling into Hunsford after the wedding and the arrival of her friends and family in March, only a few weeks had elapsed, and so Charlotte had not yet had much opportunity to experience what her new life really felt like, day to day.

Spring slid into a warm summer, and just as Charlotte's garden began to bloom and flourish, so she found herself growing into her new life with more colour and more vigour than before. She found a routine which suited her well: her visits to the village, looking after the church, keeping house, gardening and writing letters to her mother and sister and to Elizabeth kept her occupied – though Elizabeth was more lax in replying than usual.

Charlotte walked a great deal. The countryside around Hunsford was stunning in the summer. The parkland around Rosings led right to their gate at the parsonage. Before nearing the grand house itself, there were acres of land that they were welcome to enjoy freely. A long avenue of beech trees led the way through the estate, with paths leading off it into the lawns and woods that made up the farthermost gardens.

One part of those grounds, which she had stumbled upon in February and was keen to revisit, was an area of woodland that she found enchanting. Trails led up high to rocky outcrops and down to cave-like hollows beset with knotted roots and tangled undergrowth, the thicket dotted with rhododendron bushes that decorated the wood with flashes of colour when in bloom. In winter, it had been a fairyland – dark, shadowy, mysterious. In summer, it was a playground – splashes of pink, purple and blue, lit by shafts of sunlight which burst through the canopy making them glow. It was a special place, and all her own.

On the other side of the parsonage was farmland – yellow fields stretching out for miles, divided by country lanes and footpaths, some of which led into Hunsford or other neighbouring villages (if you welcomed a long walk) or allowed one to simply wander through the fields in the hazy air of high summer.

Charlotte explored it all, little by little, savouring each new part of it, unwrapping the gifts of her surroundings one at a time.

She had occasionally shared these walks with Mr Collins and had hoped it might be a pastime that would bind them closer. She did not expect a marital miracle, but in her modest hopes, she imagined there would be a rare accord between them. As it was, her husband was not very comfortable on country walks. His eyes seemed to squint in the sun or be bothered by the breeze, blinking and watering. His clothing itched and chafed and it was too much, or too scant. He would stumble and trip often, but that owed as much to his lack of attention as it did to a want for surefootedness – his gaze was never expanded out but kept close to his own person, or to Charlotte's. He could not keep pace with her, even though he was taller, because he walked in small steps and with hesitations and interruptions, fiddling with a shoe or moving a twig or turning to check on his wife.

Therefore, they now had an unspoken agreement that country walks were mostly taken by Charlotte alone. She was grateful for solitude over a poorly matched companion. However, in the recent days of bright sunshine, when she could wander freely, bare-shouldered and freckled and sweaty, glorying in the sights around her, she wished so much that she had someone with whom to share it all.

There was a development in her situation that she had not expected, which was that, at the invitation of Lady Catherine, she began visiting Rosings every week, alone, to practise the pianoforte. She let herself in by a side door, as instructed, and crept to the little square pianoforte in Mrs Jenkinson's room, which was a good, basic instrument. She had a few sheets of music herself, brought from her home in Hertfordshire, but she found a large and up-to-date collection of music left for her on the instrument, varying from country dances to the latest Beethoven sonata.

After a few weeks, she encountered Lady Catherine as she was leaving the house.

'Next time you come, Mrs Collins, play on the Broadwood grand in the drawing room. It is a superior instrument, and I think you would feel the benefit.'

'Oh, I am very happy where I am, Lady Catherine—'

'Nonsense. You are becoming a fine pianist, and you should play on a fine instrument. And a pianoforte needs playing, or it will go out of tune, so it would be a favour to me if you would play it.'

Lady Catherine did not look as if she were requesting a favour; Charlotte took it as an order but soon came to appreciate being pushed towards the scheme. She had enjoyed the privacy that came with her upstairs practise sessions but she found, to her surprise, that it was gratifying to be heard by the household. Lady Catherine often made herself absent for these times, and Charlotte could only guess at whether this was due to a surprising sensitivity – acknowledging that always having an audience was not helpful for improvement – or because she did not have such a 'true enjoyment of music' as she once claimed. Either way, it suited Charlotte well. She was transported on these visits. Her passion and her skill at the instrument were secrets she held for herself, and she treasured them.

Her contentment came from everything in her life, excepting her marriage, but she had not yet wholly resigned herself to despair on that front. She knew that her husband was not a sensible man – she had always known that. But neither was he a cruel man; he could be judgemental but never towards her, and she found that her hopes for the marriage continued to evolve. During weeks when she had not spent many hours with him, she could think that, in time, she might come to love him, in a companionable sort of way. On days when he was buzzing around her, like a persistent wasp, she thought that, at most, she would be able to tolerate him indefinitely. And at other times, she pinned her hopes on the notion that a sudden apoplexy would carry him off. Her thoughts were uncharitable, but they were private, so she let them be and tried not to think them in church. This was difficult, because listening to his poorly written sermons was one of the chief agitators for her.

Each month, she waited to see whether her courses would be late, if her body would swell, if her face would glow as she had been told it might.

But each month her body – her healthy, robust body – remained the same, running like clockwork. It was a disappointment. She knew that six months was not a long time to wait for a child, but she felt a need for her life to advance, and this seemed like the natural next step. She did not feel a longing for a child – not yet. If solitude was her comfort, she knew a baby would be its thief, and she was in no hurry for that. But she had no idea what a married life looked like without children. A life spent with Mr Collins, with just each other for company, did not appeal.

Meanwhile, Mr Collins's appetite in the bedchamber had increased. He grew in confidence, though little in skill. One mark of this evolution was that, while formerly he had attempted to make love while wearing his nightgown, he would now, at least, disrobe before the act. He did so in a rather ceremonial way, folding each item of clothing after he had removed it and placing it on a chair. He did not require the same from Charlotte, apparently preferring for her to remain in her nightgown and for him to work around it. Charlotte did not have the experience to know what was and was not standard practice, but she felt instinctively that she would rather clothes were removed or cast aside in the heat of passion, rather than as a pre-ritual formality.

She had hoped she would grow more used to it, but as time went on, the opposite happened. Their communion felt more wrong each time; while her mind accepted it, knowing it to be a requisite of a stable marriage, her body did not, and at times she had to force herself not to pull away, not to stiffen in her body.

But Charlotte had always been a fast learner and resourceful, so she began to seek out ways of making it all more comfortable for herself. She experimented while alone, until she found a few methods which she could employ to ensure that marital relations were, at the very least, physically endurable. But any pleasure she was able to find she owed entirely to herself and always in spite of Mr Collins rather than because of him.

So, while Charlotte was keen to be with child, she found she could not match her husband's enthusiasm for what he insisted on calling their 'delightful duty'. Her consolation was that this was only a small part of what marriage to Collins afforded her, and so it could be endured. It must be.

✣ 1803
OXFORD

The dining hall of Merton College was rowdy and stifling. A rowing victory had the boys in high spirits, and a lot of the crew were drunk on bad wine and triumph. The end of Trinity term often saw a lot of students neglect their studies for the river, and a crew from Merton, a college not known for sporting prowess, had beaten Magdalen that day in what was meant to be a friendly skirmish but was taken as seriously as the Battle of Bosworth Field. There were more races expected in the days to come.

'If we can bump Magdalen, we can take on bloody Christ Church!' jeered a bunch of damp boys, their voices easily cutting through the clamour of the hall, the clanking of their glasses and the screeches of their chair legs echoing around its high ceilings.

Magdalen and Christ Church, with their 'small-chinned pampered princes', were not well liked in this company, so a victory over them was even sweeter. This cohort of Merton loyalists would enjoy the moment, before they were, in all likelihood, bumped themselves tomorrow.

William Collins sat at one end of the long, dark wooden table, eating his meal and trying hard to avoid the attention of the others. This was his third term at Oxford, and it continued much like the previous two: eight weeks of intense study, working late into the night, his cheap tallow candles making his eyes water with smoke.

'You finishing that, *Scholar*?' came a rough voice from close behind his head.

Henry Russell, still smelling of river water and sweat, was not much taller than William but held himself with all the confidence of an Eton boy. Add to that the bulk of a powerful rower (he was a natural in seat five), a meagre intellect and a history of boorish behaviour – which, in a poorer boy, would have landed him in front of the magistrate, but which, with his family connections, had always been dealt with quietly – and you would find a young brute who would inherit Wiltshire before he had finished growing.

He was the same age as William, but seemed older than his sixteen years, partly because of his aforementioned confidence, and partly because he had the facial hair of a much older man, stubble arriving daily and thickly. Unchecked, he would resemble Captain Blackbeard – fitting for someone whose actions were not far from those of a pirate.

'Er – yes?' replied William, unsure of the answer least likely to cause a stir.

'What do you need game pie for? Keep you strong for sitting inside reading the Bible? Or will you take some home to send back to your mother?' Russell laughed at his own words, so often the preserve of people who cannot make others laugh. 'Come on, Moonface – give it to me.'

Russell pulled the plate towards himself, and plucking William's fork from his hand without compunction, he stabbed at the pie, shovelling what remained into his mouth while dropping crumbs onto William's shoulder and into his hair. He met William's eyes as he ate, which was intended to be threatening but was also rather disgusting. William could hardly look away from the meat globules catching around the whiskers on his top lip. William said nothing, but looked over Russell's shoulder, seeing most of his peers watching the scene and grinning.

William Collins was known around the college as an odd fellow and an easy target. He had arrived at Merton with little luggage, no reputation and no established friendships – unlike most boys there, who knew each other from one school or another. Apart from his academic dress, he had brought mostly black clothing, as befitted his intended profession. But this was a practical choice also, because stains and dirt would not show as easily on black, and he could not afford to often change his clothes.

It was quickly learnt that he was there on a scholarship, which only added to his isolation, and his habits of reading indoors, alone, became a self-fulfilling prophecy. He had grown pale and thin; as the dining hall became a place of danger to him, his appetite had waned. *Scholar* and *Moonface* were not as offensive as some names he had been called in his life – being, respectively, factual and descriptive – but the name-calling signified to him the same thing it always had: that he was strange to them and not wanted.

He was a brilliant student. His memory for whole passages of the classics or philosophical texts or the scripture was a marvel. His Latin took some work – he had not the early training in it that most of these boys had – but he learnt it well enough and quickly.

At first, he had struggled to speak up in tutorials, afraid of nasty comments or being shouted down by a peer or a tutor (he had not been raised to think his voice worth hearing). But as time went on, and he saw that one of the tutors actually wanted to listen to him, he began to speak more. At first, he would tremble as he spoke, but as months went on, he trained himself to keep his voice steady. He achieved this most often by not stopping; a pause gave him too much time to overthink, which led to further hesitation. Better to plough on, he discovered, and he became more adept at speaking in front of people, though not so adept at speaking *to* people. He had made few friends during his months of study, but in tutorials, asked to monologue on a particular subject, citing references and proffering opinions, he was in his element.

He watched Russell chomping his venison and glowering at him. A shiver ran through his shoulders, and he hoped that Russell would not see it. He could think of nothing to say, and feared whatever he did say would earn him another beating.

But he knew he must speak, to save himself.

'Of course you must have it,' said William obsequiously. 'You need it much more than I, having achieved so much for the college today. I imagine you made the Magdalen boys feel very small, and I think there is a good chance you'll do the same tomorrow. I wish that I had the vigour for rowing, but alas, it is the reserve of gentlemen like yourself. Have my wine; I'm not drinking it.'

Russell, nonplussed, looked him up and down. He went to say something but, having been beaten to the line on every point, uttered lamely, 'Yes, that's right.' He grabbed William's drink and downed it, unnecessarily, and returned to his company.

William, looking at his plate and fixing an odd smile on his face to deflect any further attentions, waited ten minutes for the moment to fully pass. When he felt sure the waters were quiet, he stood and walked the long way out of the hall and back to his room.

He lit just two candles, sat and opened his Bible, finding a part that comforted him lately.

'And he said unto me, "My grace is sufficient for thee: for my strength is made perfect in weakness."'

28th July 1812

Dear Charlotte,

I write to you from Longbourn, for I am brought home from the Peaks earlier than anticipated due to some very bad news, which I will tell you of now.

You will remember Mr Wickham from his time in Hertfordshire with the militia. You did not care for him, I think. I, who fell for his tales so easily, should have listened to you.

He is a liar, Charlotte, and a villain. I knew some of this even when I was with you in Kent – I wish I had confided in you, but so much was happening during that time.

I am writing this all in a muddle – forgive me; there is much to relate.

I must tell you first, before the pressing news, that when I was staying with you in the spring, Mr Darcy asked me to marry him. I turned him down.

You will wonder why I did not tell you at the time, and the answer is here: the morning after his proposal, he handed me a letter that contained such revelations that I was in a stupor of a kind, wrestling with the mistakes I had made – including, perhaps, my refusal of him. It was shortly before I was due to leave, and I was quite ill with it, Charlotte, as you will recall. I could not add to that the task of sharing it – I have told no one but Jane, and even she had to wait a few days.

In short, the letter marked Wickham as a cad – I cannot go into the particulars, but it confirmed he has seduced young women, racked up large debts, is a drinker, a gambler and lied with such ease about his relations with Darcy that I know not how he maintained his composure. The Wickham I knew was a fantasy, a concoction, but recent events must confirm that he is not imaginary but all too real: a living, breathing monster.

My opinion of Mr Darcy changed upon reading his history. I have had cause to spend more time with him in Derbyshire, and either he has altered or I have understood him better. Perhaps a little of both.

Anyway, that is all for nought now, because he will never ask me again once I tell you what has come to pass.

The militia were posted to Brighton. Lydia was allowed to go with them, as the special companion to Colonel Forster's wife, which I counselled my father against. But even I could not have predicted what has since come to pass.

We have lately learned that Lydia and Wickham have eloped. They have not even gone to Gretna Green as everyone supposed but are residing in London. You can imagine the rest. They have been there a fortnight and, as far as we know, remain unmarried.

She is lost, Charlotte, and I know not how we can forgive her. I cannot say this to Jane; she is all sympathy and 'Poor Lydia', but I hope I can say to you that I am so angry with her, I feel like my skin must be hot to the touch. You know her – silly, foolish, thoughtless Lydia! – all her instincts were always to do something daring and outlandish that would amaze us all, and now she has. She will have no thought of what it will cost us, what it already has. Not just reputationally but in body, in spirit.

My mother has taken to her bed – that will not surprise you, but Jane tells me that my father visibly shrank upon hearing the news. She says that, before he left for London (he is there now), his skin turned grey. He was weakened, could hardly walk. I fear what will greet us upon his return.

Oh Lydia! I should pity her, but I cannot help but rail against her stupidity, her selfishness. And when we meet her – God knows when that may be – she will laugh about it. I know her too well to doubt otherwise.

Of course, of course, I am angrier at Wickham — he will have seduced her using all the charms at his disposal, of which I have been party to and fallen for, and which you, so wisely, never did. It need not be said that I will now despise him always. But I also cannot imagine finding love for Lydia. I can say these dreadful things to you only — they are unchristian and unsisterly and probably unfair. But I can say them to you, my dear friend, for I know you will not judge me.

I am sorry for not writing to you before catastrophe has befallen us. I should have. I will write again soon, when we have more news.

Your affectionate friend,
Eliza

CHAPTER XI

Charlotte sat with her mouth open. This was shocking indeed, and she grieved for her friend's prospects – but then she also was astounded at the revelation of Darcy's proposal. *When I was staying with you,* the letter said. But how? Where? Was it here, under this roof? Charlotte had guessed at an attachment on his part but not that he would go so far, and with so little encouragement. But now, she feared such an advantageous match would be impossible. If Lydia truly was lost – if she did not marry Wickham – it would bring the whole family down. Bingley would not be allowed near Jane; nor would any other gentleman of good standing.

And she felt, too, her friend's anger at Lydia. She had always thought Lydia foolish – she had even said so to Mr Collins once. But in the moment, now, she had the distance to feel sorry for her. Wickham, it seemed, was practised at this – Lydia had not stood a chance against his persuasion. He would have chosen a vulnerable animal for his prey and recognised such a one in Lydia. She might not have been weak in body or in spirit, but she was vulnerable to flattery and to desire.

Charlotte wished to reply immediately, so she left her sitting room to look for a pen in the study, taking the letter with her.

She returned to her sitting room with a clean sheet and a pen and began her response. It took over an hour, on and off; the balance of reassurance and honesty was difficult to get right.

Introducing Mrs Collins

When the letter was nearly complete, she heard the front door open and close and stood up to see whom it was. As she passed into the hall, she saw Mr Collins through the open doorway to his study, reading something and making small exclamations.

Curious, she went over and asked, 'Mr Collins? What is it you are—'

And then she paused, for she saw that it was her letter from Elizabeth.

'How did you get that?' she asked crossly.

'Why, I found it here on my desk, my dear. I assumed it must be intended for me, and then, after reading a very little, I considered it my duty to continue – this is, after all, *my* family.'

Charlotte must have left it on the desk when she had been searching for a pen, but it should have been obvious that an opened, crumpled letter was not for him. She was incensed.

'That is private correspondence, Mr Collins – it is for my eyes only.'

'I'm afraid news such as this will not long be concealed.'

She looked at him very sternly. 'That is private – please stop reading it.'

'I'm afraid it is too late for that, my dear; this is my second perusal, and I assure you, what it relates is even more shocking the second time.'

'Then, I ask you this, very seriously: if you value me, do not act on this. Tell no one, I beg you. It is not finished yet – we do not know the outcome. The Bennets' reputation will be harmed, yes, but more grievously if news gets out prematurely.'

'But I must console with them, as a minister! I must help them in their hour of need.'

'I promise you that your consolation will not be welcome.'

He lay down the letter, and she walked over and picked it up, folding it roughly, anxious that she get control of the situation.

'I have already written to Mr Bennet.'

Charlotte was puzzled. '… When?'

'I wrote to them within this hour, as soon as I read of their predicament. The balm of ministerly concern cannot be delayed. I sent Brooke out with the letter a few minutes ago.'

Charlotte's face flushed with anger. He had schemed to accomplish this quickly, before she could stop him. It was a deception, and a deliberate one. This was a side of Collins which was mercifully rare but which she detested. She did not trust him to have written a good letter. She felt sure, in fact, that it would have been at worst hurtful and at best absurd. She saw in his face that he revelled in the downfall of a family who, as he saw it, had rejected him. He believed that Elizabeth had thought herself above him, and now, with this, the opposite was true, or so he would see it.

Charlotte walked out of the room and went to their bedroom, not trusting herself to say anything to him. All she could do was hope that the letter was taken as a curio and not as an affront, and she hoped she would not be tainted by the words written by her husband. This was not a position she wished to be in, as a wife.

She felt suddenly nauseous and faint, and she lay on the bed until dusk, when she realised she was ravenous and made her way downstairs to supper, sitting opposite a quiet, guilty-looking husband.

Charlotte felt unwell for the next few days and put it down to the shock of Elizabeth's news and the argument with Collins. But when she had to leave the Sunday church service in the middle of a hymn to expel the entire contents of her stomach on somebody's unfortunate grave, she started to take more notice. It was not her favourite hymn, but it did not merit quite this reaction. The whole congregation had seen her squeeze out from the front pews and run down the aisle. And so, to avoid the pointed enquiries from parishioners, she did not return to the service but walked home, appreciating the fresh air.

Mrs Brooke was surprised to see her back early and enquired if she was well. Upon discovering what had happened, she raised her eyebrows and cast her eyes down to Charlotte's belly.

Charlotte paused, accepting it herself for the first time, and gave a rueful smile. 'Yes, I think it must be that. I am ... rather late,' she said with a meaningful look.

Brooke nodded, understanding, and smiled warmly. 'Oh, I am happy, Mrs Collins. A little one in the house! I have been hoping! Shall you inform Mr Collins?'

'No!' Charlotte replied sharply. She softened herself, smiling. 'I would rather wait until the outcome is more certain. I do not want to disappoint him.'

'Of course, Mrs Collins. I will say nothing. May I bring you something to eat and some water?'

'Thank you. I will go to my bedroom; I am still a little unsteady.'

Charlotte lay on the bed, her hands on her stomach. It was, of course, still perfectly flat, but she noted that – yes, her breasts were very tender, and her stomach still roiled. This must be it, she thought. There was no official moment to know for certain – merely the collection of signs and feelings put together to form a good guess. A baby. She would have a *baby*. How tiny it must be, she thought. The size of a walnut, perhaps, or maybe even smaller. Her baby. All of her own. Well ...

Her mind clouded a little as she thought with whom she would share it. But the doubt passed quickly. This was a new start for her. Her body would change; her thinking would change. She already felt protective of her little walnut, a feeling she had never experienced before.

She felt instinctively that she would have a girl – she could only picture a girl. What might she show her? What stories might she tell her? What songs might she sing her? *Hmm. I do not have a voice for lullabies,* thought Charlotte, wondering if such a skill was a key part of motherhood. Her mind rested on a happy thought: *I will play for her.*

Over the weeks that followed, Charlotte continued her visits through the gate, down the drive, across the lawn, into the back door of Rosings and to the grand piano that awaited her. She played sonatas and waltzes and scherzos and preludes and bagatelles – all the music she could find.

She played with joy, with abandon, and she played for *her*. She did not know whether her baby could hear her yet, but she played all for her.

CHAPTER XII

Mr Collins was seated in the drawing room, in one of the less comfortable chairs, reading a book of sermons. He would occasionally pick up the biscuit resting on the table to his side, taking a single bite – each time scattering crumbs upon his page every time and each time, with mild surprised and faint annoyance, brushing them briskly off.

Charlotte was on a chaise-longue, considering her husband. In the few weeks since she had first known, she had been choosing her moment. 'My dear, I have some news.'

Mr Collins looked up over his book, eyebrows raised. She waited for him as he put down his reading, then beckoned for him to join her on the chaise-longue.

She did not wish to waver, so she said simply, 'I believe I am with child.'

He did not seem to comprehend her words for half a minute, but then, as their meaning settled upon him, his eyes widened, and tears came to them. A giddy smile formed as his lips trembled with emotion. He gently took her hands and, bringing them up to his face, kissed them.

For once, he did not have a speech prepared. 'Oh, my dear Charlotte. Such joy. How lucky we are. How lucky I am.'

Charlotte waited for him to descend into trivialities or a speech about the fate we are handed by God or the best way to position a crib, or to suggest a list of terrible names, but he did not. He just kept holding her hands and smiling, and he looked down at her not-yet-rounded belly and smiled more.

'I wonder if it will be a boy or a girl.'

'We can have no way of knowing,' began Charlotte, a little shyly, 'but I have a feeling it will be a girl. I do not know why.'

Collins beamed. 'A little girl. Yes.' He was quiet again, painting a picture in his head.

He was so uniquely enchanted by what was being presented to him that Charlotte wondered, as she often did, what occupied his mind on a daily basis. It was as if, despite their marriage and shared bed, and his sermons on the importance of family and even his remarks about his hopes for one – spoken in his very proposal – he had never, until this moment, considered that it would come to pass. The idea seemed brand new to him, and the effect of it was not unpleasant. Charlotte saw that he was utterly delighted. He had been stopped short by it, and it softened her towards him.

She rather liked this version of her husband.

'The sun is very sharp in here, Mrs Collins. I know not how you can stand it. I shall have to look away from you.'

'Oh, pray, let me move so that you are not looking at the sun.'

Charlotte took the footstool by the fire, the only other possible place to sit in the room that was not in front of the window. She would not have asked Lady Catherine to swap seats with her for all the world – once Lady Catherine was seated, she would not be moved, even for her own convenience.

'You ought to fit the windows with thicker drapery – these fine, thin curtains do no good.'

'I rather like the sun streaming in, Lady Catherine, but I can easily see it is not to everyone's taste.'

'Well, I am glad you can easily see – even if, owing to the ineptitude of your curtains, I cannot.' Lady Catherine paused to ensure her barb had landed, before continuing. 'Now, I come to see you because—'

Lady Catherine had a useful habit of always telling someone explicitly, at the start of her visit, why she had deigned to come – as if to acknowledge to her host that it was indeed an honour and she would not have done so without valid reason. Charlotte did not mind this habit; she found it gratifying. To be told someone's intention and objective, particularly if that person was otherwise rather difficult, was a gift.

'I have lately heard from Mr Collins that you are with child.' She paused a moment, waiting for Charlotte to confirm or deny.

Charlotte was surprised that her husband had told his patron so soon – a mere matter of days since she had disclosed the matter to him – but then, at the same time, she was entirely unsurprised. Nothing could be more in character.

She nodded, so Lady Catherine continued, 'And I come to offer my advice.'

Not, notably, her congratulations.

'How are you feeling? You look very green.'

'Oh, how kind of you!' said Charlotte, daring to be a little playful.

'Well, you will find I do not mince my words, and I do not believe you to be missish about these things. You do not ordinarily look green, therefore there is no offence to be taken, Mrs Collins. Is your hue merely down to sickness, which is to be expected?'

'Yes, my lady, I believe it is.'

Lady Catherine nodded but did not look satisfied. 'Well, as time goes on, I offer the services of my physician, Dr Chappell, who is excellent in all these matters' – Lady Catherine made a small hand gesture at Charlotte's abdomen – 'having studied in Edinburgh.'

Charlotte was rather bewildered by the interest that Lady Catherine seemed to have in her pregnancy; she had given more thought to the practicalities than Charlotte had.

'Oh, well, I thank you, Lady Catherine. I had not – that is, I assume all will be well.'

Lady Catherine fixed her eye on Charlotte and nodded sharply, continuing, 'Well, the doctor will be present at Rosings a great deal, so you will most likely meet at some point. He will tend to my nephew, who is lately returned.'

Charlotte's brain had four or five questions at once, rendering her unable to ask any one of them, so she merely blinked. Just as she opened her mouth, Lady Catherine ploughed on.

'Colonel Fitzwilliam – you will remember. He was injured last month and has come back here to recover. I am sure I have told you that my nephews are particularly attached to Rosings.' Lady Catherine smiled as if she had won her point.

'How badly is he injured?'

Lady Catherine looked surprised by the question. 'It should hardly be a topic of conversation between us, Mrs Collins.'

Charlotte was blindsided by this about-turn in the rules of conversational intimacy, given the last few minutes.

'Of course, but – he will live?'

'Oh! Yes, he will live.' Lady Catherine paused for a moment with her lips pursed, in an uncharacteristic display of uncertainty. 'He would benefit from an uplift of spirits. Dr Chappell can tend to his wound but is not a source of comfort or levity, if truth be told.' She frowned for a moment, looked at Charlotte and then raised her eyebrows; she made her thought processes very visible, like seeing the machinery of an open clock. 'You make visits around Hunsford, I think, to those who need help?'

'I do.'

'I wonder if you might add Rosings to your list – we would welcome your company. Occasionally.'

Charlotte dared not demur and replied, 'Certainly.'

She felt a brief jolt of excitement at the idea of seeing him again, but it was complicated by the thought of both his physical state and her own.

With a satisfied nod, Lady Catherine went to rise, but then said, 'Your husband must be delighted.'

This must relate, Charlotte quickly calculated, to the earlier topic of conversation.

'Yes, he is. He really is.'

'It is a very fine thing for him. And a very good thing for *you*.'

Lady Catherine seemed to imply a mysterious higher meaning, more than the usual congratulatory sentiment, but Charlotte was too tired to wonder at what she meant. She simply thanked her ladyship and saw her out to her carriage before Mr Collins could arrive home and extend the visit by an hour.

2nd September 1812

Dear Mr Collins,

I was delayed in reading your letter but now reply to it with haste, in the hope that I might catch you before I lose your approval of yet another of my daughters. Perhaps Kitty will be next; I hardly know whether to expect you to propose to her or condemn her; either seems possible, or perhaps both. Thank you for your condolences and your fears on my behalf. I was of a mind to throw off my youngest daughter's affections, as you so keenly suggest, but after reading your letter, I no longer feel inclined to. She will have plenty in the world who will do that, you and your patroness chief among them, and I think I shall not add to their ranks. By the by, my youngest daughter is lately married; I can assure you that has no effect on my shift in sentiments. Lydia is not the most sensible of young ladies, but she is of good heart, and she does not judge others for their errors, as some do. "Judge not, that ye be not judged" in Matthew is a passage well-thumbed in my Bible; presumably that chapter remains pristine in your own copy.

I suspect we will have little to do with each other these next few years, until that time arrives when you will be seated here at the very desk where I now sit. I wish you, and more particularly your wife, happiness. I have learnt many lessons these last few weeks, and I continue to do so as I reflect on the whole affair. My situation would not have been happier had I chained my daughter to my hearth but might have been improved had I educated her better, and not only with the word of God. Should you be blessed with a daughter, I hope that she thrives and that she breaks every expectation you have of her – and is all the better for it.

My best to Mrs Collins.

P. Bennet Esq.

CHAPTER XIII

It was a few days after that – in the first week of September, with the air still warm – that Charlotte headed to the 'big house next door', as she and Brooke called it. Charlotte felt like quite the regular at Rosings. Between social occasions and her piano practise, and now with the addition of her first pastoral visit, she almost felt she ought to start paying rent. As she walked down the beech-lined drive, she considered what might await her upon her arrival. She not only wondered what might have befallen Colonel Fitzwilliam, but could not help recalling their last meeting.

In the days after he left in the spring, she had, in her modesty, persuaded herself that she had imagined any provocation or suggestion from him that was out of the ordinary. She first told herself that she was a married woman, and any gentleman of sound mind would see she was unavailable. She also reminded herself that she was plain. She was not likely to be the object of an inconvenient lust or a wanton frisson – it was fantastical. Such was what her modesty told her.

But as well as being modest, Charlotte was also logical, and when her brain took inventory of his actions and words, she decided that, yes, there had been something. What it amounted to was probably very little, but it was not nothing – he had alluded to something more than ordinary acquaintance. But, she comforted herself, it was a fancy of his, and it was fleeting. She had no doubt it would have been forgotten, swept away by his experiences since then. As for her own feelings – well, her mind was now set on the future: her tiny bump and how her life was soon to change. She needed no other intrigue to occupy her. She trusted her emotions would not betray her.

She did not slip in the back door, as she did on her piano practice days, for this was a different kind of visit, the rules of which she did not know. She was shown into the morning room by Figgis and found Lady Catherine in her usual chair, with a recumbent Colonel Fitzwilliam on a large chaise-longue near the fire, a blanket over his lower body.

His face was worn, tanned and leathery, and there were hard lines and small scars where there had been none before. His hair was shorter than the last time she had seen him, roughly cut. Instead of wearing his uniform, he was now clad in a crumpled banyan, wrapped tightly about him.

Her first feeling upon setting eyes on him was a fierce protectiveness. She fought an urge to go straight to him, to tend him. But as she watched him closer, she came to suspect that such feelings from her would not have been welcome.

When Charlotte had been announced, he had smiled politely, but as she drew nearer, she saw a look of disquiet in his face.

Charlotte was invited by Lady Catherine to sit on a chair nearby; she did so, placing the basket she carried to one side. Not knowing what might greet her, she had brought some scones and a tincture for fever – items she might take on her other visits – but she did not feel inclined to offer up anything here and now. The atmosphere was awkward; she felt she was intruding on what should be private.

'Good day, Lady Catherine,' she said and, turning to him, 'Colonel Fitzwilliam.'

He cleared his throat, 'Good day, Mrs Collins. My aunt told me you might visit us one day this week. I hope you will forgive my appearance.'

'Of course. I am sorry you are in discomfort.'

'Discomfort is a luxury I now enjoy, following its predecessor – bloody agony.'

Charlotte was shocked at his language and visibly so; this was rather rough talk that she had not been used to – common among soldiers in barracks perhaps but not in a morning room, to a lady. He did not retract it or apologise, however, but stared into the fire, troubled.

'My nephew has been poor company in the last few weeks, Mrs Collins – I am hopeful you might improve his mood.'

'Quite a task to set her, Aunt.'

'It is, but I know she does such things for others who are embittered by their circumstances; I have seen it in the village. You, nephew, might begin by asking Mrs Collins how she is. Though you are injured, you are not the only person in the world with news to tell.'

Colonel Fitzwilliam looked chastened and sat up a little more. 'Forgive me, Mrs Collins. It is good of you to come. I did not want to receive you in such a state, but my aunt insisted.'

'Please, do not make yourself uneasy on that score. I have seen people in worse states than yours.'

Fitzwilliam nodded graciously but remained a little detached.

'May I ask,' Charlotte began, then hesitated, glancing at Lady Catherine, as if seeking permission to ask, before continuing, 'what has happened to you?'

Colonel Fitzwilliam looked surprised. 'I thought my aunt would have told you. Shot in the leg.'

'I am sure Mrs Collins need not know the details of your injury, Nephew. You forget you are not in company with your men now,' warned Lady Catherine sternly.

Charlotte dared not reply after witnessing such a rebuke, but Colonel Fitzwilliam, visibly irritated by this, said tersely to his aunt, 'I can hardly forget that.' He then turned to Charlotte. 'Are you shocked, Mrs Collins?' he asked roughly.

'I am not.' She looked apologetically at Lady Catherine at this minor betrayal. 'I have seen all kinds of injuries on my visits, so I am unlikely to swoon from mere words.'

Colonel Fitzwilliam nodded, as if he had won an argument. 'I expected as much.'

Charlotte dared to ask, 'Is it healing well?'

'It got the bone. It's not shattered, thank God, but it's ... I know not – *they* know not the extent of the damage, for sure. But there's a break of some sort, and it will take its time to heal. I cannot walk on it, which is galling.'

He rambled this off while not looking at her, as if ranting to himself. It was clear to her that he was in very poor spirits, and she was silent, allowing him to rail against his condition. She knew not what he had suffered through, and it seemed fair to her that he would be agitated. But it troubled her that she did not wholly recognise him.

He fell quiet then, taking a breath, and said, 'It has robbed me of my manners, Mrs Collins. How are you?'

'I am well, thank you,' Charlotte replied. 'I have not been shot in the leg.'

Colonel Fitzwilliam laughed at this, then winced, the movement evidently triggering a pain somewhere.

Lady Catherine looked unhappy at the levity.

'I am glad to hear it,' he answered, then asked, with visible effort, 'Your husband is well?'

The door opened at that moment, and Figgis walked in and whispered something to Lady Catherine.

The great lady rolled her eyes and sighed with exaggerated exasperation. 'Can not Mrs Jenkinson deal with such things?' she said, in what seemed as quiet a voice as she could muster, which was loud.

Figgis replied again, close to her ear; his ability to convey a message soundlessly was a marvel.

Lady Catherine gave another large sigh and heaved herself from her chair. 'I must attend to something, Mrs Collins. Pray do not leave; I will return shortly. Figgis, it is very stuffy in here; please open a window – Mrs Collins will be hot.'

Figgis did so, before both he and Lady Catherine left the room. Fitzwilliam and Charlotte looked at each other, smiled awkwardly and looked away again.

It was only now, when they were alone, that the memory of their last meeting rose briefly as a spectre between them. But, as Charlotte had predicted, something had shifted since then. His injury – or rather, his incapacity due to it – had altered him, and it loomed in the room. It was as if he was still at battle, and she could not get near him. She, of course, had her own reason to feel distanced from him, but she would keep it to herself for now.

'I am glad to be alone with you,' the colonel started.

Charlotte flushed, thinking that surely he would not now continue in that vein.

Fitzwilliam, seeing her expression, realised how it sounded, and hurriedly continued, 'That is, I am glad to spend time with someone other than my aunt.'

Charlotte breathed out with relief; she had assigned great effort to putting that intrigue firmly away, for her own well-being, and was not prepared to unearth it.

'Lady Catherine has been so good as to allow me to convalesce here. She has brought in her doctor and keeps me company daily. But, I confess, to be *this often* in her company is—' He struggled for the word.

'Character-building?' offered Charlotte.

He smiled with gratitude. 'Yes,' he affirmed, with a wry grin, 'character-building.'

Charlotte looked around the large, ornate room. 'This is a grand place to convalesce. How is it you are here and not at your family home?'

'This is by far the better option – the only one, really – so I am grateful to Lady Catherine for taking me in; she does me a great service. Rosings is an easy distance from the port – they brought me to Dover – whereas Tolbrooke Hall is exceedingly far north; I would not have withstood the journey.'

'Ah, I see. A shame for you, though, not to be at home.'

He hesitated before replying, then shook his head. 'My *home* is not … Tolbrooke is not as it should be. It was never a grand house, nothing like this.' He gestured at the majestic room around him. 'But as things are now, I am not even convinced of it having the fires lit, nor would I expect an entirely warm welcome.'

Charlotte was intrigued. 'Why not?'

'My brother and I are not on friendly terms.' Charlotte frowned, inviting him to elaborate. 'I blame him for what has happened to Tolbrooke, and he knows it. It may be his now, but I remember how cherished it was while my mother lived: the care she took of it, the pride she had for it. He has run roughshod over her legacy, gambling away much of what was needed to maintain the house, and it is now in a terrible state. His wife and children suffer for *the earl's* itinerant habits.'

His lips curled in disgust as he spoke of his brother, and Charlotte was shocked to hear him being so damning; this darkness in him was a revelation.

Seeing her reaction, he adopted a more cheerful tone. 'Staying there would be a more humbling existence, certainly. On the other hand, it might urge me to hasten my recovery, simply to be able to leave.' He tried to make a joke, but the bitterness beneath it was evident.

In other circumstances, Charlotte would have asked many more questions, but she could hear his desire to move on and acquiesced. 'Then it is well that you are here,' she said, smiling at him.

After a moment's silence, as Fitzwilliam looked absorbed in his own thoughts, Charlotte dared press him a little further on the cause of his abstraction. 'Do you want to tell me about your time in Spain?'

He shook his head. 'I think I will not speak of it today. I am glad to see you, and if I begin to open my mind to that, we will not ... I would be glad not to think of it for a while.'

'Of course. But tell me this – is there anything I can bring you that will make you more comfortable? I can see Lady Catherine has the advantage of me in most things, but is there any way that I may help? That is why I am here after all – to be of service.'

'Oh. Yes, of course. But I hope you come here as a friend also, not just to fulfil a duty?'

'Yes. As a friend, of course.'

He considered her shrewdly. 'You look very well, Mrs Collins. I mean, you look in good health.'

'I thank you, sir,' she replied guardedly. If she were truly honest with herself, Charlotte did feel something for Colonel Fitzwilliam; that instinctive attraction she felt towards him, her interest in him, had not disappeared, in the wake of her pregnancy or his injury. However, she felt less disquieted by it now, because she felt more sure of her own ability to ignore it, given her new circumstances. She only hoped that he would do the same.

He looked down pensively and seemed to be considering what next to say. Charlotte was nervous of what his speech might contain. When he spoke, his words set off an alarm in her.

'When last we met, I began to tell you—'

But she would not let him finish. 'I have some news of my own,' she blurted out, and found herself saying. 'My family is soon to grow.'

A breath escaped him and for a moment, as he gazed at her, his eyes betrayed a thousand varying, complicated reactions. And then he blinked, and his eyes looked only kind. Certainly, he had been a little taken aback, not least because such things were not often spoken of between men and women, but then the two of them had always been more direct with one another than was quite proper.

The slight frown had disappeared, and he smiled warmly, if perhaps a little sadly. 'Mrs Collins, that is wonderful news. You are happy?'

She read in his look a genuine enquiry, and trying to reassure him with her own expression, she answered with equal sincerity, 'I am, Colonel. I am very happy in this.' She said it firmly, deliberately.

He nodded and was quiet, as if accepting a truth he could not argue with. He had weathered the blow quickly, for her sake. 'I am so glad for you. It already suits you. Mr Collins must be delighted?'

'He is. In fact, I must take my leave, to be back for supper with him.'

'Of course, of course. But my aunt has not returned yet.'

He looked anxiously at the door, unsure of the etiquette. Charlotte thought he seemed a little child-like, if truth be told. Here was this brave, injured officer, who had seen foreign lands and led men into battle, but who was now like a lost boy in his aunt's care.

'I'm sure she will forgive me. Would you please pass on my regards?'

'I will. I am only sorry I cannot stand to see you out.'

'You are much better where you are. Do not rush to recover, sir; take your time and be fully healed before you test it.'

'I know not how I will ever be fully …' He started to speak bitterly, but tailed off. 'I will not hurry it, Mrs Collins. I thank you very much for visiting. I will be appreciative indeed of your company in the weeks to come, if you can spare it.'

'I can, and I will. May I bring you anything to comfort you, or amuse you? A book? Or some other pastime?'

'I can do little but read. I am struggling to name another pastime I could enjoy in this state.'

Charlotte thought. 'You might sew.'

He guffawed and winced again. 'Sew?!'

'And why not? Because you think it so much a lady's activity? You think it trivial perhaps? Or easy?' She was provoking him, but in good humour.

'No, it is only that I have done enough of that on campaign.'

'Sewing?' she asked incredulously.

'Most soldiers know how to sew. I do not know how to embroider a pattern, but I take some pride in my skill with repairs and patches. My stitching is better than most.'

She looked at him curiously. 'I should have thought, as a colonel, that would be done for you.'

'Ordinarily, it is, but I have always done my own if there is time. When on campaign, I find it curative.'

She smiled and nodded. She added this to the little library of information she had of him.

'But I have no uniform to patch at present.'

'Well then, there is nothing for it. I will teach you the piano.'

'Oh my!' he exclaimed good-humouredly.

She laughed, curtsied and exited.

As she walked home, she felt very satisfied with the meeting. She recognised a healthier accord between them, provided by their changed circumstances, though she could hardly rejoice in the reason for his change. He was, understandably, very different from how he had been in the spring, less able to put on a mask of well-being, and even before she delivered her own news, he seemed ill-equipped to deal with anything other than companionship at present. Although it was not planned, the revelation of her pregnancy had worked as intended: it had drawn a line between them. She could be a friend to him now, a companion, a nurse at times, but all from a place of safety – she had seen from him that he would respect it.

She pulled her shawl close about her as the evening breeze grew harsher. Catching a thread on the button of her dress, she was reminded of his admission, which conjured in her mind the image of a weary soldier sitting in his quarters, patiently sewing a patch onto the sleeve of his torn shirt.

10th September 1812

Dear Charlotte,

Thank you for your letter of last month. It was a consolation to Jane and myself in such a time of turmoil. We also received the letter from your husband, which was interesting, and which gave comfort in a way unique to himself. I am inclined to think you perhaps did not have a hand in its writing.

I promised to write when there was better news, and I am glad to say – there is! Although our measure for what is good news is set very low at the moment. Lydia and Wickham are married. Perhaps you already know for I believe my father wrote it to Mr Collins. It is not what anyone with sense would wish for, but given the prospect of a far worse outcome, most of us feel grateful.

We have so many to thank for the achievement of the scheme: certainly my uncle, Mr Gardiner, but chiefly, it was arranged by – you will not believe it – Mr Darcy! He who I imagined had sighed with relief to be out of my sphere when he heard the story. He must have paid Wickham a great deal to persuade him to marry, and he has bought him a commission in the regulars – a regiment up in Northumberland, far away by design. The thought of Wickham sharing that uniform with the calibre of men we know to serve the army is galling. But it is done, and I will never have the words to thank Mr Darcy. But, my friend, you must be thinking, Eliza, do not pretend you do not know why he acted so.

Let me be truthful with you, then, and tell you that I hope so much it is for me that he acts. But I cannot be sure of it. He certainly had his own motives; I believe he wanted to play a part in taming Wickham and lessening any further crimes he might commit. Therefore, I cannot know that his acting in my interests was for me, or if my interests merely coincided with his own wishes.

You will already know that Jane and I would wish the whole affair to be as little known as is possible. The marriage must be announced, because any suspicion that they remain unmarried is intolerable, and yet we still fear the looks and whispers of society that are bound to come. When I think of that, it seems even less likely that a man such as Mr Darcy would attach himself to me.

My father is still very unwell. This matter has shocked the life from him; he walks slowly, he eats little, and his humour is much reduced. He blames himself, I know, but I have never seen someone take on such guilt and worry into their bones as he has.

Your mother and father have visited us, which was kind and timely; their show of support helps lessen our status as pariahs, as I am sure they knew. Was it at your request that they visited? That is just the sort of clever thing you would think of.

You said little of your own news in your last, which was unsurprising given its purpose to comfort, but I would be glad to know more of my friend. Are you well? Have you spent more time at Rosings? Do you expect any visitors during the winter months? Even in these last weeks, I have thought of you, Charlotte. I cling to Jane for comfort, but I miss your honest counsel – and your wit. Perhaps I could visit you in the coming months, depending on your plans, and providing Mr Collins will allow the association.

Your affectionate friend,
Eliza

15th September 1812

Dearest Eliza,

I am delighted to hear that a conclusion has been drawn on such a difficult matter and wish you all as much comfort as can be found at this time. I am not as astonished by Mr Darcy's involvement as you are. From what I have heard from Colonel Fitzwilliam, Mr Darcy appears to be a man who takes action to help a friend, and I admire him for it. I look forward to meeting him again, which I have reason to think I shall, for several reasons. Forgive me, Eliza, but I am hardly being fanciful when I say I believe he will apply to you again. I am sure he acted, at least in part, to win your approval. He has his honour, but he is not a saint.

You might already know some of the news I can impart? Our friend aforementioned, Colonel Fitzwilliam, was injured at Salamanca (you will have read about the battle, perhaps?) and is recovering at Rosings. His leg is badly injured, so he is rather trapped inside with his aunt. I have offered the best remedy I can, which is to provide alternative company, for which he seems grateful.

My other news, which is much more mine to tell, is that I am with child. Among all of the upheaval you have experienced in recent weeks, I hope this makes you glad. It certainly makes me so.

I send my fondest regards to your family, but especially to your dear father, whom I hate to hear of as being unwell. I will be thinking of him. Pray do not mention me to your mother, as I do not think she welcomes my regards.

Yours in affection,
Charlotte

CHAPTER XIV

On something of a whim, shortly after finding out about his impending fatherhood, Mr Collins decided to start employing a curate. There was no real need for this, for there was very little to take him out of the parish and prevent his fulfilling his role. And, after all, the wages would come out of his own living, which did not seem to Charlotte to be entirely helpful. However, when a polite, red-headed young man arrived at the church, with a charm that won over the elderly ladies and a gift for preaching that won over everybody else, it seemed like a decision well made. Mr Smithson was a good conversationalist, if a little over-pious, and was able to occupy a useful position at the parsonage as well as at the church, possessing as he did an unusual capacity for listening to Mr Collins at length. This was as much a help to Charlotte as it was to Mr Collins.

September proceeded with unusual sluggishness; Charlotte felt so eager for the next stages of her own journey – to have the shape and glow of a mother, to feel her baby move – that the weeks passed slowly to her mind. Having never before felt a yearning for it, she now felt as if it were the most natural thing to happen to her. It felt entirely right.

She filled her time with pastoral visits, including those to Rosings. She had visited Colonel Fitzwilliam three times since his return, and his improvement was slow: he seemed to wince a little less each time and had more mobility in his upper body, but his spirit remained rather dimmed.

And yet on her fourth visit, she immediately saw there was a marked change: he was now dressed for visitors, in a smart brown tailcoat and cream breeches.

'You look well, Colonel,' she said upon entering.

He turned to her and said drily, 'I have always thought that a cravat becomes me better than a coverlet. Your comment gives me confidence that I am correct.'

This attempt at good humour was an effort made for Charlotte, but as the other visitors poured into the room behind her – namely her husband and Mr Smithson – he retreated back into silence. Lady Catherine had invited the new curate to Rosings, which was quite an honour. She put great esteem in the clergy and, though poor, a curate's position was adjacent to that of a gentleman, as far as she was concerned – far beneath her, of course, but worthy of attention.

Mr Collins began, 'Mr Smithson has been a worthy addition to the parish, Lady Catherine, and if I may be so bold as to make such a judgement, I believe it reflects well on Hunsford as a parish that we value the workings of the church highly enough to have acquired one.'

'I think you are correct, Mr Collins. And you, Mr Smithson, where did you study? Oxford?'

'Cambridge, Lady Catherine.'

'Oh dear,' replied Lady Catherine, wrinkling her nose. 'Well, it will suffice, though I have always thought it far inferior. Which college?'

'St John's, my lady.'

She nodded – this answer, it seemed, was satisfactory. 'Good,' she said sagely, as if he had narrowly avoided a calamity. 'And where are your family?'

'In Lincolnshire,' Smithson replied hesitantly.

'Lincolnshire is a fine part of the country,' Lady Catherine declared. Charlotte could not help but wonder on what criteria these judgments were formed but was relieved that, with no other information, families across Lincolnshire had been declared fit for purpose.

Mr Smithson ventured, 'I have had the good fortune to have spent a great deal of time with the Russells of Shepton Court. They have supported me since I was fourteen.'

This information had not been previously supplied to Charlotte or her husband; if Mr Smithson had kept it specially to present to Lady Catherine, it seemed a rather calculated move – but, Charlotte had to concede, a successful one.

'The Russells?' exclaimed Lady Catherine. 'Very fine people. I have dined with them – at Shepton – many years ago. The sons are old friends of Fitzwilliam.' Lady Catherine glanced over at her nephew, who nodded noncommittally. 'Mrs Russell's brother went to *Oxford* with my late husband. Are you still connected with that family?'

'I am, and they delight in my appointment here.'

'Very good,' said Lady Catherine, exceedingly pleased with this news. She eyed Mr Collins at this moment, as if thinking to herself how disappointing his connections had turned out to be.

Mr Collins flushed, presumably falling on the same thought himself: the shame occasioned by his youngest cousin's recent actions. Once Lady Catherine has returned her focus to the curate, Charlotte put a reassuring hand into her husband's, which he accepted gratefully.

'Are your lodgings satisfactory?' continued Lady Catherine in her interrogation of the curate. To an outsider's eye, the great lady could almost appear altruistic in her enthusiasm to know about the comfort of other people's houses.

'Yes, indeed. I am living, in fact, in the house of Colonel Raeworth. I owe the arrangement to Mrs Collins, who recognised so cleverly that I was in need of somewhere to live and he in need of someone to assist him.'

Colonel Fitzwilliam, who had otherwise been somewhat taciturn, roused a little at this and leaned forward. 'Lieutenant Colonel Raeworth? Of the 50th Foot?' he asked.

Mr Smithson looked unsure and turned to Charlotte for the answer.

'Yes, I believe so,' said Charlotte. 'He is a colonel now though – since he came home. He told me when we first met.'

'Why is he no longer serving?'

'He lost his leg in battle.'

'When?' Fitzwilliam was almost badgering Charlotte.

'I am not certain, but I believe it was a few years ago.'

Fitzwilliam refused to abandon his line of questioning. 'Corunna? Talavera?'

'Yes,' said Charlotte, glad to have something for him, 'I think he said Talavera.'

'Talavera,' he repeated, nodding. 'So, they gave him a promotion after that, did they? A leg for a title. A fair swap.'

'A shank for a rank,' added Charlotte, stumbling on the wordplay and speaking it almost without thinking.

To everyone's surprise, Colonel Fitzwilliam broke out in almost violent laughter, and as his reaction faded, he gave Charlotte an approving nod.

She smiled tightly, secretly pleased. It was clear that the rest of the party had been left behind in this moment of levity.

Mr Smithson, however, was undaunted and would not be distracted by the lightened mood. 'I believe, from what I have seen of Colonel Raeworth, that he is honoured to have served his country so valiantly. He takes solace from this and from his faith. "I beseech you therefore ... that ye present your bodies a living sacrifice, holy, acceptable unto God, which is your reasonable service."' Mr Smithson held an unusual expression as he said this to Colonel Fitzwilliam. It was that of a teacher, giving a difficult lesson.

Fitzwilliam returned his look with some distaste. 'Many young men carry a Bible with them on campaign, Mr Smithson, and it has been a great help to some.'

Mr Smithson smiled wider, until the colonel continued, 'If worn in the front pocket, it can sometimes stop a bullet from a musket blast.'

Mr Collins gasped, scandalised. Mr Smithson did not look shocked but calmly understanding, which Charlotte imagined was even more irritating to Fitzwilliam.

'*If we may* talk of something else,' Lady Catherine broke in, looking sternly at her nephew, then turning to Charlotte, 'what of your friend, Miss Elizabeth Bennet? I have heard something about her sister being lately married?'

'Yes, I believe so.'

'To a Mr Wickham?'

'Indeed,' returned Charlotte, determined to close down any further discussion.

Lady Catherine sensed her reticence but was equally determined in the opposite direction. 'It was a very short courtship, I have heard. This is what comes of girls being allowed out before they are ready. She was out at fifteen! And now look.'

'And now she is married to an officer in the army. I think her mother is well pleased with the outcome.'

'The outcome, perhaps, but not the method.' Lady Catherine spoke these words pointedly and looked at Charlotte, as if she were somehow responsible for this scandal. 'And your friend, Miss Elizabeth. Has she hopes of matrimony? This must affect her chances.'

Charlotte looked at her and blinked, refusing to rise to the bait. 'I do not know.'

Lady Catherine held her gaze, her eyes demanding a more complete answer, but Charlotte would give none. Turning to Mr Smithson and Mr Collins, Lady Catherine continued, 'I have always been concerned for the care of young women. When they are neglected and allowed to go to ruin, I feel it very deeply.'

'Indeed, your compassion is evident, my lady,' simpered Mr Collins, in an attempt to make up for his stiff, unsmiling wife. 'Society owes you a debt for the interest you have taken in families that have not been steered as well as you have steered your own.'

'On Sunday, I plan to speak of the importance of protecting the morality of young women,' spoke up Mr Smithson boldly.

As Lady Catherine smiled approvingly at him, Colonel Fitzwilliam broke his silence, with, 'But nothing on the morality of young men?'

Mr Smithson was caught off guard. He turned to the colonel. 'Of course, both the sexes have an obligation to adhere to godly behaviour, but the sanctity of womanly virtue must be protected.'

'Is it not men who are the chief risk to womanly virtue? You might as well preach that message exclusively to a congregation of gentlemen on Sunday and let the ladies enjoy a walk outside, if such an activity does not threaten their moral standing.'

Mr Smithson was not cowed by this challenge. He looked as if he enjoyed it. 'I abide by the Bible, sir. "Who can find a virtuous woman, for her price is far above rubies."' Smithson smiled beatifically, as if he were speaking as a prophet himself.

'And I choose not to talk about women having a price,' countered the colonel, pushing himself up straighter to better stare down the young curate. 'Morality is all very well, sir, as far as it serves us and God, but I tell you I have seen women punished for behaviour far less immoral than that of the gentlemen who judge them. I have known men, braggards, who have stolen that "sanctity" women are supposed to hold so carefully, then walked away with their reputations intact. Equally, I have seen boys as young as fourteen, encouraged to drink and swear and take their pleasures with women, all so that they be hardened up for battle and made ready to die. I would pray for *their* sanctity. I think you have it the wrong way round, sir: keep our boys pure and give the girls a little freedom.'

He slumped back in his chair. Charlotte thought that if he could have taken his leave, he would, and she felt disappointed for him that such a moment of drama was denied him. She was rather struck by him in that instant: his vigour. She liked what he said very much. She tried to catch his eye to communicate this to him, but he had retreated into himself and was now determined not to look anyone in the face.

Lady Catherine turned to the Collinses and Mr Smithson. 'I think it is time that we bid you good day.'

One of the things Charlotte admired about her husband's patroness was her readiness to dismiss her guests when the time was right. It was a talent she hoped to learn herself.

She went to take her leave of Colonel Fitzwilliam and found him looking at the back of Mr Smithson's head with some distaste.

1802
LONDON

Miss Eleanor Trowbridge, dressed in a pink satin dress and white gloves, with a pearl-encrusted bandeau across her blonde hair, skipped gracefully down the line of gentleman. Then, after rounding the corner, she took her partner's hand once more and ducked under an archway formed above them by another couple's hands.

Eleanor grinned at Captain Fitzwilliam as they emerged and settled back into their line. The final strains of the music sounded, and she curtsied; her partner bowed and offered his arm, leading her to the side of the ballroom. Her face was flushed with the movement and with the heat of a summer's evening.

'You do not know that dance,' she teased him.

'I truly do not. I was following Lord Archer for most of it, but he abandoned me at the third section.'

'I saw it happen. That is when you trod on Miss Palmer.'

They both laughed. 'You shall not want to stand up with me again,' challenged Fitzwilliam, knowing what her answer would be.

'I think I shall bear it. I shall just have to teach you more steps.'

He tilted his head down to whisper in her ear, 'I shall be a willing pupil.'

She looked up at him, her eyes fiery with anticipation, and he felt no less excitement.

While no official engagement had taken place, there was an understanding between them that it would be secured soon. One full season might, to one couple, seem too short a time to be sure of a courtship; but to another, it could feel as long as a lifetime. He was ready, and she was hopeful.

It had been early in the season that Captain Fitzwilliam had spotted a pretty girl whose eyes seemed to be challenging him across the ballroom and had entreated his brother to make the introduction.

Thomas, the elder Fitzwilliam brother, had laughed, 'You make quick work of the London scene, Richard. She certainly seems interested. One moment …'

In a matter of minutes, Miss Trowbridge and her mother were talking to Captain Fitzwilliam and his brother, who was styled Lord Charlton. The mother's eyes widened considerably when she heard the title of the elder brother, and there was no doubt she was keen to secure his interest for her daughter, but Miss Trowbridge had eyes for no one but the young soldier.

As her mother engaged his brother in conversation, Captain Fitzwilliam had the attention of Miss Trowbridge to himself. She began, 'I have not seen you around the town before, sir. How can that be?'

'I have been posted in Gibraltar, Miss Trowbridge, but now that we are peace, I am happily returned.'

'And do you enjoy ballrooms, when you are used to barracks?'

'I like both well enough. I am certainly appreciative of varied and lively company, having spent a year with a hundred men on a rock. I welcome new acquaintances.'

'I am glad to hear it,' she replied.

Their initial attraction had given way, over the coming weeks, to a very real attachment between them. He admired how unafraid she was – bold in her actions as well as her conversation. Some evenings, she danced with nobody but him, and touched his arm as she spoke to him. She was not afraid for people to see how attached she was, and that made him love her more.

She noticed how he went out of his way to put people at ease; he was well-mannered, but he also seemed principled; she had seen him argue a point with gentlemen far senior to him, and she liked him all the more for it. He occasionally drank too much, but

Introducing Mrs Collins

she supposed this would improve with a more settled life. More than anything, she liked his steadfastness towards her; he had not looked with interest at another since the first moment they met, and nor had she.

When Captain Fitzwilliam called at the family's townhouse late in the summer, he was shown into her father's study. He was a large, balding man in his sixties, with a genial look and a low, calm voice. He did not look horrified to see the young man at his door, which seemed to Fitzwilliam a good start.

'Come in,' he beckoned, his smile one of resignation.

'Thank you.' Fitzwilliam walked in stiffly, stood opposite the desk, and announced rather formally, 'Sir, I come to ask for your daughter's hand in marriage.'

Mr Trowbridge sighed. 'Yes, I thought as much.'

Fitzwilliam said falteringly, 'I – I love her very much. I would endeavour to take good care of her. I only have an income of—'

'Captain Fitzwilliam, I know what your income is, approximately. It is that of an officer in the army, and not yet a very senior one. I have seen you with my daughter, and I have asked around about you.'

Mr Trowbridge proceeded to deliver a painfully accurate report of the captain's fortune, prospects, character – he had heard reports of Fitzwilliam's drinking and fighting within his barracks – and his ability to provide for a wife.

'I intend to take a house as soon as I am able—' interjected Fitzwilliam rather desperately.

'It could be ten years before you can do so.'

Fitzwilliam had no answer: it was true. He felt suddenly foolish, like a love-struck boy with nothing to recommend him. Mr Trowbridge's manner was not unkind, but it was unyielding, and the truths it held fell like blows.

'My own estate is only of modest means, Captain Fitzwilliam – much like your own family. Certainly, your father holds the earldom, but there is not a great deal of wealth, I believe. And what wealth there is will never come to you, as the younger son. My daughter must marry well. I do not have a substantial dowry for her, and I want her to be comfortable.'

'But—'

Trowbridge held up his hand to indicate that he had not finished. 'Were it merely this reason, I might be willing to overlook your lack of fortune. But you are a soldier.'

Here, Fitzwilliam did object – and fiercely! – asking through gritted teeth, 'And is there no honour in that, sir? In a man who fights to protect his country?'

'There is great honour in it, Captain.' Mr Trowbridge looked weary. 'But if you truly love my daughter, what life do you hope for her, while you fight or march or conquer?'

'My life has not been so much abroad – a stint in Gibraltar, which held little danger, but otherwise, I have been stationed at home.'

The other man nodded. 'It will change.'

Fitzwilliam looked puzzled.

'You know that I sit in the Commons. I hear what is happening; I follow it closely. We know that this peace will not last. It was fragile from the moment it was agreed. The French have no interest in the treaty, and it is simply a matter of time before we are at war again. It shall not be long. Where will you be then?'

Fitzwilliam looked at him, taking in what he had said. 'I do not know.'

'No. You do not. Perhaps Europe. Perhaps the Indies. Perhaps dead.'

Fitzwilliam stared at him, struggling.

'I want better for Eleanor, and so should you.'

Fitzwilliam's breathing was heavy. He felt the truth of what had been said, but it did not help. He wanted to push the desk over, to rail against the man. He needed a drink. He felt he must leave before he said or did something he would later regret, and so, forcing himself to look Trowbridge in the eye, he curtly said, 'If the matter is lost, I will take my leave.'

Mr Trowbridge nodded. He felt genuine sympathy for this smart, earnest, rather naive young man. 'I wish you well, Captain Fitzwilliam. I think you will do great things.'

Seven months after this embarrassing refusal, Fitzwilliam was at another ball. He stood to the side of the room, conveniently near to the table where a large bowl of punch was sitting. He swayed a little, watching the cotillion taking place in the centre of the room. He was accompanied by two old friends, but not ones he was very fond of – Thomas Russell, whom he had known since his brief few terms at Eton, and a fellow officer, Captain Radlett. All three were rather drunk and getting disapproving looks from better-behaved guests. Russell, in particular, was blessed with the naturally resonant voice of the upper classes, and it was in full effect tonight.

Fitzwilliam had spent a miserable winter on garrison duty with the 149th, bored, restless and hopeless. He might better have borne his failure with Eleanor, and the loss of his future prospects, as he saw it, had he been active and useful. But he felt worthless doing drills and exercises in barracks. He had not felt that before; he had not felt the call to fight so keenly. But now – it was galling to be stuck here, when the obstacle that prevented him from her was his call to duty.

It was the first event of the season, and he had attended in some desperate hope of seeing her.

Just as he was considering leaving, he saw her, on the arm of her mother, dressed in ivory and with the same pearls, the same locks of fine blonde hair and that same smile. He resented that she looked the same: he knew that he did not. Ravaged by drink and regret, he was not the sunny boy she had met last year. They had written to each other after her father's refusal: loving words full of passion and sorrow. But ultimately, she had listened to her father and abided by his decision.

Now, she looked at him with such concern and compassion that it hurt his heart. He must look wretched indeed.

'Who's that?' asked Russell loudly, seeing the girl look at his friend.

She heard him and turned away, back to her group. Fitzwilliam ignored him.

'Come, who is she?' asked Radlett. 'That blonde piece over there – pretty. She's an interest in you, Fitz.'

'It is Miss Trowbridge,' answered Fitzwilliam wearily.

'Trowbridge …' Russell seemed to be dredging some memory up from his drunken brain. 'Eleanor Trowbridge! I've heard about her.'

Fitzwilliam frowned at him. 'What have you heard?'

'Quite a lot of fun, I think,' said Russell lasciviously, raising an eyebrow and warming to his subject. 'Made quite a spectacle of herself last season over someone, maybe a soldier actually – I'm not certain. They weren't engaged, but I hear she has a light skirt!'

'Ah, a shame. So pretty,' said Radlett priggishly, 'but no one will want a girl who's lost her virtue.'

Radlett heard a sound beside him, like a low growl, and found himself pulled up by his collar and shoved against the wall, pinned, his feet only just touching the ground. Fitzwilliam held him roughly, saying nothing but pushing so hard against his gullet that Radlett could hardly breathe. Unable to speak, he grabbed at Fitzwilliam, pulling at his lapel, trying to break free, but to no avail. He remained suspended for a few seconds until, all at once, Fitzwilliam let him go. He slumped to the ground, bending at the knee, recovering.

'What the devil, Fitz?!' cried Russell, as Radlett got his breath back.

Everyone in the room was staring at the display, and there was a hushed excitement. This kind of event would be the talk of the season, and they were grateful to have witnessed it.

Fitzwilliam looked around the room and saw Miss Trowbridge staring at him, horrified. He looked back, trying to convey some meaning to her with his eyes – sorrow, apology, farewell – but she continued to look mortified. He heaved a sigh and, with bent shoulders, hurried from the room, taking no leave of his friends.

Late that night, upon returning to his barracks, he found he had torn his jacket in the skirmish. Looking in his kit, he found the needle and thread he always kept, but rarely used, and started roughly tacking the fabric seams back together. His mother had taught him to sew, much to the disapproval of his father. She had shown him running stitch, back stitch, tent stitch. She had told him to be slow and patient when his frustrated hands wanted to race. He did not easily get to grips with the intricacy of the task, and once, in frustration, had declared it was not a job for a man. His mother, though indignant, had laughed at her little eight-year-old proclaiming himself a 'man' so soon. But she told him that you needed strong hands to sew, which he had. She patiently, determinedly taught him this skill, saying that he should learn to take care of himself. She was already preparing him for life without her.

He looked down at his work and thought that she would not be especially proud of it. It was sloppy, rushed. He pulled out the thread and started again with a neater stitch. Once completed, he cast off and, happy with his work, put on his jacket. He thought about his mother. He thought about Eleanor. He thought about going to war, and he found that he was suddenly eager for it.

He would not have long to wait.

CHAPTER XV

It was late in September that Lady Catherine next invited Mr and Mrs Collins to dine with her, in a fairly informal setting – or as informal as dinner at Rosings could be. At the head of table sat Lady Catherine, who, as she often did, invited Mr Collins to sit at the opposite end – a privileged position which he relished. He did not let her down; before she had taken her seat, he had already remarked upon the grandeur of the table arrangements, the finery of her gown and even how perfectly suited the weather was, as if she might merit praise for having arranged that, too. Lady Catherine took his flattery in good grace, always appreciative of admiration and deference in equal measure.

Colonel Fitzwilliam sat next to his aunt, with Mrs Jenkinson on his other side, while Charlotte found herself placed between Lady Catherine and her daughter, Miss Anne de Bourgh, whom she had not spoken to for some months. Charlotte knew her to be about six-and-twenty, but she appeared younger, with fine wispy blonde hair, a thin frame and a very pale complexion – unsurprising for someone who seemed not to have set foot outside for as long as Charlotte had known her. Charlotte had often found her difficult to converse with, sometimes hardly uttering a word, but this evening, she was determined to bring her out. She had grown in confidence these last months and felt more able to urge a conversation, even a reluctant one. But as it turned out, her efforts were not required, as her companion spoke first, albeit very softly.

Charlotte craned to hear her quiet voice over the hubbub of dinner. 'I'm sorry, Miss de Bourgh, I did not hear you.'

'I said: you play extremely well, Mrs Collins.'

Charlotte looked puzzled, then said, 'Oh! The pianoforte? Thank you, that is kind. I am very grateful to play on the instruments here.'

'You are most welcome. It is a pleasure to hear you – I am in my rooms a good deal, so I heard better when you played on Mrs Jenkinson's, but I can still make you out a little on the grand downstairs.'

'You enjoy music?'

'A great deal. I used to play – very well they told me – but I find it too tiring now.'

Charlotte refrained from asking her what ailed her, but tentatively asked whether it might yet be possible to play if it were for short periods only, urging that it would be a shame to let the talent slip.

'You sound like my cousin,' Anne replied, nodding at Fitzwilliam opposite. 'He is the only person in this house who does not treat me like a flower threatening to wilt at any moment. If there is draught in the hall, Mrs Jenkinson believes it will blow me over.'

Charlotte pondered this for a moment or two. 'You are – more robust than they think?'

'Yes,' said Anne, taking a moment to chew. 'I will never be hearty, Mrs Collins. I was very ill when I was a child – they tell me I nearly died. But I am not so useless as they believe. My mother has never even let me dance,' she added quietly.

Hesitatingly, Charlotte asked, 'Could you dance?'

Anne blinked. 'I could not dance two fast reels in a row, but I am sure I could walk a quadrille.'

Charlotte could not pair this open young woman with the silent creature she had encountered on previous occasions. She had always assumed that Anne must be very sickly indeed; she kept so much to herself, often not appearing downstairs at all when there was company.

'You keep to your rooms a great deal,' Charlotte stated, hoping the observation formed the question she wished to ask.

Anne nodded. 'That is when my spirits are low. My body, I think, could rally well enough but my spirits are' – she searched for the word – 'hard to predict. Some days, I feel very well and full of ideas – and glad of company. Today is such a one.' She smiled at Charlotte. 'But at other times, I feel unable to even face the day.'

Charlotte imagined what it might be to feel so utterly desolate but to have to entertain virtual strangers in your home at the invitation of your mother. She started to have an idea of why she'd had so little conversation from Miss de Bourgh on past occasions. 'That must be very difficult,' she said.

'I *am* very difficult,' said Anne, 'but I have given up trying to be otherwise.'

They sat quietly for a minute or two. Charlotte, at every step, felt the danger of overstepping her place, but Anne seemed willing, on this occasion at least, to talk candidly.

'Have you … thoughts of marriage?' she asked softly.

'I think it is too late for that.'

'You are but six-and-twenty?'

Anne looked at her, and Charlotte caught a little of her mother's hauteur in her manner. 'You know yourself that six-and-twenty is not young, Mrs Collins.'

Charlotte's cheeks reddened.

Anne continued, 'My mother still talks of me marrying Fitzwilliam, which is absurd.'

Charlotte frowned. 'Marrying Colonel Fitzwilliam?'

'Oh! No! I mean Darcy; he is *Fitzwilliam* Darcy.' She chuckled at the error.

Charlotte laughed, too, but thought it rather careless to throw around so many Fitzwilliams in one family.

Introducing Mrs Collins

'Why is it absurd?' Charlotte asked carefully, knowing at least one reason why it was; She knew enough of Darcy's latest ventures to merit caution on the topic.

'If Fitz— Sorry, if *Darcy* planned to ask for my hand, he would have done so years ago. He will not do so by choice, and I would not want him forced.'

'Would you have him if he asked you?'

Anne looked askance at Charlotte, who wondered if she had finally gone too far. Anne thought about it. 'No. He is too cross and serious. I would need someone more gentle. Like your Mr Collins.'

Charlotte's fork paused over her plate. She had never heard her husband endorsed as a preferred choice of partner. She looked over at him. He was spooning some potatoes onto Lady Catherine's plate. It was enlightening to think that, from another's eye, he was worthy of notice. As she so often did, she questioned her feelings towards her husband: could she yet feel more for him? Had her feelings from the start been guided only by the judgment of her friends, when first they had met? There would be many opportunities to know him more, she realised, in the years to come – to know him as a father might alter their relationship altogether.

Feeling confident that they were now conversing as women of a certain age, Charlotte coyly asked, 'Has there been any man you have liked?'

'I have hardly met any. I have hardly been out. And here at Rosings, it is nearly always cousins. My cousin Thomas used to visit – Richard's elder brother.'

Charlotte was confused again. 'Richard?' she asked.

'Fitzwilliam.'

'Darcy?'

'No! Colonel Fitzwilliam – Richard.'

'Oh, yes,' said Charlotte. She had heard the colonel's first name before in conversation but had never spoken it herself.

'So, the colonel's brother used to visit? But not so often now?' asked Charlotte, determined to keep up with the dialogue.

'Well, Thomas is the earl now and has a wife and children. Their father died a few years past, and now Thomas has an estate to manage. He struggles to maintain it, in truth. It never had a vast income, as I understand it, and it was fortunate that my mother and her sister married well; my uncle would not have had much spare income to dispose upon his sisters. But the estate has shrunk further since Thomas took it over. But enough of that, Mrs Collins. How is your family?'

Charlotte answered her questions, but she saw Miss de Bourgh's energy begin to wane, and fortunately it was not long before it was time to retire to the drawing room. This transition was quite an event, because Colonel Fitzwilliam still could not walk and so it was the work of Mr Collins and Figgis to help him from his seat in the dining room to the room next door. This required the colonel to stretch out his arms and lean heavily on the shoulders of his two aides, both of whom nearly buckled under his weight.

All observers – for nobody was polite enough not to watch such a sight – were holding their breath for the duration of the process, praying he would not be dropped and break his other leg. Finally, the colonel was lowered (with not quite enough care) onto a settee, where he could raise and rest his leg. It was clear from his face that his pride was wounded by the charade.

Charlotte sat herself in the chair next to his.

The evening felt pleasingly relaxed, given the setting, and even egalitarian – an assembly of people of different stations who all now knew each other well enough to dispense with undue formality and reserve.

Lady Catherine asked Mr Collins to pull the fireguard around and then engaged him in conversation, having been parted from her preferred companion for all of dinner.

'Are you feeling well, Mrs Collins?' asked the colonel.

Charlotte moved her chair a little so she could address him more easily, as he could hardly turn to her in his position. 'I am, sir, thank you.' She guessed at a greater importance behind the question than normal, given her recent revelation. 'But as I have just seen my husband acting as your sedan chair – and a rather shaky one at that – I will immediately return the question.'

Colonel Fitzwilliam smiled ruefully and looked down at his leg with a sigh. 'I am as well as can be expected.'

'*As well as can be expected* is the answer people give when they are not well at all. Now I think on it, the question in your situation is not a good fit. I can see you are not "well"– you are not healed, but ... I would ask, are you in good spirits? You may be frank.'

'I always feel I may be, with you. I thank you for that. I think, considering my situation, I am content enough. On the one hand, I am pampered here, and I can hardly complain of it. I am very bored, certainly, and probably rather difficult company for my aunt and for Anne. If I am not useful, I am miserable. But your visits have been very welcome. I would be glad of a visit from Darcy, but he seems to be embroiled in some business in London.'

'You enjoyed an interesting conversation with our new curate?' Charlotte asked, raising an eyebrow.

Fitzwilliam smiled ruefully. 'I was perhaps a little harsh the other day. I do not like people who sermonise about things they do not understand.'

'One might say that a curate has an obligation to sermonise.' But Charlotte was only teasing him, for she knew what he meant.

He only gave her a rakish half-grin. He was not up to a battle of wits, and she saw that and relented.

'I think you did not care for him?'

'I did not. I would have liked to exit theatrically but I could not.'

'I thought that was the case!' said Charlotte, with some force. 'I wished you could!' She laughed a little, and he watched her closely, enjoying her reaction. She gathered herself and asked, 'Has Dr Chappell given you any indication of how soon you might walk?'

'Yes, and he thinks it will not be soon. I may hobble in a few weeks, but it will be months before I can walk well enough to be on campaign.'

'Are you keen to return?'

He looked puzzled by the question. He turned from her, taking a moment to consider. 'Yes,' he said plainly, then, 'No. Well, it is my life. I have known little else. I joined at sixteen, and I have not veered off course. So, I suppose I am keen to continue with my life.'

Charlotte nodded. 'You once asked me what would I do, if every freedom was afforded to me – ignoring what present circumstances dictated. May I ask you the same question?'

She thought he might be unwilling to engage with this exercise, as he did not reply immediately but then he raised his eyes to her and asked, in mock-seriousness, 'Do I have two working legs in this scenario?'

She grinned. 'You may have full use of your legs.'

He nodded. 'I would like not to travel far—'

'But you must say what you *do* want, not what you do *not*!'

'You are very particular!' cut in Fitzwilliam, quite entertained.

'I am,' returned Charlotte, enjoying her own folly.

He seemed to be struggling with the question. To prompt him, she offered, 'Perhaps you should start with something small. What is one object you would like to possess in your life?'

He furrowed his brow in thought. 'A mantelpiece.'

Charlotte looked at him quizzically. 'A particular mantelpiece?'

'Not any particular style, but large enough that it might hold a vase or two. The picture I have is me standing at the mantelpiece, resting my glass on it and stoking the fire.'

'Is the mantelpiece in a study or a drawing room, or neither?'

'It is in a drawing room.'

'So, there is a fireguard, perhaps, and a rug?'

'Of course – a large rug, a little worn at the edges from use.'

'What colour are the walls of this room?'

He smiled slowly, realising they were playing a game. He had mentioned his boredom, and she had risen to the challenge. He played along. 'It is blue. Light blue.'

She frowned.

Colonel Fitzwilliam chuckled. 'No?'

'I do not think it is light blue. Sage green, perhaps?'

'Yes,' he said, accepting it in a serious manner. 'It is a sage-green room.'

'And this room is in a house? A large house?'

'Not too large.'

'What else would you have?'

'Grounds where I may ride for miles.'

'Large grounds. Stables and large grounds, but only a modest house?' she said sarcastically.

'You mock me?'

'Only a little,' replied Charlotte, smiling at him. 'They are your choices.'

'They are indeed! And this game was your idea. But I shall finish: I would have a soft bed, a fountain in the gardens, and … chickens.'

'Chickens?'

'Chickens,' he confirmed.

'So, a home then? You wish for a home.'

His eyes glazed a little. 'Yes. I suppose I do.'

Charlotte paused, considering this, then said gently, 'There is nowhere you would call home at present?'

He shook his head. 'I have had nowhere to call home for most of my life. I left my father's house at twelve. A few terms at Eton – I did not excel.' He grinned self-effacingly here. 'And then I joined the army as an ensign at sixteen. I have lived in barracks or in quarters for nearly eighteen years. When on leave, I have visited friends' homes and stayed with family. I have been up to Tolbrooke over the years, of course, but that is my brother's home now, not mine. I have spent months walking, marching, from one unknown place to another, and what greets you at your destination is more unfamiliar than the last. When they brought me back this time, on a stretcher, they told me they would send me "home". But I did not know where that would be. I had nowhere to picture in my head.'

Charlotte, after a moment, tentatively asked, 'Could you not take a house?'

'No.' The colonel gave a bitter laugh at this. 'It is only recently that I have had the means, but while the war continues, it would be a wasted venture. Why hold a house that would sit empty all year long and go to ruin? Besides, I still owe some debt for one of my commissions, so it is unwise altogether in my current state.'

Charlotte nodded. 'But if your life were your own—'

'Is my life not my own?' he interrupted.

She opened her mouth and shut it again. The answer was *no*. In his current circumstances, he was not free to make his own choices: to freely marry or take a home or leave his position. But none of this was cheering or helpful, so Charlotte said instead, 'I do not know that any of our lives are our own. We are all subjects to circumstance, are we not? I, for example, might wish to join the army, but I am not allowed.' She was being playful again.

Colonel Fitzwilliam smiled at this. 'I have said it before, and I maintain that you would excel in the army. I can see you looking well in regimental dress.'

He was lost in that picture for a brief moment, then struggled to regain his train of thought, but Charlotte was already moving the conversation forward briskly. 'So,' she summarised, 'you would wish for a modest house, with a green drawing room and a mantelpiece, and you would live there with your horse?'

'And, God willing, a wife!' he added defensively. 'I do not plan to make my life with a horse!'

Charlotte laughed. 'Well, you have only mentioned the horse!'

'Well, that is because I already know my horse.' He was pensive for a moment. 'Yes, a home, with a wife, and ...' He tapered off for a moment.

'And children?' suggested Charlotte— it seemed the natural missing piece from the picture he had painted.

He considered and replied, non-committal, 'Oh. Yes, perhaps. I would be glad to have children, if they came. But I do not value the prospect of children as keenly as I do the prospect of companionship. And I have never had that desperation for legacy that some men have – my brother being one ... But who knows! All of this may be nonsense, Mrs Collins. As I said at the start, how can I know what I want when my only experience of life is what I have lived?'

Charlotte wrinkled her brow in scepticism. 'That is not as unique as you think.'

'Living an army life?'

'No, I mean, that we all of us are limited in our scope. None of us know the full breadth of experience that the world has to offer. But we may still make an educated guess at what we want and strive to achieve it.'

He listened to her attentively and nodded, then seemed to turn in on himself. 'It is not always possible to live the life you wish,' he said, with some degree of melancholy.

Charlotte looked at him in his damaged state and did not begrudge him such a gloomy statement. He had earnt the right to it, she thought.

'Mrs Collins, you must play for us,' came the invitation – or rather instruction – from her hostess across the room. The great favour that Lady Catherine had bestowed on her, in letting her use the piano, had to be repaid somehow, and one public performance seemed a fair price for the privilege. But Charlotte felt the weight of Lady Catherine's expectations – as if the hours spent practising on this instrument ought to be on display here, as proof of her hostess's magnanimity. It was the first time most of the guests here would have heard Charlotte play, which added another pressure, if one were needed. Nervously, she rose and made her way to the piano.

She sat and considered what she could play, and play well. She decided on an andante movement by Pleyel – the mood in the room did not feel as if it would suit a sudden burst of lively music. She played it with feeling and felt pleased with her performance.

As she finished, her audience applauded, but Lady Catherine called out, 'That was very good, Mrs Collins, but I know you have much more to show us. Play again. I would enjoy something rousing.'

In truth, Charlotte was glad of the push. She acquiesced to the request and, after a moment, settled on an elaborate sonatina by Clementi. With runs and trills and fast arpeggios, it was a fine showcase for her.

If she had been able to look out while she was playing, she would have seen the reactions of her audience: Miss Anne de Bourgh was delighted; Lady Catherine was smug, taking some of the credit for this; Colonel Fitzwilliam looked as if he were in awe of her, and Mr Collins wore a peculiar expression on his face. It might have been shock; it certainly was not joy.

Early on in his acquaintance with Charlotte, Mr Collins had a feeling that they were a fine match – and an equal match. His sense of worth was now innately tied to his marriage; he had found his place in life and been accepted. He had always believed that he and Charlotte were on a similar plane, physically and intellectually, and that was a comforting thought.

As he watched his wife play, he did not feel that comfort. He did not recognise her. This poised, assertive woman was a vision, undaunted by entertaining a room of high-born people in a house such as this, with a talent he had had no idea she possessed. She was radiating energy, joy and purpose, all while carrying his child. She was splendid, and her splendour shook the foundations of his peace of mind. Whereas another man might have felt only pride in his wife, for Collins, this feeling was mixed with something much more disquieting.

What he felt was: *She is beyond me.* What he felt was: *I will not be able to keep her.*

1800

MAIDENHEAD

William Collins walked the mile from the vicarage to his home in the centre of the town. For three years now – since he was ten – he had been having lessons twice a week with Mr Poulteney, the vicar, with four other local boys. Mr Poulteney was a kind, highly educated man of about forty, with an interest in many things beyond the scripture. Those he taught were local boys who might go on to be farmers, soldiers, shopkeepers or work in service. He therefore did not waste his time or theirs teaching them what boys at Harrow or Eton would be studying. He could not resist teaching them a little Latin but did not go beyond the basics: *amo, amas, amat,* and a few fun phrases for them to throw in to impress a stranger. But he did teach mathematics, as well as botany and geography – skills that might be applied broadly and which were useful in all walks of life.

With some help from his wife, he even taught them some simple country dances. It was quite a sight: thirteen-year-old boys self-consciously holding one another's hands in a square formation, walking in a circle around a vicar's small drawing room. William had a feeling his father would not approve of this activity, and fearful he might somehow catch wind of it – or worse, see it! – he always chose to bow out of the lesson, standing at the side and claiming a bad leg. He was short for his age and had no skill for sport; in times outside of study – when the boys would run or tussle or shout well-meaning insults at each other – he always felt a little out of place.

He made up for it in his studies. He learnt the Bible very well, having an unusual capacity for memorising verses. He also had a fine hand for sketching, which was nurtured by his tutor. Mr Poulteney had given him sheaves of paper, expensive paper, to draw studies of the plants and flowers from his garden that they were learning about. His botanical drawings, unlike his peers', were intricate, more like art than science; they were carefully shaded, using a mixture of a soft and heavy touch of the pencil.

One afternoon, his tutor gave him his drawings to take home to show his father, and some blank pages besides to fill in his own time. William felt proud of his work and pleased with the gift; such paper was a real luxury.

On entering his home, he could see his father through an open doorway, sitting in the front room. It was neither a study nor a drawing room, containing both a desk and an old settee, and the family had always simply called it the 'front room'. The house only consisted of five rooms in total so they each needed to perform overlapping functions. There was no room in the house whose sole purpose was repose.

His father was seated behind the desk and seemed to be leafing through some letters, emitting angry grunts, a heavy frown etched into his forehead. The fire wasn't lit. No fires in the house were lit, despite the chill. Recently, William had formed the impression that his family were poorer than they had been a few years previously, but he did not know why. He knew that Eton used to be talked of for him, and no longer was. He knew that the house used to be warm, and no longer was. He knew that his father used to smile at him, and no longer could.

Since his mother died, his father had changed. He had always been serious, but now he was surly. His temper could rise at the drop of a crumb from the table. He would snap at the maid and dismiss visitors boorishly. But then there had been some callers who were very unfriendly, arriving late at night, and whom William had overheard making demands of money – and making threats. His father had not been boorish with these men, instead pleading quietly for them to leave. William did not like seeing his father desperate and decided he preferred him boorish. That preference came with its limits, however.

William knocked at the open door and entered at his father's command.

'I am back from my lessons, sir.'

'I can see that.'

'Mr Poulteney told me to show you these. He said … he said they were exemplary.'

'What are they?'

'Drawings.'

'Drawings! What is he teaching you there?' The elder Mr Collins unfolded the sheets and looked at his son's sketches, still frowning. 'What are these?' he asked quietly, pointing at the middle of one page.

William peered over to see what he was looking at. 'Er, those are foxgloves, sir.' Greeted with silence, and finding that his sketches held no interest, William tried to appeal to his father's thrift by adding, 'Mr Poulteney gave me some spare paper to draw on at home.' William held up the other two sheets to show him.

'Good.'

William's spirits rose a little.

'We are out of paper.' His father took the empty sheets and placed them in the drawer. He then returned his attention to his son's sketches and, after gathering them all up into a pile, he slowly ripped them in half. Taking one of the torn scraps, he lifted his pen, dipped it in black ink and started writing in a thick, unrefined hand, across the lower half of a pencilled foxglove. He dragged the nib of the pen heavily, and it scratched loudly against the paper, leaving blots and leaks blighting the handwriting, pouring more scorn on the care with which the underlying image had been drawn.

He let it dry for a moment, then folded it in half and handed it to William. 'You give this to your Mr Poulteney.'

William took the note, cradling what was left of his artwork in his hands, now a blotted mess of a letter. He blinked tears back from his eyes before his father could see them.

He went to leave, but his father called him back. 'Read it aloud.'

William was shaking. He didn't move.

His father lurched suddenly across the desk and slapped him, once, hard across the face. It nearly knocked Willliam over, and the letter flew out of his hand onto the floor.

'Pick it up and read it.'

William, his cheek burning and his head pounding, scrambled to pick up the paper, and opened it. In a quiet voice, he started to read, 'Mr Poulteney.'

'Speak UP! Speak like a MAN!'

'Mr Poulteney,' William tried again, his still-unbroken voice trying for a volume he could not achieve. 'In the future, I would appreciate you t-teaching my son skills that will be useful to him in his life, not … training …' He broke off, his chest heaving.

'Not training him,' picked up his father, his voice rising, 'in the frivolous pursuits of a woman!' He shouted the last few words, then collapsed back in his chair.

William took this as an opportunity to flee the room, knowing too well what treatment might befall him if he stayed until his father's temper reached its peak.

He sought solace in his bedroom, still trying to stop his tears, even now he was alone. His father had always tried to shape him into the image of the son he wanted. He had tried to beat the softness out of his body and make him sturdier by withholding affection. But the beatings had made him stoop, and the coldness had made him desperate.

His mother had arranged these lessons with Mr Poulteney before she died, and his father, thus far, had honoured the arrangement. But if he handed his tutor this letter, he feared it would bring about an end to them, and so an end to his hopes of Oxford and beyond – of escape. He would end up like his father, perhaps. But if his father found out he had not handed the vicar his letter, he would beat him and probably end the lessons anyway. So what choice was there?

After reading the missive, the Reverend Poulteney refolded Mr Collins's note and placed it on his desk. He looked at William, then let his eyes roam across the room. His study was generously appointed and filled with objects of interest: ornate Chinese vases, a large globe, an ivory elephant, a tin whistle, a chunk of amethyst; the rare sitting side by side with the mundane. Poulteney was well travelled and enjoyed having reminders of his former adventures around him. But he was settled now. His living was a good one; he had a large income and lived in a fine house, and he enjoyed the free time his income allowed to do things like teach poor boys how to dance a quadrille.

He seemed to be ruminating on something, and after a few minutes, he pulled out a clean sheet of paper, wrote a letter on it and went to hand it to William. But then, looking at this desperate messenger, weary from delivering difficult messages between two figures of authority, he said kindly, 'I will return to your house with you today, William, to visit your father.'

William never knew what occurred between his father and his tutor that day, but it caused a change in his life for which he was to be forever grateful for. Whether the vicar threatened his father with the threat of hell, shamed him, invoking his mother's memory, or, as William sometimes wondered might be the case, offered to pay some of his debts, he knew not. What he did know was that Mr Poulteney walked out of the front room looking victorious, holding a piece of paper, and told William he would see him tomorrow.

William's father never hit him again; William saw him fight the impulse on occasion, but he never rose to it. Furthermore, from that day, William was allowed to spend a great deal of his time with Mr Poulteney and his wife. While he still slept in his father's house, he visited the vicarage daily. The couple had no children of their own, so there was ample room in their life for a rather strange, lost young boy with a dead mother, beautiful manners and bruises on his body.

The week following Mr Poulteney's visit to his father, William returned to the vicarage for a lesson and walked into the study as usual. He had often peered at the interesting items around the room, so different from the bare surfaces of his own home. But today, William's eyes fell on an addition to its walls. Above the fireplace hung a newly framed picture: a finely drawn pencil sketch, torn at the bottom, of the top half of a foxglove.

CHAPTER XVI

Mrs Brooke sat in the kitchen, finishing a large cup of tea and some fruitcake, made the evening before by Mrs Windham, the cook. A mid-morning tea was a ritual they adhered to daily. They had worked together, in this house, for decades now, and such routines had become a necessity. It used to be tea and a gossip, or tea and a joke, or occasionally tea and a cry, but these days, as they were both older, a lot of the dramas of their youth had passed them by. Now, more often, it was tea and an easy silence.

Mrs Brooke dabbed the crumbs from her mouth and rose slowly. 'Well, I had better get on. Wash day! Where is Sally?'

'She's just finishing sweeping.'

Sally was the housemaid, but her routine would be a little different today. Laundry day, every two weeks, was a substantial chore within the household, and all the staff pitched in.

'Well, I'll get started. I'll bring the first pile down after I've taken the master his toast,' said Mrs Brooke.

Mrs Windham chuckled. 'Mood he's been in, he'll praise God for the best butter he has ever tasted. High as a kite these last weeks.'

Mrs Brooke grinned. 'Make the most of it. Good to have a happy house.'

She deposited Mr Collins's toast in the study and, glancing through a window, noticed Mrs Collins in the garden. Next, the housekeeper went upstairs to the master bedroom to gather up the sheets to launder. As she pulled the blankets off the bed, Brooke saw a watery reddish-brown stain on the bedsheet. She let out a small, 'Oh,' before pulling the sheet off the bed quickly and taking it down to the washroom. She dumped it unceremoniously in the large tub, then stood there for a minute, considering what to do.

'Bess!' she called out, and she heard the cook tutting, drying her hands and coming to her.

'What?'

Mrs Brooke said nothing but held up the stained patch for her to see.

Mrs Windham looked at it, frowning. Then her expression changing to worry. 'How far gone is she now?'

'Coming up on three months,' replied Mrs Brooke. She had been keeping track, almost as keenly as Charlotte had.

'You should go and speak with her,' said Mrs Windham. 'She'll be worried, it being her first.'

Mrs Brooke nodded. She put down the sheets and made her way out to the garden. Charlotte was kneeling, performing some end-of-summer pruning and seeming, from this angle, as serene as she had on previous days.

'Mrs Collins, I have gathered the sheets for washing.'

'Thank you, Brooke,' replied Charlotte, smiling politely but not looking at her, still leaning over her plants.

Brooke did not know what to say. Obviously, she could not be explicit. She stood but remained conspicuously unmoving. She was about to leave when Charlotte turned to her.

'I had a little bleeding last night; you probably saw.' Her voice was tight. 'But none today, so I think all will be well. I do not feel anything different. I am sure all will be well.'

But now that Mrs Brooke could see Charlotte properly, she saw that her mistress did not seem as calm as her words implied. Her face was quite pale and blank, but her eyes were busy, darting.

'Perhaps you ought to have an easy day today, madam. Inside? I could bring you something to eat and light a fire?'

Charlotte nodded limply. She removed her gloves and, placing her pruning shears on the ground, walked calmly, rather primly, indoors.

Mrs Brooke treated her as tenderly as she could. She had seen enough pregnancies in her time to know that Charlotte was quite right – all might yet be well, for blood can come and go sometimes.

Brooke had seen the dried blood of monthly courses on the clothes and sheets of three different mistresses and their daughters. She had seen blood in chamber pots and blood coughed into handkerchiefs. She had seen blood on the sheets after wedding nights and blood let by a physician. Her previous mistress had borne four babies, but only three had lived. So Brooke had come to know the blood of childbirth and the blood of loss.

Not for the first time, she considered how much a woman could withstand in the natural course of her life, and how much of that life was stained with red. She had not been on the battlefield and seen the wounds of soldiers, but what she had seen in the bedroom of this very house could, she thought, rival any man at war.

The next night, Charlotte woke up and found herself wet. It was in the early hours of the morning, and Collins lay asleep beside her. As carefully as she could, she crept out of bed, trying not to wake him, holding up her heavy damp nightgown so it did not drag. As her eyes adjusted to the little light peeping through the curtains, she was able to see the shade of what had saturated her nightgown. It was much darker, and more in abundance, than the previous night.

She did not know what to do. She stood, paralysed, until the tears came to her. She tried not to make a sound, endeavouring to dampen her sobs; she did not feel ready to contend with her husband in this moment. She wished her mother were here.

She wrapped an extra gown around her bottom half and carefully left the room, closing the door quietly, and made her way to the staircase that led to Brooke's door. She did not feel capable of walking up any stairs. She stood at the bottom, feeling utterly desperate. The household was asleep and, although she urgently needed help, she did not want the attention of all.

She called up the stairs, in a voice she knew, even as she spoke, would be too quiet, 'Brooke? Mrs Brooke?' She was sure she would not be heard.

And yet, in what struck Charlotte as nothing short of a miracle, Brooke opened her door almost immediately, appearing before her fully clothed and carrying a candle. She took in Charlotte's tear-stained face and state of undress and hurried down her small staircase to her.

'Did you ... ?' asked Charlotte.

'I have been waiting up, madam, just in case.'

At this kindness, Charlotte's face and body crumpled, and Brooke, though petite, held her firmly. After a moment or two, she helped her mistress to sit on the stair. Charlotte, usually so resolute and decisive, felt entirely helpless in the face of what was happening to her. 'I do not know what to do ...'

'Let me put you in the blue bedroom, madam. Come with me.' She helped Charlotte up and led her into the guest bedroom down the corridor.

When Charlotte was safely installed in bed, Brooke took her hands, saying, 'I will stay with you, madam.' She gently smoothed Charlotte's hair back from her face.

Charlotte kept trying to say that she did not know what to do, and on top of her current distress, she seemed alarmed that she could not direct what was to happen.

Mrs Brooke tried to reassure her, on that score at least, where no other consolation could be given. 'I have helped others with this before; I know what to do. Let me look after you.'

Charlotte nodded limply, her eyes dull.

Brooke looked at Charlotte, her face sweating with effort, her cheek stained with tears. She was already very fond of her mistress. Although the loss of a baby was all too common, it was not any less catastrophic each and every time. She knew too well the toll it would take on Charlotte, on her feelings and on her body.

After some time, Charlotte's eyes closed, and she seemed to have drifted off, her body and mind demanding a moment of recovery, in spite of it all. *Let her sleep,* thought Mrs Brooke, *while she can.* She leant over and kissed her young mistress on the forehead and went to fetch some water.

The days that followed were a lesson in kindness and cooperation. A time that is among life's worst can bring out the very best in people, and so it proved.

Mr Collins was roused from his bed early by Mrs Brooke (who wisely predicted he would panic upon waking and discovering the state of his bed and Charlotte gone), and he was in need of comfort also. His first thought was of Charlotte, but she did not wish to see him as she was, so he was sent to the village to fetch the local midwife. He returned with her within the hour.

Whenever he was in the house, he could hear that Charlotte was in a great deal of pain, and yet he was not admitted to the room. It was hard on him; banned from the entire upstairs, he was left alone, while the women pulled together tightly.

He retreated to his study to pray and was left alone with his thoughts, desperate for something to do, to help. There was very little.

Two days later, when Collins was finally admitted to see Charlotte, he found her looking blankly out of the window. Her face was as pale as the pillow she leant on. She had been dressed warmly, a gown covering her up to her neck, but her body was still shaken at intervals by a shiver that came and went.

He walked to the end of the bed, not daring to approach her.

She still didn't look at him, so he cleared his throat and said softly, 'Charlotte? My dear?'

She glanced at him but could not hold his gaze, turning quickly to stare at the wall. Her eyes were now bone dry, but his filled with tears to see her like this.

Mr Collins knelt at his wife's side. 'I am most sorry for it,' he said, with all the compassion he could pour on her.

She could only nod.

'We will try again.'

He offered this as a comfort, but it was not a solace at this moment. She had no thoughts to spare for the future – only for what she had lost.

Seeing that he had not helped, he pivoted to the practical. 'Is there anything I can fetch you, for your comfort?'

Charlotte shook her head but then stopped herself. 'My mother. I would like to see my mother.'

'I took the liberty of writing to her when first – that is, I wrote to her two days ago. I hope she may arrive today.'

Charlotte looked at him in amazement. She grasped his hands. 'Thank you,' she said earnestly. She had never appreciated him more than in that moment.

In the days following her mother's arrival, Charlotte took up the task of writing to Elizabeth. She found the letter surprisingly tiring to compose, but once accomplished, she was glad of it.

10th October 1812

Dear Eliza,

I write to you with bad news. I am no longer with child. I had the first signs that this was happening a few days ago, and my body has now given it up. Mrs Brooke tended me with great care, and my mother is now here and will stay a while. Her absence in Meryton may be noticed. She suggested I write to you. I do not think she had in mind a full confessional but, if I write to you, I must tell the truth, or else why make the effort at all.

I have always known, as you must have, that this kind of loss is common enough, which always made me think (if I did ever think about it – I hardly did) that the feelings connected to it would also be common enough. I was wrong. My world feels overturned, and I do not know where to place my hopes now. I feel at sea, unrooted. Nothing holds meaning for me. My husband, my home, my friends, leave me cold. I can attach to nothing.

My body is very weak. Mrs Brooke says all situations like this are very different, but mine has taken a lot from me. I should feel pity for my body, perhaps, and want to care for it. I feel only anger at it. It has let me down so badly. I should never have trusted it. I feel empty, Eliza, so empty and so pointless. I should not write to you in this state, I know, but I know not how else to write.

I am assured I will rally. I assume I shall. If you have any news, I would welcome a distraction.

Yours in friendship,
Charlotte

However, just as Charlotte was preparing to have it posted, she was pre-empted by her friend: a letter arrived from Longbourn.

8th October 1812

My dear Charlotte,

This is only a short letter, so forgive me for reaching the point so quickly, but – I am engaged to Mr Darcy! You may enjoy the pleasure of saying 'I was right!' to me for the rest of our days! I am more happy than I can comprehend. You will have heard of Jane's engagement already, perhaps, which only adds to my joy! There is much to organise, and so I cannot write much more at present – except to say, thank you for telling me your news, and I am tremendously happy for you! It feels like the lives of all around me are suddenly working out just as they ought!

I send you all my warmest wishes for health and happiness, my dear friend.

Yours, in affection,

Eliza (soon to be Darcy!)

After reading her friend's news, Charlotte knew she could not send her own missive. She folded it carefully and kept it in her drawer: a small piece of her own history, told, in the end, to no one but herself.

CHAPTER XVII

Life at Hunsford felt strange over the following days. It was as if the household were suspended in time, removed from the ordinary goings on of the outside world. Lady Lucas stayed with her daughter, alongside an ever-attentive Mrs Brooke. Both of them knew, from experience, that Charlotte's body would not recover until her spirits did. They tried to allow her time to mourn her loss, while keeping her mind a little occupied so that she might not fall further into malaise. Charlotte was, naturally, not herself. She was vacant, dry-eyed, often silent and eerily acquiescent.

If she ventured into the garden, she would walk without purpose, round in circles, not really looking at her plants. Encouraged by her mother to take up her sewing, Charlotte asked Brooke for things to mend, rather than her embroidery; she had no capacity for creativity.

Her mother's presence gave Charlotte licence to become a little girl again, and she did, placing herself entirely into her mother's hands. Lady Lucas gave orders for the household, was the one to get Charlotte up in the mornings and sit with her at night. Each day, Charlotte performed the activity her mother suggested. She ate whatever her mother told her to and took what remedies her mother bid her. In truth, she had never been this obedient as a child, so it was a new state for her.

At first, Lady Lucas was glad to be of use. That she could offer any comfort to her daughter was a blessing indeed in the circumstances, but as days turned into weeks, she started to realise that her presence was not helping Charlotte any longer. While she was standing firm for her daughter, Charlotte was standing still; stuck in a state of child-like dependency. Charlotte needed to come back to her own life and with so constant a prop at her disposal, she never would.

It was with conflicting emotions that Lady Lucas informed her daughter she must return to Hertfordshire within the week. If she expected Charlotte to react like her old self – practical and capable – she was mistaken. Her daughter railed against her departure. She accused her mother of abandoning her, begging her to stay with increasing desperation. Charlotte was indignant, and she remained in a state of helplessness until the day her mother's carriage drew up to the drive.

The trunks were loaded aboard, and her mother came to the little sitting room to bid her daughter farewell. They sat opposite each other, Charlotte unspeaking as she mostly had been of late, looking so much smaller than she had the year before.

'Before I go—' Lady Lucas began.

Charlotte raised her eyebrows wearily. 'I know what you are going to say.'

'Oh, do you? Pray, what will I say?'

'That I must not be disheartened, and that children will come in time.'

Lady Lucas looked at her closely and took her hands. 'I do not know whether children will come in time, my darling.'

Charlotte looked up sharply.

'Only God can know that. I do not comfort you with a promise that it is not in my power to keep. You might have children, and you might not. But I promise you that you will find your happiness again. Whether with children or not. There is not one path to happiness. You must find yours.'

Charlotte did not react.

Her mother, frustrated, reached out and held her chin, making her look at her. 'You *must*,' she said again, more firmly.

Charlotte shook her hand away.

Her mother took a deep breath and sighed. 'I have something for you.' She removed an item from her reticule and placed it in her daughter's hand.

Charlotte, puzzled, looked down and saw the emerald snake ring her mother had lent her many years before. 'Why are you giving me this?'

'Did you not once tell me it was a symbol of life carrying on?'

The gesture was not lost on Charlotte, but her own exactness could not allow for misrepresentation. 'Well, no, that's not quite it.' She broke a smile at her own pedantry and then, surprising herself, she actually laughed.

Her mother joined her, delighted to see a glimpse of her daughter returning to herself. 'Whatever it means, my dear girl, you liked this ring,' said Lady Lucas.

'It is rather daring, isn't it? Dazzling,' said Charlotte rather disapprovingly. 'I don't think it really suits me.'

'It used to.' Her mother said it as a challenge. She reached out and closed Charlotte's palm over the ring, shutting it tight.

As Lady Lucas's carriage pulled away, Charlotte walked back into the house and closed the door with one hand, looking at the small golden ring in the other. She placed it on her finger and took in its effect. As if suddenly coming to herself, she hurried upstairs, threw her old grey shawl on her bed, then began rifling through her cupboards.

Mrs Brooke was in the kitchen, finishing her morning tea, when she heard her mistress call out, 'Brooke! I am going out for a walk!'

She was surprised – Mrs Collins had not ventured beyond the garden for a long time. Assuming her mistress would need help preparing, Mrs Brooke made her way upstairs, only to find the bedroom in disarray and the window left ajar to allow some air in. From downstairs, she heard the front door close with a thud.

Looking out of the open window, Mrs Brooke watched her mistress striding purposefully down the lane, a basket on her arm and a bright-green shawl wrapped around her shoulders.

VOLUME
TWO

1811
MERYTON

'Must I attend, Mother? I have nothing to say to soldiers, you know; and they rarely have anything to say for themselves.'

'I see you are an expert on military men. I had no idea,' replied Lady Lucas drily.

Mother and daughter were stood in front of Charlotte's open wardrobe, selecting a dress for her. Tonight's dance at the assembly rooms had been arranged by Colonel Forster to provide some entertainment for his militia regiment, who had been recently installed in the area, and to introduce them to the people of Meryton. It would be fairly relaxed – not a grand occasion, but a chance to be seen.

Lady Lucas picked out a pretty peach gown for Charlotte, with puffed sleeves and lace detail – which Charlotte rejected in favour of a simple, pale-blue dress that bordered on day wear.

Her mother was not pleased. 'Perhaps if you gave them your time more generously, and actually listened, you might find they *do* have something to say – perhaps you would learn something about the war.'

'From the militia? I hardly think so. Although it is true that I have been hoping for instruction in shining buttons and drinking ale very quickly.'

'Charlotte!' Her mother was usually amused by her daughter's quips about their acquaintance, but tonight, she was in a mood to be irked by them. 'You cannot set yourself against entire groups of gentlemen on the strength of but one or two encounters. Your judgements are formed too hastily; no man is likely to approach you if you look closed to the very notion.'

'I ought to be grateful for the attentions of just anyone?'

'No. Only of someone good and worthy, but you will never be approached by that person if you wear anything like the expression on your face at this moment.'

Perhaps it was the act of being forced by her parents to attend an assembly that was making Charlotte feel like a child tonight, but she was in a mood to be difficult. She had grown accustomed to being allowed some agency over which social events she attended, but since her last birthday – as if the particular age of twenty-seven held some distinct horror – her mother had suddenly been more insistent on her attendance at *every* occasion.

Tonight was one that Charlotte would certainly have foregone. She had no interest in the militia, and she did not anticipate Elizabeth or Jane attending. She had received a note from her friend earlier today to inform her that, owing to the arrival of a cousin who had come to visit, the whole family would be absent. Without the hope of their company for diversion, the evening held little prospect of enjoyment.

'Even if I *were* noticed by a soldier, you would not have me marry a member of the *militia*, would you? How generous a dowry is Father willing to give me that I might support a handsome captain with no house?'

'I am not trying to marry you off to a soldier! I only think it wise to be seen among all sorts of people and be known as pleasant company.'

Charlotte sighed. 'Very well. Although you know they will only have eyes for Maria.'

'You and Maria are very different.'

'Oh, I am aware of that.'

'I know her features have invited compliments, but you have many qualities she does not.'

'I do not have the ample qualities she possesses, which most of those soldiers will be looking at instead of her face.'

'Charlotte Lucas!'

Lady Lucas playfully slapped Charlotte's arm and exited the room, shaking her head.

Charlotte grinned and sat down, allowing Alice to begin curling her hair.

Charlotte, in pale-blue muslin and with neatly curled hair, stood alone – contentedly so – watching the dancing and sipping some punch. She had positioned herself in the corner of the hall, avoiding the eyes of her mother, who was beckoning her over with a curt tilt of her chin. Lady Lucas and Maria were standing with Colonel Forster and two young gentlemen, one of them dressed in regimentals, the other in cream breeches and a smart navy tail-coat. The latter rather stood out, as every other man here was in uniform; the hall was a sea of red, white and gold. Tonight's assembly was a diplomatic venture of sorts, smoothing relations between the soldiers and the town, and Colonel Forster's efforts in this were aided by Sir William Lucas, who cut a fine figure as he moved through the gathering, making introductions with practised ease.

'Ah, and here she is!' exclaimed Lady Lucas, when Charlotte, relenting, joined the group. 'May I introduce my eldest daughter? Charlotte, this is Mr Denny, and Mr—' She looked questioningly at the gentleman in navy. 'Oh, forgive me?'

He smiled warmly and supplied, 'Wickham, my lady. And a pleasure to meet you, Miss Lucas.' He bowed low, and Charlotte gave a small curtsy in return.

'How are your men enjoying Meryton so far, Colonel?' Charlotte asked Colonel Forster, already an acquaintance after he had visited Lucas Lodge a few weeks ago, when the regiment had first arrived.

'Oh, very well, I thank you. There are many pleasant people here who have welcomed them generously. And a lot of pretty young ladies to keep them entertained!' he added, with a chuckle and a sideways look at Maria.

Charlotte did not like seeing her sister – and, by implication, many other girls in the village – treated as a plaything for amorous soldiers. That said, she knew for certain that several of the ladies in question treated the soldiers with the same attitude, that those of the militia were there to be gawped at and flirted with but rarely considered for serious attachment. Perhaps, therefore, the furtive looks being exchanged between Denny and her sister represented some kind of equality. But even so, Charlotte did not care for them.

Charlotte turned to the gentleman on her right, Mr Wickham. 'Pray forgive the question, sir, but are you with the regiment? Only, you stand out a little, without a red coat.'

'I am aware of the contrast,' he said, smiling. 'I receive my uniform soon, and then I shall look more the part and be glad of it.'

'You are a new recruit, then?'

'Indeed. I arrived from London just today.'

'Well, I hope you will enjoy Meryton. It boasts little beyond a very fine ribbon selection at the milliner's, if that is of interest to you?' said Charlotte playfully. She had not the will to engage in the usual dull small talk, which such an occasion often demanded.

Mr Wickham looked a little confused at the suggestion, then, catching the tone, he laughed. He seemed surprised to have found humour in his new acquaintance. 'Ah, you know me well – my uniform will no doubt benefit from some trimming.'

Yet even as he spoke, he leant back slightly, his eyes moving quickly as he surveyed the room. Charlotte felt that Mr Wickham's attention was already starting to wane. She had no inclination to detain him, but until he excused himself, she did not wish to stand in silence – so, as the others in the circle seemed occupied, she went on, 'Do you come from Hertfordshire, sir?'

'No, Derbyshire,' he answered.

'Oh – splendid. I have not travelled far myself, but I have been to the Peaks and enjoyed the vistas very much.'

'It is a beautiful part of the country,' he said distractedly. 'But I now prefer London, in truth.'

'Oh, really? You must enjoy events like this then. You prefer a country dance to a country mile?'

'I suppose I do.' His gaze, having found no better prospect, returned now to Charlotte and he seemed decided to enter again more fully into the conversation. 'There are other pursuits I should have enjoyed even more, had life been kinder to me. But' – he drew in a breath, offering a faint, rueful smile – 'I am not one to dwell on past ills.'

Charlotte suspected he was inviting her to enquire further, but finding herself unwilling to satisfy him, she instead replied briskly, 'Good for you,' with a smile.

He took a breath to begin his story before realising what she had said. His expression was as if she had shut a door in his face. He was not happy. He looked around the room once more and, clearly seeing something more to his liking, said, 'If you will forgive me, Miss Lucas, I believe it is my duty to make myself known to as many people as possible tonight.' He put on a face of regret, as if it were a sacrifice for him to leave her side, which struck Charlotte as very false.

She smiled however, saying, 'Of course, Mr Wickham,' and curtsied.

She watched him as he traversed the room towards a group of pretty girls giggling in a corner. The young women – and they *were* young; they must be only just out – stopped giggling with each other and started to laugh instead at whatever Mr Wickham was saying.

How interesting, thought Charlotte. He had not seemed especially humorous, and yet they were all greeting him with gales of appreciative laughter. He seemed much more at ease with this situation than he had been with Charlotte.

The evening passed as she had expected; she danced once with Colonel Forster and once with Mr Denny, who was now well liked by her parents and appeared rather taken with her sister, whom he stood up with more than once. Her expectations of the militia were surpassed on this occasion; she enjoyed some lively conversations and met with some interesting characters, whom she was eager to tell Elizabeth about when she next saw her.

Word quickly spread through the village that there would be a ball at Netherfield the next Tuesday, held by Mr Bingley and his sisters. It was an event that had the mothers of Meryton in thrall, posing as it did such a fine opportunity for their unmarried offspring to encounter new, wealthy potential suitors. Perhaps related to this, Lady Lucas determined that Maria needed new gloves.

The weather was grumbling on the Saturday morning when the ladies all walked down the lane of Lucas Lodge towards Meryton. In the milliner's, Lady Lucas inspected gloves, fans and hair-combs. There was not time – or money, frankly – for a new dress to be made, but she thought she could afford to supplement her daughters' attire.

'Charlotte, come here – what if we trimmed your rose dress with this?' Lady Lucas proposed, holding up some fine lace.

Charlotte glanced over. 'My dress will do well as it is, will it not?'

'No, it will not – not for Netherfield,' replied her mother. 'Come, stand here; take off your coat. What you are wearing now has the same fit. I can measure it out.'

Charlotte acquiesced, removing her pelisse and standing on a small stool, while her mother tried the lace against her hem.

Maria had been looking at some gloves laid out near the window and, glancing up, exclaimed in some excitement, 'Oh look, there is Mr Denny!'

Charlotte was suddenly grabbed by her sister and ushered out of the door with great urgency. She tried to go back for her coat, but Maria hissed, 'Leave it! We will only be a moment!'

Seconds later, the two sisters almost bumped into Mr Denny, as they 'accidentally' crossed his path. Charlotte was both surprised and impressed by Maria's artfulness.

She did not mind being a prop in her sister's courtship; while Maria and Mr Denny made conversation, she wrapped her arms tighter around herself against the chill and found her eye wandering down the lively high street, which bustled with locals, soldiers, carts and carriages.

In the distance, she spied a uniformed officer on horseback, looking keenly towards Mr Denny. As she trained her eyes on him, she recognised that it was Mr Wickham, having now been granted his regimentals. He looked as if he were in two minds about whether to approach the party, but he remained loitering a little way off. This was either a mark of his friendship with Denny – affording him time with an admirer – or, perhaps more tellingly, a mark of his lack of interest in Charlotte.

Just as Maria and Denny's conversation seemed to be nearing a conclusion, light raindrops started to fall. Charlotte, who remained coatless, was keen to get back inside. She stirred with agitation, prompting Maria to begin her say farewells; but Mr Denny took a step forward and said, 'Before you go—', which led to a final entreaty, much to Charlotte's dismay, as the rain was beginning to fall in earnest.

Denny rather haltingly requested Maria's hand for the first dance at Netherfield, and she delightedly agreed. Charlotte hoped now to escape, but as Denny took his leave, he caught sight of Wickham and beckoned him over. Charlotte and Maria were both shivering by this point, so to Wickham's credit, he did not invite much further delay. He approached carefully, then dismounted and bowed.

'Ladies, I will not keep you out in this weather. I hope you have found everything you were looking for.' He addressed this to Maria with a smirk, then, turning to Charlotte, added, 'And I hope you shall soon locate your coat, Miss Lucas,' with a mocking grin at her state.

She did not respond directly, but said only, 'Until Tuesday then, Mr Denny, Mr Wickham.' Her dress was drenched by this point, the rain plastering her hair to her face and running down her neck. Even Maria appeared bedraggled, despite having her coat and bonnet.

The sisters returned to the shop, and the two men, after performing deep bows, went back to their horses.

Charlotte and Maria found Lady Lucas standing outside the milliner's, under a small canopy that offered shelter over the doorway, having finished her purchases. She held out Charlotte's coat, which she started to put on with some difficulty, dragging it over her soggy dress; as she did, the two soldiers rode by, with a final, pleasant nod from Denny towards Maria, and from Mr Wickham, a lingering look towards Charlotte, in her damp, dishevelled state, taking in her body from head to toe. He then met her gaze, with something resembling disgust, though there was a flicker of something else, and nothing that could be called gentlemanly. It was only a look, she told herself, but it made an impression on her. She could not help but feel he had intended it to. But what was it exactly that his look held?

She pondered the question when they arrived home, as she changed her clothes and warmed herself by the fire. Then she forgot about it until dinner time, when she held a torn piece of red meat on her fork, about to put it in her mouth, and the answer came to her. *That's it*, she thought. *Carrion. He looked at me as if I were a piece of prey.*

On Tuesday evening, at the Netherfield Ball, she had every intention of telling Elizabeth about the assembly with the militia, including the strange Mr Wickham. But before she could do so, she found that Elizabeth was keen to tell her about her own week. Once Eliza started to talk, with great animation, of meeting a handsome, charming man – one who had been, she believed, most unjustly mistreated and whose presence she had so wished for that evening – Charlotte felt, in that moment, that she could not tell of her own, now seemingly insignificant, encounters with the very same Mr Wickham.

She would not pour water on her friend's new passion, but she felt relieved that the gentleman in question was not present at the ball. And soon enough, she was distracted from unpleasant thoughts of him by her engagement in a lively reel, partnered by a certain Mr Collins, to whom she had just been introduced.

18th October 1812

Dear Mr and Mrs Collins,

I trust you are both in good health. I am eager to hear your news, but let us set that aside while I tell you tidings of our family, which may be of interest to you, because whether we would wish it or not, you have both been closely connected to us in one way or another, and I trust the news will bring you joy, or something like it.

It is thus: my two eldest daughters, both of whom were of particular interest to you at one time, Mr Collins, are both now engaged! Jane, whose looks I had always thought must not be for nothing, is to marry Mr Bingley of Netherfield Park, who has five thousand a year. Elizabeth, who has always had luck on her side, is to marry Mr Darcy of Pemberley in Derbyshire, who has ten thousand a year. I tell you of the gentlemen's fortunes because I wish to set your minds at rest should you harbour any feelings of guilt about the entail of Longbourn; it is only Christian that you should feel that way and it is right. But now the blow will be somewhat cushioned, at least for my girls. They will have a comfortable home when the time comes, and what will become of me, I am sure is the least of anyone's concerns. And so it should be: a mother can have no concerns about her own destitution, so long as her children are safe.

I had the good fortune to meet Lady Catherine de Bourgh not long since; she was good enough to visit us at Longbourn. She had some business with Lizzy, which chiefly took up her time with us, and that vexed me, but before that, she was very gracious, and it was an honour to welcome her. I see why you spoke about her so much, Mr Collins; she is very grand indeed. Please do give her my regards when you next see her and be sure to tell her about Jane and Lizzy's engagements.

Mrs Collins, I saw your mother in Meryton this week, and she said you had been unwell. I am sorry to hear it; there is a vicious influenza around, which has brought down half of Hertfordshire. Perhaps you have had that, but in Kent. My sister, Mrs Philips, has been in bed for two weeks, and while it looks like indulgence – and so I told her – she assured me she was really very ill indeed, and I am of half a mind to believe her. Mrs Collins, you must be grateful you do not suffer with your nerves, as I do: the summer was a very bad time for me, but I am improved in recent weeks, and it is a good job, too, as Mr Bennet is in rather a malaise, considering what reasons he has to be cheerful.

But I have said enough. I thank you for welcoming our Lizzy in the spring, and perhaps now you will like to visit her instead, as she will soon have vastly more rooms to offer you.

Yours joyfully,
Mrs Bennet

P.S. I saw your Maria this week at church, and she is become such a beauty! What a pleasant girl – always with a smile and a manner that puts one at ease. You would not think you were sisters! But then my Lydia could not be more different from Mary, so that is families for you.

20th October 1812

Dear Mr Collins,

I am given to understand that an event is to take place greatly to my dissatisfaction. That is, the wedding of my nephew, Mr Fitzwilliam Darcy, to Miss Elizabeth Bennet. I have put forward every objection to the match most keenly, and I am shocked with the response I have received from them both. I do not condone the marriage and will not send them my good wishes.

Further to my other objections, it has been hinted that they are to marry from Pemberley, not from Longbourn, which is most unseemly. Worse still they have chosen to invite guests well beyond immediate family to join them for the ceremony, which I find vulgar, bordering on vain. My dear sister Lady Anne would not have approved. I can only assume these theatrics stem from the habits of Miss Elizabeth Bennet and not from my nephew, who has a more modest sensibility, like his dear mother. Should you receive such an invitation, I assume I may rely upon your loyalty in ignoring it or, perhaps more wisely, writing to decline your attendance. I will be extremely disappointed if I discover you have been part of a union which has brought great unhappiness on my family.

My daughter Anne rallies well enough, but inwardly, she must suffer greatly from this blow, even while she insists that she does not. The betrothal of my nephew and my daughter has been in place since their infancy, and for Darcy to throw her off now is a disgrace. I do not solely blame him, however: I witnessed for myself how artful Miss Elizabeth might be when she visited you last. I have met pretty girls before, but she was pretty in a rather underhand way.

When I think that you might have been tied to such a girl! What fortune that this was avoided, and that you were guided instead to dear

Mrs Collins, who is a far superior creature to her friend – or rather, erstwhile friend – Miss Bennet.

I am sorry indeed to add this calamity to the other difficulties which have recently beset you both. I enclose a secondary letter for Mrs Collins to read privately at her discretion, if you would be so kind as to pass it on.

Yours sincerely,
Lady Catherine de Bourgh

20th October 1812

Dear Mrs Collins,

No doubt your husband has disclosed the contents of my letter regarding the forthcoming marriage of my nephew; I urge you to encourage him down the sensible path. I know I may rely on your spousal influence, as well as your moral conduct.

But the reason I am writing is that I have heard of your recent loss. I hope you will forgive my being frank in addressing it directly; I have been in the same position several times, and I have never found delicate words to be of much use in dulling the pain.

You will by now be operating your life at a normal pace, I think, and appear to others to be quite recovered. I know that in truth you will be still in some turmoil, carrying a weight with you, which, though it will become lighter and easier to manage, you will always carry.

If I may, I offer the following advice: to include your husband in your grief. While Mr Collins's feelings will not be the same as your own, he, too, will be suffering, and he has the potential to be a sympathetic ear to you. He is a man of unique skills, not all of them suited to marriage, but he loves you very dearly – that much is clear – and I suspect he would be a comfort to you, if you would let him.

I expect this letter to remain strictly between us, and I shall not remark upon it when I see you next.

I am reliably informed that the poplars at the bottom of your drive are overgrown and are now encroaching upon Rosings parkland, so my gardener will cut them back at some point this week or the next.

Yours sincerely,
Lady Catherine de Bourgh

CHAPTER I

'I will go if I am invited, William.'

'But, my dear, please consider,' began Mr Collins desperately, 'We owe a great deal to her ladyship, and she has made her feelings very clear—'

'And I am making my own feelings clear,' replied Charlotte, her knitting needles striking one another with some fervour. Knitting was a rare discipline which Charlote did not excel at, and it was not soothing her mood.

Mr Collins involuntarily leant away from her. He was in some turmoil. He had never before had so stark a choice to make between his patroness and his wife. But while he was used to Lady Catherine being forthright and obstinate (which he rather considered her natural right), he had not come to expect it from Charlotte.

Something had shifted in their relationship since their loss a few weeks earlier. Sometimes, when trouble strikes in a marriage, there is an opportunity for a couple to grow closer from it, in the shared task of holding their grief and their disappointment together. But for Mr and Mrs Collins, the chance to truly share that loss passed them by. Charlotte often thought about Lady Catherine's advice, but although she tried to act upon it, she could somehow never find the right words or the appropriate moment.

Mr Collins had, in those first few days, keenly wished to be a support for Charlotte, but as it was, she had been quite apart from him, surrounded by women, tended by Mrs Brooke, protected by her mother. When Lady Lucas left, he had seen a chance to swoop in, in her absence, to be Charlotte's protector and comforter. He had rather looked forward to the opportunity to be so. But it was at that very moment that Charlotte had seemed to strengthen, or harden, and she had had no need of tending or consolation. She had started to dress differently; her tone was slightly sharper, her movements brisker. She seemed filled with a vigorous energy, to which he did not know how to respond. He did not want to upset her and was largely glad to see that her spirits seemed recovered, but he feared this change; he felt more than ever that he did not know how to reach her, and certainly not how to influence her.

In truth, he had received little word of consolation himself for the loss of his expected child. He had been much on his own and, apart from a few kind words from Mrs Brooke or the occasional holding of hands from his wife, he had not had any comfort. He was not adept at guessing other people's thoughts, but even he sensed well enough that his wife was not able to talk to him about it yet. Perhaps she never would. But while Charlotte had spoken about it to her mother, and to Mrs Brooke, he had not a soul he felt he could mention it to, and so it remained trapped within him: not only an unspoken sadness but one about which he had absolutely no understanding. The way in which he had been raised by his father, and the dearth of women close to him in his life, meant that he did not know how often this happened, or why it happened or what it meant for the future.

With his wife seeming so far away from him, his chief anchor in life was in the form of Lady Catherine de Bourgh. And to threaten that accord, as odd a connection as it was, was a grave concern for him.

The afternoon had grown dark, yet Charlotte seemed resolved to keep knitting in the dim light. Her hands moved as determinedly as she spoke. 'I will not be dictated to by Lady Catherine,

William. She is kind to us in many ways, but in this matter, she is displaying a profound lack of rationality, and I will not bow to it.'

Charlotte did not appear to require a response, and Mr Collins felt unwilling to proffer one, particularly while his wife was armed.

He slipped out of the room and found refuge in his study, consulting the Bible on what best to do.

30th October 1812

Dearest Charlotte,

I saw your mother in Meryton this week, and she told me (not in explicit terms, but it was understood) that you are no longer with child. I am so sorry, my dear friend. I wish I were there to soothe you in whatever way I might. I hope very much that I will see you soon and can be a better friend to you once you are close by (I do not offer this hope idly – read on).

Things have been very busy here – Jane is married already. She and Bingley wed from the church at Longbourn as soon as the banns were read and are now travelling, visiting various members of his family – she was in Cheshire the last I heard, with plans for the Welsh borders: not my idea of post-marital delight, but she sounds, from her letters, exceedingly happy. I have been rather putting off naming the day of my own wedding until I know for certain when she will return. However, I will not wait longer; Mr Darcy and I are both keen to settle it, given the objections still standing. So, Darcy has applied for a licence and wishes to marry at Pemberley, and having seen the chapel there, I am more than happy to oblige him. And so I come to another purpose to my letter.

I invite Mr Collins and yourself to join us at Pemberley on 20th November, to attend our wedding and to stay for two weeks after – or three if you can spare the time. My hope is that this might be a welcome distraction from your troubles and that it will be a comfort to be in one another's company (and possibly Jane's, too, if she ever leaves the alluring realm of Bolton). Darcy is in accord with my wish that you should stay on after the wedding, for I have told him you are in need of friendship more now than ever, and he is most eager that you should come. And your husband, of course.

It is not to be a large party. Apart from immediate family, we have invited only you (and Mr Collins, naturally) and Colonel Richard Fitzwilliam, who will be Darcy's best man. I am acutely aware that their aunt, Lady Catherine, is against the match, and I have no doubt she will put obstacles in the way of any scheme of mine. Therefore, I do not know whether Colonel Fitzwilliam will feel he can attend, but I hope he may, out of loyalty to Darcy. (I also suspect he rather likes an adventure?) That is, as long as his leg is up to it. I hear reports that he is doing better in that regard.

If you should feel able to come – and I so hope you shall – it is in my power (ha! It is in Darcy's power, but now that is one and the same) to send a carriage for you. Please write back and tell me that you may!

Oh, I feel I have not said the right thing to you, or enough. Forgive me. I do not know what is best to say, but when I see you, I trust I shall know how to comfort you.

Your loving friend,
Eliza

CHAPTER II

It was still early in the morning, not quite light, when Charlotte's trunk was loaded onto the carriage that waited in the drive of Hunsford Parsonage. Mr Collins fretted around, checking the wheels, tapping the doors, and then, realising he had little input into the workings of the vehicle, he went back into the house and brought out an extra shawl for Charlotte, which was an unnecessary but kind gesture. He wore a look of great concern, while she wore one of cheerful determination. She knew that if she showed even a hint of apprehension about the plan, he would falter, so she showed even more confidence than she felt.

'I do not like the scheme, Charlotte. What if you are set upon by highwaymen? Mr Darcy's carriage is extremely provocative in that regard.'

'What have I to offer highwaymen, my dear? They should find themselves terribly disappointed.'

'It is no laughing matter. The highways are safer than they were, but it is by no means guaranteed that you will find safe passage – the Great Dover Road used to be notorious!'

'William, I shall be at Lucas Lodge by this afternoon, and from there onwards, I will be accompanied by Alice.'

'You will allow me to remain apprehensive; Alice will be a comfort but hardly a protector. Perhaps I should, after all, go with you.' He glanced towards the house, wringing his hands.

Introducing Mrs Collins

After Elizabeth's letter had been received, a decision had had to be reached: whether the Collinses should attend the wedding and stay for a fortnight after, or not. Their respective positions seemed to oppose one another.

In the dilemma this presented, Charlotte saw a chance for something she now realised she had longed for: some time alone – some time apart. So, she had set herself to making it happen. Instead of allaying her husband's fears about Lady Catherine, she concurred with them. The only sensible option, she argued, was for Collins to remain. Meanwhile, she pointed out the courtesy due to Mr Darcy, as her ladyship's nephew; was it not sensible to retain his favour, thinking ahead to a future where he and his aunt would certainly be reunited? The only sensible option, she argued, was for her to go.

Charlotte was calculating. She felt some guilt about that, but not an abundance: being clever about her life had been a necessity so far, and her scheming was, after all, what had brought her and Collins together. Was it so bad to use the same tools to give her some time away from him?

There were several reasons why Collins did not want to come, even setting aside his patron's disapproval; he did not feel at ease with Elizabeth Bennet or her family, and he suffered with sickness on long journeys. None of it appealed to him. And yet Charlotte knew that all those issues would have been nothing to him, had she asked him to come with her. He would have done so in an instant. But she did not ask him.

As the practicalities of such a long journey might yet have swayed the decision, Charlotte used all the administrative powers she had to make the journey appear achievable, writing promptly to her mother, and to Elizabeth, to settle the finer details of the journey. To Elizabeth, she did not state clearly that she would attend alone, preferring to explain Collins's position in person and not wishing to invite any questions.

In due course, all was arranged: Darcy would send a carriage for her (indeed, for both the Collinses, as was presumed by he and Elizabeth), and Charlotte would travel to Derbyshire via her family home in Hertfordshire, and then, accompanied by Alice, her old maid from Lucas Lodge, she would travel on to Pemberley. It was a substantial undertaking, and Charlotte had needed to stay very firm in her convictions to persuade all involved that she could do it. But she could. And she would.

Just as she was about to take her leave of Mr Collins, another carriage was heard approaching. Turning, she saw a small gig rounding the corner of the drive. It settled not far from where they stood, and with some help from the coachman, the figure of Colonel Fitzwilliam descended from the carriage and stood in front of them. He wore a long green coat and top hat and leant on a walking stick. He appeared in good spirits and was looking expectantly at them and at the larger carriage in front of him.

Neither party had seen the other for many weeks, and much had transpired in the interval; some degree of awkwardness was to be expected – though perhaps not quite so much as presently prevailed.

Mr Collins, to hide his confusion, launched immediately into formalities, bowing low. 'Colonel Fitzwilliam! An unexpected honour. How may we help you at such an early hour?'

Fitzwilliam was thrown by the question. 'Unexpected? But—' He sensed something had gone amiss. 'You are travelling to Pemberley, I think? I have not misremembered the day? The presence of the chaise suggests I have not.'

'This carriage goes to Pemberley, yes,' answered Charlotte uncertainly.

'And I am to share it with you both. Were you unaware of the scheme? Darcy told me that he was sending a carriage for the Collinses and that I should travel with you, as we make the same journey.' He looked at their blank faces. 'I see that you were unaware. That, I am afraid, is an oversight on the part of my cousin. I thought he had written to you.'

Charlotte recovered herself a little, seeing how uncomfortable he was, saying, 'It is quite possible he has, sir. The scheme is all so lately made that the letter may have not reached us yet.'

He nodded gratefully. 'So ... I may join you?' asked the colonel tentatively, reading uncertainty on their faces that he could not fully explain.

'Forgive my hesitation, sir,' stepped in Mr Collins, finding his voice. He walked towards the colonel somewhat deferentially, glancing between him and Charlotte. 'But the facts are a little more complicated than you have them. I am not attending the' – he cleared his throat – 'happy occasion. My wife has made plans to travel alone and visit her family on the way. I have been a little uneasy on account of the great distance, but my wife has assured me she will be quite safe.'

Colonel Fitzwilliam raised his eyebrows. 'Indeed,' he replied. The idea was singular, but then he had come to expect that from Mrs Collins.

Mr Collins looked enquiringly at Colonel Fitzwilliam. 'Can I take it, from your presence, that Lady Catherine has softened in her attitude towards the match? She is apprised of your attendance?'

Fitzwilliam paused before replying, considering how honest to be. 'My aunt is aware.'

Mr Collins looked delighted.

'She does not condone it.'

Mr Collins looked deflated. 'Then, I am once again conflicted. Knowing that she has been abandoned by you,' said Collins, eyeing Fitzwilliam as he would an unfortunate sinner, 'makes me feel I must persist in my conviction to remain. Lady Catherine must have one ally in this matter, I feel.' He breathed a sigh and looked at Charlotte. 'But, for you to travel ...' Here, Mr Collins was rather stuck, trapped between his wish for his wife's safety and his desire for her not to be in close proximity with a soldier for a lengthy period.

'If I may, Mr Collins,' said Colonel Fitzwilliam, 'it sounds as if my presence might be a benefit to you both. You may remain here, strong in your convictions, and Mrs Collins will find safe passage with me; your fears for her will be allayed.'

If Colonel Fitzwilliam had any thoughts of spending a prolonged amount of time in a small space with Charlotte, he made a gallant attempt to push them to the back of his mind. He genuinely wished to be of help, although to Charlotte rather than to her husband.

Mr Collins looked doubtful. 'I confess it seems rather irregular for you to travel together. What should Lady Catherine say? I have some misgivings, naturally, albeit—'

'I will offer my own thoughts on the matter, if I may,' Charlotte said archly.

She was truly thrown by this new development. She had spent two weeks manufacturing this opportunity for independence, and the appearance of a companion, albeit one she liked a great deal, was not immediately welcome – even if a flutter of excitement passed through her at the prospect. But setting that aside, the situation was what it was, and there was only one logical conclusion.

'Colonel Fitzwilliam, you have been expecting to travel today, and in this carriage. Therefore, it would be insupportable to ask you to delay or find an alternative route, particularly given your condition.'

She then turned to her husband and took his hands. 'My dear, it is an unusual circumstance, but it solves a problem, does it not? I will not be alone, should anything happen.'

Mr Collins still looked concerned, and she added, suspecting where his discomfort lay, 'And this afternoon, I shall be with my family, and then accompanied by Alice for the remainder.'

This thought cheered him very little, but he felt that he could not object, with everyone standing there in the cold and the horses ready to leave.

As Colonel Fitzwilliam's trunk was loaded onto the carriage, Charlotte embraced her husband, who needed more reassurance than she, and bid him farewell, kissing him lightly on the lips. He did not want to part with her, and his concerned expression did not ease.

He studied his wife, who had a vigour about her this morning, undimmed by the alteration to her plans. Her eyes sparkled, and there was a good colour to her face, no hesitation in her movements. Who was this adventurer he had married, thought Collins, in wonder and in worry.

Charlotte let go of her husband's hand, turned to the door of the carriage and saw Colonel Fitzwilliam's hand held out, waiting to help her up. She ignored it, bracing her hand on the door instead, and pulling herself inside. She took a seat opposite the colonel and looked out at her husband.

Her heart felt a pull, seeing how lost he looked. But so had she been. She had lost herself, she realised. Whether it was in the last month or the last year, something had gone amiss.

And as she rode out of Hunsford, out of Kent and onto the long road north, she felt some hope that she might find it again.

CHAPTER III

'I can only apologise for surprising you in this way, Mrs Collins; it was not my intention.'

Colonel Fitzwilliam sat back, his shoulders braced against the plush burgundy fabric of the interior, attempting to occupy as little space in the coach as he could. Charlotte was sitting formally and stiffly, as if her stillness could render her invisible. In both cases, it was a futile exercise: each of them was acutely aware of the other's presence. Charlotte wilfully ignored how close her legs were to his, while he tried not to notice how her hem had ridden up to show a glimpse of her ankle. He looked anywhere but at her ankle.

She replied in a manner that betrayed nothing of her private thoughts. 'Please do not make yourself uneasy – a quirk of the post, or an oversight on Elizabeth's part. She may have thought that my husband and I were both travelling together, in which case the need to inform us of a companion would have been less pressing.'

'I see. Were you both intending to attend originally, then?' asked the colonel curiously.

Charlotte went red. 'I kept our response a little vague, being unsure how matters would fall out.'

Fitzwilliam nodded, sensing that she did not wish to explain herself. 'I attempted some discretion myself, when it came to leaving Rosings. But the fact of my going could not escape the ever-vigilant attention of my aunt.'

Charlotte grinned. 'Is she furious?'

'She is. But I am sure it will pass. It will have to – she will want to be involved with any children Elizabeth might have – a potential heir to Pemberley! – so she will have to make it up with them before that happens.'

His countenance sobered, and there was a certain intent in his manner – as though he sought to leave the present subject behind and venture into more personal territory. Charlotte knew why he was discomforted but did not have the words either.

Taking a deep breath, Fitzwilliam said, 'I have not seen you since' – he hesitated again – 'since you were with child. I have been wanting to tell you that I am very sorry for what has happened – and to know whether you are well, or well enough. I have thought of you often. It is not a gentleman's place to enquire, but I have wanted to.' He looked pained but genuine.

Charlotte took a moment. Knowing the frankness that had played out between herself and Fitzwilliam previously, she had wondered if he might mention this, and she was not averse to it. In fact, she thought it was brave.

'Thank you.' She rearranged her skirts distractedly. 'I was not well, or happy. But I am "well enough", now, as you have put it: well enough to travel, well enough to partake in other people's joys, which is my hope for this trip.'

He did not attempt to move on but looked at her still, in case she should say more.

Charlotte made a show of being stoic. 'I am told to look to the future, not dwell too long on the past.'

'I have heard such things said,' replied Colonel Fitzwilliam earnestly. 'It is not always possible.'

'No,' said Charlotte, meeting his eyes in understanding. 'Not always.'

A good deal of their journey was spent in companiable silence, looking out of the window at the sights as their surroundings changed from the countryside of Kent to the pretty villages on the outskirts of London, and then through the loud bustling streets of the capital itself.

Fitzwilliam was used to travel, but he found new joy in it upon seeing Charlotte's delight. Her face was craned around, staring out, her eyes hungry for new sights. While she was so happily occupied, Fitzwilliam was able to observe her at leisure, without causing discomfort. Her enthusiasm for these passing scenes came from a curious mind, but he speculated that it also spoke of what her life had been lately. *She has been bored,* he thought. The first time he met her he had recognised someone with a superior mind, and from talking with her since then, he knew she had a lively spirit, needed diverting conversation and new things to learn. Her eager eyes looking out at the mundanity of life – cows, farmers, trees, bridges – spoke of someone who was starving for new experiences.

As he watched her, her hand folded over the top of the window, her dark hair blowing onto her face, Charlotte shut her eyes and took a deep breath in, then released it slowly. She looked happy.

He was reminded of something she had once said to him at Rosings: that she wanted a peaceful life, but that peace must include passion. He understood that sentiment now, as he looked at her. Amid the noise of the wheels rattling and the bumps of the road jolting her, with the cool autumn wind flying in her face, unsettling her bonnet and her hair, she looked entirely at peace.

He was struck by an urge to reach out to her, to cup her wind-beaten cheek in his hands, to turn her face towards him, to kiss her. It felt more possible here, in this moment, loud and blustering, than it ever had. But he knew now was not the time. Such a time probably did not exist. *Of course it does not exist,* he thought.

'You are a fool,' he muttered to himself, the words lost against the clamour around them.

But then she turned to him. Had she heard? He was not sure. Her head was still at the window but looking at him very directly.

She held his gaze and smiled so warmly, so broadly, at him that he felt a lightness in his chest.

He could not smile back, so surprised was he by how much he felt for her in that moment. He had not expected it. He held her eyes, and his seriousness did not dim her expression. She did not seem to be asking anything of him in return. She offered her smile to him as a gift, with no expectations.

Just when he thought he could stay still no longer and would rise from his seat, it was she who was launched at him, as the carriage jolted, passing over a bump, and she hurtled forward. His rescue was ungainly; he caught her fall by her arm on one side, and her hand on the other.

Once the carriage was steady, he helped her into her seat, holding both her hands, arguably a moment longer than necessary. Once she was settled, Colonel Fitzwilliam pushed his back hard into the seat, dropped his shoulders and closed his eyes.

Had he known what Charlotte was feeling on that journey, he would not have been so restrained. The touch of his hand had kindled a fire in her that had been long dormant. She was feeling truly alive for the first time in months.

They reached Lucas Lodge early that afternoon, as Charlotte had hoped. Fitzwilliam, before the surprises of the morning, had intended to find an inn in Dunstable, but Charlotte now invited him to stay with her family in Meryton, and he gratefully accepted. He wanted to prolong their time together by whatever means possible.

When the carriage arrived outside the house, her mother and Maria came out to greet her. Charlotte climbed out, and as she did so, her family saw, to their surprise, another figure in the carriage. They looked a little quizzical until Maria exclaimed, 'Colonel Fitzwilliam!' in delight.

Charlotte met her mother's enquiring eye with an expression that indicated *I will explain later*. And Lady Lucas, excellent host that she was, welcomed the unexpected guest into her home with great warmth, holding back her many questions.

Luncheon was waiting for them, and they were a merry party: Sir William and Lady Lucas, Charlotte, Colonel Fitzwilliam, Maria and Edward, the youngest of the Lucas children – who, at fourteen, was in awe of being at a table with a 'real' colonel from the regulars. He peppered Fitzwilliam with questions, which he answered as best he could. Every member of the Lucas family had questions for the colonel, and Charlotte was nervous for him, imagining he would be exhausted by the interrogation. But he answered them all with enthusiasm and as much truth as could be borne at a mealtime.

'May I ask about your injury, sir?' ventured Sir William Lucas.

'Father—' Charlotte began to interrupt.

But Fitzwilliam shook his head, content to answer. 'I was shot in the leg at Salamanca, sir.'

'I read a little about Salamanca in *The Times*. A great victory; you must be very proud.'

Colonel Fitzwilliam poked at his meal, considering what to reply. 'I am proud of my men, whatever the outcome. The battles drawn up as victories are not always as victorious as they sound.'

Sir William looked a little confused. 'Ah – but we won, yes?'

The colonel glanced briefly at Charlotte, trying to convey a question with his eyes – the question being, *Ought I to continue?* – and she gave him a small nod of encouragement.

'What I mean to say, sir, is that we are advancing well, but each battle or siege must be chalked up to one side in the newspapers and reports. But that is not always an indication of triumph. Salamanca was more reasonably hailed as a win, even though we lost thousands. But the reason I was able to meet your daughters in the spring was because I was sent back home with what remained of my regiment after Albuera. Did you hear of that battle?'

Sir William nodded, tentatively saying, 'I believe I did. Hard fought?'

'Hard fought indeed, on both sides.'

This got a frown from young Edward, incensed that the French might be considered for praise in any circumstance.

As he appeared to have the attention of the table, Colonel Fitzwilliam continued, 'It was hard fought but not *well* fought. It was a mess. We were led by fools, generals replacing generals even while we were fighting. Our orders changed throughout, and no man knew what was happening. We didn't have enough guns or a clear line of sight. We lost as many as the French, and that was a great many, and it was needless. No side won that day.'

The table was quiet. Charlotte wanted to meet his eye, but he looked down.

'Their poor families,' said Lady Lucas quietly. 'Imagine having a son out there, under such threat.' She leant over to squeeze Edward's hand, and he pulled away in embarrassment. 'I have had friends separated for years from their military husbands, never knowing when the letter might come that brings bad news. I would not wish such a fate on my daughters.'

How particularly Lady Lucas intended those words was not clear to Charlotte. She thought she saw her mother give a side glance to Maria as she spoke, but if she intended the warning for her youngest daughter, it was felt keenly by Charlotte also, and by their guest.

A silence fell after she spoke.

Colonel Fitzwilliam broke it. 'I agree with you, madam. It is a cruelty, I believe, to ask such a life of someone you love.'

Lady Lucas nodded, satisfied, while Charlotte stared at her plate, deep in thought.

'There are exceptions, however,' continued the colonel. 'Susannah – I mean, Mrs Fontaine – came with us on campaign – through several campaigns actually, to be alongside her husband, Lieutenant Colonel Fontaine.

Charlotte was intrigued. 'She did? How did she manage it?'

'No one knows, really; she's only a slight little thing, not built for that life at all. But she did it. She was at Salamanca; I mean to say, she was there, in the thick of it. In the night, she searched the battlefield, tending to those who had fallen but ultimately seeking her husband. She wouldn't stop until she found him.'

The Lucas family were rapt by the story, awaiting the next sentence.

'Was he dead?' asked Edward loudly.

Lady Lucas tutted and shushed him.

Fitzwilliam grinned. 'No. He was alive but gravely wounded; she took him back and tended to him, and they now live together, here. He does not serve any more.'

'He was one of the lucky ones,' said Lady Lucas.

'In every sense,' replied Fitzwilliam. 'Lucky to live, lucky to find someone so devoted. I rather envied him,' he said, giving a rueful smile.

He bashfully looked down now, the conversation coming to a close; they would soon leave the table. Lady Lucas watched him.

'Thank you for sparing Alice, Mother. She will be a great help.'

Charlotte and her mother walked the grounds of Lucas Lodge, wrapped up against the late autumn chill. It was not really weather for a turn outside, but Lady Lucas had been rather firm in inviting Charlotte to accompany her.

'Of course I can spare her, and it is the least nod towards propriety you can afford, Charlotte.' From her daughter's letter until this moment, Lady Lucas had not been afforded a chance to speak honestly to her. She did so now, in no uncertain terms. 'What are you thinking, Charlotte – travelling half the length of the country with an unmarried man – part of it with no chaperone! What will people say?'

'It was an unusual circumstance – there was a miscommunication—'

'Even so, even before this, you had planned to come alone – that, too, is very odd behaviour and not safe.' She pulled her shawl around her. 'You seem … different.'

'If I am different from how you left me, that is exactly what you asked of me.'

'I do not mean that. I mean, different from the daughter I know. That person would not ride miles in a carriage, either alone *or* with a stranger.'

'He is not a stranger.'

'No, I can see that.'

That stopped Charlotte short. Carefully, she replied, 'We are neighbours. Over these past months, we have naturally become well acquainted.'

Lady Lucas turned to her daughter with a raised eyebrow.

'Why do you keep looking at me so?' cried Charlotte.

Her mother took her hands, standing in front of her. They stood in the same pose as they had almost a year ago, after Mr Collins's proposal. 'Charlotte, I will only say this. You are married. You are not wealthy enough to withstand a scandal, and neither are we.'

Charlotte scoffed. 'And this is what you will "only say". Mother, honestly—'

'Let me say my piece first – then you may reply. Think hard on the consequences of any foolishness. The Bennets survived Lydia's disgrace only because of the good luck of Eliza's and Jane's matches. If a scandal hit our family, Maria's chances, Edward's chances, would all be destroyed. Not to mention, you would be ruined.'

'Mother!' cried Charlotte. 'This is too much! Your warning is unnecessary. I value my marriage too highly to—' She hesitated, then reconfigured her response. 'And besides, there are no such feelings. You must know me well enough not to doubt it; I am not romantic. I have never had an interest in such matters.'

'Yes you *have*. You have. You have not always been as averse to the attentions of men as you claim, or to your own desires. You have learnt to ignore this part of yourself, but you are a woman with feelings, just as I am, and I see some feelings there. I see it, Charlotte.'

Charlotte could not reply. Her mouth was set tight, as if holding in a response.

'Alice will be with us for the remainder of the journey,' said Charlotte rather lamely, as to do so seemed a tacit acknowledgment that her mother was right.

Lady Lucas nodded. 'And I am glad. I really do wish that you enjoy your time away, my darling. I know you need it, and I understand why. Relish it. See your friend, share her joy, take in all that Pemberley has to offer. And then, go home.' She said the final words with some meaning.

The next day, the carriage was packed and ready by eight, and Fitzwilliam, Charlotte, and Alice made themselves comfortable within it. Alice, only slightly older than Charlotte, had been with the Lucas family for many years and knew Charlotte well. She therefore noted the awkwardness between her mistress and her travelling companion, but she decided that was to be expected, given the length of the journey and what she presumed to be a lack of acquaintance between them.

On the second night of the trip, the ladies found lodgings at an inn in Leicester while the colonel stayed at a barracks nearby. They reunited for the final day's journey, which held a sense of anticipation for all. The scenery through the Midlands was stunning, and when the first glimpse of Pemberley came, it was worth the wait.

Charlotte had never seen a house so grand; it rivalled even Rosings in stature, and it held a grace and proportion that Rosings lacked. Alice blew out a whistling sound as she saw it, the first time she had dared utter a sound all journey, and the other pair laughed, agreeing with the sentiment.

As the carriage approached, they were greeted by Darcy, while Elizabeth stood back a little on the drive, with a girl Charlotte assumed to be his sister Georgiana. Some surprise was expressed at finding no Mr Collins present, and Charlotte received a piercing look of curiosity from Elizabeth. But it all passed smoothly, and they were welcomed affectionately, Darcy heartily embracing Fitzwilliam which made Charlotte wince slightly on his behalf, considering his injury.

Elizabeth hugged Charlotte closely, giving the latter the opportunity to whisper into her friend's ear, 'I like your house.'

'It is not mine yet.'

They walked idly through the grand entrance of Pemberley, Charlotte looking up and all around. 'It is as good as yours! How many rooms do you have? Will you sleep in a different bedroom each night?'

'I will certainly try, which is bound to make me popular with the maids.' Elizabeth grinned. As she led Charlotte into a drawing room, she said quietly but emphatically, 'You must tell me about your journey ...'

CHAPTER IV

The bride wore white and a bonnet tied with lace the colour of claret and held a bouquet of eucalyptus, veronica and dark red roses. She smiled warmly as she walked down the aisle, despite shivering a little from the chill in the chapel.

While Pemberley was braced for the coolness of late November – every fire lit – the chapel, with its high ceilings and marble pillars, remained stubbornly chilly, even when bedecked with flowers and candles and filled with an excited congregation. Charlotte sat next to Jane, who had arrived with Bingley just in time to see her sister wed.

Mr Darcy stood at the front, looking resplendent in a crisp navy tail-coat, with Colonel Fitzwilliam next to him in his regimentals. Charlotte had stirred slightly at the sight of him in his uniform, which she had not seen him don since the spring. Darcy had looked a little nervous moments before, and it had warmed her to see Colonel Fitzwilliam cheering him with a joke and a pat on the shoulder. Her thoughts had been interrupted by the strains of the organ and the turning of heads.

Now, as Elizabeth made the short walk to the front of the chapel on her father's arm, Charlotte was struck by how certain she looked, and how comfortable. She considered how she had felt on her own wedding day, walking towards Mr Collins. She turned her mind away from that thought; she wanted to enjoy the moment.

Charlotte had not seen Mr Bennet for some time, and he looked a different man – thin and pale. Eliza was on his arm as they walked, but it seemed she supported him, not the other way around. But he still made funny expressions at his daughter, making her laugh, and his pride in her was clear.

Kitty, Mary and Georgiana, with flowers in their hair, now stood to Elizabeth's side. Kitty looked delighted and excitable. She was turning into a very pretty girl, thought Charlotte, and seemed more confident now she was out of Lydia's shadow. Georgiana was smiling and demure, while Mary ... Charlotte thought that Mary looked as if she were working out a particularly difficult sum, except that doing such an activity would have brought her some joy, and this did not.

Elizabeth had also invited her aunt and uncle, Mr and Mrs Gardiner, who sat just behind Mrs Bennet and looked for all the world like proud parents. Charlotte was glad Eliza had *some* sensible adults in her life.

The happy party of just a dozen guests (hardly the Bacchanal that Lady Catherine had implied it would be) made its way from the chapel to the drawing room, which was elegantly appointed. High windows allowed views down the length of the gardens towards the lake. The walls were panelled in cream and gold, and the room's aspect was more bright and airy than grand.

Charlotte chose a seat facing the window. She expected Jane to find her husband or speak to the Gardiners, but she took a seat next to Charlotte instead. It seemed Jane was eager for her companionship, having been with her new husband and his relatives for several weeks. Though Charlotte had never been as close to Jane as she was to Elizabeth, Jane had been a good friend, and it was only during this last life-altering year that the two had lost touch. Jane therefore had much to tell her, and both were in a mood to share confidences, which they did and at length.

Before long, Elizabeth joined them, and the three were raucous for a few minutes; overcome with the simple joy of being reunited.

'When were we last together, all three?' asked Jane.

'Before my marriage, I suppose, so almost a year ago,' Charlotte replied. 'And look now: all of us married. Quite a feat for one year!'

'Yes, and this now makes three Bennet sisters married off, for better or for worse,' said Elizabeth wryly. 'Mother is beside herself and somehow takes a great deal of credit for it. But as for that other case, I cannot think its achievement merits *any* credit.' Her face clouded, and Jane patted her hand.

'We will be happy today. And you must brighten before she arrives,' said the elder sister, the mediator as ever.

Elizabeth gave a sigh and looked apprehensively at the door.

Charlotte learnt that the 'she' was Lydia, who would be joining them at some point in the day. She was making her way down from Newcastle but had, characteristically, missed the service. Elizabeth had received a letter from her only the day before, saying she would come, but it was clear then that she had not made the necessary arrangements and that it was likely she would be late. None of this surprised her sisters; it confirmed that marriage had not changed Lydia.

'Will she come with her husband?' enquired Charlotte carefully, aware of the toll Mr Wickham's designs on Lydia had taken on the Bennet family.

The sisters shook their heads. It was not in their power to reveal the whole truth of why Wickham would never be welcome at Pemberley, as that would implicate Darcy's sister, Georgiana. A naturally protective brother, Darcy would not permit the presence of the man who had almost succeeded in eloping with Georgiana when she was but fifteen. But Charlotte knew enough of his character as a rogue, gambler and liar not to question this any further.

A happy afternoon passed: games of cards, turns around the house, and musical entertainments provided by either those who could play well – Georgiana and Charlotte – or those who were willing – Mary. By early evening, the drawing room at Pemberley was buzzing with conversation, the table decked with sugar decorations, bon-bons, cakes and, crucially, bowls of punch. This was the Darcys' first experience of entertaining in their married life, and they wanted to impress.

Charlotte felt elated. Did she feel like herself, she wondered, or did she feel not at all like herself, and that was the joy? Why did she revel in being far from her home and from all that she had come to make her own? She did not want to think of the answer. But she knew it.

She shook it off, determined not to overthink her pleasure and thereby tarnish it. She wore a fine green silk dress that she had worn in her youth, and had rediscovered at Lucas Lodge during her recent visit. Her mother had gladly packed it in her trunk to take with her. She enjoyed the feeling of wearing a dress she'd worn as a girl. She let herself be giddy. There was a rose to her cheeks and an easy laugh on her face all evening – she was glowing, and for once, she knew it.

Once or twice, she caught Colonel Fitzwilliam looking at her, but she knew better than to invite his attentions; she did not want to be the subject of any intrigue, and she heeded her mother's warning. After all, tonight was for Elizabeth, and she made efforts to keep her eyes and her conversation for her friends.

Around eight o'clock that evening, Elizabeth heard a carriage outside and readied herself for Lydia's arrival – a mere ten hours later than expected. The butler entered to announce her, but instead of doing so, he walked uncomfortably over to Darcy and whispered in his ear. Darcy's face turned to thunder, and he went to Elizabeth and said something quietly in her ear. A look of shock briefly crossed her face, and she muttered, 'Excuse me,' to Charlotte and quickly left the room with Darcy.

Their exchange did not go unnoticed. Most of the guests continued their conversations, despite their curiosity, but Charlotte, left alone by her friend's sudden departure, stepped out of the drawing room and lingered in the hallway, observing from a distance what had caused her friend's distress.

Far down the corridor, in the entrance hall, stood Lydia, and beside her, a tall, grinning figure whom Charlotte had not seen for over a year. He was looking around with pleasure, taking in every detail that would have once been so familiar to him.

'Why are you here, Wickham?' demanded Darcy.

'What a cold greeting, Darcy, my God! What an abominable host!' Wickham laughed. 'I am, of course, here to celebrate your nuptials – my warmest congratulations to you.'

There had long been an understanding between Darcy and Wickham that the latter would never return to Pemberley, and Wickham had agreed to facilitate that arrangement, in return for Darcy's financial support and his silence on certain matters. Wickham had in fact confirmed in writing that he was unable to attend today; his only duty was to maintain his own absence.

Yet here he stood, bold and unabashed, acting for all the world as if that understanding between them did not exist. He knew his presence here was not only unwelcome but shocking, and he revelled in the effect it had on both Darcy and Elizabeth.

'Lizzy, stop being silly,' cried Lydia petulantly. 'You should be glad my husband is here, and you are not being very nice, if I may say so. Poor Wickham. We have had a terrible journey – we ran out of brandy two hours ago, and we haven't eaten since luncheon.'

They went to step farther into the hall, but Darcy stopped them. 'Mrs Wickham, you are welcome to join us, but your husband is not.' He turned to Wickham directly. 'You must know why it is impossible. I will not have you anywhere near my' – he paused – 'my guests.'

Lydia was outraged, and her voice reached fever pitch. 'I shall cry, Lizzy, if your husband is this rude and inhospitable. I am your sister! Wickham is my husband! It is too much!' She was overcome – and also drunk – and began to wail.

The maid carrying food from the drawing room nearly dropped her tray at the racket, and the eyes of those in the entrance hall turned towards her and thus in the direction of Charlotte, who, just in time, ducked back into the room.

She crossed the room to Jane and whispered, 'Wickham is here.'

Jane's eyes widened, but, always calm, always collected, she replied, 'Lizzy will know what to do.'

Indeed, back in the hall, Elizabeth acted swiftly to limit scandal or mischief, persuading her husband, who was shaking with rage, that they should secrete the pair in another room until Georgiana had retired for the evening, and then, for the remainder of their stay, sober them up and keep a close eye on them.

An hour later, the Wickhams were admitted to the drawing room, after Elizabeth and Darcy had discreetly alerted their guests as to who was about to join them.

Wickham's expression as he entered was smug. He had got his way and was happy to be the centre of attention. He left his wife immediately and, spotting a fellow officer, settled himself down next to Fitzwilliam. He beckoned over a servant and asked for two glasses of brandy. The colonel was cool and unsmiling with him but seemed to understand that keeping the peace was in everyone's best interests at present.

As the night wore on, the jubilant, easy atmosphere of the earlier evening returned. The disruption caused by the arrival of the Wickhams had now dissipated, and lively conversation had ensued again, lubricated by punch, port and wine. Lydia was in a corner, chatting gleefully with Kitty, and Mr Wickham was being talked at by Mrs Bennet. The Gardiners were settled happily on the settee, satisfied as ever with only one another's company but

Mr Bennet had announced he must retire before either he finished off the port, or the port finished him.

Charlotte, for once, had allowed herself to indulge, and while she was not quite drunk, the mix of the punch had given her a bad headache, and she said to Elizabeth that she, too, had better retire, loath as she was to miss the fun.

'Oh, stay, Charlotte – do not retire yet!' protested her friend.

'I do not wish to, but my head is swimming, Eliza! I am making a spectacle, wincing and holding my temple as I have been! I just need a little quiet – perhaps if I step onto the terrace and get some fresh air ...'

'You'll freeze! Come with me'

Elizabeth dragged her friend out and down a corridor, then pushed open two large doors, showing the small music room where they had heard some of the ladies play earlier. In it was a piano, a harp, and an inviting settee. The fire was still lit, and Eliza set about lighting a few candles.

'There. Sit here and regain yourself, then come back and join us – it is still early!'

'Early, do you call it? It is past eleven! But I thank you; this is perfect.'

'Should you like me to play the pianoforte to soothe you?' asked Elizabeth, grinning.

'Not unless you wish my headache to worsen.'

'Charlotte!'

'Forgive me, Eliza, but I am not friends with you for your musical ability.'

'But for my wisdom?'

'No, for your wealth,' replied Charlotte quickly.

Elizabeth laughed, and she squeezed her friend's shoulder. 'Come and find me when you feel better.'

'Go – I will recline here like a fine lady. *Oh, my nerves!*'

'Now you mock my mother! It is too much!'

It was not too much, and she heard Eliza giggling as she stepped down the corridor. Charlotte closed the doors and moved to the settee, where she slumped down heavily, enjoying the chance to fully relax, unseen by anyone. The day had been very long, and the drink very strong, and only a few moments after closing her eyes, sleep took her.

'It has been a long time, Miss Lucas.'

Charlotte was jolted awake by the words and scrambled to sit up. The fire had gone out, and only candlelight remained.

'Who is there?'

Slowly, her eyes attuned to the dim light enough to see Mr Wickham standing in the entrance, the dark corridor behind him. She already felt the awkwardness, the impropriety of them being removed from the party, alone. She could hear the distant sound of lively conversation from the room at the other end of the hall, and she looked in that direction, as if she could transport herself there by willing it.

He saw her looking and smiled. He stepped farther into the room and closed the door behind him. 'Why are you in here, all alone?'

'I felt a little unwell and was seeking solitude. I have not been successful, it would appear.'

'Ha! You are as sharp as you ever were, I see, Miss Lucas.'

'Mrs Collins.'

He paused. 'Ah yes. Mrs Collins. You are married now. Quite unchanged, though. You know, you always looked young for your age, and you look quite the same as when I last saw you, if a little less damp.' He smirked and looked her up and down.

Charlotte recognised that look from the last time she had seen him.

'That is to say, you look very well,' he said, his voice low and a little slurred from drink.

'You speak as if we have met several times, Sir, and in fact we have met but twice, and briefly,' Charlotte said lightly, seeking to diffuse the situation that she could feel rapidly slipping from her control.

'True. Why did you not tell Lizzy that we had met before? She introduced us as strangers tonight. Why would you keep it a secret?'

'It is no secret; it is only of no consequence. I talk to my friends about things that interest me.'

His smile remained fixed, but she could tell he was irritated. 'I do interest you a little, though. I saw you earlier, in the hall, peeping,' he said, his eyes challenging hers.

Charlotte's brisk smile faded. She felt him provoking her, but did not know how to respond.

He continued to goad her. 'You were watching us from the shadows. Rather prying, but then, you are a rather watchful person, I think. So am I.'

Wickham began to walk towards the settee, so Charlotte rose from it quickly, not wishing to share a seat with him. He was enjoying her nervousness. As he sat, he seemed struck by genuine exhaustion for a moment, and he rubbed his hands over his face and groaned.

Charlotte, now standing, felt chiefly the impropriety of the situation, and more disgust *towards* him than any threat *from* him: she knew too well that his interest was in young girls, and she had always felt far beneath his attention – a lucky escape on her part, she thought. She did not wish to be alone with him, but she also sought not to incite his temper or make a scene, which she knew Elizabeth and Darcy were keen to avoid. She was treading a fine social balance.

'Marriage disappoints us, does it not, *Mrs* Collins? I always thought a wife would be a firm companion, a match for my own spirits – you understand? I thought I would have a wife who was my intellectual equal. But that has not proven to be the case.'

'You are lucky in your marriage, sir. Lydia is very devoted to you.'

'Yes. Devoted, besotted, *easy*. She was easy to catch, and she remains eminently available. But I have known enough women now to know the value of a real lady – a woman of *substance*. You must know a man wants some mystery, a lady who holds something back, someone modest, demure ... a little hard to get.'

He was looking at her again, his eyelids low and his breath heavy. She felt a shift in his intentions, and she wished to be away from him. But she felt afraid and incapacitated by her fear. Her instinct told her to keep him talking.

'I do not know what a man wants, sir,' she answered, distracted, looking at the closed door.

Wickham grinned, wolf-like, and said, 'So you claim. But you're clever; I bet you could learn.'

Charlotte heard the implication, felt the alarm. She wished to leave now and did not know why her body felt so paralysed when urgency was required.

Wickham rose surprisingly quickly from the settee and started to approach her. 'As a man, you want to feel you are uncovering something that hasn't been seen before, that you are making a discovery, Miss Lucas—'

'Mrs Colli—' she automatically corrected him. He was standing in front of her now. She felt her hands grow rigid with anxiety.

'Yes, yes, *Mrs Collins*,' he said irritably, then, with a sneer, 'Yes, you have some experience now, although I can't imagine it has been very satisfying.'

'I will not talk to you further,' she said abruptly, wrenching her feet from where they had felt stuck to the floor and turned from him.

Charlotte made quick progress towards the door, but a moment later, she felt her wrist caught firmly and pulled back. She cried out in surprise. Wickham spun her around and pushed her back, and back again, nearly tripping her, pinning her against the wall. His body was now pressed firm against hers, and her face craned away from his as he loomed over her, close enough that she could smell his sour, stale breath.

'But I want to talk to you, Miss Lucas. You think you are better than me. I saw it the first time we met. You judged me then, and you're judging me now.' He was ranting. His eyes looked wild, and he spat as he talked. He looked as if reason had left him entirely. Disdain, anger and drunken lust were a terrifying combination to see up close.

'Let me go,' she managed to utter.

It was as if he did not hear her. 'You do not like me, but you *do* want me, do you not?'

Charlotte's breathe was short; she could hardly reply. 'I do not,' she managed to utter.

'I know you do. Always so detached, so proper, but I bet you were burning for me.'

One of his hands gripped her at the waist, squeezing painfully, while his other held her arm against the wall. She was pushing with her other hand at his chest, but it was pointless.

'Please!' she cried. She closed her eyes tightly, wishing herself away.

His lower body pinned her against the wall, and his hands pulled sharply at the neckline of her dress, grabbing at her breasts. As he did so, he slammed his lips hard against hers, knocking her head back against the wood. She turned her face to the side, his lips dragging across her cheek. He grabbed her jaw and painfully turned her face back to his.

And then, suddenly, she felt herself free. She opened her eyes to see Wickham's face moving quickly backwards, away from her, his mouth open in shock. Only then did she see a strong hand around his neck, pulling him back by the throat.

Wickham staggered, losing his footing, even before Colonel Fitzwilliam threw him to the floor. The colonel then positioned himself between Charlotte and the rather pathetic figure now panting on the ground.

A few tense moments passed, only the sound of ragged breaths from all breaking the silence.

Wickham slowly rallied himself, stood up, rubbing his neck, and turned to look at Fitzwilliam, then at Charlotte. 'Is this your protector, Miss Lucas?' He laughed. 'I had no idea you would be so *gallantly* defended!' He started to walk towards Charlotte, his eyes on her, as if Fitzwilliam were not present. 'We could ask him to leave again?' He chuckled to himself.

Charlotte would not look away. She met his eyes without blinking or response.

Irritated by this, Wickham turned his gaze to Fitzwilliam and said, 'What a fuss, Colonel. Is it just that you hoped to have a go yourself? I warn you, she's a little frigid at first but—'

Fitzwilliam's fist had met Wickham's face before he uttered the last word, and Wickham's body had twisted and fallen from the blow before Charlotte fully knew what had happened.

This time, Wickham remained down.

Fitzwilliam turned now, to look at Charlotte fully for the first time. He sought her eyes, and she, seeing his concern, felt the force of the moment upon her, and her composure broke. She sobbed, and her body was wracked by trembling as she stood. Her shoulders rounded over, and her arms folded in, as if making a protective shell.

He so wanted to wrap his arms around her, to be an armour for her, a shield, but that seemed like the last thing she would want in this moment.

Charlotte felt flooded by feelings, and she had neither the capacity nor the desire to convey them to Fitzwilliam; she did not wish to be close to any man at this moment.

Just then, as if a silent prayer had been answered, Elizabeth entered the room. 'Charlotte, I heard—' She paused at the threshold, saw Wickham on the floor, not moving, and then turned and took in Charlotte, huddled over, in tears, and Fitzwilliam, standing a little way from her. Within a moment, she had an idea of what had happened. It was something like what she had always feared.

Elizabeth was enraged and brimming with feeling, but like Charlotte, she could be relied upon in a crisis. She did not give in to her inner wish – to walk over to Wickham and stamp on his neck. It would help neither her friend nor the situation.

She was decisive. She deftly took Charlotte's arm, gently moved her hair from her face, put a firm hand on her waist and said, 'Come with me, Charlotte.' And then, turning back to Fitzwilliam, 'Find Darcy, please – tell him what has happened, and he will know what to do ...' She paused a moment, and added, 'I am glad you were here.'

Fitzwilliam, himself rather shaken, simply nodded, but his eyes were only on Charlotte as she was led out the room.

CHAPTER V

Charlotte sat up in bed, fiddling idly with her emerald ring, which she had taken to wearing every day since the morning her mother had left Hunsford. She was still in her nightdress. She looked around the room. She had been here a few nights now and was growing more used to the grandeur of her surroundings, but it still felt odd. The four posts of her bed loomed above her, draped in red, matching the vast Persian rug covering the floor, on which sat a mahogany table and four chairs. Charlotte had laughed at the set-up when she first arrived: who was inviting four people into their bedroom of an evening?

Her eyes fell on the dress that lay over one of the chairs, the one she had worn last night. It would need mending. It had gotten torn a little at the waist and at the neckline. 'Or rather, *he* had torn it,' she thought. It hadn't torn all by itself.

She looked away from the dress.

Breakfast had been brought to her room at Elizabeth's suggestion, and she was grateful – not that she had much appetite, but she was glad not to have to face anybody yet, especially those who had witnessed, or knew about, the events of last night. Those people numbered no more than three, she hoped: Fitzwilliam, Elizabeth and Darcy. She would certainly not be adding to that. Alice had brought her breakfast, and as glad as she was to see her, Charlotte counted her as yet another person from whom she must conceal the truth.

She heard a clattering and rumbling outside her window – a carriage arriving? Ah yes, she remembered: the Bennet family were to return to Longbourn after breakfast, having already stayed for a week or so. It brought back to Charlotte the very same sounds she had heard in the early hours.

Charlotte had not been party to all that had occurred after Eliza took her from the music room. She had brought Charlotte up here to her bedroom and stayed with her a little while before finally leaving her friend to rest. Charlotte had not been able to sleep at first, reliving the scene in her head and wondering where Wickham was now and what was happening downstairs. But twenty minutes later, alerted by noises outside, Charlotte had watched from the window as a weeping Lydia and the stumbling figure of her husband were put into a carriage and driven away at speed.

After that, Charlotte's body had surrendered itself to a deep, heavy sleep that had carried her easily into mid-morning the next day.

When she had first woken, she hadn't recognised where she was and had a pleasant moment or two of recollecting whose house she was in, enjoying the comfort of the bed and the light shining into the room. And then the memory of the night before descended on her, like a cloud across the sun. She grew a little colder, and felt a tremble return to her body, and her heart starting to beat faster.

She had managed to calm herself before her body overtook her, but now, a little numb, she was left alone with her feelings.

What consumed her most was anger: anger at him, but also a little at herself. She berated herself for indulging him as long as she had; why had she not left the room as soon as he entered? Why had she conversed with him at all? Her cautiousness in not causing offence had played directly against any cautiousness in protecting her person.

Charlotte could not help but think that her experiences of intimacy were cursed: Mr Collins had been her first and only physical encounter with a gentleman, and the attempts in the marital bed had been perfunctory and uninspiring, but they had at least been gentle at every step, even to the point of her frustration. Her consent had been based on a sense of obligation, but she had, at least, given it.

To go from that to the actions of last night, with no other experience in between, was a bitter revelation. She knew instinctively that the attack from Wickham was not based on desire for her but a desire to win and to belittle. And on the other side, she had never even felt much longing from her husband in his overtures, only something closer to a duty well observed. Therefore, at this moment, she felt entirely unwanted and small and weak. She had never been truly desired by anyone, she thought, and last night's act seemed to prove it, though the appearance of it would betray otherwise.

It was as if her view of the world had been a little broken, and she with it.

Her thoughts were interrupted, perhaps fortuitously, by Elizabeth, who knocked and entered, treading softly. 'You are awake. How do you feel?'

Charlotte considered. 'I do not know. Not well.' She shrugged.

Elizabeth nodded. 'Might you come down? You do not have to, but ... a continuing absence will be asked about, and to avoid the effort of lying, it might be easier to ...' Elizabeth struggled to complete her point.

'I know what you mean. And you are right. I will be down shortly.'

Elizabeth hesitated. Her brow was crinkled, and tears formed in her eyes. 'I should never have let him in. Darcy warned me. It was my idea to allow it.'

Charlotte shook her head and said, 'It is not your fault, Eliza.'

Elizabeth looked into her eyes. 'Nor yours.'

Charlotte didn't reply.

'I'll see you downstairs then. We will be in the parlour.'

'Yes. I shall not be long.'

Elizabeth, who last night had been swift and certain in her reactions, this morning seemed unsure how to behave. She would usually have hugged her friend and sat with her, but Charlotte felt that Elizabeth seemed a little afraid of her – afraid to touch her or get too close, perhaps even slightly repulsed, as people often are of things that are wounded.

As it turned out, few questions were asked about Charlotte's late appearance – it was easily put down to the same headache she had had last night. Present in the parlour were the only guests remaining at Pemberley: Jane, Mr Bingley and Colonel Fitzwilliam, and its residents: Mr Darcy, Elizabeth and Georgiana.

Charlotte sat next to Jane again and drank tea, careful as she moved her arms not to pull too much on the long sleeves she had worn to conceal the bruises on her wrist. She was determined not to catch the eye of Colonel Fitzwilliam, who was, rather unhelpfully, staring at her with a grim, stern look. An outsider might have thought he was angry at her, but Charlotte guessed at his feelings.

She let her eyes wander around the room, trying to focus on something other than her own thoughts. She eyed the paintings, the curtains, the fire. The fire proved a winning option. It held her gaze and her interest. She stood up, and grabbing a poker, she started to stoke the flames, lightly at first, and then, in something of a daze, she began jabbing at the coals harder, until one fell over the grate onto the hearth.

Charlotte, unthinking, went to pick it up with her bare hand, and Fitzwilliam, the only person with eyes directly on her, vaulted forward from his seat and grabbed her other hand, pulling her backwards.

She looked around, shocked, and then seemed to come back to herself.

'Allow me,' Fitzwilliam said, and reaching down, he grabbed the pair of tongs and carefully returned the coal.

They both now stood by the mantelpiece, not knowing what to say.

'Thank you,' she said.

'It is nothing.'

'It is not nothing. I am grateful,' she said, turning her face up to finally meet his eyes.

Colonel Fitzwilliam had spent a restless night. While Charlotte was taken upstairs, he had found Darcy, as instructed, and they had gone together to where Wickham still lay. Darcy, taking advantage of the man's inert state, had quickly formulated a plan, giving several directions to his butler and informing Fitzwilliam of his intentions. When Wickham's eyes started to open, Darcy and Fitzwilliam pulled him to sitting, which wrenched him into consciousness.

Once Wickham was able to hear and respond, Darcy said simply, 'You are leaving. Tonight.'

Wickham grinned and then winced; a purple bruise was already forming across one side of his face. 'Absurd. What a hysterical reaction, Darcy! Why are you involving yourself in this petty argument?'

Darcy certainly did not look hysterical. He was entirely composed and seemingly emotionless. He had been dealing with Wickham his whole life, and it showed; he indulged none of his talk, letting his words slide away into nothing.

Elizabeth entered, soft-footed and efficient, and whispered in Darcy's ear.

Darcy turned to Wickham and said, 'Your trunks are loaded. The carriage is ready. Your wife is waiting. Go.'

And after a few spluttered protestations, he did. A wailing, reluctant Lydia accompanied him, and Pemberley was rid of them both before the morning light broke through.

Now, in the parlour, Darcy looked at his cousin, standing by the fireplace next to Charlotte. He considered the fortune of Fitzwilliam's presence last night; what luck that he had been near the music room and heard the commotion. Had he gone looking for Charlotte, he wondered? He lost the thought, as Bingley asked him a question and he allowed his attention to be drawn.

Fitzwilliam, oblivious to his cousin's observation, had eyes only for Charlotte, who had taken her place next to Jane once again. Having been so radiant last night, she now looked pale and drawn. She had been putting on a show of being only tired, but he saw the effort she was making to keep that up.

Thank you, she had said, but what had she to really thank him for? For throwing a punch, for losing his temper, for brawling and, in truth, enjoying the win. He did not feel heroic now. He felt rather dirty and like his old self. But would he do it again? Of course. He was fighting an instinct, now, to sit with her, to comfort her, to be close to her – which was, he surmised, probably the last thing she would want.

So, he remained standing a while, a safe distance from her, feeling as uncomfortable as he appeared.

CHAPTER VI

Jane and Bingley left Pemberley the next morning; they were both keen to get back to Netherfield, having not had the chance to settle properly before their travels. Heartfelt goodbyes were made between all: Elizabeth and Jane, Darcy and Bingley, all of whose fates had been intertwined and come out for the better. Charlotte hugged Jane tightly, and they assured each other they would write more and make plans to visit.

And with that, just two guests remained at Pemberley.

The house that had been brimming with activity had shed its guests quickly and efficiently over the course of two days, as if in harmony with the falling leaves outside its windows, and was left in a state of relative quiet and welcome peace. The household now comprised Mr Darcy and Elizabeth, Georgiana, and Charlotte and Colonel Fitzwilliam.

As the days moved onwards, this grouping proved to be an easy fit. The two gentlemen got on as well as they always had, and found their best conversations took place when they were occupied by other pursuits: playing a game of billiards or fishing in the lake. Charlotte and Elizabeth needed no such prop. They talked together with neither prompt nor pause, for hours at a time but also often sat companionably in silence, reading or sewing. Long walks in the day, and languid evenings in were enjoyed by the whole party. Georgiana seemed to find an affinity with Charlotte; she shared many of her traits, being easy in solitude and a diligent reader, more interested in intimate conversations than in holding the attention of the group. She fitted in well with them all, content to be a little separated by age and experience. All in all, the household was so well suited, it could have been by design.

As the shadow cast by Wickham lightened day by day, Charlotte began to relax into the happiness of her situation, and in her stronger moments, she found that she was in her element. The days were passed too quickly until she must return, and she wished she could stop time and remain here, suspended from her life. Pemberley already seemed otherworldly in its aspect, and to imagine it existing outside of the ordinary progression of time, was only a small leap in her imagination.

The ease of manner between herself and Colonel Fitzwilliam was notable to the others. It was hard not to observe that they fell into step with a married couple without any difficulty.

'I wonder at how acquainted Charlotte and my cousin have been in Kent,' Darcy remarked to his wife one evening, after retiring to bed.

'They met but two or three times while I was there. They must have met more often since then, to be so familiar. They talk very frankly with each other, do they not?'

'They do; one might think they were long married.'

'Except, if they were long married, they would not have the spark they have now.'

'Oh, I don't know,' said Darcy, seizing her at the waist. 'I think we shall have the spark for a few years yet'.

'Oh, *we* shall. I shall always strive to be the exception to any rule,' she said with a mischievous grin, and Darcy leant over and kissed her.

She let herself be distracted by him then, but she had already added *Colonel Fitzwilliam?* to a growing list of concerns that she had about her friend. But it was not the most pressing.

'I keep thinking about Wickham,' Elizabeth said to Charlotte, rather unexpectedly, as they sat in the parlour one afternoon. Elizabeth was attempting some embroidery, which always made her irritable.

Charlotte looked up, closing her book. Her silence invited Elizabeth to go on.

'He must surely suffer some consequence to his behaviour. And yet, it is his attachment to my family that means he cannot. What disgraces him also disgraces my sister and myself. It infuriates me,' she said, stabbing at her sampler.

Charlote nodded. She was well aware of the predicament and the injustice of it. 'My hope – and I can only say this to you and you alone – is that, in his new position in the regulars, he is sent abroad and proves useful to his country.'

Elizabeth, not looking up, idly replied, 'Yes, yes, I'm sure he will be of some use.'

'And then gets shot.'

Elizabeth's head jolted up. She caught Charlotte's grim expression and laughed uncertainly. 'Charlotte!'

Charlotte shrugged and held her look. 'Do you not?'

Elizabeth grinned slowly. 'I do.'

'Pretty good chances of it,' said Charlotte darkly, with the smallest grin.

Elizabeth chuckled, shaking her head in disbelief. 'You always surprise me.'

'I will take the compliment.'

A moment later, Elizabeth asked, 'But are you well, in yourself? After what occurred?'

Charlotte took a moment to think, then replied with clear eyes and firm voice. 'I am.'

The answer surprised even herself.

Ten days after their wedding, the new Mrs Darcy accompanied her husband on a long day of visits, in which she would be introduced to his tenants, leaving a slightly depleted party at the house. As luncheon was cleared, Colonel Fitzwilliam asked if Charlotte or Georgiana would like to accompany him for a walk through the grounds. It was a bright day, though cold, and there was much he wanted to explore, he told them, as far as his legs would take him. Even though he was still unsteady, and his body tired easily, he could now walk without the aid of a stick, and he was keen to make the most of his new faculty. Georgiana declined, preferring to stay inside and practise the pianoforte, but Charlotte accepted.

The grounds of Pemberley were breathtaking; there was so much to remark upon, to delight in, as they progressed, that Charlotte and Fitzwilliam hardly needed to discuss any subject beyond what was in front of them. They walked through the herb garden, then the orangery, across the sweeping lawns, past the lake and beyond. At points, they were child-like, rendered so by the playfulness of the landscape; Charlotte jumped from side to side of a hillside cascade, Fitzwilliam splashing the water with a stick.

They reached the *labyrinth*; a thick, tall hedge maze, known for its difficulty.

'Shall we?' asked Fitzwilliam, expecting a demurral.

Charlotte grinned. 'Let's.'

Upon entering the maze, Charlotte turned a sharp right, as he took the left. Charlotte got immediately lost, taking sudden turns, going back and trying again, and to no avail.

After five minutes, she heard him.

'Where are you?' came his voice, from some way off.

'Obviously, I do not know!' she exclaimed into the air, laughing a little, breathless.

'I have found the middle!'

'Good for you!'

'It is very nice here; I recommend it,' he said drily.

'I would love to join you! But the hedge seems to want my company.'

'I'll try to find you!' he called back.

She continued in one direction, then, finding a dead end, turned back. It was hard to believe that so small an area could cause her to feel so disorientated. Thick clouds had now covered the waning afternoon sun, and she felt rather cold. The tall hedge close around her cast the narrow paths into shadow, and even as she cursed herself for being foolish, she started to feel a little panicked. She was truly lost and had been for some time now.

She picked up her pace and called out again, 'I cannot find my way!' She felt foolish and a little desperate. She heard no reply.

Perhaps it was the sudden shade or the cold or an after-effect of her encounter with Wickham, but she felt suddenly emotional, and tears pricked her eyes. She was running in a panic now, turning corner after corner – until, taking one more left turn, she ran headlong into the chest of Colonel Fitzwilliam.

He grasped her arms, steadying her, then looking down and seeing her distress and her shivers, he wrapped his arms around her, gently cradling her head as she pressed it into his chest. She clung to him while her panic abated, appreciating the sturdiness of him. After a few moments, she was recovered, but she did not loosen her grip. She wanted to stay this close, or closer, to let him enfold her, to lift her up. She did not want to wait any longer. She did not want to hesitate.

She pushed just far enough from him to be able to look up and see his face. He was peering down with fierce intensity.

'Charlotte,' he said, almost to himself, his voice rough and low, tasting how her name sounded on his lips.

She grasped onto his jacket, holding him to her. She knew she had his attention and his affection and his protection. But was there more than that? Could there be?

His hair had fallen over his brow, and she brought her hand up and gently pushed it back, then let her hand fall to his neck. She stood on tiptoes and, rising up, pressed her lips to his.

He responded gently, politely – so lightly at first that she felt she had made a mistake. He matched her, but as she fell back onto her heels, he did not reciprocate. She looked down, embarrassed, and tried to pull away from him, but he held onto her.

In a strained voice, he said, 'I do not want to hurt you.' With one arm still around her, he brought a hand up to echo her own action and slowly brushed away a stray lock of her hair. She put her hand over his and pulled it down firmly and placed it on her waist.

Her breath was heavy, and she looked him in the eye as she replied, with a clear voice, 'I will not break.'

She felt a change then. She felt the hand on her waist hold her tighter through the many layers of her coat and dress, his strong fingers clamping the gathered fabric into her skin. His other hand was behind her neck then, and with his fingers entwined in her hair, he pulled her face firmly to his, craning over to envelope her in a deep kiss.

Had Charlotte had the mental capacity to think about it, she might have considered that this was her first proper kiss: her first kiss fired by mutual desire. But she had not the room for reflection in this moment, she had only her instincts, which were strong and clear; she wanted to be as close to Colonel Fitzwilliam, in whatever way she could, as soon as she could.

She pulled at his lapels, grabbed at his hair as he tugged at her coat, impatiently undoing the buttons, then straining at the final one, which eventually burst off. The isolation of where they were was intoxicating: no onlookers, no coachman, no servant or eavesdroppers. They were half a mile from anyone, and anyone who came to find them would fail.

How they revelled in being lost. Her coat was on the ground, his jacket off, his shirt loose and neckcloth untied so that she saw the flush at the top of his chest. She felt his hand move down her back, drawing her still nearer to him. His mouth was now at her neck, seemingly as eager as she was, needing to find and touch every inch of her that he could see, and those he could not.

They both knew what came next – no need for words, only instinct. They both were thinking of skirts gathered, a shirt ripped open, the frantic need for something to lie down upon or press against. They might have. They nearly did. One moment more, and they'd have fallen to their knees on that cold ground – pulling, unfastening, casting off – had not a few drops of rain started to fall.

Just one or two at first – Charlotte blinked as a raindrop fell on her forehead and ran down into her eye. Heavier drops began to fall then, on Fitzwilliam's chest or the back of Charlotte's neck, more and more, marking the beginnings of a downpour. They acted to douse the fire that had consumed them, for long enough to give them pause – to really consider what was next.

His hands stilled; she pulled her mouth from his, and they stood, heads close, holding on tightly in the rain, breathing and staring, daring the other not to stop. But they were both too intelligent not to think of the consequences, now that their minds had a second to do so. Practicalities that a moment before had been swept aside now resumed their significance. The ground they were to use as a bed was fast becoming swamped. The coats that lay on the ground were getting drenched. They were expected back. They would be missed. They would be noticed.

A decision seemed to have been reached silently, and recognising a surrender of sorts, Charlotte flung herself into his chest, her head under his chin, in a gesture of affection over desire. Her arms encircled him under his jacket, and he put his around her shoulders, kissing her head. Locked there for a few minutes, both of them thought of all that had just happened, their brains fizzing with the unknown that was before them. Then they slowly unwound, retrieved their coats and started to make their way back.

Fitzwilliam knew the route and, holding her hand, led her out, until she could see the gardens and the house beyond.

They started walking, but then, pelted by the rain, they half-ran, half-stumbled, their shoes soaked, their clothes dripping, hair slick on their faces, shivering with cold but laughing like children at their own disarray.

As they got closer to the house, Charlotte saw figures waiting for them. Alice was at the back entrance with some towels, looking concerned and then amused, and Darcy waited just behind her.

The pair sobered a little as they were greeted.

'Quite the downpour,' said Darcy stiffly.

'Yes! We were at the other end of the estate when it began. The run back has rather dishevelled us,' Fitzwilliam replied, trying for nonchalance.

Darcy nodded and watched as Charlotte handed her wet, muddy coat to Alice. She was trembling now with the cold. With a backward glance at the colonel, she exited the room and made her way upstairs.

Fitzwilliam stood in front of Darcy, damp and undone, and felt oddly exposed. Darcy's dark eyes were sharp and seemed to be probing him.

'What?'

Darcy did not answer the question, instead stating, 'You seem to have forgotten your injury.'

'I—' Fitzwilliam began, then faltered, looking down at his leg as if that would provide an explanation. 'Yes, I suppose I did. It has not pained me all afternoon. I have not given it any thought.'

Darcy raised an eyebrow. 'You must have had much to distract you.'

Fitzwilliam was about to reply when Darcy said quickly, 'Richard, I—' then hesitated and continued in another tone, 'I will have them bring up hot water to your room.'

The moment Darcy's footsteps faded down the hall, as if by dark magic, Fitzwilliam felt the pain returning to his leg – and in abundance. He had put extra weight on it in the maze, using it to bear the weight of two bodies. Perhaps he should have been more careful, but he had felt nothing in the moment, nor in the cold, giddy rush towards the house.

He winced as he began to ascend the stairs, and pain darted down his leg. But on balance, he thought with a grin, it was well worth it.

30th November 1812

My dear Charlotte,

I do hope that your visit to your friend has provided you with succour and that you feel ready to soon return home, refreshed and healed. To bear witness to a marriage, even a marriage that has been censured by many, is a blessing, and I trust the Darcys are grateful for your presence there, which will have added considerably to the happiness and the respectability of the occasion.

All is well here. Mrs Brooke is doing more than usual to make up for any household duties of yours that lay derelict. I am requested to pass on good wishes from the following:

Brooke sent her 'warmest wishes';

Colonel Raeworth, whom I saw at church, said you were 'much missed';

Anne de Bourgh, whom I saw also at church, which is rare, sent you her 'fondest regards', which was unexpected;

And finally, Mr Smithson sends his 'best wishes' and suggests you return as soon as may be, for your community needs you, which I thought was thoughtful.

Mr Smithson has proven to be a real boon here in Hunsford. The parishioners like him a great deal, and I confess I sometimes feel envious of how easy he is with them. I personally do not like his style of sermon; it is rather informal and plain-speaking; it suggests to the congregation that he is their friend, which is misleading and will confuse them. However, they seem to respond well to it, so on the occasions when he leads the service, I need not worry that my flock will be despondent. Quite the opposite.

Smithson has visited me at the parsonage most days. We get along famously, and he has joined me once in a visit to Rosings, in which,

I must observe, he was wont to dominate the conversation with Lady Catherine. But such a connection is, to him, still a novelty, and therefore I can understand that he cannot temper his enthusiasm. She seems to respond well to him also, which, I will confess only to you, my dearest, also sparks the faint beginnings of jealousy in me. But I know that such feelings are beneath me, and thus, I endeavour to tamp them down firmly, as if pushing unwanted items into the back of a cupboard, so that they are unseen day to day. Although, considering it now, perhaps it would be more prudent to rid oneself of unwelcome items rather than keeping them in a cupboard, where one may accidentally discover them one day when searching for a fresh handkerchief. (A metaphorical handkerchief, you understand.) I shall think on this further.

I have missed you a great deal. The house is rather cold without you here (not literally cold, for Brooke is keeping the fire well stocked, as I mentioned earlier). There is a quietness that I have not grown used to and do not care for. Also, your dahlias have died.

Come home soon please.
Your ever-loving husband,
William

CHAPTER VII

There were various people in states of undress, fabric falling off their bodies, some of them playing the lute and some of them the harp. Charlotte did not know who they were. *Perhaps angels,* she thought. She rubbed the back of her aching neck, sore from looking up at the painted ceiling of the chapel. Her eyes turned instead to the image over the altar, which dominated the front of the chapel. It was framed by intricate marble carvings, and primarily depicted two men, one of whom was standing as the other knelt in front of him.

She had not taken in much of the detail of the chapel during Elizabeth's wedding; there had been much more to look at than fat cherubs and harp-playing angels, but now, with only a few days left to make the most of Pemberley, she had taken herself on an early morning private tour, enjoying the opportunity to take in its grandeur in solitude. She felt she ought to pay attention to the chapel; it was, the housekeeper had assured her, *of great artistic importance.*

Looking again, she believed the standing man was Jesus. She did not know the identity of the kneeling man but he looked very sorry for himself and was touching Jesus's torso. Jesus's torso was quite a spectacle. Really, Charlotte thought, she had never seen such a broad, muscular Jesus. His legs were as thick as tree trunks, and he wore only a thin blue cloth over his lower half. No wonder this other man was touching him.

Right, that's enough of that, Charlotte thought, blinking herself out of the moment and turning to leave. She knew she could not help the urges she had been having these last few days, but she drew the line at lusting after Christ. She silently told herself to gain some control.

In the days that had passed since their encounter in the maze, Charlotte and Fitzwilliam had not had the opportunity to be alone again. They had passed each other in corridors or been the first to arrive in the drawing room, but the plentiful staff that Pemberley boasted meant the chances of being overlooked were very high. They were cautious. They were cautious not only for fear of discovery but for fear of the other's feelings.

It had been left unclear whether the kiss, the embraces that had so stirred them both in the moment, would be looked on by one or the other as something to regret, or to forget. Fitzwilliam wondered whether Charlotte would think of it as a terrible mistake, while Charlotte, at her more vulnerable moments, persuaded herself that Fitzwilliam might not think about it much at all – viewing it as a brief, meaningless tryst which hardly affected his feelings, or his life. Such a response would be in keeping with many rumours she had heard of military men, even if she could not really believe that Fitzwilliam was such a man.

These thoughts crossed her mind as she made her way to the breakfast room. Elizabeth, Darcy and Georgiana were already seated, the two ladies serving one another, while Darcy read a newspaper.

A few minutes later, Colonel Fitzwilliam entered the room.

'Good morning!' he said amiably and sat down opposite Charlotte.

She smiled tightly and looked down, busying herself with her cutlery.

'I have been feeling rather forlorn at the prospect of your leaving, Charlotte,' said Elizabeth, quickly adding, 'and you, of course, Richard.'

Fitzwilliam smiled. 'I take no offence, madam – I am aware that I cannot be an equal part in your friendship with Charlo— Mrs Collins.' He felt a flicker of the eyes from Mr Darcy. 'I hope that my cousin will be just as heartsore over my departure!' he continued lightly, trying to mask his mistake in addressing Charlotte so informally.

Darcy gave a short laugh, then folded his newspaper as if coming to a sudden decision. 'Actually, I have a request. I have some business interests to attend to rather urgently in London, and I would appreciate a second eye on them. Would you accompany me, cousin? You could then make your way back down to Kent at your leisure.'

It was clear from Darcy's tone that this was not an idle request. Fitzwilliam was surprised by the scheme, which would mean his departing a day earlier than planned, and crucially, not with Charlotte. He guessed at his cousin's motive, and he acquiesced.

Charlotte, not oblivious to the sudden change, saw fit to be nonchalant about it, saying that she would travel on the 5th as planned, with Alice.

'We will be comfortable companions and will benefit from the extra space,' she said in good humour.

Darcy nodded sharply. 'Good. Then it is arranged. We will leave tomorrow morning, Richard.'

That night, the party enjoyed a fine dinner and a relaxed, happy evening together, albeit one tinged with melancholy for the ending to what had been a period of great contentment for all. Elizabeth and Darcy would now embark on their married life without their oldest friends' presence to disguise the huge change that meant. Fitzwilliam would return to what now felt like a rather odd existence: convalescing with his elderly aunt until the call of war beckoned again – and until he was well enough to answer. And Charlotte, of course, must go home. She must remember that she was married.

During the course of the evening, Charlotte played them a slow adagio on the piano. As she played, she felt Fitzwilliam's eyes on her, and a flush crept up her neck as she tried to keep time.

When Charlotte finished, Georgiana applauded her, and Elizabeth, walking towards the piano, declared, 'I am sure you have never been such a talent as you are now, Charlotte. Where have you been hiding your skills? None of us knew you could play like that.'

'I did,' declared Fitzwilliam rather defensively, from across the room.

Elizabeth looked over. 'I beg your pardon?'

Fitzwilliam, slightly regretting speaking up, continued, 'I only mean to say that Mrs Collins has been practising at Rosings and has entertained us there, and so she has not been hiding her talents. Her talent is no secret.'

Elizabeth looked rather irritated by this. 'Well, thank you for that. No, indeed. I only meant, Charlotte, that *we* have not had the pleasure of hearing you play for a long time. Those at Rosings obviously know you much better than I,' she said, with perhaps a hint of petulance.

'You know me better than anyone,' said Charlotte to Elizabeth, keen to soothe any upset. 'And I, you. I recall how you hated your own pianoforte lessons with Mrs Timpson.'

Elizabeth was mollified, saying, 'Who now has ten children.' With a raised eyebrow to Charlotte. 'Imagine!'

Elizabeth was oblivious to the insensitivity of her remark, but Colonel Fitzwilliam glanced at Charlotte, recognising the pain it might elicit.

Charlotte met his eyes and gave him a crinkled smile of acknowledgement, and replied evenly, 'I hardly can.'

Later that evening, when everyone had retired to their rooms, Charlotte sat plaiting her hair for bed. Her room was lit only by a single candle, which she was about to blow out when she heard a knock on her door.

She rose and tentatively went to the door. When she opened it a crack, she saw Colonel Fitzwilliam standing before her, still dressed.

'You cannot be here,' Charlotte said immediately.

'No, I know, it is only ... I am sorry to greet you at such an hour. But – I do not know when I will next see you ...' Fitzwilliam spoke urgently but quietly.

'You ... you cannot come in.'

'Of course not; I do not ask it.' He lowered his voice yet further. 'I do not want to cause trouble for you. I only wanted to say goodbye.'

Charlotte opened her door further.

He looked at the long plait that fell over her shoulder and onto the edge of her white nightgown and thought about stepping over the threshold, loosening it, putting his hands through that thick hair and pulling it back—

'Colonel?'

His mind jumped back. 'When we return,' he continued, 'I know that we will see one another in company. But this cannot be the last time I see you alone. It must not. I ask you now, Charlotte. Will you meet me again?'

She hesitated. This was not sensible. It posed a great risk to herself, and it had the potential to cause great hurt to her husband and her family. She was not given to rash courses of action based on nothing but feeling. She had never been led by her feelings. Never.

Perhaps, she thought, *it is about time.*

CHAPTER VIII

Fitzwilliam put on a long, thick greatcoat and set out, with his walking stick, from the back doors of Rosings. He could now walk, albeit uncertainly, without the stick, but on the uneven terrain of the gardens and the woods beyond, he thought he had better be sensible. In this, at least.

Winter had arrived in earnest – mid-December had brought cold rains and bitter winds, but none of this had deterred Colonel Fitzwilliam from venturing out on his daily walks through the grounds. Lady Catherine and Anne found it puzzling, but as they saw it, a wounded soldier, a little lost without his purpose, must be allowed some quirks. He never invited anyone to join him, and luckily nobody in the household had any inclination to.

He made his way past the rose gardens, through the orchards and across the sweeping expanse of lawn – then, just as he was about to turn back despondently, disappointed not to have found his quarry, he decided he would push on just a little farther. He did not usually venture into the thick woodland that sat on the farthermost patch of Rosings land. This was due to his last vestiges of self-preservation; the steeply rising peaks and sudden drops in the wood, all of it darkened by rhododendron bushes ten feet tall, meant it was a hazard, even to someone who was being as stubborn as he.

But today he did go in, making his way carefully over fallen pinecones, twisting roots hidden by fallen leaves; he was glad of his stick. A few minutes in, he saw a glimpse of something through the trees – or someone. A flash of blue.

'Hallo there?' he shouted.

There was a sudden stillness; then he heard twigs snapping underfoot and saw Charlotte emerging through the trees, coming towards him. She walked quickly and with purpose. Her face was a little ruddy from the cold, and her hair was messy, blown about by the wind. She looked wonderful to him.

He spoke first. 'I have been hoping to see you.'

She did not reply immediately. They had not met since leaving Pemberley, two weeks earlier, and formality had crept back during that time apart.

'I, too,' she said simply.

'I have taken walks with, frankly, suspicious frequency, in the hope that I might happen upon you,' he said, with a nervous laugh. 'The effort has been in vain, until today.'

'I am glad you found me.'

They stood a few yards apart.

He looked around the dense wood, squinting. 'I am surprised I did. This has all the hallmarks of a good hiding place.'

She grinned. 'True.' She mimicked his movement – looking all around. 'I find a peculiar charm in this place.' She turned to one side and beckoned. 'Shall we walk? Can you?'

He nodded and offered her his arm, which she took gladly, as much for his support as her own. 'You have walked here before then?' he asked.

'I have. Many times. I like the secrecy of it. It feels unexplored. And I know I won't be disturbed.'

'Until today.'

'Today, I wished to be. I allowed myself to be found,' she said impishly.

As they picked their way through the trees, they spoke of this and of that: their respective journeys from Pemberley, the health of their households, the bitterness of the weather. Fitzwilliam, in truth, would have picked up where they left off and kissed Charlotte where she stood; but he sensed that she needed space – some small retreat before anything more could be ventured.

'May I ask you something?' said Charlotte.

'Of course.'

'You can now walk and will soon, perhaps in a month or two, be able to walk well enough to rejoin your regiment?'

He made a sound of agreement.

'But – must you go?'

Colonel Fitzwilliam had asked himself this question a thousand times. 'Eventually, I must.'

'Have you not done enough?' said Charlotte heatedly. 'Have you not lost enough?'

Fitzwilliam sighed. 'To put it simply, no. I have not lost enough – not officially. I am still relatively young, and I will be well enough to fight – and so I shall have to fight. The army is in need of experienced men – I am one, and better trained than most. In that sense, it is right that I should go.'

'And in another sense?'

'In another sense, I would give anything not to go.'

Charlotte looked sideways at him and patted his arm. 'You'd give your right arm?'

He gave a small laugh. 'My leg, at the least.'

She felt a little regret for having made a joke when he was trying to be earnest. She stopped walking, turning so she could meet his eye. 'Are you afraid?'

The colonel drew in a breath, and he glanced around the wood – up at the grey sky, the dark canopy of trees – and then down to her. His gaze roamed over her hair, her face, the curve of her neck, yet it faltered before meeting her eyes. Instead, he turned back to the path, his movement gently urging them on. 'No,' he replied at last, with a tight, unreadable smile.

After a few minutes more, Charlotte suggested they sit down on a tree-stump to give the colonel's leg some respite, and she pulled some biscuits from her pocket, wrapped in a handkerchief.

This greatly amused Fitzwilliam. 'You smuggled these well. Did you bake them?'

She shook her head, grinning. 'Since my cook makes such superior ones, I see no reason to bake ever again.'

He returned her grin and took a bite. 'I can see what you mean,' he said, through a mouthful. He was lost in thought for a moment as he continued to chew.

'You look far away,' observed Charlotte.

He seemed a little shy, answering, 'I was reminded of something. Someone.'

'Who?'

'I once told you that I lost someone – someone in particular – at Albuera. Parker was his name. We used to share food like this on campaign – he always squirrelled something away for later and would share it with me when we stopped for a break.' He took another bite.

'Tell me about him,' Charlotte pressed softly.

He began, a little self-consciously at first, 'Well … I had known him since we were ensigns at sixteen. He was a clown.' Fitzwilliam chuckled. 'He liked practical jokes – which in our barracks could be pretty dangerous. He did voices, too, with rather alarming accuracy. He could even imitate our colonel, which landed him in a chokehold on more than one occasion. He wasn't – or I should say, we weren't of the same station or upbringing. His family was of more modest means, so there were fewer expectations on him, and I found myself, at times, envying the freedom of that – which he found irritating, understandably. He called me 'The Prince'. The unfairness of it was that I rose through the ranks quickly – my father was generous while he lived – and soon, we were in separate regiments and saw each other rarely. Parker remained two ranks behind me, for no reason but the system itself. He performed the same drills as I, took the same risks, gave up the same freedoms. But by the age of twenty, I was his superior.'

'And yet you were still friends?'

'Oh yes. He never allowed the injustice of it to get in the way of our friendship, nor our separation; he would write to me. He was diligent about it. I was less so, rather lax in my replies. He would chide me for it. "Not even the French can stop you writing a letter," he would say. But when the war began in Spain, we found ourselves thrown together. I was able to offer him a battlefield commission in my regiment, and he took it. He had a sweetheart – they were betrothed, in fact. He was very taken with her, quite changed. I saw a more serious side to him.'

Charlotte pulled her coat around her, and he caught her shivering.

'Forgive me. I have never spoken of him, and so I have not learnt to be brief. I should not have entered into this when we are both sitting in the cold. You must be freezing.' He shook his head, feeling foolish.

'I invited you to do so, and I ask you to continue.'

He did not immediately but stood to remove his coat and wrap it around her. She accepted it, pulling it tight. It swamped her frame, but she was glad of it. She looked at him expectantly. 'What happened?'

He took his place next to her again. 'Well, there is little left to tell.' He paused, thoughtful. 'A cannonball took him down. Decisive.' Fitzwilliam smiled grimly, but Charlotte saw the pain behind it. 'I knew he wouldn't survive it. I found him, after the battle, which in itself was a miracle, and he hadn't long left, and he knew it. He couldn't say much, only, "Not now" – which I didn't understand at the time – and then, at the very end, "Sarah". I think I understand him now.'

He took a deep breath before continuing, 'I told you I wasn't afraid of going back, because that used to be true. But that was a falsehood. I am now afraid. I fear the loss of you – the hours, days we might have had. I have not been accustomed to any particular connection in this world. I am, I think, generally well liked and at ease with most – but there has been no one I want to live for. Until you. And now, I find I am not ready to go. Not now.'

He looked straight ahead, afraid of her reaction. She didn't know how to express the emotions that rose within her at this speech – or, indeed, if she should say anything. Instead, she brought her hand to rest on his, where it gripped the edge of the log.

Eventually, when Charlotte remarked that she would soon be missed at home, they roused themselves to leave the wood; at the prospect of returning, there came a tension between them again. It was not easy, as it had been at Pemberley. Their first touch there had been like a spring uncoiling or water bursting forth from a valve – urgent, unstoppable, no question of when or how or whether it should cease. But now, that initial spark released, they were realising this was something deeper that neither knew how to navigate yet – or when or whether they should.

Fitzwilliam raised her gloved hand and kissed it tenderly. 'I shall return here tomorrow and every day if I can.'

'I will try, also,' Charlotte said simply. She felt tears spring to her eyes. 'But what will we …' She faltered. 'What can come of this?'

He put his hand on one side of her face, feeling the cold of it, and held it there, stroking her cheek. 'I wish I had the answer. All I know is this: I want to know every part of you. I want to be as close to you as I am able. I want you. But that is all nothing if you do not share the same feelings.'

'I do share them.' She shook her head in frustration. Her practical mind could not simply give in to the moment, even a moment such as this. 'But that is not enough. What of my marriage? What of God? What of our future?'

They both paused, considering that unholy trinity of obstacles, which were almost too great to contemplate.

'I know not,' he said. 'I have no answer. If you wish to stop this now, I understand why. And I will honour whatever you choose – I swear it.'

In the end, she answered her own question. 'I do not want to stop seeing you. I cannot. If God made me capable of love, then it must be his will that I find it. Even if I left it later than most.'

Colonel Fitzwilliam looked into her eyes searchingly, his brow furrowed with curiosity. 'Love?' he asked.

She nodded.

His features relaxed then into an expression of warm, easy delight – as if the summer sun had shone on his face.

Charlotte reached up to kiss him – which he returned with energy.

After a few moments, he stopped to pull her gently to him. She nestled her head under his chin, and he whispered, 'Love,' into her ear, like a secret shared between them.

CHAPTER IX

'Your modesty does you credit, sir, but I must be allowed to offer what I consider a well-deserved compliment on your execution of the cotillion. A fine example of precision, while wholly devoid of undue flamboyance. As clergymen, we are tasked with a role that is, at times, a difficult one to balance, but I congratulate you on treading that line between what is diverting and what is dutiful with uncommon finesse. Or, if I may use the word, with elan.'

'I thank you, Mr Collins. It must be said that one could not dance finely without a fine dance partner.' At this, Mr Smithson gave Charlotte a rather obsequious little bow.

She had in fact found the dance rather exhausting, due to Mr Smithson's incessant questions. He had asked about Mr Collins, about how they had met, about her family, about Lady Catherine and Anne de Bourgh and the Darcy connection and her friendship with Elizabeth. One would think he were writing a chapter in *Debrett's*, and Charlotte bet to herself that he wished he could note some of it down with a pen. What an odd character he was turning out to be, she thought: well-liked, seemingly, in the village, harmless enough perhaps, but she could not make him out. He seemed to indulge her husband excessively, which, though obviously not an evil in itself, led her to wonder at his motives, for it was not only her husband that he indulged.

Mr Smithson was already crossing the room to linger close to Lady Catherine, who soon bestowed her attention on him. They had quite a rapport, those two, which made Charlotte nervous somehow. Was it that he seemed to be replacing her husband in Lady Catherine's affections and that Charlotte feared how such a loss would affect her husband? That was part of it perhaps, but not the whole.

Lady Catherine's decision to hold a ball for the New Year had been a highly surprising decision; she had not thrown such an event for many years and disliked large crowds of people, especially when they might disturb the order of her house. This much Charlotte knew. She also knew that, a few weeks prior, Mr Smithson had mentioned to Lady Catherine that he had never been to a ball before. He had spoken also of the grandeur of Rosings and what a shame it was that such a pearl was left unseen by so many who might admire it. His sycophancy hit its mark, and Lady Catherine sent out invitations within the week. Charlotte realised that her husband had unwittingly taught his curate a great many lessons – and not all of them liturgical.

Rosings looked splendid, decked out in all its finery for the occasion. The cavernous rooms, which Charlotte had always thought rather gloomy and foreboding, were now transformed. Enormous chandeliers blazed with light overhead, and candles set in gleaming wall sconces brightened every corridor. Tonight, the house had taken on a dreamlike softness; white fabric was swathed across mirrors, and giant urns filled with greenery and trailing ivy sat in the corners of every room. The musicians, seated at the far end of the ballroom, were attired in coats richly embroidered with gold, while many of the guests had chosen to dress in jewel tones in keeping with the season. Charlotte marvelled at the gowns of emerald, sapphire and rich ruby red.

Charlotte herself was in white; she had chosen it in the hope of blending in, white usually being such a popular choice for a ball. But she had not anticipated that so many other guests would wear such vivid colours. For once, quite unintentionally, she stood out.

She loitered now, on the side of the room, watching Colonel Fitzwilliam talk to Anne de Bourgh. Miss de Bourgh's presence had caused something of a stir. She was so rarely seen in society that even a ball thrown in her own house had not guaranteed her attendance. Yet here she was, looking more at ease than ever. She and Colonel Fitzwilliam were fitting dance partners; Anne could not manage a fast reel, for she would soon be out of breath, but she could move steadily through the more sedate dances. Fitzwilliam, for his part, could step with care, but his leg would not permit him to jump or skip. They had therefore stood up together more than once, grateful for the other's limitations.

Charlotte felt a little jealous. She would have liked to dance with Fitzwilliam, but they were both aware of the risks; while it would not be improper to dance with him, she feared their mutual regard would somehow be noticed. Presumably because of the same caution, he had not asked her. *Which is wise,* she convinced herself; in this of all places, she should look to her husband.

She observed Mr Collins now, queuing for a glass of punch. He was humming along to the tune of a jig, tapping his foot and glancing around the room, an idle smile on his face.

Charlotte berated herself, not for the first time. *What sort of woman are you, that you can betray him like this?*

She found it impossible to reconcile the person she had always believed herself to be with the one who was now acting so recklessly, so selfishly. When she reflected on how cursed she must be for her actions – when she allowed herself the indulgence of self-censure – she saw Collins in her mind, as he appeared before her now: a blameless innocent. That was not a true depiction of him – he, like anyone, was capable of hurting others – but no matter his faults, Charlotte knew for certain he would never betray her in the way she was betraying him.

Yet she had not stopped. She had continued to meet Fitzwilliam whenever she could these last few weeks: a snatched hour here, a moment in the street, a shared look across the church. Christmas had come and gone, and at a time when others pulled their family closer, she had pulled away from her husband and even been disappointed that the festive period limited her freedom to roam. There was no defending it.

And yet, she knew why she was doing it: because it hurt not to. Because she felt like she had unlocked a part of herself that had been buried. Because she felt, after years of duty and modesty and sense, an irresistible desire to be a little daring. Because, after months that had encompassed trauma and loss and shock, it felt like a kindness to herself.

But what of all that? She was an adulteress. She did not think too deeply about the sin of it or of going to hell; her faith was not so dramatic. But she did think of Mr Collins, who had pulled her from an unwanted spinsterhood, who had arranged his home for her, made room in his life for her, and who loved her as well as he could, even though she could not love him.

It was not a passing thought but had been a constant stream of inward dialogue over the past few weeks. The guilt was a part of her daily routine now. It was her morning prayer and her afternoon indigestion. It accompanied her on walks, sat next to her at church and invaded her dreams at night. Shame was her solid companion, and she did not wish it gone, because when guilt left, she would know she had truly lost herself. She might not have integrity, she thought, but at least she still knew what it was.

As the Rosings ball wore on, a whirlwind of country dances, gossip and punch, Charlotte found herself standing in a group with her husband, Colonel Fitzwilliam, Anne de Bourgh and Mr Smithson, who had danced all but one of the dances, with an array of ladies. It had not gone unnoticed.

'You have been lucky to find so many willing partners, Mr Smithson. You must be very persuasive,' said Miss de Bourgh playfully.

Mr Smithson smiled smoothly, replying, 'I have no particular ways, madam, but I presume ladies feel that having a man of God as a dance partner renders them relatively safe.'

Charlotte wrinkled her brow. 'Safe? From what, sir? Being trodden on? Because I have known more than one wrong-footed vicar.'

Smithson did not laugh with her. 'I meant, safe from any unwelcome attentions and from any questions about her reputation.'

Colonel Fitzwilliam joined the conversation, adding, a little provocatively, 'I think you do yourself a disservice when it comes to the latter, sir. You are a young, fine-looking man. You are as likely to stir a heart as anyone here tonight, and gossips will find your position in the Church only adds to the intrigue.'

Smithson gave him an odd, piercing look. 'Perhaps you know more of such matters, Colonel. I would bow to your knowledge. I lead a simple life here in Hunsford. You must be finding yourself quite at home here, by now.'

Colonel Fitzwilliam felt the sting. Smithson certainly knew how to rankle people and he had hit the spot with Fitzwilliam. Since he had been able to walk, albeit still in pain and with an unsteady step, Fitzwilliam had felt the weight of guilt for not having returned to the front. Being practical, he knew that until he could march for miles, every day, there was little purpose in turning his steps in the direction of war. But the shame still weighed on him, and he felt too much, in that moment, to respond to Smithson – Smithson, who had never taken up arms or set foot on foreign soil, whose hands were soft and whose legs were unbroken, able to dance every dance with ease.

'It has not been his home of late,' interjected Miss de Bourgh, who seemed oblivious to the tension. 'It is not so very long ago that we got him back from Derbyshire.'

'Ah yes,' replied Smithson, looking now at Charlotte. 'With Mrs Collins.'

Charlotte glanced at Fitzwilliam briefly, then looked squarely at Smithson, 'With my friend, Elizabeth Darcy, and Mr Darcy and his sister.'

Mr Smithson nodded. 'I kept your husband company in your absence, Mrs Collins, and helped with any tasks that might otherwise have gone unattended while you were away, lest you should be concerned.'

Charlotte stared at him, aware that he now seemed to be turning his sharp claws to her. 'I was not worried. I know my husband to be both capable and understanding.'

'He is very understanding,' said Mr Smithson boldly.

Mr Collins was studiously looking into his glass of punch.

'I thought it a little odd that a wife would go so far away, without her husband,' continued Mr Smithson, 'but he has explained to me that you are rather ... independently minded.'

Charlotte looked at her husband.

He knew he must say something. 'I said ...' Mr Collins faltered. 'I said that you enjoyed your solitude, my dear, and were very adept at taking care of yourself, which I admire.' He smiled at her, seeking assurance.

'A very understanding husband. How lucky you are,' said Smithson to Charlotte. He was relentless.

She regarded him with a cool and measured gaze. 'I am blessed, sir.'

Miss de Bourgh, who had been rather distracted during the interchange, looking across the room at one of the other gentlemen she had danced with, now re-entered the conversation, saying blithely, 'Oh, a cotillion is starting! Look, they need a final couple to begin. You must retain your record Mr Smithson – you cannot miss this one!'

'Gladly, Miss de Bourgh, if you would honour me,' he said, bowing low.

'Oh, I had not intended ...' Miss de Bourgh was reluctant – not merely from fatigue but from possessing just enough of her mother's snobbery to baulk, ever so slightly, at the prospect of dancing with the local curate. 'I am not well enough to participate at this moment, sir, but I thank you. You danced so well with Mrs Collins earlier; perhaps she will agree?' She shifted her question from Smithson to Charlotte, expectantly. All eyes were on her.

Charlotte, not wishing to cause a scene after what had already been a needlessly tense conversation, acquiesced. She passed Anne her fan and shawl and began to walk towards the other dancers, bracing herself for further interrogation from her partner.

When she was just a few steps away from the formation, Mr Smithson, who had not moved from his spot, quietly uttered, 'I will forego this dance. I hope you will forgive me.'

He backed away towards the other end of the room, but Charlotte, not having heard him over the general hubbub of the dancers, was surprised when she looked back and found he had not followed her. She was all confusion and so did not immediately retreat back to her circle. Instead, she looked around the room frantically, eventually spotting him at a distance next to Lady Catherine.

Charlotte became suddenly aware that she was now standing up alone, without a partner, and the sensation of exposure was swift and mortifying. Her cheeks flushed with colour; she saw the other dancers looking at her awkwardly, wondering what she planned to do. Mr Collins was slow to react and, if anything, embarrassed by Charlotte, and he beckoned her back to him like a dog.

Instead, it was Colonel Fitzwilliam who walked forward boldly and took his place proudly next to her, readying himself for the first step. They turned to face one another, and as she curtsied in answer to his bow, she tried to convey gratitude in her eyes. But he either did not see it or did not require it; this was not a favour but, rather, the opportunity he had hoped for all night.

Introducing Mrs Collins

As the music began, she took his hand, and they moved together seamlessly.

They did not speak during the dance. It was difficult to feign small talk when they enjoyed rich conversation in private. And they dared not speak freely in case they betrayed a detail or a level of intimacy that could be overheard. And so they danced quietly, glad just to be near each other. Their steps aligned with natural ease, and they fell into rhythm with one another and with the other dancers.

Charlotte had never felt elegant during a dance; her height often made her feel ungainly, and her steps always seemed heavy. But now, she felt ... graceful. She knew that she and Fitzwilliam were dancing particularly well together; she felt eyes on them, onlookers watching and smiling. She knew what they were doing was dangerous, foolish, and this attention should be unwanted. But her only thought was: *Let them look*. If she enjoyed how firmly he held her right hand behind her back, while they promenaded smoothly, she hoped it was not apparent. If he gazed at the fall of her shoulders as she skipped away from him, he trusted it was not noticed.

But it was. Not by everyone assembled, but by someone with a keen eye, who observed from the other side of the hall. At this very moment, that gentleman's eyes were narrowed in speculation, though he turned his face back politely as he resumed his conversation with Lady Catherine de Bourgh.

4th January 1813

Dear Charlotte,

 Let me, for the sake of clarity – and all that is romantic – first state that I am very happy in my marriage and blessed in my position and that I am as much in love with Darcy as ever, etc. But now, that achieved, may I also declare that I miss you intolerably!

 As much as I am enjoying my time with my husband, I cannot help but mourn the loss of our delightful November days. Being removed from my family home, and especially since Jane has married, I miss having such kinship at close quarters. Having you near reminded me of such sisterly comfort. It is a shame, indeed, that friendship should have to make way for matrimony. But to have good friends to stay was a balm indeed; I feel rather proud of myself for having manufactured such an excellent scheme, and I hope we shall do it again soon.

 I do not wish to draw your mind to unwelcome thoughts, but I wanted to inform you that Wickham has been censured by superiors within his regiment. He cannot be demoted without drawing attention to his specific actions (and thereby to ourselves and to you), but he will never rise to any rank beyond where he is now; both Darcy and Fitzwilliam have set about ensuring this. He will soon be in Spain, so he will at least be put to some use. It is small consolation, but to know he will never truly thrive makes me glad.

 It is a unique situation we are in. We must support them financially, or Lydia – and any children that follow, and I bet that will be soon – would fall into ruin. But he must be humbled in some way. Therefore, it has been a difficult balance. I hope we have done right.

 But tell me, how is Mr Collins? And how do you fare? I heard that Lady Catherine held a ball. Were you invited? We were not, and quite pointedly so! She invited Georgiana, but not Darcy! Can you imagine?

She is wilful and petty as ever, but her attempts to offend only serve to divert me. If only she knew.

Ah, it is a comfort to write to you. I wished to write cheerfully, but I know you would wish to know the truth: that my father is very unwell. You may have noticed in November that he was a good deal changed. I had thought it was the shock of Lydia, etc. and that he might recover, but now I think on it, he was not truly well before that occurred. He is thin now and easily wearied. Jane assures me he is being tended to. He has seen Bingley's physician — a good one — but they cannot detect anything. Jane keeps me well informed; she is at home with them often, as Netherfield is so near. We do not know how it will go.

I am to travel to Longbourn to stay with them next week, and I think I will be there for some time, so you may write to me there.

Your loving friend,
Eliza

CHAPTER X

A week after the ball, Rosings was back to its usual state – still grandiose as ever, but darker, quieter, even peaceful. It was rendered especially so since Lady Catherine and her daughter, along with Mrs Jenkinson and several staff, had decamped to London for a fortnight. The reason for this was ostensibly for Lady Catherine to see a particular physician, but her true motive was rather more intriguing. At the ball, Miss Anne de Bourgh had caught the eye of a certain Lord Chartwell – a respectable, genteel man in his forties – and his affections had been returned. January was not the ideal time for courtship, being outside of the social season, but Lady Catherine wished to move swiftly in the hopes of securing him.

This past year had seen a happy change in Anne's condition and in her disposition. How this had come about was not known; she had seen fewer doctors than ever and certainly been bled less often. And yet, she walked outdoors more and had regained her appetite. The states of panic that used to rule her seemed to come less frequently, and that, in itself, made her less prone to them. Anne was on an upward cycle, which her mother was loathe to interfere with but could not help but take advantage of. Lady Catherine had long grown reconciled to the idea that her daughter would live alongside her at Rosings in respectable spinsterhood, but she had recognised the change in Anne, and acted upon it. Her design in throwing a ball had not been to satisfy the whim of

Mr Smithson, as Charlotte had thought, but to display her daughter to a generation of eligible men yet to meet her.

It was a successful scheme; there was much interest, and, after sifting out the mercenary, the dull and the poor, her daughter had found Lord Chartwell. He was a handsome, wealthy widower, with a fine reputation, three estates and still a good head of hair.

This was an opportunity not to be wasted. The carriages were packed, their London residence prepared, and they departed within the week with plans to linger – with dignity, naturally – in the vicinity of an eligible man. Lady Catherine had done it before and it had worked then. She had no qualms about repeating the scheme for her daughter.

Meanwhile, Charlotte was eager to renew her visits to Rosings to practise the pianoforte. Preparations for the ball had so far delayed the possibility, but on the day after the household had departed for London, Charlotte headed to the great house and the staff, who knew her well by now, let her in the back door without fuss, as she wished.

As she made her way up the stairs discreetly, she could not help but wonder whether she would encounter the colonel. She did not think it very likely, her being tucked away upstairs, and he being, presumably, occupied downstairs. But it was possible, and while it was not her intention on this visit, she found it hard to erase him from her thoughts.

She arrived at Mrs Jenkinson's room and, making her way to the small pianoforte, she removed her coat and bonnet, placing them to one side. She peeled off her gloves and lay them on the top of the instrument.

Leafing through the music in the cupboard, she found a sonata in C sharp minor by Beethoven, a piece she had enjoyed playing a number of times before. It was slow and sombre, well-suited to deep winter, but also rich and romantic to her ears. She placed the sheets on the stand and sat down on the long piano stool, arranging her skirts and making herself comfortable.

Her fingers found the keys as though no time had passed and, as the melody built, she allowed her eyes to close; she knew the notes well enough now not to need the sheets. She lost herself in the music, her body swaying with the movement of the melody as she felt herself drawn in by something deep and instinctive.

As she approached the middle section, she opened her eyes and saw Colonel Fitzwilliam standing in the doorway, openly watching her. She was not startled by it; perhaps she had felt his eyes on her. She kept on playing, enjoying the sensation of being observed while indulging in this passion.

He slowly moved towards her. She did not look at him but at the keys. He sat next to her on the stool, and she paused.

'Keep playing,' he whispered gruffly in her ear as he leant closer towards her. 'Please'.

She did so, and as her fingers found the keys, he moved closer still to kiss the back of her neck, his arms moving about her waist. She struggled to continue, her breaths coming faster now. He could sense the growing excitement in her, and it served only to increase his own; his hands gripped her tighter; his kisses became more urgent.

As her hands rested on the final chords, his own heavy hands touched hers, pressing between her fingers, until they clutched together at the keyboard. She turned to him then, and he kissed her, lightly at first and then with increasing urgency. A dissonant chord sounded as she mashed the piano keys, before pulling her hands away and threading her fingers through his hair, hungry for him.

They both became aware that a servant could discover them at any moment. Fitzwilliam rose to shut the door, but as he reached the threshold, he paused, looking across the landing and then back at Charlotte. He pointed at a door on the opposite side of the landing.

'Those are my rooms,' he said simply. He was not asking but offering.

Charlotte looked at his closed door and then back at him. He returned to the piano, sitting again next to her. His blue eyes met hers with a softness that she appreciated. Where previously there had been fire – an urgency that had guided their hands, their lips, their every movement – in this moment there was something quieter, steadier. What she read in his expression was a fierce desire but also something gentle and tender. His eyes seemed to say, *There is no rush.*

She took a moment to consider, her desire tempered by self-consciousness. 'It has been a long time since I ... practised,' she said quietly.

He nodded, stroking the hair from her face. 'Then we can wait.'

He held her tightly for a moment, then left her at the piano, walked slowly to his room and pulled the door to. It was her choice. She could stay here, continue playing and then return to Hunsford. Or she could cross the landing and open a door.

CHAPTER XI

Charlotte sat at the front of the church, on one of the hard little pews, training her eyes on her husband up in the pulpit. While she was now practised at appearing attentive, her mind had wandered from what Mr Collins was saying, lulled by the droning of his 'church voice' – which was, inconveniently, more monotonous than his 'everyday voice'. When she tried to force her thoughts into concentration once more, he seemed to be speaking about the undue influence of modern novels on young women – a niche topic that had been stirred up by Mr Smithson's influence – and was reading an extract from *Fordyce's Sermons*.

'*What shall we say of certain books, which we are assured (for we have not read them) are in their nature so shameful, and contain such rank treason against the royalty of Virtue, that she who can bear to peruse them must in her soul be a prostitute!*'

At this, Colonel Raeworth, sitting behind her, coughed, while an elderly lady at the back of the church gave a small whimper.

Mr Collins, looking down from his elevated position, seemed to enjoy the effect. He continued with vigour, '*Let her reputation in life be what it will. But can it be true that any young woman, pretending to decency, should endure for a moment to look on this infernal brood of futility and lewdness?*' He looked rather proud of himself, which Charlotte thought undeserving on several fronts, not least because his words were not his own.

However, even though the words belonged to another, the phrase *any young woman pretending to decency* affected her deeply. That was her, was it not? She was sat here reverently in a pew: the rector's wife, wearing a high-necked dress with hair pinned back neatly, all signs pointing to her morality and modesty – when only a few days earlier, she had braced her hands against a wall while her stays were hastily unlaced.

Her thoughts were consumed by Colonel Fitzwilliam, who sat in his family's box to the side of the nave, at a right angle to Charlotte. She resolutely avoided his eye, though it felt quite unnatural and gave her the beginnings of a squint. From time to time, she felt his gaze settle on her, which was unhelpful to her resolve. She could not help but wonder where his own thoughts tended.

Perhaps they were thinking of the same thing: the moment when her dress and stays had slipped to the floor, leaving her standing in only the lightest of petticoats. Through it, he could see almost the entirety of her body, and he had to restrain himself from moving too quickly, too ravenously. Instead, he had sat down on the edge of the bed, looking at her, drinking her in.

At first, she had felt too vulnerable. She had never undressed with a man before like that. Relations with Mr Collins had been under the covers, and partially clothed. Little had been seen; little had been explored. And so, to be so exposed felt startlingly new, oddly thrilling and not a little disorientating.

A hundred thoughts had flooded her mind then – complicated, disordered thoughts. When fully faced with the truth of her body, she thought of what it had endured since the summer – and she felt overwhelmed by it in the moment, as if her disrobing had somehow laid her whole soul bare.

Fitzwilliam saw this. He gently pulled Charlotte to him, sitting on the edge of the bed, holding her close, making room for her to feel this wave of emotion without expectation from him. She let herself fall into him.

Fitzwilliam, too, was feeling a great deal. He was remembering what intimacy felt like; it had been a long time. In his youth, he had taken any opportunity that was laid before him, and there had been several for a young soldier; his charm and his uniform made a winning combination. But in recent years, he had lost his taste for any such encounters. He had not had the time nor the opportunity to form a true connection with anyone, and anything less had felt rather unsatisfying.

Since meeting Charlotte, he had felt things he had thought long dormant: not only desire, but desire tempered with care, ferocity met with delicacy. He wanted to protect her and consume her in equal measure. But at present, protection won out.

As Charlotte raised her head from his shoulder, he was ready to help her get dressed again, thinking that this had been too soon, too much. But when he reached to pick up her clothes, she stopped him, holding his arm, then she slowly traced trembling fingers up and across his broad shoulders and then moved down his front. He did not touch her yet; he was not sure whether she would want to continue and wished to let her guide the speed of their first steps, if there were to be any.

Just as Charlotte's mind lingered on the image of her slowly unbuttoning Fitzwilliam's shirt, revealing the dark hair across his chest and the warm skin beneath, Mr Collins voice broke into her thoughts: '*Their descriptions are often loose and luscious in a high degree; their representations of love between the sexes are almost universally overstrained. All is dotage, or despair; or else ranting swelled into burlesque.*' His throat was a little clogged, and he had to clear it a few times between these phrases.

She hid a smirk and let her mind return.

It had not felt *overstrained* when Charlotte had risen slowly, drawing away from Fitzwilliam to loosen the final ribbon on her petticoat and lift it over her head. Her hair hung loose about her shoulders as she moved towards him, where he sat watching with an unreadable expression. She straddled his lap, her knees pressing into the bed on either side of him, and kissed him – long and deep. His hands came to her back with surprising gentleness, and he kissed her in return, though he did not press for more.

After a moment, she pulled back just enough to search his face. 'Are you – do you want to?' She asked it genuinely, suddenly uncertain whether she had misread him entirely.

He gave a short laugh and said in a low tone, 'Yes, I want to.'

She looked a little puzzled. Then, with cool, clear eyes, she said to him, 'You are still afraid to hurt me. But I know you will not.' She put one hand on his cheek. 'Others have thought me weak. You do not. You know I am strong.'

'I do,' he replied hoarsely.

'Treat me as such, I beg you.'

And as she kissed him now, he grabbed her by the waist, lifted her up off her feet and laid her down on the bed, his hands, his face, his body now moving as powerfully as they had wished to.

Charlotte's hymn-book nearly fell from her hands, as she lost herself briefly in the memory, and as she pulled herself back to the present, she felt Colonel Fitzwilliam's eyes upon her, staring. She blinked rapidly, trying to alert him to it, and he averted his gaze hurriedly.

The sermon had finished, and after they had sung the final hymn, the congregation began moving towards the door. As she filed out, Charlotte passed the pillar where she and Fitzwilliam had once fallen against each other, and she had first felt his hands on her. She felt a rush of blood surge within her but also the swell of a deeper emotion.

For perhaps the most intimate moment of their union had come not in the heat of passion but afterwards, when they had lain for some minutes on the bed together. Charlotte had felt changed – not by Fitzwilliam but by herself. She had so often felt let down by her body: by its appearance, lean and neat, with no soft abundance of flesh; by its failure to respond to her husband; by its slowness to carry a child and its readiness to part with it; by its inability to defend itself.

But then – this. How her body had danced. How it had moved, reacted and rejoiced. Her body worked! And how it worked. How it worked with his: in tandem, in harmony. She felt a new understanding of herself, and it was bold, and it was physical. But she wrestled with it. This was new.

They were not able to remain there long; Charlotte's absence would soon be felt, and they were fearful of rousing suspicion among the staff. Charlotte, suddenly restive, rose and began to dress herself.

The light from the window shone brightly on her, casting her in silhouette before the colonel's eyes. He gazed lazily at her and she enjoyed his stares.

'You do not tire of the sight? You have seen it all now,' she said mischievously.

'I do not. I never will. You are beautiful.'

Her grin dropped at this. 'I am not beautiful. You can flatter me without falsehood.'

He frowned, feeling stung. 'I am not false. Why do you say that?'

'I must say it, when you say things that do not suit me. To say I am beautiful is not—' She hesitated as she pulled her dress back on. 'You must have said that to other women, and perhaps *they* were, but I need no such lie. I know you like me for what I am. I need no flowery phrases.'

He sighed gruffly. All had been well, and he did not understand how this outburst had been provoked. 'Charlotte, I do not like you: I love you. And I do not lie when I say you are beautiful.'

'I am a fully grown woman—'

'Do you not think that grown women can be beautiful?' he asked, exasperated.

'I mean – this – what we have – is not ... it is not because you are so handsome and you think me so beautiful. It is *more* than that; it has to be. It has to be worth more than that.'

For once, he did not understand her, and she didn't entirely blame him. She was wrestling with her feelings and not conveying them clearly.

'Are you suggesting,' he asked, his face contorted in confusion, 'that as long as you are plain, then our actions are less scandalous somehow? More noble?'

'No, of course not. It is only ... I must know myself, or I am lost! I am plain, and I had found peace with that. I am unromantic, and I had found peace with that!'

He was quiet at first, as though weighing her words. 'You are neither. And you know it yourself.'

She offered no reply, so he continued, more softly than before, 'You had not found peace with that. You told me that when we first met. Because you cannot have peace without passion. Some can; you cannot. Because you are passionate. And you are beautiful.'

Charlotte longed to go to him, to let his quiet reassurances wash over her – but she found she could not soften. She squeezed her eyes shut and shook her head vigorously, as if shaking a thought from her head, and walked swiftly to the door. After listening for a moment, she hurried through it and disappeared down the corridor.

He could not follow her at such speed, for he was not yet dressed. She had left him baffled and hurt. Their time together had been a blend of tenderness and fierceness that seemed to have suited them both. She had been giddy, happy, serene, but this reaction had stirred discord into their alliance. Their first argument, and he did not even understand what it was about.

He watched Charlotte from his window, striding out the back door, now in her coat and gloves, the wind beating against her, the turn of her lip stubborn against the bluster. God but she was beautiful. Why would she not hear it?

Outside the church, as Charlotte stood near Mr Collins, who was greeting the parishioners as they left, she saw Mr Smithson approaching.

'Did you enjoy the sermon?' he solicited, 'It is one I introduced to Mr Collins myself.'

Charlotte answered as diplomatically as she could. 'It is not a favourite of mine, but then I have never read many novels, old or new.'

'But the lessons to be learnt from those words apply to the corporal world, not merely the literary.'

'I am sure.' Charlotte smiled broadly and excused herself, keen not to be drawn into her second sermon of the day.

She went back inside the church and began gathering up the hymn-books left in the pews, but a moment later, she was surprised by Colonel Fitzwilliam hurriedly stepping back inside.

He moved quickly towards her and handed her his hymn-book. 'I almost left with it! Foolish! Good day, Mrs Collins.'

His eyes seemed to say more than his words did, and Charlotte, looking down at the book in her hands, saw that it was not closed fully, that some of its pages seeming to be folded. She had the quick sense not to investigate now, so, curtsying to Fitzwilliam and taking her leave, she took it to the vestry. There, she discovered a letter enfolded in the pages. She removed it, folded it tighter still and pushed it up the sleeve of her coat.

When she exited the vestry, she found Mr Smithson had taken over her job of collecting up the hymn-books. His eyes followed her from the vestry, back up the aisle of the church, narrowed suspiciously. She returned the book she was holding, placing it into his hands, and he idly glanced down at it before putting it on the pile.

'Did you find what you needed?' he asked.

'No.' She thought quickly. 'I was looking for my husband.'

Smithson raised an eyebrow. 'Why, he is still in the churchyard.'

Charlotte hurried from the church, which felt chillier than outside. She found her husband conversing with a parishioner and stood by his side, talking politely and nodding, all while the letter in her sleeve burnt into her skin.

29th January 1813

Charlotte,

I have thought of nothing but you. I know not how I offended you, but my soul aches with the sorrow of it. I had never known such joy as when I last held you, and I have never known such agony as when you left me. Any words I said, I will retract; it is done. Anything I did, I will swear never to repeat. I may not understand all your feelings, but I will endeavour to, and until I do, I will do whatever I can to be near you again and to be worthy of you.

Say that you forgive me. Say that we may meet again. Say that you are still mine, for I am yours.

RF

CHAPTER XII

Smithson was waiting in the parlour at Rosings, standing up straight, running over his lines in his head. He looked around the room, at the high walls, gilded portraits and ornate furniture, and for once, he felt a little nervous, but he quickly gathered up his confidence for the task ahead. He had been preparing for this interview ever since her ladyship's return from London.

Lady Catherine entered, and he bowed low. She gathered a smile for him – she had grown almost as fond of him as she had of Collins. Yes, he was perhaps a little sterner in his faith than was fashionable, but that need not affect her. For him to call on her uninvited, however, was very unexpected and not a habit she wished to encourage. It was four o'clock; a time when she would ordinarily call for tea, but she put off doing so, in order not to delay his departure.

She sat but did not invite him to do so. She made a beckoning gesture with her hand which indicated he should begin. He hesitated, fiddling with his cuff.

'You seem rather unsettled, Mr Smithson. You have been enough in this house, surely, to be able to overcome any natural timidity? Pray tell me the purpose of your visit, for I feel certain you would not have presumed to call on me without one.'

'Thank you, Lady Catherine,' he said, giving another small bow. He made his face very sombre. 'If I am unsettled, my lady, it is because I am the bearer of unsettling intelligence, which, though painful to relate, I am compelled – by both duty and conscience – to disclose.'

Lady Catherine replied with one long blink.

Taking this as encouragement, though her cues were often inscrutable at best, he continued, 'You know how I have esteemed Mr Collins and have been so grateful to him for my position here. He has been a guide and a friend to me, and I would protect him at any cost, if it were in my capacity.'

After a pause, Lady Catherine said, 'Some concision would be appreciated, so that you might reach a conclusion before supper.'

After clearing his throat, Smithson hurried on, 'What I have to say concerns Mrs Collins.'

Lady Catherine raised an eyebrow.

'And, well, this is delicate, because it also concerns your nephew, Colonel Fitzwilliam.'

Lady Catherine frowned now, and colour rose to her powdered face. She picked up the bell that sat on a tray near her chair and rang it. She kept her eyes fixed on Smithson's face as she awaited her butler's entrance, and when he appeared, she requested tea without diverting her stare.

Figgis left, and the door was closed.

'Continue.'

Without the need for further encouragement, Mr Smithson launched into the speech he had prepared and practised; he was excited to begin. 'I know for certain that there is an understanding between Mrs Collins and Colonel Fitzwilliam, and I can offer you evidence of it. I would be loath to bring such tidings to you if it were not for a lack of discretion on their part, which I fear invites scandal into our community. I value Mr Collins so very highly, and I also value the good reputation of our parish, so much so that I did not feel I could be idle while such a threat to our village – and an affront to God – is taking place.'

'What is this evidence you speak of?'

'Well, firstly that of my own observations: their connection is clear if one is looking for it.'

'And you were looking for it?'

Mr Smithson faltered. 'Y-yes. Once I sensed something amiss.'

'What are these observations?'

'You know yourself that they spent several weeks together at Pemberley.'

'Alongside my other nephew, Mr Darcy, and my niece, Georgiana. Have you any accusations to set against *them*?'

'No indeed! But I also saw an accord between Mrs Collins and Colonel Fitzwilliam at the ball here – a closeness in their dancing, an intimate look.'

Lady Catherine's face was stony as she said, 'Mr Smithson, you bring me nothing but the excitable gossip of a young girl in her first season. None of what you have said has any substance, and what you are suggesting is grave indeed. I am disappointed that you would so easily slander two people of whom I am very fond.' Her voice was rising now, and she could hardly conceal her anger.

Mr Smithson was panicked. Without a word, he put his hand into his pocket and brought out a crumpled leaf of paper and handed it to her. She took it, handling it the way one might a dirty napkin. She unfolded it and perused it.

Nothing in her reaction was visible except for the throbbing of a vein that ran across her forehead. She read it once more, and then carefully folded it and placed it on the small table next to her.

'How did you come by this?'

'I found it on a visit to Mr Collins's house this week.'

'Left casually for all to see?'

'No.' He frowned, confused by her line of questioning. 'It was – well, it was in Mrs Collins's sitting room.'

'On a table?'

'Tucked inside a poetry book.'

Lady Catherine smirked. 'Your talents are wasted on us, Mr Smithson; you would make a fine bloodhound.'

He blanched, not sure whether to thank her for the remark or not.

Figgis entered now, set tea down on the table and stood by, ready to pour.

'Two cups please, Figgis,' said Lady Catherine.

Smithson looked grateful, though surprised, and took the proffered cup and saucer. Lady Catherine sipped her own the moment it was poured, oblivious to the heat, and then set it down. She waited until Figgis had made his exit before resuming.

'Tell me, what do *you* think the consequences of such a discovery ought to be? I would value your counsel.' She smiled at him, and he relaxed a little.

'Though I am reluctant to suggest it, I fear some damage may already have been done, and I believe you should act quickly. Unfortunately, Mr Collins is tainted by association, and the parish simply cannot be led in faith by a man who has been morally compromised in this way. While the fault lies with Mrs Collins—'

'And not with my nephew?' interrupted Lady Catherine.

'Oh, I am sure he has been persuaded into it. One cannot underestimate the powers women can wield.'

She raised an eyebrow again.

'Ungodly women, I mean,' he amended hastily. 'But as I was saying, while the fault lies with her, I am afraid Mr Collins must suffer the consequences equally. I believe you must ask him to leave his post, for the good of the Church – and for the protection of your own good name, your ladyship.'

'Please do not concern yourself with my good name, Mr Smithson,' she said sweetly, smiling again. 'And what would I do for a rector, were I to act upon your counsel? The living would be sitting empty, and I should be quite bereft.'

Mr Smithson gave a passable impression of nonchalance, offering a mild shrug and saying, with carefully measured hesitation, 'I know not, Lady Catherine. I am, of course, ever ready to be of service in whatever way I am called. The parish has, I believe, embraced me as something of a second son, and I would be more than happy to step in – should it be of help to you, and if it please God.'

Lady Catherine gave a small nod. And then, quite unexpectedly, she stood. 'Would you join me for a turn, Mr Smithson?'

Puzzled but delighted, he rose and walked alongside her across the room. To his surprise, she opened the door, and together they started to travel slowly down the long corridor.

'I thank you for bringing this to me, Mr Smithson.'

'I considered it my duty, your ladyship.'

'This is your first post as curate, is it not?'

'It is, and what luck that it is such a fortunate placing.'

'You are fortunate indeed. If only Mr Collins were so fortunate.'

'Quite.'

'Poor Mr Collins has been burdened with a curate who would concoct stories about his wife, disparage his name, and go behind his back to oust him from his own house and steal his living. I call that most unfortunate.'

Mr Smithson spluttered. 'I concocted nothing.'

Lady Catherine did not slow her pace to accommodate his increasing levels of agitation as they turned down a narrower, less ornate corridor. She spoke in a controlled, measured tone. 'I do not believe you, Mr Smithson; let me be very clear on that. The observations you have made amount to nothing and owe themselves to a wild and malicious imagination.'

'But the letter—'

'The letter is as fictitious as the rest – a theatre prop. It is not difficult to fabricate a love letter and to sign it with someone else's name.'

'I have done NO SUCH—'

Lady Catherine turned suddenly, her movement now sharp as a whippet. She held his gaze, whispering with icy clarity, 'I suggest that you do not raise your voice to me, Mr Smithson.'

Smithson visibly folded. 'My apologies.'

She resumed her former demeanour and continued walking, forcing him to keep pace. When they reached a plain-looking wooden door at the end of another hall, she stopped and turned to face him. 'Now we have established that I have no intention of acting on your little fiction, I will say this to you: I have been surprised by your visit, Mr Smithson, and I have reached an age at which I had not thought surprises possible. That you – a young, inexperienced man of twenty years of age, who has seen nothing of the world and added little of value to it – should see fit to enter my home, uninvited, and proceed to advise me on how to best run my estate and manage my affairs – which I have done single-handedly for many years – astonishes me. Had you brought this nonsense to my late husband, Sir Lewis de Bourgh, I think it unlikely that you would have been allowed through the door. But then, I do not believe you would have attempted such a feat with my husband, would you? To manipulate and then offer advice to the *master* of this house? No, you would not. But you would offer it to the *lady*.'

'I assure you, I have the utmost respect for your ladyship, and I wished only to act in service of the Church—'

Lady Catherine's sharp intake of breath was enough to cut him off, and stepping closer to him, she spoke in a low but steady voice. 'If I should hear even a whisper on the wind of this tale, from anyone in the parish or from farther afield, I shall know it was you who spread it. Should that occur, you will not only be immediately removed from your position, but I will ensure that you never hold any in the Church again. The Church that I know has no place within its ministry for slanderers or dissemblers – or for those who delight in the downfall of others. I will see to it that you are not welcomed by any good family again, not even your friends the Russells. It will be as if you have not a friend in the world – not a penny, nor a prospect. I think you know I *can* do this, but I wish to assure you that I *will*. If you give me reason.'

Mr Smithson's mouth hung open, his eyes wide with horror. He seemed quite at a loss for words.

Lady Catherine, however, did not require a response at this juncture. 'As for bringing my nephew into this equation – that shows a shameful lack of foresight. You mark yourself as rather stupid by such a suggestion. That said, cleverness is not something I value in a clergyman, or in an acquaintance. Shall I tell you what I do value, Mr Smithson?'

He nodded limply.

'Loyalty and discretion.'

He blinked.

'Might I assume that you will cease your … *holy mission* now? Or should I write to the archbishop this evening?'

Mr Smithson had no fight left in him. 'I will cease.'

Lady Catherine nodded. 'Now, I doubt I will see you here again, Mr Smithson. But might I advise you never to call on a lady at teatime in the future? It is most disturbing.'

She knocked loudly on the wooden door, and a moment later, a maid appeared, shocked to find her mistress at the door. 'My lady?'

'Maud, please escort Mr Smithson from the house, via the back stairs. He will not be returning.'

With that, Lady Catherine swept away without a backwards glance at Mr Smithson, who stood, shaking, before being led out like an obedient dog, through the servants' kitchen, down a set of stairs and to the back door. As soon as he had set both feet on the ground outside, he heard the key turn in the lock.

Back in the parlour, Lady Catherine sat heavily in her chair, as shaken and as weakened as her guest was. Lifting the letter from the table, she read it once more and, wearily, pushed herself up out of her chair.

She took a step towards the fire and threw the letter into the hot flames. She watched it closely, until it was burnt to nothing.

CHAPTER XIII

Charlotte pressed her head to the floor in her bedroom, lifting the blankets to peer under the bed. Nothing. She had checked every drawer, every bag and pocket, though she knew that was silly. She *knew* where she had left it; it simply wasn't there.

She hurriedly walked downstairs again and entered her sitting room. Flicking through her poetry books again, she made a sound of exasperation, loud enough that Mr Collins poked his head around the door, enquiring, 'Are you well, my dear?'

'Oh, I have lost something, but it is not of great import.'

'My dear, why did you not say? What is it?'

'Just a ... poem that I have written. It is nothing.'

'You have written a poem? You are uniformly charming. It must certainly be found – Brooke!' he called with urgency.

But Brooke could not reply, for at that moment, the bell for the door sounded. Mr and Mrs Collins looked at one another and, establishing neither was expecting a visitor, quickly made their way to the drawing room, Charlotte removing her apron as she went, Collins smoothing his hair so it lay even flatter on his head.

Once seated, they immediately rose again, as Brooke entered and announced Lady Catherine de Bourgh. She came in wearing her usual expression of distaste, peering around the room, finding little to her liking.

Mr Collins practically jumped forward to greet her. 'What an honour, Lady Catherine! Tea, please, Brooke. Would you care to sit here, your ladyship? This is our best chair. But perhaps the light is in your eyes? This room can be dreadfully bright.'

'It is all perfectly acceptable,' returned Lady Catherine.

This was an honour indeed. Lady Catherine rarely visited them in their home.

'May I enquire after Miss de Bourgh, your ladyship? I do hope you both had a pleasant time in London.'

At this, Lady Catherine looked pleased for the first time since her arrival. 'My daughter is well – particularly well at present, Mrs Collins. But I will say no more on the subject of Anne.' She took a sip of tea, before proceeding to say more on the subject of Anne. 'I have reason to feel hopeful for her future, but all of us know that nothing can be guaranteed.'

'Indeed!' Mr Collins picked up the reins of the exchange. 'Miss Anne de Bourgh has long been considered one of the brightest stars in the firmament of greater Kent, but if she should see fit to shine that light elsewhere, we should all—'

'I understand from my nephew, Mr Darcy,' Lady Catherine cut in, 'that Mr Bennet is not in good health. Has this intelligence reached you, Mrs Collins?'

'Indeed. I did not know that it was widely known. Eliza told me in a letter.'

Lady Catherine said sharply, 'It is not *widely known*. I have been told privately by my nephew about his father-in-law. I did not hear it from a village gossip.'

Mr Collins leapt in. 'Of course, and how pleasing it is to know that you are on good terms once more with your nephew. The Darcys were gracious, indeed, in hosting my wife, and with your permission only, it will be a pleasure to welcome them back into our acquaintance. But should you say the word, we would strike them from our lips and never speak of them again.' Collins was in fine dramatic form, emboldened by the honour of his patron's visit.

'You exaggerate the situation, Mr Collins. I never had any quarrel with the Darcys; I only wished they had consulted me more in their plans.'

Charlotte had to work hard to mask the incredulity she felt. Only Lady Catherine could deny entirely a fall-out so expansive that most of the Home Counties had heard of it.

'I suppose you have considered the consequences of Mr Bennet's ill health?' asked Lady Catherine, posing the question more to Charlotte than to her husband.

Charlotte hesitated. She had not; her mind had been preoccupied of late. 'I do not know yet how serious it is.'

'I believe it is very serious,' replied Lady Catherine quickly. 'I believe it is getting more serious by the day.'

Charlotte suddenly felt a great weight upon her, that of having neglected her friend. While she *had* replied to Eliza's last letter, she had allowed the contents of it to slip from her mind amid her own exploits. Should she have gone to visit the Bennets? Would she be welcome?

But clearly, Lady Catherine was speaking of the more material consequences: the entailment of Longbourn. 'It seems likely that you may have a time of change coming, Mr and Mrs Collins. It behoves you both to be ready for it.'

They were silent, Mr Collins readying himself, as ordered, for such a change of circumstance, Charlotte not ready at all, thinking only of what she would be leaving behind.

Lady Catherine broke into their thoughts. 'I have not seen the gardens of the parsonage for many years, and I am reliably informed that you have improved them, Mrs Collins. Though it is a cold day, perhaps you might grant me a tour of them?'

'They hardly look their best in February!' began Charlotte, but she was silenced by a look from Lady Catherine and added, 'But, of course, it would be my pleasure.'

Mr Collins went to rise but was discouraged by Lady Catherine. 'I will feel rather crowded on your small paths with two guides, Mr Collins. I wish to take the air with Mrs Collins alone.'

Mr Collins acquiesced but not without a good deal of curiosity. As Charlotte followed Lady Catherine from the room, she turned and pulled a face that clearly said, *I haven't the faintest idea either!* He mirrored it instinctively, and they exchanged a brief grin – grateful for a moment of shared levity. They had not had many, in recent months. They had not had many at all.

Just past the herb garden, Lady Catherine began. 'You may be surprised, Mrs Collins, to learn that I consider Mr Collins to be … I care what happens to Mr Collins. I did not appoint him at random, and I had many other candidates. He is a good man, whom I trust, which is rare, and one of whom I have grown fond.' Lady Catherine looked pained by what she was admitting and added, 'I care about his interests.' She spoke this statement as though to replace the previous, more sentimental one.

'As do I,' said Charlotte uncertainly.

'Do you?'

Charlotte had some degree of alarm, but more than anything, she was tired of the obfuscation. 'What is the matter, Lady Catherine?'

Lady Catherine sighed, as if Charlotte's question disappointed her. 'The matter,' she returned, feeling the labour of the words, 'is the affiliation between yourself and my nephew. It must come to an end.'

Charlotte stopped breathing. Her vision clouded, and she nearly stumbled. She reached out instinctively, and Lady Catherine allowed her to steady herself on her arm. She waited with uncharacteristic patience for a response.

Charlotte's thoughts ran with an impossible speed. It was obvious that this was not a guess; Lady Catherine seemed sure. She would not take action in this way unless she was. Charlotte therefore asked the first thing that came to her, which was, 'How did you know?'

'I know more than you think I do, Mrs Collins. I see more than you think I do. I know that you are, in all other circumstances, a sensible woman. I know you are clever. I know you married someone beneath your intellect. I know your chances at marriage were low when you met him, and I know what freedoms he has afforded you. I know that there is some depth to the *feelings* between you and my nephew. I also know that there is no future there for you. I know you will make a wise decision.'

Charlotte blinked tears out of her eyes, tears formed from finally confronting the hopelessness of the case – and in such company, under such pressure.

After a moment, Lady Catherine encouraged them to continue walking. 'Do I have your assurance that this *situation* will end?'

'Do you have his?'

Lady Catherine was not pleased with this spark of defiance. She snapped back, 'I do not. I consider you, like any woman, infinitely more capable of taking charge of the situation. And it is in *your* interests to do so. What do you think my nephew risks in this? Nothing. He will return to war within the year. His life will continue unaffected. Were his name linked to a married woman, what harm would it do to him, a single, eligible colonel, honoured by Wellington? No harm at all. He will be unchanged.' Lady Catherine leant in closer to Charlotte's ear as she said, vigorously, 'And you will be ruined. You will have no place in society, either disgraced in divorce or tortured in your marriage. It is not he but you who will pay the price for this. So, I come to you, not him, to solve it.'

Charlotte looked at her, clear-eyed, and nodded.

'But let me be clear: I am not persuading you; I am telling you. I will not brook further harm to Mr Collins. I will not have my parish be the subject of gossip and scandal. I will not have my family brought into disrepute. I ask you, finally: do you agree to put a stop to any connection between yourself and Fitzwilliam?'

Charlotte could not help but think of a similar scene that she had heard about in detail from her dearest friend. Lady Catherine had, only months before, paid a visit to Longbourn to entreat Miss Elizabeth Bennet to drop her connection to another one of her nephews. Charlotte almost found it funny to think that Lady Catherine was having to repeat the same threats, the same tactics, to persuade Charlotte now.

And yet, unlike Elizabeth, Charlotte knew Lady Catherine well enough to place some trust in her motives.

Unlike Elizabeth, Charlotte had half-expected this question to arise and had prepared herself for it.

Unlike Elizabeth, her answer would be, 'Yes.'

CHAPTER XIV

Snow had fallen and settled overnight across Hunsford and Rosings Park. From her vantage point, Charlotte could see the village in the distance, lying still and peaceful but for the church bell ringing for eight o'clock. She had set off early, before Mr Collins had awoken, determined to face the task ahead without distraction. She had taken herself on a long walk through the grounds to gather her thoughts and prepare her words. She turned off the hill now and walked down to the copse below, her feet treading deeply into the snow, her face red from the cold.

She did not have long to wait. She knew his routine well enough now; he often walked the grounds before breakfast, his military training not allowing him to sleep in late. He saw her through the trees and came to her.

She was interested to see how well he walked now: hardly a hesitation, even on this rough ground. There was nothing to delay his return to the front then, she thought. This would be timely. It seemed as if it were God's will that it should end now, if God's will spared no thought for love.

'Charlotte!' His smile was broad, and under the cover of the trees, he kissed her and then held her in an embrace so encompassing, she no longer felt the cold in the air. She let herself be enveloped in him, knowing this might be the last time.

The letter he had passed her in church two weeks earlier had served its purpose and soothed their quarrel. She had set out to meet him the day after receiving it; he, eager for reconciliation, had been waiting. They had met twice more since then, in the same spot where they stood now, and they likely would have continued their meetings as the snowdrops faded and bluebells started springing up around them – were it not for Lady Catherine's visit.

He loosened his hold now to better look at her, and she took his hands. She could not meet his eyes, and he noticed immediately.

'What is wrong?'

'You are walking well.'

He frowned, puzzled by the comment. 'Yes,' he replied uncertainly.

'You will have to return to campaign.'

His face relaxed. 'Is that what troubles you? But I found out only this week that I have some grace before I am called; they have been willing to take my word on the subject of my own recovery.'

Charlotte nodded, still not looking at him.

He was dismayed that this did nothing to alleviate her low mood. He tried again. 'It is unlikely I will be on the front lines, at any rate. I could request a strategic role when I return.'

She looked up at him. 'Richard.'

He met her eyes, and he knew then, more or less, what was to come. Both of them had always known, if they allowed their minds to travel to it, that what had happened between them could only ever be temporary. It had to be. Therefore, both had been awaiting the hammer-blow. It had just been a matter of who would do it and how soon.

Fitzwilliam had lived a strange existence this year. He had been in uniform since the age of sixteen and had quickly become accustomed to, even reliant on, routine. Drills, exercises and marching, first in barracks and then, at the turn of the war, on garrison in Gibraltar. Always drills, exercises and marching. He had then fought in Spain, but even that was no great break from what he knew: he had his orders, his regiment, his red coat, his destination and his purpose. When the terrain was new and tough, he returned to shining his boots, sewing his patches, following orders, issuing orders and marching. Always marching.

Since Albuera, all had been chaos. It started with the chaos of the battle itself: total disorder, man after man cut down, achieving nothing. He lost so many. He lost Parker. The return journey had been long and sombre; all regiments had suffered such great losses that those who survived travelled in a state of shock. His regiment had been decimated, and on return, they had been tasked with rebuilding their ranks for a few months. Initially, they were on leave but then barracked, so it was back to drills, exercises and marching.

Fitzwilliam had received a promotion during this period at home – reward for his leadership during Albuera. It was laughable to him that any praise should be meted out following such a catastrophe. He had therefore been in a sort of limbo when he first went to stay at Rosings.

It was during this time of stasis that he visited Hunsford and first met Charlotte. Although Elizabeth had initially drawn his eye, with Charlotte he had immediately felt something new, something comforting. She put him at ease, which, given his circumstances, was radical to him. But he did not consider at that point that there might be any deeper feelings; she was married, and he was a soldier. He directed some half-hearted flirtation towards her single friend, albeit with no serious intent. But he could not stop his mind wandering towards Charlotte, no matter how pointless it seemed. He masked his feelings well enough, at first.

He could not forget that day at the church last spring. She had so easily laughed off the debacle that caused them to collide, but he did not forget it. He had almost declared himself that day. She had caught him before he could. Had she not, he would have told her how he felt drawn to her, how he felt sure of her, and how he had never been so loath to leave someone when his orders came.

Salamanca had been a very different affair from Albuera — brutal, of course, but the campaign, taken as a whole, had been more familiar to him. He had started to feel as though he were returning to a life he recognised, the life of a soldier: following orders, issuing orders and marching. Always marching.

Then he was shot, and he could march no longer.

When Charlotte first visited him at Rosings after his injury, he was wretched. Ashamed of his broken state and reluctant to let her see him so weak, he had been rude and agitated. When she told him she was pregnant, he saw that she had found the peace she had once spoken of. She looked serene, contented. He knew to leave her well alone, to leave her to her happiness so that she could build her family.

And so he had intended — until Pemberley. Until he found her, lost in a maze, and she found him, and he wanted the hedges to grow and entwine and close over the pathways so that they might never find their way out.

And when the rain came down on them, he found that he could not only march but run.

As he strode back towards Rosings now, his thick coat rippling in the winter wind, he blinked back tears and felt every crack, every strain, every stab of pain in his shattered leg. But he did not slacken his speed. He moved like a tempest, and the ache only spurred him on. As he walked purposefully into the house, his aunt called, 'Richard, is that you?'

He did not reply.

'Come into breakfast; you are late.'

He still did not reply. Instead, he turned away from the breakfast room, made his way to the drawing room and the inviting drinks table. He grabbed the decanter of brandy and set about pouring a very large glass. His chest was heaving as he lifted it, the strong vapours hitting the back of his throat like a violent old friend — but did not yet drink.

His eyes fell on the grand piano in the corner of the room. He imagined Charlotte seated there, effortlessly playing a melody that dazzled the assembled company. He pictured her hands, her delicate fingers, which had held his face so gently just now in the woods as she had said goodbye.

He looked down at his own trembling hands, wrapped tightly around the glass, hands that had held her – sturdily but with great care. His hands, though rough and calloused, could both wield a sabre or thread a needle – hands practised in repair, in steadying what was broken.

He put the glass down.

He walked away from the drinks table and up to his rooms, where he set his troubled mind to something more practical – which is what, he imagined, Charlotte would do.

28th February 1813

Sir,

I have received and laid before the commander-in-chief your letter of the 18th Instant and am directed to grant your request to return to duty. You are to proceed by the earliest opportunity to Lisbon and to report your embarkation to this department, in conformity to the directions hereby enclosed. You will seek Lord Wellington's pleasure as to the nature of your command.

Yours,
Lieutenant Colonel Henry Torrens

VOLUME
THREE

6th March 1813

Dear Mr Collins,

I thank you for your last letter; I am now in a better position to advise on the matters you mention, with regards to the recent passing of Mr Bennet. The estate of Longbourn will fall in its entirety to you, as you expected, and once the papers enclosed are signed, it is done.

As to the practicalities: it is customary to wait at least a month before taking the house. I am in correspondence with a Mr Bingley, who is handling the affairs on behalf of the Bennets. If you wish to move to Longbourn before that period, please inform me, and I shall ask him to speak to the family; it may be possible. There are some details of the entail I wish to speak to you about, but for now, it is all in hand.

Your servant,
Mr Noakes

CHAPTER I

'This is strange,' said Charlotte, as she walked with Elizabeth through the wilderness at the back of the house. 'Does it feel strange to you? Awkward?'

'It should,' replied her friend, touching the bark of a tree she had climbed many times when she was a child. Elizabeth stopped walking to take in the rest of the gardens, her gaze sweeping the estate. 'It should feel peculiar, and yet somehow, it does not. This – you, here – seems fitting somehow, Charlotte. I believe you suit being the mistress of Longbourn better than my mother ever did. I always loved the house; it is understated and elegant. It did not deserve the howls and conniptions of my mother's tenure.'

'Eliza! Your poor mother. How is she?'

'Settled, thank you. In truth, I think she is very content, considering everything. In living with her sister, she has a like-minded companion available at all hours, to share gossip and forceful opinions, to visit other families with. It suits them all very well. That is – I do not say that she does not miss my father, but all things considered, she is in a happy situation.'

'Good. And it sounds as if Kitty will be content at Pemberley?'

'Not only content but, if I may sound like my mother for a moment, rather advantaged by it. We are seeing to it that she belatedly enjoys some tuition, and her friendship with Georgiana is growing, so she has a companion close to her own age … We are all still learning to do without father – she feels it keenly, as we all do – but, materially, she is well placed. As is Mary, in a different way.'

'Will Jane like having Mary with her at Netherfield, do you think?' asked Charlotte, looking sideways at Elizabeth.

Elizabeth grinned guiltily. 'She will be a much better guardian for her than I ever could. Jane is so tolerant; Mary has been greeted with kindness and joined a gentle household, which suits her. Lord knows if she will ever embrace a dance, but she has as good a chance now as ever.'

'But – how are you, Eliza? You must miss him terribly.'

Elizabeth sighed, looking back at the tree. 'My mother never wanted us to climb trees as girls. Jane and I were good climbers – I know, Jane! Who should have thought it? But mother had a great fear that we would fall. She got less protective the more daughters she had,' said Elizabeth dryly. 'It did not stop us; it just meant we would climb it when she was not looking, to save the argument. Father initially waded into the discussion to defend our right to be adventurous but quickly gave it up for some peace. The next time Jane and I climbed this tree, we went farther than before, having spied something in the high branches. I reached it; it was a note, a little faded and folded, tied with coloured string to a branch, presumably so we would not miss it. It read: *You are not allowed to be up here.*' She chuckled as she remembered it.

'He was a good father.'

'Not entirely,' said Elizabeth, 'but he loved us. And he tried his best.'

'Things turned out very well for his daughters, in the end.'

'Some of them ...' returned Eliza. She breathed in deeply. 'I just so wish he had got to meet—' Her face dissolved into tears now, and Charlotte moved quickly to hold her.

'Sorry,' whispered Elizabeth, her voice muffled against Charlotte's dress.

'You need not apologise.' Charlotte held her friend as well as she could, allowing room for Elizabeth's now prominent bump.

'He would have suited being a grandfather.'

'He would indeed,' said Charlotte.

They stood for a moment and just took each other in. They were both thinking something similar: that girlhood was now firmly behind them. Adulthood pressed upon them more keenly than it ever had.

Elizabeth roused them both from their reverie. 'Shall we return to the house? To *your* house?'

'Only if you're ready?'

'I am ready.'

'Thank goodness, because I do not want to leave Darcy alone with my husband for too much longer. I am afflicted, after all, with compassion.'

Eliza laughed but then, as they set off, observed, 'But you seem more settled now, together. Perhaps I imagine it, but there is a calmness between you that I had not observed before. What has changed?'

Charlotte had so much to say to her dearest friend. Were she to tell anyone, it would be Elizabeth, but if she began to divulge any part of it, the dam might break. She feared she would start to proclaim all her secrets to the whole of Hertfordshire.

'It is true, as you say. We are simply more settled together. That is marriage, I suppose – growing to understand each other better over time.'

Elizabeth looked archly at her friend. 'You are concealing something, but you are not very adept at it. And yet we do not have time to investigate it at present; Darcy and I need to set off shortly. Perhaps you will have more to say when I next see you.'

Presently, the Darcys were to make their way back to Derbyshire, via Meryton, as Mr Collins had requested a ride in their carriage as far as there. He needed to deliver a letter urgently, and it also afforded him more time to converse with – or rather, talk at – Mr Darcy, which was one of his favourite pastimes, and one of Darcy's least.

As Charlotte watched the carriage depart, she smiled to herself. An afternoon of solitude – blissful. Elizabeth was not wrong on one score; she was calm, and in many ways, she was content.

Since the cold morning when she had severed relations with Colonel Fitzwilliam, she had made no contact with him and neither had he with her. It had been understood, in their parting, that this was how it should be. She had heard nothing of his life – Lady Catherine and Mr Darcy were the only people of her acquaintance who might know anything of his movements, and they had no reason to share this intelligence with her, and she certainly dared not ask. But above that, she actively decided she did not wish to know. She had closed that chapter – the most thrilling chapter of her life, certainly, but she'd known it could only ever have been a short one, and it had now run its course.

Since their parting in February, many things had occurred: a death, a will, another new home. They had taken up residence in Longbourn at the very start of May, allowing two months for the Bennets to make their arrangements. Charlotte would have given them longer, but their attorney, Noakes, advised against.

It should have felt odd moving again so soon, but it did not. It felt like coming home. She knew every room, every path, every nook and cranny of Longbourn.

Charlotte summoned the memories now: she and Jane and Eliza entering the hall dripping with mud after a long walk, playing charades by firelight in the drawing room, snow falling across the garden and the thick ice that formed over the pond, newly baked cakes smuggled from the kitchen by Elizabeth, and the three of them huddled on the bench under the stairs, sharing whispered secrets as the night drew closer. She had come to know Longbourn well. And now it was all hers.

Charlotte still had secrets to hold in this house, but she would no longer be sharing them with anyone.

CHAPTER II

Two months earlier, Mrs Bennet had stood alongside her five daughters, all dressed in black, watching her husband's coffin be carried down the aisle of the small church in the village of Longbourn.

In her married life, Mrs Bennet had been criticised and sometimes ridiculed for the way she had raised her daughters. Despite being an ambitious mother, she was not willing to bow to the expectations of the society to which she aspired. She had no time for those rules that curtailed her daughters' freedoms and natural urges. She had not been strict with their education; some showed aptitude for study (Mary) and some showed more aptitude for dancing (Lydia) – she let those natural proclivities fall where they may. She had not adhered to the rule that younger sisters should not come out into society before the elder were married; this seemed unfair on the younger, and after all, her youngest daughters enjoyed society more actively than any of them!

And she certainly did not adhere to the custom which suggested that women should not attend a funeral, but stay at home, while the men represented them in church. The idea that her husband should be led to his grave by the likes of Mr Gardiner, Mr Phillips and Mr Darcy – and even Mr Collins, who was stealing their own house out from under them! – while Mr Bennet's own wife and daughters were left to watch from behind the curtains, seemed absurd to her. An unsympathetic witness might have said that she could not bear to be left out, but as ridiculous as her behaviour could be at times, Mrs Bennet had always had a strong sense of her rights and needs, and those of her daughters, even when it flew in the face of decorum. To some, she might have been viewed as rather modern.

Mr and Mrs Collins had travelled to Hertfordshire to attend the funeral; it was fitting for Collins to do so, as the heir to Longbourn, and Charlotte was glad to be of some comfort for Elizabeth and Jane. She did not attend the church service that morning but stayed back with a handful of other ladies.

When it was finished, Mrs Bennet and her daughters returned to the house while the gentlemen attended the burial. Upon entering, she set eyes on Charlotte and was immediately incensed.

'Oh! I see Mrs *Collins* is here already. But of course she is – it is her house now, after all!'

'Mother! Stop! Charlotte is here to help,' cried Jane, horribly embarrassed.

Charlotte was not overly offended, having known Mrs Bennet and her ways for many years. With grace, she stepped back and gave Mrs Bennet some space. She had half expected this reaction, and furthermore, she did not disagree with Mrs Bennet that the entail was unjust. She would have felt the same, under the circumstances, although she would not have been quite as outspoken.

'Well, Mrs Collins,' Mrs Bennet continued, undeterred, 'I am mistress of Longbourn for a short while yet, thank you. I do not require your help in any regard. I will take my place as usual.' At this, she sat in her preferred chaise-longue. 'And ask that someone other than Mrs Collins pass me a biscuit?' With that said, and the biscuit consumed, she regained her strength and held court in the parlour until the last guest left.

In the light of the early afternoon, Charlotte took a turn in the garden alone, requiring some fresh air and solitude. As she neared the house again, she found herself confronted by Mr Wickham, who had loosened himself from Lydia and apparently come out purposefully to greet Charlotte. He did so as if nothing untoward had ever passed between them, an aggravating smirk fixed on his face, even under these sombre circumstances.

'And how have you faired, Mrs Collins, since our last meeting?'

Charlotte did not feel afraid of him; they were within easy distance of people who, though indoors, could step in at any moment if Charlotte were to call for them. Added to this, she now considered Longbourn more her territory than his, which gave her some confidence.

'I am well, Mr Wickham. I trust you and your wife are also in good health?'

'Oh yes, all well. Lydia is with child.'

'What happy news,' returned Charlotte evenly.

He screwed up his face as if mocking the idea. 'Certainly. Inevitable, of course. She's pleased. I can't help but be grateful I ship out before it arrives. I am needed in Spain; I sail to Lisbon in a fortnight.' He spoke with some bravado before adding, 'I shall relish the chance to distinguish myself. By the time I return, you may be addressing me as *Captain* Wickham, and after that, who knows? I know how you appreciate a high-ranking officer.'

Charlotte ignored the innuendo and said, smiling gently, 'I do not think you will make Captain, nor even Lieutenant.'

'Why should you say that?' he said, unease plain in his tone.

'Let us say that I have an intuition about it.' She shrugged. 'I predict you will be a lowly ensign for these ten years at least. I do hope it is not embarrassing for you? An educated man of nearly thirty years old, serving as an ensign?'

Her words took effect. A suspicion was forming in Wickham's mind that made a vein in his forehead start throbbing. In spite of this, he was still trying for nonchalance as he said, with a tight grin, 'You can have no power over such things.'

'Oh no. I, a woman? I have no power in such matters. But I know better men than you. And they do.'

Wickham was outraged. He spoke quietly but with fury, trying to loom over her. 'A woman who would tear down a man's livelihood on a whim might remember that he has a wife and family who rely on his income, so who is she truly punishing?'

Charlotte inwardly scoffed to hear how quickly he brought to mind his child, whom he had only a moment ago been so keen to leave the country to get away from.

'Your wife and child are amply provided for by their relations. This has always been assured. Any hardship arising from a lack of position and income is felt only by you. This does not give me pause.'

'All because of – nothing! It was nothing; you flatter yourself that I made any serious advance!'

Charlotte had never seen him so worked up, spitting and floundering, losing the cool nonchalance that he usually wore like a uniform.

'And are you so afraid of a man's company that you should react so? Or perhaps, as I always suspected, you prefer the company of—'

'I do not think of you as a man.'

Wickham scoffed, then paused, desperately seeking a rejoinder. Swaggering, he offered, 'As a beast, I imagine.' He looked pleased with this.

Charlotte turned her face up to meet his, unflinching. 'Nothing so exciting. A mouse – small and grubby. There are thousands like you, and just when you think you have rid the world of one, another appears. You are an irritation, Mr Wickham, but ultimately you make no more impact on a person than to occasionally put them off their dinner. And what you will leave behind in this life, when you are dead, is only crumbs.'

Charlotte exited his orbit quickly, without taking leave, and did not look back to see his face.

If she had, she would have seen a man turning from red to grey. His energy left him for a moment, and he was deflated. But a minute later, another guest approached him, and his devilish smile returned. Men like he are not easily depleted. Charlotte's words and actions would make a notch in his esteem and make his life materially more difficult, but here was a man who would grin even while the noose was around his neck. The best one could hope for was that he be humbled by circumstance, encountered as seldom as possible – or that he, one day, be put out of his misery while he scrambled for a piece of cheese.

CHAPTER III

Mr Collins had thrown himself with vigour into the work of managing the estate. It was still early in his tenure and he had much to learn, but he had always been a quick study. With the help of Mr Bennet's land steward, a Mr Thacker, he was introduced to the duties and people he would be managing. If the tenants and the staff thought Mr Collins eccentric, they also saw a man who was trying. This was a new world for him, and he was daunted but excited. In fact, the spring of 1813 was perhaps the happiest season Mr Collins had ever passed. Every day, he was learning something new, was tested and was pleased to find himself mostly up to the task.

This applied not only to his new position but to his marriage. He fancied that he was, belatedly, learning how to be a good husband – finally understanding Charlotte's ways and anticipating her needs. He could not quite term his last year with Charotte *tumultuous* – the shifting ground of their marriage had not been an earthquake, but it had felt continually rocked by small yet constant tremors. He had felt, at times, as if her heart were miles from him, and he had worried, on more than one occasion, that she regretted marrying him. He had wondered if the lack of children was a cause for this. They had tried again, sporadically, in the months after their loss, but to no avail. He was sorry indeed for that.

But around the time of Mr Bennet's death, she had started to come back to him. The timing made him think that perhaps she had been homesick and missing her family and that the move back to Hertfordshire would be a return to familiarity. Or perhaps she had simply disliked living at Hunsford and needed a fresh start. But speculation as to the reason was now futile: his wife was more content than he had seen her; he would not waste time wondering why.

One of the lessons he had learnt was that she needed to see her family and friends more often. Never having had any family whom he would wish to see, he had overlooked that aspect of her life. He now understood that she needed to visit Lucas Lodge or Netherfield and eventually even Pemberley again – and that, sometimes, *he* should not be present.

She had told him, one evening, that she did not care for hearing the Bible read aloud, nor even *Fordyce's Sermons*. This had shocked him at first, but when she offered other choices of text – poems and histories – he had been willing to try them. He found little pleasure in poetry, not understanding its meaning or purpose. He got on better with her historical texts, which sometimes *she* would read aloud to *him*. He was aware that their interests did not align perfectly, but they had found a middle ground that suited their purpose well enough.

Theirs was not a passionate marriage. Intimacy, in that regard, was always something of an arduous duty. He had never experienced that act as being comfortable or satisfying, so clouded was it by uncertainty and awkwardness. He had not had a father, brother or friend to whom he could talk about such matters, so he had no means of comparison and continued in ignorance. Relations were infrequent – he would not allow them to cease entirely, mindful of his duty as a husband – but his wife neither pressed for more nor seemed discontented by its diminution. He, for his part, was equally content with their almost platonic day-to-day, and he felt no less intimate with her for it.

'Have you received word from anyone in Hunsford yet, my dear?' asked Mr Collins, as they sat in the drawing room one balmy evening in early June.

'I have. Mrs Taylor sent me news of what the ladies of the church are undertaking and their plans for the summer fair. And I have had a letter from Miss de Bourgh.'

'Miss *Anne* de Bourgh?'

'The very same.'

'But what can she have to say to you, my dear? I am surprised that, considering matters in her life must be so elevated, she should deign to share them. What condescension!'

'They are not so elevated, William. She shares some of the same concerns we once did: courtship, a desire to marry … and I believe her desire may be fulfilled before long.'

Collins's eyes widened further at this. 'And she has confided this to *you*?'

Charlotte was not offended at his amazement; it spoke more of his own humility than his opinion of her. 'She has confided some things. Nothing is certain. We must not speak of it to anyone.'

'No indeed,' replied Collins with vigour. He looked briefly down at his book, then ponderously asked, 'Have you had any correspondence pertaining to Mr Smithson?'

'No. Why?'

'Well, I only wondered what news he brought of the church and, well …' He faltered. 'I was curious about his affairs.'

Charlotte thought about Mr Smithson's time at Hunsford. Although she had disliked him, he had invigorated Mr Collins's spirits. He was the only person she had ever known who had called on her husband at home, for no special reason beyond the social. 'He was your friend,' she said simply.

Mr Collins considered this, not sure whether he approved of it. 'He was my curate,' he corrected.

'Might he have been both?'

After a moment of deliberation, Mr Collins nodded. 'Yes. He might have been.'

'And you miss him.' Charlotte was treading carefully.

'I merely wish to know whether he is well and how he takes care of the church.'

'William, you should write to him.'

'Perhaps. I suppose I could enquire about some clerical matters?'

'You could, but you can also write to him purely to maintain the friendship. I would not like you to lose a friend.'

She did not say *your first friend*, although that is what she imagined he was. If Mr Collins had ever enjoyed a lasting friendship, he had never mentioned it. So while Mr Smithson was not the company she would have chosen for her husband, she would far rather he had a friend than not.

The next day, as she passed the study, she saw Mr Collins writing diligently and asked him what his business was.

'I am writing to Mr Smithson,' he replied with a sheepish smile.

She walked behind his desk and, placing her hands on his shoulders, gently kissed the top of his head. He reached up to put his hand atop hers and gave it a squeeze.

By the summer, Charlotte felt, as several people had commented, *settled*.

She had never had cause to so examine a word before. She had now heard it so many times and from so many different quarters that it had almost ceased to hold any meaning. But it was the right word. She had settled; but also, perhaps, she was settling.

Her decision to halt contact with Fitzwilliam had been supported in every way by the events that occurred around it – which, she reflected, rather lessened her achievement in doing the right thing. She hoped that she would have acted the same, no matter how things had fallen, but as it was, the death of Mr Bennet, coming so soon after their farewell, removed her from temptation. The inheritance and the business of moving to a new home was a useful distraction and a welcome one. It also felt like a sign; it seemed that she was always fated to be parted from him.

On her first night at Longbourn, she had been hit with a wave of grief: grief for the love she would not have, for the regret she held. She felt all the unfairness of not having met Fitzwilliam a year sooner, that she might have had a very different choice to make.

Also, simply, she missed him. She had not been able to conceal her sadness, but she could not reveal to anyone the reason for it. Elizabeth had comforted her, putting it down to the emotion of being once again removed from a home and starting anew. Darcy had noticed Charlotte's red-rimmed eyes and, having some idea of their cause, been gentle with her.

And yet, after a little time, Charlotte strived to embrace those qualities that she had always prized in herself: stoicism, pragmatism, steadiness. She set about making Longbourn her home – an occupation she greatly enjoyed. She resumed her involvement with the church, this time free from the obligations and expectations that had accompanied her role as the rector's wife. She was also pleased to learn about some aspects of managing the estate alongside her husband.

Charlotte was, she hoped, a determined person. And she had determined – resolutely – to shut off the part of herself that had been set alight in the last few months. That flickering, reckless flame, once welcomed, must now be extinguished, or at least carefully smothered beneath routine, propriety and purpose. She determined to keep herself from dwelling on that time or that man – or on the person she had then become. She determined to remember who she had been when she married, because that person had been grateful. That person had been content. That person had *settled*.

So, she now lived her life at a lower temperature and a slower rate. If she lacked fire, then she could be thankful not to be burnt. If she lacked speed, she was grateful never to trip. She saw her mother and her siblings with welcome regularity. She spent time with her friends. She embraced her new home. She cultivated her garden. And she tended to her marriage, which was in great need of nurture. She turned her face fully towards Mr Collins for the first time in a long time and allowed him to truly see her.

She reminded herself that she had not chosen badly in accepting him. He was a good man, a gentle man, who worked hard and loved her. These things she held to – and week by week, month by month, she settled.

CHAPTER IV

'She is here! Rouse yourself, Charlotte, she is here!'

Mr Collins was even more at sea than he usually was in the anticipation of Lady Catherine. For her to honour them with a visit, now that they lived so far from Kent, showed an unprecedented level of condescension that Charlotte found puzzling and Mr Collins found thrilling. They had received the letter two weeks prior, reporting her plans to visit her nephew in Derbyshire and to call on them en route. (Fortunately, her chaise, Mr Collins assured Charlotte, had such excellent suspension as to make the journey comfortable enough.)

That great lady arrived promptly in the early afternoon, and Charlotte and Mr Collins, in their best dress, stood outside to greet her. Unsmiling, as she always was, Lady Catherine descended from the carriage, looking up at Longbourn as if it were an old enemy come back to challenge her. She wore an expensive-looking but heavy gown, bordered with an immaculate lace trim.

They took her into the sitting room and Mrs Brooke brought in tea.

'Good day, Brooke,' said Lady Catherine, exhibiting her unparalleled memory for names – a skill she quite regularly, and audibly, congratulated herself on.

'Good afternoon, my lady.'

Lady Catherine proceeded to make herself entirely at home, dismissing Brooke with a regal wave and assuming command of the tea-tray as if it were her birthright. The moment she had poured she took a sip of tea, though it must have still been boiling hot. She didn't flinch as she swallowed. Charlotte wondered, not for the first time, what this woman was made of. Literally.

She was staring at Lady Catherine's gullet when that lady launched straight into her favourite pastime – gentle interrogation – with all the interest of a general inspecting the troops.

'You now have a full staff, here, do you not, Mrs Collins? It appears so. Did the majority stay on when the Bennets vacated?'

'Indeed, most of them did, which made the transition much easier. Indeed, all stayed but Mrs Hill, who has gone with Mrs Bennet. So, it worked out very well for us that Mrs Brooke was willing to come to be with us from Kent. We are very fond of her.'

Apparently satisfied, Lady Catherine pivoted to a new topic. 'You have seen Mr Darcy and his wife, I believe?'

'We have indeed had that great pleasure, your ladyship,' began Collins, 'and we hope it was apparent the extent to which myself and Mrs Collins are natural and sympathetic successors to the legacy of the estate. In time, we—'

'When did they depart?'

Charlotte answered now. 'About six weeks ago, Lady Catherine. Elizabeth was the last of the family to remain in the house, even while Mr Collins and I settled in. Her presence in that period was comforting for both of us – she was able to say farewell to the house, while I had company and guidance while learning the shape and running of a new household.'

'And was it a comfort for *you*, Mr Collins, to have Mrs Darcy here?' asked Lady Catherine pointedly.

Mr Collins hesitated before saying, 'To be sure, my lady. I was pleased to be able to accommodate the wishes of both ladies.'

Lady Catherine raised an eyebrow.

My, she is in a mood to stir the pot today, thought Charlotte, but a part of her reflected guiltily on what had just been said. How *had* it been for her husband to have the woman who rejected his proposal stay in his house, with her more handsome, more wealthy husband? She had hardly considered it.

She inwardly berated herself, while Lady Catherine's conversation moved on to Elizabeth's impending child. Charlotte was pleased to note a surprising warmth from her on the subject. Apparently, all past resentments were forgotten in light of the promise of a Rosings grand-nephew. And yet Charlotte had the distinct feeling that her remarks on the subject of offspring contained a subtle barb meant for her.

While Lady Catherine paused, Mr Collins tentatively ventured a question of his own. 'If I may ask, how fares Mr Smithson? I do hope he is guiding the parish well?'

'You may ask.' Lady Catherine seemed to give such a simple question rather a lot of thought. 'He is a little less fervent than he was when he first arrived, and I think it no bad thing. He is surprisingly keen on his pastoral role. He has been present at three deaths already.'

'An impressive record, my lady,' attempted Collins. 'May I enquire as to who it is that has—'

'I believe he will hold the fort very well, Mr Collins, until such time as I find the appropriate person to take the living.'

'Oh,' said Collins shortly. 'I had assumed you would bestow it on him?'

Lady Catherine lifted her teacup. 'No,' she returned, without further explanation.

She took another sip, placed her cup down and announced, 'I would rather not remain any longer in this sitting room, which I remember and dislike. I would welcome a turn around your grounds, if you would honour me.'

'Gladly,' said Charlotte.

Mr Collins also expressed approval of the plan, but in many more words.

*

'You are settled well here then, Mrs Collins? You look settled,' observed Lady Catherine, as the three of them wandered across the lawn.

Charlotte laughed out loud at her observation and could not explain the reason.

It was Mr Collins who replied, abashed at his wife's irreverence. 'We are happy indeed, your ladyship, and consider ourselves blessed. There is still much to learn, but I relish it, for God did not mean us to sit idly.'

'No, indeed.'

Once Lady Catherine had seen all that the gardens had to offer and adequately passed judgement on them – the rose garden's scent was deemed rather overpowering, and the trees in the orchard had been too sparsely planted – she stated that she would bid them farewell. They all made their way to the drive, where Lady Catherine's maid and carriage awaited her.

As they neared, she sighed. 'Ah, I have dropped my glove somewhere. I believe it must have been in the rose garden, when I took my handkerchief out to sneeze; they really were pungent. Would you be so good as to retrieve it, Mr Collins? You know best what route we took.'

Once Mr Collins, who naturally leapt at the opportunity, was a safe distance away, Lady Catherine invited Charlotte to take a turn with her around the drive.

'I am glad to have a moment alone with you, Mrs Collins. I think you have made some wise decisions recently, for the benefit of all. I wished only to commend you on your resolve.'

Charlotte found it hard to believe this was all Lady Catherine wished to say. After a moment, she was proved right, as Lady Catherine proceeded to make enquiries which were well beyond the bounds of propriety: asking whether Charlotte was with child.

Startled into answering, Charlotte replied in the negative, and Lady Catherine's next remark was as sudden as it was baffling.

'Go to Bath.'

Charlotte blinked. 'I beg your pardon?'

'Go to Bath. Take the waters.'

'Why? I am not ill.'

'I understand the waters help all kinds of maladies – rheumatism, low spirits, and difficulties of your kind. My sister took them.'

Charlotte wondered if Lady Catherine had laced her tea with gin. 'I do not wish to go to Bath. I do not believe water can change my situation.' She added, rather piously, 'I do not think it is God's will for me to be a mother.'

Lady Catherine pulled an incredulous face. 'God's will? You sound like your husband, Mrs Collins. I had not marked you down as being so' – she searched for the word – 'passive.'

'Passive! How can I be otherwise?' cried Charlotte. 'You know how I fared last time.'

'Yes, I do,' replied Lady Catherine, calmly and unsentimentally. 'Are there efforts in the marriage to try again?'

Charlotte shook her head in disbelief at the temerity of her companion but found herself responding. 'Yes. Some. But it is to no avail. Therefore, I confess, we have largely ceased to try, to save ourselves the heartache—'

'Oh, come, Mrs Collins – you are not the first wife to have difficulties getting with child.'

Charlotte had mostly restrained her anger thus far, but it began to find some momentum. 'This is too much! You keep saying "difficulties"; I do not know whether I have difficulties – the difficulties may not be *mine*! What if the difficulties are *his*?'

Her voice grew louder as she raised a concern that had preyed on her mind since the first months of her marriage.

Lady Catherine paused, upon receiving this. 'You may well be right. But it does not matter. It is always us who have difficulties, Mrs Collins. It is always the woman's problem, in the end. I know you studied your history books, so I am sure you realise that the

Church upon which your husband's former livelihood rests was founded because of a king's desire to remarry in order that he might get himself a son. That king tried six different wives, and five of them received the blame when male heirs were not forthcoming. Yet what is more likely? That all those healthy women had *difficulties*, or that an old king, bloated, gouty and probably diseased, was not up to the task?'

Lady Catherine fell silent for a moment, before continuing in a voice low but unflinching, edged with a pride that had weathered sorrow. 'I wanted more children. It took five years to get Anne. I lost three before her. No more children were to be mine. My husband wanted a boy, of course. But it wasn't to be. He barely looked at her, at first. Too small, too sickly. But I loved Anne fiercely, to make up for his dismissal of her. She was not meant to survive, but I made certain she did. She was all I had. All I *have*.'

Lady Catherine turned to Charlotte now. 'People think me strong. And I am. I am strong – for her.'

'That was your path,' said Charlotte. 'I do not know whether I want the same.'

Lady Catherine came back to herself and said sharply, 'Nevertheless, children will be the best way out of your current predicament.'

Charlotte looked puzzled. 'I am not in a predicament.'

'Oh, but you are, Mrs Collins.' Lady Catherine breathed out of her nose, apparently exasperated by the conversation that no one was pushing to continue but herself. 'You may think you are content for the time being, but marriages such as yours cannot sustain happily without the addition of children. I speak as a widow and a dowager. When your husband is no longer there, what are you left with?'

'A peaceful life and a comfortable home,' replied Charlotte, her chin jutting out in defiance.

'No,' replied Lady Catherine firmly. 'You shall be left with neither. This comfortable home' – she gestured at the house that loomed in front of them – 'is not yours. Your previous home was not yours. The house you grew up in was not yours. This house belongs to your *husband*, while he lives. And *if* you have a son, it will belong to him, and you may live in it. If you have neither husband nor son, you have no comfortable home. You would be all alone and reliant on the charity and pity of others. Would that afford you a *peaceful life*?' She allowed the impact of her words to settle, before adding, more gently now, 'Go to Bath, Mrs Collins. Take the waters.'

With that, she took her servant's hand and climbed into her carriage. She waited a moment until Mr Collins returned, deeply apologetic for not having found her glove.

'No matter, Mr Collins; I thank you for your efforts. It is always worth trying, even when the task seems hopeless. I bid you good day.'

And with that, the carriage wheels turned, and Charlotte watched the vehicle sweep out of the drive – but not before seeing Lady Catherine adjust her bonnet, give instruction to her coachman, and proceed to don a pair of immaculate white gloves.

CHAPTER V

It was a hot, sticky summer's day at Lucas Lodge. The air was thick with warmth, and the dining room windows, though open, let in no breeze. The Collinses had been invited to take luncheon with the family, and Charlotte, ever polite, had eaten more than she had really fancied of the generous helpings of roast chicken and potatoes. The meal sat heavily on her, and, feeling languid and uncomfortable, she longed for a walk outside.

'An excellent choice of meal, Lady Lucas, well suited to the day,' Mr Collins simpered untruthfully.

Lady Lucas accepted the small compliment graciously, accustomed to Mr Collins's manners by now. The company all reclined a little in their chairs as Sir William Lucas muttered something to their butler.

'Have you any plans for the remainder of the summer?' asked Charlotte of her mother. 'Might you and Maria take in the end of the season in London?'

'No, we have no plans to. We may visit Bath in September – your aunt is keen to see Edward before he goes back to Eton.'

'I don't want to go back!' interjected Edward petulantly.

'Don't be silly, Edward,' his mother chided.

'I am not being silly. I do not like it.' He suddenly looked much younger than his fourteen years.

Lady Lucas softened in tone. 'Darling, you still have much to learn, and not all of it academic. Do you not miss your friends?'

'I do not have friends,' the boy returned sullenly. Suddenly, tears pricked his eyes, and the mood around the table changed.

Lady Lucas realised this was not now a topic for general discussion. 'We shall discuss it later.'

Determining a change of subject was needed, Charlotte said lightly, 'If you do go to Bath, we may accompany you.'

'Oh?' said Lady Lucas, rather put off by the word *we* in that offer.

'Yes, it would be pleasant to take a trip together, would it not, my dear?'

'Certainly,' replied Collins, happily surprised by the suggestion. 'I have long desired to visit the Pump Rooms.'

Lady Lucas blinked. 'Well, I will tell you when our plans are fixed.'

At this point, their butler entered with a bottle of champagne and began pouring it into their glasses. Charlotte's initial confusion at such decadence was quickly supplanted by joy as her father shared the news that Maria was engaged to be married to Mr Denny.

While Denny's less savoury connections had given Charlotte pause in the past, one look at Maria's blushing, giddy face allowed her to set those concerns aside, and she determined to focus on how well-mannered and honourable he had always proved himself. It was clearly a love-match, something she had always prayed her sister might be able to have.

'How wonderful,' said Mr Collins, who had evidently been preparing what he would say for some minutes. 'May God bless your union, as he has blessed ours.' It was more succinct than anyone had expected. He looked at Charlotte then, with such love, and as she met his eyes, she was surprised to feel tears coming. She blinked them back and raised her glass with him.

Walking with her mother in the garden that afternoon, Charlotte launched her interrogation. 'Has the courtship been going on all this time? The last occasion I saw them together was before I was engaged. She has not mentioned him since – not last year, or since I returned. It seems odd.'

Lady Lucas nodded. 'I know. She has been secretive about it, or she thought she had; I had some inclination. You see, at the start, your father and I were not encouraging of the match. You can imagine why.'

Charlotte could indeed. Life in the militia shared many of the same shortcomings as life in the regulars: absence from home, unpredictability and a lean income.

'When the militia removed to Brighton, we expected their courtship would come to a natural end. But then, of course, there followed the events concerning Lydia Bennet and Wickham.'

Charlotte felt herself lean in.

'You will remember, Denny and Wickham were friends, but Wickham's behaviour in Brighton, even before he left with Lydia, was shocking, and Denny had started to distance himself from him. When Lydia and Wickham eloped, it was Denny who alerted Colonel Forster to Wickham's nature, albeit too late. I cannot know the truth of it, but I believe if Denny were guilty of anything, it is being too slow to react.'

'But what of Maria?'

'Ah, yes. He had seen Maria that summer, when she was in London with the Miss Ainshaws, and he still liked her very much, and she him. In October, he presented himself here, to your father.'

'In October! Why have you not told me this before?'

'Because you have had plenty to think about, my darling – last October was not an easy time for you – and because I did not know how it would play out.'

'So, he asked permission to marry Maria?'

'Yes, but your father said no.'

Charlotte gasped.

'He said no, conditionally. He said that a life in the militia was not one fit for marriage, and he offered to help Denny into a career in trade; your father has excellent connections there.'

Charlotte looked sceptical. 'But does Mr Denny want this?'

'He does. He did. He had grown rather disillusioned with the militia since Brighton. He is now well established in London; he is at Berry's in St James's, with a good starting income and the prospect of taking a house within the next two years. So, your father and I have relented. Thank goodness, because Maria would have been furious. It will be a fairly long engagement, but they are happy enough with that.'

Charlotte leant back, finally satisfied with the information provided. So, a sister engaged – and not to a soldier after all but to a merchant. She wished it could have been simpler for Maria: that her beloved, in regimentals, might have asked her freely, and she might have been able to accept, immediately, without a care. But this was romantic nonsense; they would have had nowhere to live. Maria would have been galloping around the country, with no money, no friends. Charlotte also felt relieved, in a way, that even marrying a handsome soldier whom you loved entailed planning, changes, sacrifices and patience. Few unions were immediately perfect.

She looked towards the house and saw Mr Collins sitting with Edward on the terrace. It was an unusual pairing; Collins always seemed a little afraid of children, especially confident schoolboys, and Edward had always thought her husband a little odd.

Before they left later that afternoon, Lady Lucas took Mr Collins's hand warmly and said, 'Thank you for talking to Edward,' before bidding them both farewell.

They walked slowly home to Longbourn – it was a beautiful evening and the path was dry, and there was nothing to hurry or compel them. Charlotte took the opportunity to question her husband on the substance of his conversation with her young brother.

After some reticence, he answered, 'I asked him what he had meant when he said he had no friends.'

'Oh, yes. An odd thing to say – of course he has friends.'

Collins looked curiously at her. 'It is very possible for a boy to go through schooling without having friends. It is not the state one hopes for, but it is very possible.'

Charlotte regretted being so dismissive, realising that her husband was more likely an authority on this matter. 'And he does not?'

'He did have, but they have begun to be unkind to him.'

'Why?' asked Charlotte incredulously.

Again, Collins looked at her as if surprised at her naivety. 'Young boys do not need a reason to turn on one another. It might be anything – one's breeding, one's voice, one's gait, reading the wrong book, wearing the wrong colour ...'

'Then, what was your advice?'

'Only to try to see it through. Their actions may stop, or they may not. But he can survive it, and that will be a path to something better – as it was for me. I told him, as I have always believed, that education is the best way of choosing the company you keep.'

Charlotte smiled and nodded; this aphorism seemed in keeping with what she might have expected him to say.

'I also told him that of the two cruellest boys who I had the misfortune to know at Oxford, one of them is now an MP, and the other drank himself into an early grave.'

Charlotte laughed, then stopped herself. 'Was that a comfort to Edward?'

'I believe it was. I find comfort knowing that there is no reasoning to who finds happiness or success – the Goliath in the schoolyard might fall into nothing, and your brother might yet tame a lion.'

'But ... will he be happy at school, do you suppose?'

Mr Collins frowned, saying, a little grandly and pompously, 'Our task in this life to is to find happiness in what we are afforded and to improve what we find.'

Charlotte turned to him curiously. 'My mother says that. She has it embroidered on a sampler.'

'I know,' replied Mr Collins, with a shy smile. 'I saw it in the parlour.'

Charlotte started to laugh, and very tentatively, as if it were a new sensation for him, Mr Collins joined her.

CHAPTER VI

Charlotte sat down heavily, her stays suffocating her. Her dress felt too hot, too tight, for the warmth of the room. September was unseasonably, unreasonably warm. In any other circumstance, she should be in a light petticoat, outside, not entombed in layers of heavy fabric, sitting in a stifling drawing room, surrounded by so many people, all of their chatter making the air even hotter.

She feared she might faint, so she pulled at the ribbons of her bonnet and removed it hurriedly. She wished her mother were next to her, but Lady Lucas had taken charge and was greeting people and directing the staff in Charlotte's stead. Maria was too overcome to be of comfort, and Elizabeth had not been able to attend, having only recently given birth.

Jane Bingley entered the room and, seeing Charlotte, came to sit beside her. Jane was perhaps the perfect friend at this moment: calm, patient, but strong. She was stronger than people gave her credit for. She took Charlotte's hand in hers and held it, saying nothing.

Two weeks earlier, Charlotte had been at breakfast with her husband, discussing their trip to Bath. 'If it is only my mother and Edward, then we should share the carriage; it will be easier travelling as one.'

'As you wish, my dear,' confirmed Collins, smiling but then wincing.

Seeing this, Charlotte enquired if he were quite well.

'Just a pain I have had in my side since last night. I am sure it will dissipate.' He smoothed his countenance and lifted his toast, but she noted that he didn't take a bite. 'I have had a letter back from Mr Smithson,' he informed her, as cheerily as his discomfort would allow.

'Oh, I am glad!' said Charlotte. 'What is his news?'

'I have not yet opened it; it arrived this morning.'

He grimaced again. She supposed that what ailed him might be indigestion or perhaps a gastric complaint, and she did not wish to embarrass him by questioning him further.

But that afternoon, upon returning from a walk into Meryton, she discovered that he had taken to his bed. She entered their bedroom quietly, finding him lying on top of the bedsheets, fully clothed, gripping his right side as he had at breakfast.

He smiled tightly at her. 'It has not dissipated. It is a little worse.'

Charlotte sat on the bed and put her hand tenderly on his arm. 'What can it be? Is it an ache?'

'It is' – he winced – 'a sharp pain.'

'Could you have broken a rib?'

He only shook his head; speaking seemed to be difficult. Instead, he groaned again, loudly, and clutched his side.

Charlotte went downstairs and asked Mrs Brooke to fetch the doctor. Brooke prepared to leave immediately, and as she turned to go, Charlotte grabbed her arm and said, in a panic, 'I do not know what to do. What can I do?'

Brooke took her hand and said, 'Just be with him, madam.'

Now, Mrs Bennet had found a comfortable seat for herself next to her sister, Mrs Philips, and was eating a sandwich and cheerily discussing how the decoration of the room had changed since she had quitted Longbourn. Lady Catherine was present, too, occupying a corner seat, sitting with an ashen-faced Maria. For the first time in all of their acquaintance, Lady Catherine looked truly grieved.

Mr Bingley stood by the fireplace, speaking seriously with an older man whom Charlotte did not recognise. She asked if Jane knew who the gentleman was but, on receiving a negative, returned to silence. She had said very little in the last few days.

But a few moments later, she was forced to engage when Mr Bingley approached her to introduce that very man as a Mr Poulteney.

The gentleman gave Charlotte a soft, kind smile, sitting down in the vacant seat next her. 'I knew your husband quite well, Mrs Collins. I was very fond of him.'

Charlotte felt tears in her eyes then, because she had not heard that sentiment expressed by anyone in the last week, and she had mourned for the lack of it. Mr Collins deserved better.

'So was I, Mr Poulteney. So was I. Tell me, how did you know him?'

She sat for half an hour, listening to the man's stories of William Collins's quirks and misfortunes, talents and gifts. It was a gift to her to receive them. If she gained a better understanding of her husband from this, it came too late to be useful in their marriage, but she was grateful all the same.

Across those next two days, Mr Collins's pains became far worse, and he had a high fever. The doctor spoke with great authority, but it was clear to Charlotte that he no more knew what to do than anyone else. He recommended cooling cloths and opening the window, both of which she and Brooke had already done. Brooke was her usual self – calm and resourceful – but even she was helpless in the face of this malady.

At points, Mr Collins was delirious and became agitated by the thought that Charlotte was not with him, even though she was; she always was. When his body was taken by dramatic tremors that seemed ungodly, she tried still to hold him. When his hair was matted to his face with sweat, she gently combed it to one side.

He was bled by the surgeon, but this did not ease him. By the fifth day, Charlotte could not help but be grateful when he seemed to be taken into sleep. His breathing was greatly laboured, so it was not the rest she would hope for him – but at least he was still.

She decided to try reading to him, in the hope he might hear her. She chose a sermon by Fordyce, passages that were written for the death of a friend, which offered words of comfort – at least, words she believed her husband would find comforting.

'*The beginnings of piety are often scarcely discernible; but being kindled by the breath of God, that spark of divinity is by degrees blown into a flame, which mounts upward, and upward, and still upward, till it reacheth to the throne of the Eternal.*'

She looked keenly at his face, but it showed no sign of understanding. Turning the page, she continued, '*Under the righteous reign of Jesus, that "everlasting righteousness" which he defended, must prevail; and neither death, nor life, shall be able to separate the pious and the just, from the love of God.*'

She closed the book and took his hand, pressing her cheek to it.

'He was not the most accomplished of dancers,' admitted Charlotte, smiling gently at her husband's childhood tutor, 'and now I understand why.'

'Curiously, while he could not retain the fixed moves of a country dance, I would, at times, observe him dancing, in his own particular mode, very happily and rather creatively, when my wife was playing the piano and he thought he was unobserved.'

'Indeed? I wonder what other talents he was hiding.'

'I would not call it a talent,' chuckled Mr Poulteney, 'but William learnt his own way of doing things. I could not be happier that he found someone like you, Mrs Collins. I was not sure that he would.'

Charlotte felt a deep stab of remorse. She felt oddly inclined to be open with this stranger, almost more than anyone else in the room. 'I have not been the wife I should have been, sir.'

Mr Poulteney did not enquire what she meant but only nodded, saying, 'None of us is perfect in our marriage. I doubt he was the perfect husband.'

Charlotte looked down but did not respond. She was shaking her head, tears in her eyes, 'But I – I was not ...' She struggled to continue.

Mr Poulteney took her hands then and said, 'Try not to dwell on what you were not, my dear, but on what you *were*. What I see from those here today is that you were loved by him. Do not underestimate the joy that can be found in bestowing your love on another. The boy I knew would never have expected such riches. It seems that he found happiness. That is no small thing. Perhaps you took longer to reach it. But were you able to find it, in the end?'

Through tears, she looked up at him and replied, truthfully, 'I was.'

It was the middle of the night. The doctor had gone home earlier that day, when Mr Collins had fallen into unconsciousness, but before he left, he had indicated to Charlotte what she already knew: that there was nothing to be done.

Charlotte had managed to fall into an uneasy sleep, kneeling on the wooden floor beside her husband's bed, her upper body slumped forward, with her head and arms resting on the mattress. The book she was reading to him had slipped from her hands and now lay open on the blanket.

Collins stirred a little, murmuring, waking her with a start. For the first time in two days, he opened his eyes a crack and appeared to show signs of understanding.

'William?' She raised herself up to sit on the edge of the bed, and took his hand, mindful that in his delirium of the last two days, his only fear had been that she was not with him. She leant over so he could see her more clearly and, through tears, smiled at him.

He attempted to return it and gave her hand the gentlest squeeze – just enough to show he was still there. He only looked at her; speech seemed beyond him. But she knew that he saw her and heard her.

She said, 'I am here.'

With that reassurance, he closed his eyes, as if satisfied, and his breathing became at first more laboured, and then lighter and lighter until she could hardly detect it.

And then it came no more.

CHAPTER VII

In the days after the funeral, Charlotte made attempts to start sorting through her husband's belongings. And as she did so, she had the realisation that she might reasonably start packing away her own things at the same time.

Although Lady Catherine had months ago issued warnings about the precariousness of her position, Charlotte had not taken them to heart at the time. She had put them down to Lady Catherine's habit for meddling. But now that distant scenario she had spoken of had come to pass, and Charlotte was quite unprepared. Longbourn was entailed, strictly, down the male line – indeed, it was this quirk that had seen her husband inherit it. But now, with Mr Collins's passing and no male heir, Charlotte would have to quit it, and quickly, just as the Bennets had. She would have to uproot herself for the third time in as many years, but on this occasion, she had no clear picture of where or how she would live.

At a time when grief should have been her chief companion, she had no choice but to turn her mind, as so many widows did, to more material matters.

As she leafed through the papers on Mr Collins's desk, she found several unopened letters. She sat down heavily in his brown leather chair and began to open them, finding a couple that pertained to the running of the estate, another concerning a business interest of which she had no knowledge – and then there was the one was from Mr Smithson, which her husband had mentioned, still unopened.

She considered reading it — Mr Smithson's character had always inspired curiosity — but decided, on reflection, that whatever Mr Smithson had to say was his own affair. If the pair had shared any confidences, she did not wish to pry. She tore the letter in two and threw it in the fire.

She felt suddenly very weary. She looked at the remaining letters for Mr Collins, still unopened, and could not face them. She was worn out. She felt every one of her nearly thirty years, and many more besides.

She tried to be pragmatic, to stave off the cloud of exhaustion and loneliness that threatened to overcome her. She took a piece of paper and a pen and started to write. The list she made comprised the following:

Lucas Lodge
New heir?
Pemberley?
Rosings?

Going through her list one point at a time, she considered her options.

Lucas Lodge. She knew that her parents would, of course, allow her to live there again; that was the most likely, most expected future for her now. She would return to her old bedroom and, like old times, go to assemblies with her mother. But now, her mother would no longer attempt to introduce her to eligible men. That chapter would be closed.

What she looked ahead to now was a life more akin to that of a spinster: she would stay with her parents until such time as her father passed, when she would need to rely on her brother's generosity for further lodgings. None of it appealed. The fact of it being such a direct backward step made this perhaps the most galling of all her options.

New heir. She had not yet heard from the attorney about the next heir to Longbourn, but she presumed she would any day now. It might be that he would bestow a small settlement on her, in acknowledgement of her situation – as Mr Collins had offered to Mrs Bennet. Even a small amount would help. She was not lacking in friends, but she was sorely deficient of independent means.

Pemberley. She knew Pemberley to be a vast estate, and Elizabeth would want to be of service however she could. She wondered whether there might be a room for her – perhaps a little cottage left empty … But now she thought about it, the idea was absurd. Pemberley was a family seat; Elizabeth had just given birth to their first child and would likely have more. They had Kitty and Georgiana already. No, it was not sensible.

She crossed it off the list.

Finally, *Rosings.* This seemed, even to her own mind, preposterous, but something gave her pause. Of all the people of her acquaintance, it was Lady Catherine who seemed to care most deeply about the plight of women – and to most ardently desire their independence. She had been very fond of Mr Collins, and she seemed to care about Charlotte – even if she displayed it rather harshly. Could Charlotte become a companion to her, if Anne should marry? It was all rather wild thinking, but Charlotte's situation required imaginative thought.

Charlotte was struck suddenly by a headache. There was too much to think about, and the idea of making such enquiries left her nauseous. She called for Brooke and asked for tea.

'Might you go and stay with your mother, madam? For a few days? You need not face all this yet, surely?'

Charlotte considered it. 'No,' she said eventually. 'I do not have much time left in this house, Brooke, and I do not intend to squander it.'

'It is such a shame, madam. You have just settled in. It is a beautiful house, and you have made it your own.'

Charlotte could only nod. She would never have anywhere of 'her own' again.

'Well, it is a large house, and it is rather wasted on just me. It deserves to be better populated, does it not? Perhaps the new heir will have a wife and a family.'

'Perhaps,' said Brooke, smiling sadly as she left the room.

25th September 1813

My dearest friend,

I am so sorry for your loss. I wish I were with you. I can hardly believe how quickly he was taken – what a cruel fate for him, and for you. How fortunate for him to have had you with him. He loved you, Charlotte, and you brought him great happiness. I only wish you could find the same happiness. I pray you do not give up on it.

You will have heard that we have a daughter, Sofia. She is wonderful. I want to tell you about her, but only when you are ready. I think of you daily.

Your loving friend,
Eliza

CHAPTER VIII

Mr Collins's study was becoming more of a home for Charlotte than she could ever have anticipated, it being a room she had barely visited when he was alive. As autumn progressed, she sat in it most days, occupying herself with correspondence and handling the estate as best she could, with the help of Mr Thacker, the steward. But it was also a place of leisure; here, she exchanged letters with Elizabeth, mostly about little Sofia. She was delighted to hear about her friend's happiness as a new mother, but that joy was tempered by a more complicated feeling – a familiar pang that always seemed to accompany news of other people's children.

She had begun to occasionally purchase *The Morning Chronicle* when she was in town, and she would sit in the study with a cup of coffee, reading the sections that most interested her. Her late husband's leather chair was too low for her, so she placed a cushion on it so she could sit more comfortably at the desk. She had found Mr Collins's university gown among his belongings and had taken to wearing it slung about her shoulders as she sat in the study. It was the right colour, after all, and it warmed her, in more ways than one. She bought new ink and paper and found herself surprised by how well-situated she was for the task of planning her future.

She wrote to Mr Noakes, their attorney, to enquire about the new heir to Longbourn, and she also wrote to Lady Catherine. She did not ask directly about the possibility of being housed at

Rosings – instead, her first action was to ask about Anne's situation, as this information would indirectly influence her own.

As days passed without a response to her letters, it seemed increasingly likely that Charlotte would follow the expected route and return to Lucas Lodge. She would have to sell the little furniture that was her own, and many possessions besides; her belongings could not all be accommodated at her parents' house. To help herself organise, she had tied a piece of ribbon onto each bit of furniture or object which would have to go. She took to walking through rooms on a kind of farewell tour of these items, saying a silent goodbye.

But then, she started a more pleasant habit – noting instead the belongings that she would keep with her: her embroidery basket; her pressed flowers; Mr Collins's Bible; her poetry books; the emerald ring her mother had given her; the blanket Mrs Brooke had knitted for a cot; and the picture that Mr Poulteney had brought her on the day of the funeral: a framed pencil drawing of some foxgloves, intricately sketched and carefully preserved. She would not part with that.

Sometimes, when a chapter of one's life closes, there is the sense of the next one beginning, to help pull one through it. And yet for Charlotte, the prospect of returning to her childhood home – now widowed, with no means and without the hope of love or marriage – held none of the novelty of a new beginning. It merely felt like rereading an old chapter of her life, but with the book rather worn and the ink faded.

One morning in the first week of October, a month after her husband's passing, she heard a rigorous knock at the front door. Charlotte arranged herself, standing up as Brooke showed a gentleman she did not recognise into the sitting room. 'Mr Noakes, madam.'

'Oh! Mr Noakes, our attorney? I am glad to meet you.'

Mr Noakes was a serious, rather nervous-looking man of around fifty. He was almost entirely bald and wore small glasses. He bowed, and Charlotte gestured for him to sit.

'Good morning, Mrs Collins. I hope I am not troubling you too much – I am most sorry for your loss – but I am here about the entail.'

'Yes! I am glad; I have been waiting to hear. You need not be concerned, for I have been preparing myself for the transition.'

'I received your letter.'

'Good,' said Charlotte, wondering why he looked a little perturbed.

Mr Noakes frowned, pausing before saying, 'It led me to think you did not receive the letter from me. That is why I am here.'

'Oh, did you send a reply? It did not reach me?'

'Er, it was not a reply, but I sent it, er, around 16th September.'

Charlotte blinked, taken by surprise. 'Oh. But that was so soon after—'

'Indeed. I was informed by Dr Barton about Mr Collins's tragic end, and so I acted quickly, assuming you would want to know where you stood as soon as might be.'

'That was even before the funeral. I was in rather a stupor, as you can imagine.'

'Oh, of course, I understand,' said Mr Noakes, looking very uncomfortable with the conversation veering into the emotional. 'If it has been lost …'

'Oh, one moment,' cried Charlotte.

She quickly rose and went to Mr Collins's study, finding the pile of letters she had abandoned days after his funeral. She leafed through them now, spotting one – poorly written – that was addressed not to Mr Collins but to Mrs Collins.

Taking it, she returned to the sitting room, tearing the envelope open. 'Found it! My apologies. Shall I read it now?'

Mr Noakes craned over to look at the two sheets she had in her hand, then pointed at one of them. 'This one, if you please.'

25th March 1813

My dear Charlotte,

I have instructed my attorney, Mr Noakes, to keep this and give it to you in the event of my passing – which, by God's grace, will be many years from now.

It is a good time to put my affairs in order; there is a great deal of decision-making to undertake now Longbourn has passed to me, and you will receive from Noakes the particulars of all that in due course. (By due course, I mean instantly, alongside this letter – it should all be within the same envelope, God willing.) These affairs turn my thoughts to you and your future – both the one shared with me and that which you may live after I have gone – for that is the very foundation upon which all these decisions rest, the reason for their being.

If I am gone – as I must presume I am, should you now be reading this (what a curious enterprise this is!) – then I will take the opportunity to say what I, alas, could never say to you in person.

When first we met, I confess I took considerable pride in my powers of expression – in having just the right thing to say to the right person, and in my studied aptitude for giving small compliments. Since our marriage, I have come to realise that I do not have the gift for flattery that I thought I possessed, and in your company, I have more than once been lost for words. I should like to explain the reason for this, which is, in fact, twofold.

Firstly, because you see me with an insight that is both piercing and rare. I have felt your cool eyes appraising me – not always fondly, I have been aware, but always fairly. Of all things, you take the time to see me and know me, and I have felt grateful for it but unable to put on any pretence. I have felt, at times, unequal to you: your wisdom, your eloquence and your grace. But then, I knew I had uncovered a hidden jewel almost as soon as when we first met. (I am sure you are sighing at such an artful phrase even as you read this.)

I have also been struck dumb, because how can I give you small, trivial compliments when the entirety of what you mean to me is so vast? How can I extol the particular shade of your hair, when your company brightens all my days? How can I compare your eyes to the colour of sea, when your counsel has led my life to be a better one? Flattery has become purposeless in the wake of what you have given me.

I know not yet whether we will be granted children in time to come. But, from where we presently stand in life, it seems not unlikely that we shall remain without. God saw fit to take one from us before it even drew breath, and He has not, as yet, seen fit to bless us with another. But I look at how good He has been to me, to bring me you, and I cannot make any complaint. I wish for your sake that I could have given you a family, but I thank you for carrying the child we had. And I pray for our future.

Longbourn is ours now, according to the entail, and I look forward to many happy years in it, by your side. If by some unhappy circumstance, those years are curtailed, I do not wish you to meet the same unhappy fate as Mrs Bennet and her daughters. Fortunately, it is within my power to ensure it does not. Mr Noakes will explain the details, but let me assure you, you will have a home here for your life.

For as much of that time as is with me, I will endeavour to make your life one of contentment and to keep you in comfort and at peace. For any years that remain after I am gone, I hope you find happiness.

I am more proud than I can tell you to have you as my wife, Mrs Collins.

Your most loving husband,
William

CHAPTER IX

Tears fell onto the page Charlotte was holding, causing the ink to run. Mr Noakes was rather alarmed by this, quickly fetching a handkerchief from his pocket and dabbing at the letter. 'We, er, we do have a copy, but it would be better if, er—'

But Charlotte held the letter to her heart, ushering Mr Noakes away. She suddenly wished he were not here in this moment – such a message should have been received in private.

Her grief at Mr Collins's passing had been accompanied by several smaller sorrows: for his suffering, for the swiftness of his decline, for the home they had created and would now lose, and for all that had gone unsaid. The manner of his death had robbed him of the chance to speak to her before he passed and left her no time to make her peace with him. But, with this, she had something like a goodbye from him – and she treasured it.

Mr Noakes's hand was hovering near her letter, desperate to return it to a place of safety – a wallet or a folder of some sort. She would not hand it over, but she did dry her eyes. She read it again, this time with greater concentration on its substance and less shock at hearing from its author.

When she had recovered herself, she said soberly, 'I am grateful for the letter, but I do not understand what it means. How can Longbourn be mine when it is entailed down the male line?'

Mr Noakes adjusted his glasses. 'Yes. Well, put simply, your husband was able to bar the entail.' Charlotte looked at him, entirely dissatisfied with that response.

'I do not wish to overwhelm you with details', he continued. 'You only need be assured that—'

'Pray, indulge me, Mr Noakes, in explaining further. I am keen to go forth with a better understanding of my own affairs.'

With a resigned sigh, he said, 'The estate *is* entailed but was also under a strict settlement; it is that—', he took out an age-worn document from his satchel and handed it to her, '—it is *this* which rendered Mr *Bennet*'s position so immovable – he was only ever a life tenant of Longbourn and, as I told him several times, when he applied to me, "there is nothing to be done!"'

Mr Noakes was warming to his task and now delivering the information with some aplomb.

'But,' he continued, 'the strict settlement was binding for four generations and your husband was …'

He paused, relishing the theatre of the moment. Charlotte imagined such opportunities were rare in his profession. But she was impatient.

'The fourth?' she proffered.

'Indeed,' replied Noakes, slightly crestfallen. 'And so your husband became tenant in tail and was in a far stronger position to …' he paused again, choosing words he thought she would understand, 'to change his fate.' He smiled here, relieved to have reached an elegant conclusion.

Charlotte blinked. 'When did he do this?'

'Oh, he first enquired about the matter quite some time ago. Before Mr Bennet's death.' The attorney stiffened a little, before adding, 'I rarely say this, but it was a pleasure to be of service to your husband; I found him very agreeable, and unusually well prepared. He took to it all with an academic rigour. He rarely required …' he looked dolefully at her, 'explanation.'

Charlotte was undaunted by his disapprobation, her thoughts more gladly occupied by his former statements.

'Thank you, Mr Noakes. Is there anything for me to do?'

He shook his head a little wearily, gathering his papers.

'And ... I can stay?'

Mr Noakes nodded, wiped his brow with his handkerchief and prepared to take his leave.

Charlotte lowered the letters to her lap, then let a breath escape her that was so large, she thought she must have been holding it for six weeks. Longbourn was hers. Her house. Her home.

After Mrs Brooke had shown out Mr Noakes, she turned to find Charlotte standing in the hall, her face ruddy with joy.

'I can stay, Mrs Brooke! *We* can stay here!'

Mrs Brooke, overjoyed to see her mistress so elated, took both Charlotte's hands in hers. 'Oh, madam! May I fetch some champagne?'

'Only if you will join me.'

With a wink, Brooke bustled away to the cellar.

Charlotte began walking around the house, admiring each room and all her belongings. In Mr Collins's study, she stroked his brown leather chair, which had come to mean so much to her in recent days. With great pleasure, she untied the ribbon from one of its arms, removing it with a satisfied flourish, before starting on the rest of the house.

In the weeks that followed, Charlotte kept busy; it was time for her to start learning how to run an estate – a daunting undertaking, certainly, but she was very glad to reflect on the example Lady Catherine had set when this felt difficult. She had help from the steward; Mr Thacker offered to run the estate almost entirely himself, without her involvement, but she declined – she wanted to be useful. While this was a change for him, and a surprise, he was glad to have a mistress who cared about the estate, and they found they worked well together. She became known to her tenant farmers, as well as those in the village of Longbourn and many in Meryton. She enjoyed the sociability it afforded her; she was meeting and befriending more people than ever, at a time when that was just what she needed.

To all outward appearance, Charlotte seemed very well. She was cheerful and talkative, singing out in church and inviting friends to dine. She walked a great deal – and fast. Considering how much her home meant to her, she was out of it a great deal. Someone who knew Charlotte very well might have noticed that she did not make room for solitude as she used to; the peace of sitting and reading a book in the quietness of her home was no longer attractive to her. When she went to assemblies and card parties, she was the last to leave. Instead of gardening by herself, she spent her time arranging flowers at the church. Instead of reading poetry in the parlour, she sat in the study and wrote letters. To all who met her, she would have seemed a contented, even buoyant, woman: always busy, often smiling, her recovery remarkable and complete.

But in truth, Charlotte was not herself. She felt very alone. The solitude that she had always thought she longed for was no longer her friend, and that unsettled her.

As she sat in the study one December morning, reading a newspaper, the black gown across her shoulders to ward off the chill, Mrs Brooke entered with the post.

'A bundle, here, madam,' she said, handing Charlotte a stack of envelopes tied together with string.

Charlotte looked at the bundle quizzically, and untied the string. It was unusual to receive so many letters at once. The top one stood out – crisp, clean, addressed in elegant handwriting. The rest were rather crumpled and dirty, clearly written by another hand. They were all unopened.

She picked up the top letter and began with that.

15th December 1813

Dear Mrs Collins,

Forgive my belated reply to your last letter. I have had a great deal to occupy me of late. Anne is to marry soon, and I have had various issues to contend with. When two great estates unite, it is both a blessing and a curse – there is much to consider. I have great hopes Lord Chartwell will eventually agree they should settle at Rosings. His home, though sizable, and of a good lineage, is in Wiltshire, which, as I am sure you will agree, is not suitable. I do hope he will be sensible – I trust that Anne will be able to work on him, if she has learnt anything from her mother.

To the main purpose of my writing: I enclose some items that ought to belong to you. They were sent to Hunsford parsonage, but because that house sits empty, they were redirected to Rosings. I have kept them here. I have not opened them, but I recognised the handwriting on the address. I do not doubt that you will understand my reasons for keeping them from you but I hope you will understand why I now feel it is time for you to have them. I judged it all as best I could, and I hope it is for the best – or that it may be, in the future.

I hear that you are now mistress of Longbourn. I am very glad of it. If you ever need advice about the estate, I am willing to bestow it. But I do not think you require it.

Yours sincerely,
Lady Catherine de Bourgh

15th March 1813, Portsmouth

Dear Charlotte,

I write to you from the offices of the harbour in Portsmouth. You might laugh to see my state at present: quite far from the smart soldier you met at Rosings a year ago. I have been here waiting for a ship for some days, but until I am called to it, my time is my own. Therefore, I have let my whiskers grow long, and I have no access to a bath: I am aware I look and probably smell somewhat like a pirate, albeit a pirate with little gusto and sadly lacking in treasure. For now, I am taking advantage of the luxury – or, more accurately, the curse – of having no one to impress.

Forgive me, Charlotte, for writing to you. I know that you wished for silence between us, for both our sakes. I want to obey you. I want to make our parting as easy as it can be for you, but I feel like I cannot breathe, cannot think, without speaking to you, even if that speech is unanswered. I see things every day that I want to tell you of. I meet people whom I wish to introduce to you. I imagine you by my side, often. If it sounds as though I am losing my senses, I do think it is possible. Being here, on the edge of the land, alone, awaiting a journey that takes me back to hell, can drive a man a little mad.

The lady who runs my lodgings reminds me of my aunt, except that she has an income of about ten shillings a week (most of those mine). She is marvellously pompous – but pomposity sounds much better in the Hampshire accent. She disapproved of me at first, but I think I have improved in her esteem the last few days. She asked if I were running away from something, and I told her no. She didn't believe me.

I have never been much of a scribe, but I think about Parker and missed opportunities. I do not intend to miss one again. And after all, not even the French can stop me writing a letter.

I hope the ship comes soon; although I am loath to travel farther from you, I have been in limbo since we parted, and I sicken of waiting for the next chapter. I think of you every moment.

Yours, always,
RF

16th April 1813, Lisbon

Dearest Charlotte,

We arrived at the port of Lisbon yesterday. It is as dirty and crowded and noisy as I remember it, and I greeted it like an old friend – an old friend whom you would not wish to see too often. It is run down but it still thrives: traders, labourers, soldiers, gentry, bustle in the streets, and if I wished to, I could attend a card party every day and a ball every night. It will not surprise you to know; I do not wish to.

I must look a little more like a colonel now and try to behave as one. With every salute and paper signed and route decided, I feel myself transforming once more into a soldier. I do not find the satisfaction in it that I once did, beyond the unimaginative relief of a return to the familiar. And yet even my jacket does not feel like a good fit any more. I used to find comfort in the manners of the army, in the rough company of men away from home, in the simplicity of being told where to go and whom to point a musket at. I asked to return because I hoped to find comfort in that once again. I do not thus far. I only find comfort in remembering you.

I know it is foolish to write, and a risk – to you, not to myself. I have always seen the threat I pose to your reputation and your future, even if I could not find the strength to break it off with you. But you, Charlotte, always stronger than I, did.

You asked me once what point there was in being together since our future was already written. I wish now that I had said to you: it is not written. It is not easy, but it is not without any choice. I should have said, 'Let us go, now, away from here! Together.' I wish I had fought harder for you.

Yours, always,
RF

10th May 1813, Freineda

Dear Charlotte,

Are you well? A small question, but the only one that occupies my mind of late. I sincerely hope you are thriving. I know you cannot tell me how you fare, and so I must imagine your answer. It is May, which suits you well, for I know you do not like the full heat of summer. You will be spending much time out in your garden in Hunsford, dirtying your hands and tending your flowers. St Thomas's will be beautifully decorated by your hand, spring blooms everywhere. When I think of you these days, it is surrounded by flowers and in that white dress you wore at the Rosings ball. It is hard to imagine that colour out here — everything is stained with orange dust.

It has been an arduous journey from Lisbon to Freineda — some 220 miles. I travelled on horseback with two other senior officers — one returning from leave, the other from an injury like myself — all of us ordered to Headquarters to receive our command. We found the horses in Lisbon, but I think we were conned — mine went lame halfway, and after making the poor thing struggle on most of the way, I got off to walk the last few miles. My uniform got rather worn from that, and I repaired it with any fabrics I could find locally. But I am here now, safe if weary, a patchwork soldier with a useless horse. I do not know what I will do with him. I rather like him — a chestnut Arab with white socks. I have called him Achilles, as it was his heel that let him down. I don't think I can stomach letting him go. Perhaps he will rally in time for our departure.

Wellington has now given me my command — I'm to lead a brigade, and I have been introduced to them. I was impressed. They have been drilled relentlessly through the winter, and any one of them is ten times the soldier I was when I first came out.

Three nights past, when I was in company with some junior officers, they asked me whether I have anyone back home — and I told them yes. I know this is not true, not any longer, but it cheers them — and me — to think it. I did not offer a name — only the letter C — but it became a game, and when one of them guessed it, I nearly spat out my drink. To hear your name spoken by another is strange indeed. Your name does not belong out here, in the heat and the dust, spoken by a rough tongue. I regretted even allowing them your initial.

I do not really think now that you are reading these letters. I write them to keep me sane, to keep me attached somehow to England, to home, to what I love.

I love you still. Oh, how I love you! As I march beneath the hot sun, I think of that smile — when it breaks free, it captures me entirely. And I think of your skin, so pale the sun glances of it like diamond. And when alone, at night, I think of your bare shoulders, the angle of your hip, ~~the sounds you made~~

I miss your company, your laughter and your spirit. And your lips. Forgive me. I am surrounded by men, none of them very pretty.

Unless we move soon, I will write again while I am here.

Yours, always,

RF

7th June 1813, Palencia

My dear Charlotte,

As I write, the sun is setting over the river Carrión, and there is a relative calm in the camp. If I walk to the perimeter and look out onto the expanse of open land to the west — and close my ears to the chatter of thousands — I can almost imagine I am here at my leisure, as part of a belated Grand Tour. It is rather beautiful: the blue skies, green hills and river sweeping through the valley. And yet I how I yearn for a cloudy sky and the middling climate of England.

Do you recall telling me once that, if you had your choice, you would run more and dance less? Where would you run? I had a dream last night that you ran to me here. I saw you in the distance, dressed in green, your hair loose over your shoulders, a tiny figure, getting closer and closer to me. But just as you arrived and I was about to catch you, you were shot down from behind.

I am sorry to describe such an image. Will I shock you? I do not think that I will. You were always able to stomach the truths of war. You were never afraid. I am afraid.

The men know something will happen soon — it must. We have the French on the run; we outflank them in numbers, in readiness. Some are excited, some resigned, some filled with bravado, desperate for victory. I hope I can lead them as they deserve, despite my mind being so far from here. Battle will be a much-needed sharpener, when it comes, bringing blood back to the limbs and away from the heart.

You said you would dance less, but I recall holding you at the ball, one arm threaded behind your back, and your other hand clutching my own. How proud I was to stand up with you. I fear, had we had the chance of a life together, I would invite you to dance more than you would like.

I will write again when I may.

Yours, always,

RF

23rd June 1813, Vitoria

My darling Charlotte,

It is done. I am just now finding the strength to write. The day of battle began strangely; a misty, grey morning, rather than the sunshine we have been used to. It was a complicated strategy — Wellington really is to be admired. We scoffed at first, but his elaborate plan was successful: a division into four columns—

I must halt myself. I am writing as if I just came home to you after finishing some business or other, sitting at our table and relating the particulars of my week and asking you for your counsel. What an idea that is. Sharing our days together ... Allow me to pretend it for a while. Let us play that it has been a hard day, and I will tell you of it as if you were mine, and as if you were here, or I there.

We were with Wellington in the centre. My brigade advanced through the village of Nanclares, and after crossing the bridge at Villodas, we were, with great effort, able to drive the French from the hill. My men were among the final push, in the late afternoon, which finally caused the French to retreat. Once the order came down from Bonaparte, it was a spectacle. How they ran! They dropped their weapons, their baggage and scattered back towards Vitoria. It was so sudden – and then, it was done.

There is hope in the camp. We might be in France in a fortnight, and from there, our usefulness will be exhausted. We will be exhausted. Those of us who return.

I do not know what the end will bring. I might come home, for as much as that means. Do you remember the home we built together, one evening at Rosings? Vases on the mantelpiece, grounds that I might ride in – and chickens! You said I would live with my horse. Perhaps I will; perhaps it will be Achilles, if he will have me.

When I return, I know not what my life will be, but I will not try to disturb you. I do not want to bring you harm. But how I should wish to see you, even from afar. I wish only to look on you, if that is all I am afforded. When this is done, they will seek to commend us for the victories, but to see you again would be a greater reward than any medal.

I will write again after the next push.

I love you.

Yours, always,

RF

CHAPTER X

Charlotte, her heart racing and her face flushed, put down the letter and searched frantically for the next. She dug through the opened sheets that lay scattered across the desk, looking for another unopened envelope.

'Where are the others? Is this all?'

There was none. This was the last.

His last was dated June, six months ago. Lady Catherine would not have known the contents, or that he had promised to write again. Why had he not written again?

The first thought in her mind was not of remembered passions or of future romance but of a desperate need to know where and *how* he was.

Since February, Charlotte had lived with a strict discipline, locking away thoughts of Fitzwilliam. At first, they came often and painfully, but she buried them, busying herself until the thoughts came less frequently and with less pain. The apparent lack of contact from him was helpful. It was exactly what she had expected and what she'd told herself she wanted. Any disappointment she felt, she dismissed as foolishness. *Of course he would not write to you,* she had thought, on the rare occasions she allowed her mind to drift into such territory. *He is at war, and you broke with him with absolute certainty. With what hope might he have written after such a parting?*

But he had. He had found some hope for her. He had found enough hope to write again and again, with no encouragement and no reciprocation. And then, he had stopped. Why?

She reasoned that if he were injured, he would most likely have been staying with Lady Catherine; she would have at least been informed and would surely have told Charlotte in her letter. But if he were still in Spain, and alive, he would have written again. Or would he? He had received no reply from her, no encouragement. Was it so hard to believe that he would grow tired of a one-sided correspondence with much greater concerns all around him? If it were any other man, she would believe it – but in her heart, she could not believe it of him.

She wanted to act; to run, to push, to shake the answer from someone – but the only powers she had were to enquire and to wait. It all felt hopelessly slow.

Taking the only action she could think of, she grasped the latest – as yet unread – copy of *The Morning Chronicle*, lying on the desk. She turned the pages feverishly until she reached the casualty listings.

It was not the first time she'd scanned the listings, eyes searching and fearing to find his name. But, as with every time before this, it was absent. Neither was it in the reports of battle. The last engagement he had mentioned in his letter was back in June. When she thought of what her life was then, it seemed a world away. Was it June that her sister got engaged, or July? She thought of that hot day at Lucas Lodge, her father's delight, Maria's shyness. In thinking of her father, a thought was sparked.

She stood and, grabbing a shawl, walked briskly to the door.

'Copies of what?' asked her father, amiable but baffled by her sudden arrival.

'Copies of *The Gazette* – you keep them, do you not?'

'Yes, mostly. But why?'

'Please may I see them?' Charlotte did not ask but demanded, already marching to his study. He followed her meekly to find her looking around the room agitatedly.

With raised eyebrows, Sir William Lucas crossed the room and took out a large pile of papers from a cupboard.

Snatching them up, Charlotte riffled through the pages with a frantic, almost feverish urgency, until her hands found a copy dated 28 June. But in the reports from Spain and the casualty lists, there was no mention of his name. She took up the next – 30 June. Again, no mention.

Her father, a little confused and wary of her mood, left the room, suspecting and rather hoping that his task was done.

She repeated the process with copies from July. Vitoria dominated the stories until she found a copy where San Sebastián was mentioned. A defeat on 25th July. Might he have been there? It seemed possible. She scanned the lists – no mention. She continued on with speed until, finding a copy issued 20th September, her eyes alighted on an article of interest.

A letter from Lieutenant General Sir Graham Thompson to the Marquess of Wellington:

I have the satisfaction to report to your lordship that the castle of San Sebastián has surrendered. And I have the honour to transmit the capitulation which, under all the circumstances of the case, I trust your lordship will think I did right to grant a garrison which certainly made a very gallant defence.

Charlotte skimmed the rest of the article then, turning to the casualty list, scanned her now-practised eyes down the page.

All at once, the urgent energy that had sustained her so vigorously left her.

Introducing Mrs Collins

Return of Killed, Wounded and Missing of the Army serving under the Command of His Excellency Field-Marshal the Marquess of Wellington, K.G., in the Siege of the Castle of San Sebastián

From the 1st to the 8th September 1813:
1st Royal Scots – 1 captain killed; 1 rank and file wounded
Royal Artillery – 1 lieutenant, 2 rank and file wounded
38th Foot, 1st Batt. – 3 rank and file wounded
59th Foot, 2d Batt. – 1 rank and file killed, 1 rank and file wounded.
47th Foot, 3rd Batt. 1 rank and file wounded.

Name of officer killed:
1st Royal Scot – Captain James Stewart

Wounded:
Royal Artillery – Lieutenant Hugh Morgan, severely
4th Division – Colonel Richard Fitzwilliam, severely

And there, Charlotte's eyes closed.

10th December 1813

Dear Mr Darcy,

 I write to you with urgency. I have heard that your cousin Colonel Fitzwilliam was badly hurt in Spain in September, but I know nothing more than this. Do you know what his injury was? Have you heard from him? Where is he? Does he live? Please share with me anything you know, however small.

 If you wonder at my asking, I beg you to delay your questions until he is found. Please help.

 Yours,
 Charlotte Collins

13th December 1813

Dear Mrs Collins,

 I sent this out with a rider to meet the morning post, in order that it reach you swiftly. It is clear that you need to hear this news urgently, but I ask something of you: that you do not match that urgency in your response but proceed with some caution. What I have to tell you is not the worst news, but it is not what you would wish to hear. However, I can reassure you on one point: I know where he is.

 Colonel Fitzwilliam was indeed injured at San Sebastián, at the second siege. He suffered a bayonet wound to his shoulder, as well as a blow to the head, and more besides, not all from the enemy. It was a very bad business all round. He was very disaffected by how the siege played out, and there was more to recover from than merely bodily injury. He was sent to Tolbrooke Hall and was not well cared for there, receiving scant attention.

 By the end of November, he was desperate to leave that place and was sufficiently recovered to be able to do so, though barely. He wrote to ask me if he could stay at Pemberley, and I of course accepted. I was shocked by his appearance when he arrived; he looked very different – scarred certainly but also unkempt, verging on wild. But it is his demeanour that has changed the most; he is not the man you knew. He is plagued by memories of the siege. He is not up to company. He wakes in fits and spends his days in a dimmed room.

 I do not know his plans; I doubt he has any. He has improved a little since he arrived, but he has no wish to see anyone and has forbidden me to write to anyone of his whereabouts for the time being, and I have agreed thus far. (I break with him in telling you of this.)

 Mrs Collins, I do not know what is or was between yourself and my cousin, but I have suspected something in the past. If you can put any faith in my judgment, I ask you to do so now. He is no state to be to you again what he once was. I care deeply for him, and what I believe he needs is to live quietly, without disturbance, in peace. I do not believe that the renewal of whatever was between you will benefit him. I _know_ it will not benefit you.

But you must do as you see fit. I only ask for your careful consideration, and as I write this, I realise I need not ask it. I have benefited from your careful consideration in the past; I have no doubt it is still your way.

Yours sincerely,
F. Darcy

CHAPTER XI

Charlotte would read the letter several times. The first was on the doorstep of Longbourn, after snatching it from the postmaster's grip. She had consumed it quickly, hungrily, her eyes only truly absorbing the words: *I know where he is*, and *Pemberley*.

Charlotte retreated to the hall, pacing quickly, and called out for Brooke. Her immediate future was clear to her: she would have the carriage readied and her trunk packed. She would wear her old green dress and the emerald ring with the ouroboros and style her hair loosely as she knew he liked it. She would get into the carriage and order the coachman to drive fast, and they would rattle down the country roads, heading towards Pemberley, and the beginning of something new.

'Yes, madam?'

As Brooke stood in front of her in the hall, Charlotte hesitated before issuing her instructions.

'Are you well, madam? Is that news of your friend?'

Mrs Brooke observed her mistress now, the letter clutched in her hand, and wondered at what it contained. She had a clearer idea of its subject than Charlotte might have guessed – servants often possess a knack for learning things that would surprise their employers. Of course, Mrs Brooke had met the colonel before on his visits to Hunsford, and she was aware that Charlotte and he had taken a carriage together to Pemberley. On their return, she had noticed Charlotte's frequent absences from the house – curiously long walks on such cold days. She had noticed Charlotte's mood change during those months, how her tastes were bolder, her steps lighter. And then, she had seen the letter, tucked into a poetry book – seen and read it, before carefully replacing it.

She was not the sort to judge; she had seen enough of life to know that you cannot understand other people's hearts. But she had been relieved when they moved, and with everything Charlotte had faced since, Brooke had felt proud of how she had handled it all.

When the bundle of letters from Lady Catherine had arrived, Charlotte had confided in Mrs Brooke only that they were from an old friend fighting in the war and that she was concerned for him. Brooke, rather daringly, had asked her if they were from Colonel Fitzwilliam – and that, with surprise at her intuition, Charlotte had confirmed.

'Is it good news, madam?' Brooke pressed her now.

Charlotte made as if to answer in the affirmative but then stopped. 'Not entirely,' she offered in its stead.

Brooke waited while Charlotte read the letter again, this time more slowly. *Careful consideration* – that is what Darcy had asked of her. That was something she was able to give.

Folding the letter, she said, 'He is not dead. So that is something.'

Brooke nodded. 'Do you need me for anything, madam?'

Charlotte paused. 'Forgive me – I think I will retire to my room.'

Sitting on her bed, she read the letter a third time – and she would read it again by dim candlelight before bed – the implications of it turning new cogs in her brain each time.

Her happiness at his survival was quickly surpassed by her grief at what had befallen him. At first, she resisted Darcy's advice to leave him be; after all, he did not know the depth of their connection, nor did he understand Fitzwilliam as she did. How could he be sure what would be to his benefit? Surely, Fitzwilliam would improve upon seeing Charlotte. Surely, she was exactly the tonic he needed.

But as she thought more and reread the letter, she began to concede. It was Darcy, after all, who had known his cousin all his life, and it was Darcy who had seen his current state.

She cast her mind to the lowest point in her own life – when she'd lost her baby and, with it, some part of herself. In the aftermath, she had wanted nothing but space to grieve and to recover. She'd had no space in her mind for complicated feelings, not even for her husband, whom she could not comfort; she had shied away from a constricting sense of obligation and guilt at having denied him a child. She had not wished to see Elizabeth, disliking her own feelings of envy for her friend's happy situation, and scorning any unwanted pity. And she had certainly had not a thought of seeing Fitzwilliam. The idea of romance, of love, of deception or regret, would have been all too, too complicated. It was not what she had needed. What she had needed was to find her way back to herself, on her own. And she had.

She pictured Fitzwilliam as Darcy described him: scarred, dishevelled, unsmiling. She then thought of Pemberley, vast and quiet, offering him space and refuge. She imagined him there, among the grounds he had loved, with his oldest friend and hers – with the cheerful company of Kitty, Georgiana and Eliza's delightful baby. She thought and thought until her brain ached and sleep overtook her, the letter still clutched in her hand.

By morning, when she awoke, the candle had burnt down to the quick, and she was still in her day dress. She rose, folded the letter and placed it carefully in her drawer. She splashed her face, smartened her hair, adjusted her black dress, made her way to the study, and wrote a reply – after *careful consideration.*

CHAPTER XII

'Beware, beware – Mr Cardew approaches,' Mrs Thacker whispered into Charlotte's ear.

They stood together in one corner of the assembly room in Meryton, Mrs Thacker in a vibrant blue dress and Charlotte in her black. She had been a widow for nearly six months and had become rather comfortable in her mourning attire. She held up her fan to hide her smile and shushed her companion.

A confident, dark-haired man of around thirty stopped in front of them – tall, thin and very well dressed. He bowed low and for too long – long enough that Charlotte almost asked if he were quite well.

As he rose, he set his eyes squarely on Charlotte. 'A pleasure to see you again, Mrs Collins.'

'And you, sir. Pray, how are you settling in?'

'Very well, I thank you. Meryton has much to offer, and business is brisk, but the change of pace from London is welcome. I must say, you are looking very well indeed, Mrs Collins.'

Both Charlotte and her companion's eyebrows rose at this impertinence, given her situation.

But the truth was, Charlotte had never looked better.

In the last few months, once recovered from the first sharp shock of loss, Charlotte had steadily bloomed. It seemed, even to her, rather inappropriate, but it was hard to deny. Her complexion had evened, her hair grown fuller, and a little added weight gave her a softer, more becoming shape; her countenance, too, was calm and content. Combined with her new position as the mistress of Longbourn, this made her a most eligible prospect for marriage among the gentry of Hertfordshire – and any man of sense would not wait until her mourning period had ended to start paying court.

Mr Cardew was such a one: an ambitious barrister, recently moved to town. With his eyes on a good prospect, he had met Charlotte before – and seemed rather taken.

'I hope I may tempt you to dance the next?' he asked.

'A rather bold hope, Mr Cardew. I am sure you know that it would not be proper for me to dance. But, considering the number of young ladies here, I am sure you will not have to look far for a partner.'

'I will settle for an inferior partner for now, Mrs Collins, but I must say that I look forward to dancing with you on a future date.'

Charlotte could think of little to say that was not blatantly rude. She had no intention of promising him any future dances, so she settled for: 'The future is such a long way away.'

He looked a little confused, it not occurring to him that he was being rejected. Instead, he took his leave and made his way across the room to a Miss Long, who had no idea she was a consolation prize.

'He is relentless!' said Mrs Thacker, when he was out of hearing. 'But you must admit he is quite handsome,' she added with a grin.

'Is he?' Charlotte appraised him from afar. 'Is he not rather too neat? And so cleanly shaven – I prefer a man who has struggled against his razor.'

Her friend laughed. 'Do you indeed? I learn more about you every day.'

Mrs Collins and Mrs Thacker had become good friends since the fate of Longbourn had been settled. Mr Thacker had been so patient in teaching Charlotte the ways of estate management that she had warmed to him immensely. Through him, she had naturally come to know his wife, and they had instantly become friends. Mrs Thacker, close to Charlotte in age, was Mr Thacker's second wife; they had a young son together, along with a daughter from his first marriage, Amelia, who was just recently out and present that evening.

'Amelia is all a-flutter for someone already,' confided Mrs Thacker.

'Oh really? But she is full young to settle! I hope it will pass. Who is it?'

'Oh, a soldier in the militia, of course.'

'Inevitable. He will likely move on soon, so perhaps that will fade.'

'It does not always,' said Mrs Thacker, with a sigh.

'Oh, I know. Just look at my sister.'

Charlotte meant the invitation literally; Maria and Mr Denny were across the room, dancing together and looking as much in love as any engaged couple ever had. They made for a very handsome pair.

'Thankfully, Maria was still in love with him even when he was out of his regimentals,' said Charlotte.

'Perhaps the prospect of him being out of his regimentals was a large part of the attraction,' said Mrs Thacker, raising an eyebrow.

'Mrs Thacker!' Charlotte exclaimed, unable to keep herself from laughing – then she caught the sound and stopped quickly; it was not decorous for her to be seen guffawing while still in mourning.

And a good thing to, for just then, they were descended upon by two ladies of around fifty with alarming coiffures – rather too many plaits and curls for one head, let alone two. Without so much as a how-do-you-do, one of these ladies swept in with, 'I see you are well, Mrs Collins – and that you know the new Mrs Thacker.'

'Mrs Bennet, what a pleasure to see you! And Mrs Philips, of course,' said Charlotte, more warmly than she felt. 'Yes, Mrs Thacker and I have become good friends. You yourself must know Mr Thacker very well.'

'Oh yes! Of course, *long* before you knew him, Mrs Collins. Our acquaintance stretches back for over twenty years!' Mrs Bennet replied with irritation, even though Charlotte had already conceded the superior acquaintance to her.

Mrs Philips then picked up the conversation, saying to Mrs Thacker, 'What a beauty Amelia is!'

Mrs Thacker smiled warmly. 'Thank you; she is indeed.'

'So much like her mother,' Mrs Philips continued.

'So I have heard,' returned Mrs Thacker, smiling beatifically.

Mrs Bennet, recognising a successful parry when she saw one, turned to re-engage her own sparring partner. 'You appear to be rather *popular* at present, Mrs Collins; it must be a novel sensation for you. It looked at one point as if you might stand up for a quadrille!'

'I have no intention of dancing tonight, Mrs Bennet.'

'But you *have* been asked,' she said accusingly.

'Yes.'

'You are looking very *well*, Mrs Collins,' Mrs Bennet continued, with evident disapproval.

'Spring agrees with me.'

'I imagine Longbourn agrees with you?' she snapped back.

'It does, thank you,' replied Charlotte calmly. 'I am very appreciative of it, and I hope I prove a worthy steward.'

Mrs Bennet managed to look mollified, albeit grudgingly so. Casting around for another area in which to be belligerent, she said, 'I suppose you have not yet met Sofia? My granddaughter, Sofia Darcy! What a fine thing.'

Charlotte tried not to betray her inward sigh. 'I have heard all about her from Eliza, and I could not be happier for them all. I will meet Sofia in May.'

Mrs Bennet's face fell once again into annoyance. 'May? Why?'

'Elizabeth is coming to visit me at Longbourn, with Sofia.'

Mrs Bennet turned puce. 'Coming to Hertfordshire, and she has not yet informed her *own mother*! That is just like Lizzy. That girl! And she would not think that I would like to perhaps see my own granddaughter? No indeed. She comes to see *you*!' She muttered a few more objections before Charlotte could attempt any consoling.

'I am sure she is coming to see you chiefly, but she consulted me first as I can more easily provide accommodation,' offered Charlotte.

Mrs Bennet looked rather pleased with the idea that Charlotte was more akin to a landlady in the arrangement. 'Well, you are probably right. At any rate, Sofia is a sweet little thing.'

'I am sure. You must be very proud.'

Once the sisters had taken their leave, Mrs Thacker said quietly to Charlotte, 'You are very patient with her. She positively goaded you.'

'I know, but ... consider her situation. She is a widow who has lost her home – the home in which she raised her five daughters – thanks to some old legal papers she has never even seen. I think I would be angry forever. And look at my situation – a widow, but with the other side of that coin. I have that home, thanks to those very same papers. I am the lucky one – so yes, I can bear her jibes.'

'Still, she has had luck of her own; some of her daughters have married very well!'

'Indeed! She is lucky in many ways. I would have liked a daughter. I'm not sure I would have wanted five, though ...' Charlotte meant the comment with levity, but it disquieted her friend.

'Yes, of course.' Mrs Thacker paused, before adding tentatively, 'You may have one yet?'

'I do not think so.' Charlotte looked at her friend with warmth, keen to ward off any pity. 'But I have other blessings to be thankful for. And I am well occupied, thanks to your husband.'

Mrs Thacker gave her a look of mock outrage, muttering, 'I beg your pardon!' and Charlotte once more laughed loudly, earning disapproving looks from Mrs Bennet and her sister.

CHAPTER XIII

Elizabeth emerged from the carriage with a red face and a fraught expression, handing a wailing infant to Charlotte with outstretched hands. Charlotte took the little girl, unsure of quite how to hold her; Sofia was bigger than expected and rather unwieldy. Elizabeth was followed by a maid with green-looking skin; both looked relieved to alight.

Elizabeth exhaled and, grinning ruefully at Charlotte, exclaimed, 'We are here! Quite a journey!'

The maid attempted a smile but, clearly suffering, begged to be excused and went inside with Mrs Brooke.

'Shall I take her back?' asked Elizabeth, arms out.

'Only if you wish to – we are comfortable enough now,' said Charlotte, and it was true; once she had worked out how not to drop the little girl, Sofia had stopped crying and seemed fairly content in her arms.

'Then I will not, and I will be grateful for it. This bodes well for my stay. You may have her whenever you wish,' Elizabeth said, grinning as she followed her friend into the house she knew so very well.

'Oh!' Elizabeth murmured as she entered, looking around. 'Oh! It is the same, but it is different. How lovely to be here!' She turned and embraced Charlotte, over Sofia's head, who made a gargle of objection. She was a charming little thing: red-cheeked and with a mop of unruly blonde hair.

'Oh, but I have not introduced you yet: Charlotte, meet Sofia; Sofia, this is Charlotte. I do hope you will be friends,' Eliza declared with exaggerated formality.

'I am sure we shall!' Charlotte craned her head back to observe Sofia's face more clearly.

Sofia regarded her, too, with serious eyes, forming a judgement of her. She looked very like her mother, but her current expression was all Darcy, Charlotte thought.

In the drawing room, Sofia crawled around, occasionally tumbling or pulling herself up into a wobbly stand like a tiny drunkard. Elizabeth filled Charlotte in on all that she had missed – which was, understandably, all about her daughter: her birth, her eating, her looks, her moods. Elizabeth leant into the difficulties and frustrations of motherhood, but it was clear from her face that she was exceedingly happy and proud.

'Only Darcy could have hired a nursemaid with such a weak stomach!' said Elizabeth, now recounting the journey they had just made. 'Honestly, I told him that I should just take Mrs Reynolds on this trip, but he said it is not her role and that the journey would be too hard on her. I wish he had seen how hard it was on Frances! She puked every third mile from Derbyshire to Dunstable.'

Charlotte laughed hard. 'Has Frances been Sofia's nursemaid since she was born?'

'No! She was hired for the trip and will likely stay on for a while, if this has not entirely put her off. We have not needed a dedicated nursemaid – which, as I am sure you can imagine, has shocked Lady Catherine out of her wits. But we have a very full household – so many staff! – including Mrs Reynolds, who adores Sofia. And then there are Georgiana and Kitty, who are also besotted, and even—'

Elizabeth stopped suddenly, quickly recovering herself before continuing, 'Even Mr Darcy agrees that a nursemaid is unnecessary, but he thought it wise to have one for this trip and was reluctant to spare Reynolds. God forbid those two should be parted. My goodness! It is sometimes like living with one's mother-in-law – if one's mother-in-law had seen you in your undergarments.'

Charlotte laughed. She was filled with joy – sitting in her own home, able to welcome her dearest friend to stay, chattering and joking like she had when they were girls.

'And what of your news? The last you wrote, you were being lectured by Mr Thacker?'

Charlotte chided her friend. 'Nonsense! I said no such thing. He has been so patient with me; I could not have done anything without his help.'

'He is a pleasant man,' Elizabeth conceded. 'And you know his wife, you said?'

'Yes! Jane – another Jane. She is very good company – but you must have met her?'

Elizabeth shook her head. 'I have not. Their marriage was still new when I was last at Longbourn and the occasion never arose. I knew the first Mrs Thacker. She was kind. She taught Jane – my Jane – and I to dance.'

'Mrs Thacker said she died when Amelia was but ten?'

'Yes. It was dreadful. Mr Thacker was …' She broke off. 'He could not be consoled, which was all the worse for him having a daughter to take care of.'

'But it seems he got through it. He is very happy now, I believe. You know they have a little son?'

Elizabeth smiled. 'I heard. I think the new Mrs Thacker, as my mother calls her, has worked miracles. For two years, he was hardly living, could not cope with his daughter and managed to do only the necessities of his work with Father. And then he met this lady, and overnight, he changed. I have often found it so; a broken man cannot rally without a woman beside him.'

'Is it not true the other way round?' pondered Charlotte.

'Not at all,' said Elizabeth, so immediately and with such conviction that it made Charlotte laugh.

Elizabeth continued on with her point. 'No, it is not the same. Look at you! You have rallied again and again, without the need of anyone beside you.'

Charlotte was rather taken aback by the sudden earnestness of her friend. She did not count herself as particularly strong or independent. But, by circumstance rather than choice, she supposed it must be conceded that she was.

She did not know what to say, so she smiled and collected up Sofia, who was grabbing at the top keys of the piano.

'That looks familiar,' Elizabeth said curiously.

'Oh, yes! It is from Rosings. Lady Catherine sent it to me at Christmas.'

Elizabeth made a face so incredulous that Charlotte had to laugh again. 'Darcy's aunt sent *you* a grand piano as a Christmas present?!'

'You need not be so very surprised. She was very fond of Mr Collins and I think has become quite fond of me. She said it was sitting going to waste in her house.'

'She has never given us a pianoforte!'

'You do not need a pianoforte! You already have – what is it, three?'

Elizabeth grinned. 'Well, I suppose it belongs with you – you are the only one of us all who can give it the life it deserves.' She touched a few keys idly, as her daughter banged a fist on it. 'But I must say Lady Catherine continues to surprise me.'

'There is a lot about her that you do not know,' said Charlotte, and then immediately regretted it.

Elizabeth, luckily, was entirely distracted by Sofia, who had just expunged a good volume of milky sick over Charlotte's settee.

The next day, Elizabeth went by carriage to visit her mother in Meryton, so Charlotte decided to drop into Lucas Lodge. Her mother greeted her with wide arms.

'How well you look.' And then, because she was her mother, after all, she added, 'But what are you wearing?'

'What do you mean? A dress!'

'But it is very severe for May, dearest! Must you really still be in black?'

'It is not black! It is grey.'

'Is it? Well, why are you in grey in May?'

'I am still in half-mourning, Mother. I can hardly walk around in a red petticoat!'

Lady Lucas gave in and led her wilful daughter into the house.

And yet, they clashed again over luncheon – a classic Lucas summer offering of rich lamb stew with buttered potatoes and green beans. Sir William had never experienced a light meal in his life and wouldn't permit one now. He quietly salted his meal, as his wife and daughter crossed words opposite him. He was not at ease with conversations of the heart during mealtimes – and certainly not before five o'clock.

'Is it so wrong to hope, Charlotte, that you might marry again? I do not hope it for myself – or for the satisfaction of society! But is it so impossible to think that it would make *you* happy? Mr Cardew is a handsome, respectable man, of about your age—'

'It will not be Mr Cardew, Mother – that much I guarantee.'

'Well, there are others in the town whom I believe have taken an interest.'

Charlotte sighed. She took a mouthful of lamb, chewed and swallowed it, while she decided how much to say. 'Mother, I have the great luxury of being content with myself and my situation. I would not risk that state for anything but the very greatest love, and I have not encountered that since—' Charlotte stopped, then corrected herself, 'I have not encountered that in Meryton.'

'When you married Mr Collins,' said Lady Lucas, proceeding carefully, 'I felt some sadness that you would not experience the ... thrill of a romance: the to and fro, the push and pull of courtship,

Introducing Mrs Collins

the fun of wondering and guessing – the drama, I suppose, of true love. That is what your father and I had, you know, at first.'

Sir William's eyes went round, and he silently skewered a potato.

'Your marriage ... Well, it was a very convenient match, and so' – Lady Lucas searched for the word – 'straightforward.'

Charlotte nodded. She was not offended.

Her mother took it as leave to continue. 'But that is why I so wish that you might find something different now. I do not say I am glad about poor Mr Collins's fate – I think he was a good husband to you – but I do not want you to shut yourself off. You might yet have that drama, that thrill.'

Charlotte thought for a moment, chewing again. The lamb was rather tough. She turned to face her mother. 'If it consoles you, then know this: I have felt some of what you describe. Do not ask me when or with whom, for I shall not tell you. I tell you only so that you may not mourn those things for me. But if you think I seek them now, you are mistaken. I do not wish to guess, nor to tease. I do not wish to chase, nor to evade. I do not wish for sport or riddles or to dance around it. When I next find love, I hope it simply walks towards me in a straight line.'

Lady Lucas listened well to her eldest daughter, her first-born – her favourite, in truth – and felt the quiet joy of truly understanding her. What she had just said was so very Charlotte, and she loved her for it.

'I am only glad,' she said, in a conciliatory tone, 'to hear you say, "next".' She patted Charlotte's arm over her grey linen sleeve, while Sir William studiously, and with great care, cut a single potato into twelve equal parts.

CHAPTER XIV

When it came time for Elizabeth and Sofia to return to Pemberley towards the end of May, Charlotte's heart was sore; they would leave such a gap, such a silence in her house. Even before they left, with the trunks packed and Sofia's gurgles quietened with sleep, the air felt cooler, thinner.

While final preparations were made for the journey, Charlotte and Elizabeth sat in the parlour, making idle chat, the way one does when procrastinating before an unwanted farewell.

'She has turned Georgiana into something of a gossip! But thankfully, they have nothing to gossip about – the county offers them little diversion, I fear,' said Elizabeth, putting her bonnet on.

'If Kitty wishes for a change of scene, she is always welcome to stay here,' offered Charlotte.

'I would not wish her upon you.'

'Eliza! You are too cruel!'

'No, I jest. She is a good girl. I will tell her – thank you.'

'And please send my best wishes to your husband.'

'I shall.'

Elizabeth tied her ribbons and stood up, preparing to leave, but Charlotte suddenly put an arm out and grabbed her wrist. Elizabeth looked down in surprise.

Speaking very quickly, as if to get her words out before she changed her mind, Charlotte asked, 'What of Colonel Fitzwilliam?'

Elizabeth's face shifted from surprise to resignation, as if she had been wondering if this moment would come. She sat again, carefully untying her bonnet.

'The coach is ready, madam,' Brooke called from the hall.

'We are a little delayed, Brooke. Please ask them to wait,' Charlotte called back. In the silence that followed, they listened to the sound of the coachman dismounting and muffled conversation in the hall.

'What do you wish to know?' Elizabeth asked, sombrely and a little coolly.

'Anything. Everything?'

Elizabeth's many thoughts and questions *and opinions* were visibly competing to be released, but she felt she owed Charlotte an answer at least, so she concentrated on delivering that first. She spoke slowly, choosing her words with deliberate economy.

'What of Colonel Fitzwilliam?' she echoed Charlotte's question. 'He was in very poor form when he first came to us. I did not know him. He did not speak, did not smile. He mostly stayed in his own quarters, and when he was present, he was … silent or gruff. I suppose we were rather afraid of him. And he saw that, which made it all worse – made him more reclusive.'

'Did his injuries ail him still?'

'Not really. He had been at Tolbrooke two months before coming to us, and physically, he was largely recovered. It was no longer his body that afflicted him. I know from what Darcy relayed that the siege was no ordinary battle. Colonel Fitzwilliam saw British soldiers behaving like animals – some of his own men, even, turned mad with it all – rioting, looting and worse; what some did to the women of the town …'

'Oh!' Charlotte muttered in shock.

'He felt as if his whole life had been for nothing; the army was a thing of disgust to him, so ashamed was he of his men and his part in it all.'

'Then, of course, he was lost,' Charlotte said, almost to herself. 'The army is all he has known since he was sixteen. It has been his home.'

Elizabeth looked at Charlotte curiously. 'Yes. But then, shortly before Christmas, something changed. He started to make an effort to recover. He began to venture out – into the grounds, attending meals. He cut his hair and, well, washed more – to be frank, the latter was appreciated by us all. It was slow progress, but it was a corner turned. He was trying. He enjoyed listening to the piano a great deal, and Georgiana was happy to oblige him. He would sit quietly, just listening to her play, saying nothing but clearly grateful. At this time, he also started to take an interest in Sofia, which pleased me and Darcy a great deal. He has been lovely with her, and she seems a balm to him. Her squalling has no impact on him, as if he does not hear it. I suppose he has heard much worse.'

As Charlotte considered this account, Elizabeth leant forward towards her greatest friend and asked the question she had longed to for months: 'Tell me, what was it between you?'

Charlotte blinked several times, trying to form an answer, before saying simply, 'Love. It was love.'

Elizabeth did not look very surprised, but she fixed her with a considered stare. 'You could have told me.'

'You know I could not,' said Charlotte quickly. 'I could not, while it was alive, and I would not, after it died – to speak of it would only have stirred the ashes. Why fan the flames of a fire you are trying to put out?'

Elizabeth nodded, as if she understood, albeit a little grudgingly. 'Of course, I guessed that there was something – some mutual fondness. But I wanted you to tell me yourself.'

'Did Darcy know?'

'No more than I. He thought that there had been some attachment. I don't believe Darcy has spoken of you to his cousin these last months, except to say that you had enquired after him.'

'And did Fitzwilliam tell Darcy then?'

'No. Nothing.'

'He has not spoken of me?'

'Never,' said Elizabeth, but seeing Charlotte's face, she added more gently, 'But neither had you of him, until just now.'

They sat in silence, both thinking, wondering, hearing the faint scuffles of staff and the whistle of birdsong from the garden.

Charlotte broke it. 'Tell me how he fares now. Is he well? Is he happy?'

Elizabeth blinked. 'Oh, I have no idea. I have not seen him for months.'

Charlotte frowned in confusion. 'He is no longer staying with you?'

'He left us in March. He was much recovered and felt he had become a burden on the household, despite our protestations to the contrary. His pride would not allow him to stay longer.'

'But where did he go?' Charlotte asked, her tone now agitated.

'I do not know,' said Elizabeth defensively. 'He told us he had business to conduct and friends he could stay with. He would not be specific, and we would not push him for a plan; it was his own business. I must say, after months of inaction, we were pleased to see him being so determined and … independent.'

'Oh.' Charlotte had a pang of that same feeling she had had after receiving Lady Catherine's bundle of letters: a feeling of being stopped in her tracks.

'Is there anything remaining between you?' asked Elizabeth. 'Do you still have … feelings for him? Your life already seems so happy and full.'

'It is,' Charlotte acknowledged, smiling. She did not add: *But a life may become happier and fuller.*

As if in confirmation of Charlotte's thoughts, Sofia's gurgles could now be heard outside in the hall. Elizabeth rose instinctively to go to her. 'I must be making my way back,' she said, walking to the door.

'Of course.'

Sofia was lying in a cosy bassinet, quite content to be placed in the carriage – Frances, by contrast, was grim-faced, anticipating the gastric horrors that awaited.

Any awkwardness of minutes ago was now forgotten. The women embraced one another before Elizabeth climbed inside – but just before the carriage door shut, she clasped Charlotte's hand in hers and said, 'I wish you joy in your life. That is all.'

Smiling back at her, Charlotte said simply, 'I have had it.'

1790
MERYTON

Mrs Lucas found her son, John, wailing in the pantry. She went to him, flooded with sorrow to see him so distressed. With some difficulty – allowing for a heavily pregnant belly – she got down on her knees. 'What is it, my darling?'

'Archie has gone! He's lost!'

She pulled her son to her and held him. Poor little John, only four, loved the family rabbit very dearly.

'I am sure he is not gone. Is he not in the run?'

Between sobs, John shook his head.

Holding his pudgy little hand, Mrs Lucas went out into their garden. Their home, a middle-size townhouse on the west side of Meryton, was a pleasant one, although she worried that it would soon become snug for their growing family, with Charlotte, John, little James in the crib, and another on the way.

She led John to the generous-sized run they had created for Archie, the black and white rabbit who had lived longer than anyone had imagined – and longer than some had hoped. But he was now a part of the family. *Archie has proportionately more generous quarters than anyone,* thought Mrs Lucas ruefully.

Archie belonged to Charlotte, really; it was to her that Mr Lucas had proudly presented the creature – a gift from an eccentric foreign trader – and Charlotte had taken to having a pet immediately, loving him wholeheartedly and kindly sharing him with her younger brother. But whereas in John's arms, the rabbit usually wriggled, terrified, with Charlotte, he would sit very still for a good length of time, assured by her steadiness and her quiet nature.

'Are you sure he is not in there somewhere?' asked Mrs Lucas, scanning the large patch of ground edged with wooden planks where Archie was often let out to enjoy some freedom, under Charlotte's supervision.

But, no, she checked all over the run and inside the hutch, and it appeared John was right: Archie was not there. And further searching of the house and grounds failed to locate him.

When she returned, Mrs Lucas found Charlotte comforting John, sitting on the steps of the terrace, her arm around his shoulders. She was a good sister – and thank heaven for that. Mrs Lucas would need help in the years to come. She hoped this would be her last; four was plenty. She was comforted to have two boys already, with only one daughter so far to marry off – that should be easy enough.

Due to some miracle – or to Archie's complete indifference to the local countryside – he was found that evening. Mr Lucas went out with fairly low expectations of success, but soon found the beloved creature, shaking and cold, hiding under a hedge about ten yards from the back of their garden. The news brought great jubilance to the household, particularly to John.

When Mrs Lucas tucked her daughter in at bedtime, she made a point of saying to her, 'You were very kind to your brother today, darling. You're a good girl.'

Charlotte smiled drowsily; she was ready for sleep. 'He was very sad.'

'He was. But were you not sad as well?

Charlotte shook her head.

'Why not? Wouldn't you miss Archie if he went away?'

'Yes,' responded her daughter, her eyes now falling shut, 'I just knew he'd come back to me.'

CHAPTER XV

'Let me know when Mr Thacker arrives, Brooke; he is a little late, and I want to be ready for him. He is taking me to see a new tenant today.'

'Yes, madam.'

Charlotte was in her study. It was a warm June day, and she was keen to get out into the sunshine, but first, she must write to Lady Catherine, who had demanded an urgent reply – indeed, she accepted no other kind – regarding Charlotte's plan for the summer.

Dear Lady Catherine,

I thank you for your kind invitation, and I would be very glad to accept, for some part of it. I am to stay with the Darcys in London for two weeks towards the end of the season, but I could come to stay at your pleasure, after that. I send on a message from—

'I see Mr Thacker approaching, madam!' said Brooke, poking her head through the door.

'Thank you.' Charlotte put her pen down and glanced through the study window as Brooke returned to her work. Yes, she could just make him out, far down the bottom of the drive.

Fetching her bonnet and her green spencer from the hook in the hall, she stood, pushed her shoes on and then stepped over the threshold. She had determined to close the distance between them to save some time. She had her eyes fixed on him now. He was on foot, leading his horse, which seemed strange; he should be in a hurry so as not to delay them further.

But then, a few steps from her front door, she slowed her pace, for she could perceive that it was not Thacker after all. The man making his way towards her had a tanned, worn face like her steward, but he was younger, with brown hair instead of grey. He walked with a slightly odd gait, heavy steps, but his eyes were looking squarely ahead. He led beside him a brown horse with white feet, and he carried his jacket slung over one shoulder.

He did not alter his pace or his course but kept on marching, marching, steadily towards her, in a straight line. As he got closer, and he could see her, he began to smile, broadly, but with tears in his eyes. The joy she saw in his face as he looked at her answered any question she had. He was her colonel. And he was here.

Charlotte made a choice. She started to walk towards him. She dropped her bonnet, dropped her spencer, and walked faster, and then she was running down the drive, almost tripping because she would not look away for a second from the man in front of her, for fear he would disappear.

He stopped a few yards short of her, readying himself to catch her because she was not going to stop. She would never stop again. She ran, and she ran, and she leapt.

✻ 1822
LONGBOURN

Longbourn was full. Mrs Brooke and all the staff were busier than ever, for every bedroom was in use and the nursery bursting at the seams. But in truth, the housekeeper was rather enjoying having a full house to serve, and the guests were almost as well known to her as her master and mistress.

It was a languid summer's day, and the hazy yellow afternoon light shone through the windows of the drawing room. Mrs Brooke served tea to the assembled party, bending to pour for Mrs Thacker and Lady Lucas, who were settled on the chaise-longue, each with an embroidery in their hand, relaxed in each other's quiet company. Mrs Thacker looked through the window to check on her son, who had fallen rather under the power of Sofia Darcy – who, at three years his junior, was quite the one in charge. They were both climbing what looked, to Brooke, like a dangerously tall tree, though their parents seemed unperturbed. Mr Thacker, looking older these days, sat heavily on a settee, deep in conversation with Mr Denny about some financial interest that sounded tedious to her ears.

Lady Catherine was positioned on the grandest chair available to her and was enjoying the attentions of Sir William Lucas. Of all the assembled party, he was the one most uniquely qualified to deal with her, being both an endlessly patient man and genuinely delighted by acquaintance with the aristocracy. Mrs Brooke was very fond of him.

Meanwhile, her mistress sat with Elizabeth, the two of them rolling with laughter as usual, while Charlotte's sister Maria was out on the terrace with the two littlest children, James and Harriet, both four years old and both fond of trouble. Brooke allowed herself a moment to regard them affectionately.

The little boy came running in and threw himself at his mother, with the abandon only an infant can muster, unsettling her tea. 'Mama, Harrie pushed me over.'

Charlotte picked him up, a groan escaping her at the effort, setting him on her knee. 'Are you hurt?'

His bottom lip protruded, and he nodded, nestling his face into her bosom.

She kissed the top of his head. 'Oh dear. Where does it hurt?'

He pointed at his knee.

Charlotte examined it – it was untouched. She kissed it. 'Is that better?'

He nodded.

'Do you want to go back and play with your cousin or stay here with me?'

He deliberated for some time. 'Go back.'

'Very well.'

She kissed him again and set him down, then watched as he bounded back outside, very nearly knocking over Harriet in the process.

Charlotte looked across the room to where Richard stood at the mantelpiece, talking to Darcy – his eyes were already on her, and he had clearly observed the little drama with their son.

Charlotte raised her eyebrows at him, and they smiled warmly at each other, Richard shaking his head and chuckling, before turning back to his cousin. Charlotte let her eyes rest on him a moment, as he stood at the mantelpiece, in their sage-green drawing room, surrounded by a family whom he never thought he would have.

Elizabeth saw her looking and poked her gently. 'Stop fixing eyes on your own husband – it is unseemly.'

Charlotte laughed. 'How do you know I was not looking at yours?'

Elizabeth smiled, and then, turning to look again at the two cousins, spoke more seriously. 'We chose wisely.'

'Not necessarily,' said Charlotte, an irreverent smile playing on her face.

Elizabeth made a show of being shocked. 'What do you mean?'

'Happiness in marriage is entirely a matter of chance.'

'You said that before you married Mr Collins ...'

'Well, I stand by it.'

Elizabeth made a face of incredulity.

'I do,' continued Charlotte. 'No choice is guaranteed to make one happy. Darcy improved between your first meeting and your engagement, but he might have turned out to be very dull.'

'That outcome remains unclear.'

Charlotte grinned. 'And dear Collins was ... priggish, but ultimately, he looked after me very well. And as for Richard ... it was a risk, was it not? A troubled, wounded soldier on half-pay? Hardly a sure bet.'

'So, you take no credit for the choices you have made?'

'I made some terrible choices,' said Charlotte, 'and some wise ones.' She looked once more at her husband, who was idly brushing his grey-streaked hair from his forehead.

'Then it would seem fortune has smiled on us both.'

Charlotte could not disagree with that. She looked around the room at the familiar faces she held dear and sipped her tea, smiling. She sat back, convinced that, whether by choice or by luck, she had found her peace.

AUTHOR'S NOTE

The description of Pemberley – in particular of the chapel, the gardens and the maze – is closely based on Chatsworth in Derbyshire. The maze there wasn't actually created until the twentieth century but it felt so right for Charlotte and Fitzwilliam's first kiss that I couldn't resist including it, and I felt that, as hedge mazes did exist at that time, such as the one at Hampton Court Palace, it wouldn't hurt.

Weddings in the Regency period were usually not large affairs, unless it was a royal wedding or similar – they were usually just a simple ceremony conducted in the local church, attended by close family. In this book, Charlotte's wedding follows this tradition. Elizabeth's does not. With an estate like Pemberley at their disposal, and with such strong affection for it, the Darcys might well have used the chapel there, and I liked the idea of Elizabeth doing something a bit different and unexpected. Similarly, while white was a popular colour of dress in this society, wedding dresses were not customarily white until later in the century so it felt fitting for Elizabeth to choose a white dress while Charlotte wore a more muted blue.

While I have attempted to be faithful to *Pride and Prejudice* wherever possible in the recounting of its events, I have erred from it in a few places, one of which is the aftermath of Elizabeth's engagement to Darcy, at the very end of the novel. Austen writes that the Collinses, as a pair, travel to Hertfordshire, escaping the anger of Lady Catherine. In my story, they remain in Hunsford immediately after the engagement, due to Charlotte's condition, and then it is Charlotte who travels to the wedding, while Mr Collins stays behind.

Colonel Fitzwilliam was presented to us in *Pride and Prejudice* as 'about thirty' years old. After a great deal of consulting, it seemed a stretch for any man, in this period, to make colonel in the regular army by thirty, even with a fortune and an impeccable reputation (neither of which Fitzwilliam had). Working closely with Dr Zack White, I pieced together a detailed career for Richard Fitzwilliam, starting as an ensign in his teens and allowing for semi-regular commissions when money and circumstances would allow. He enters my novel (and that is where we meet him in *Pride and Prejudice*) at the age of 34, which was the youngest a colonel could realistically have been, and I made it so that even then, he had achieved the rank only weeks earlier. I also killed off his father, the Earl, to better fit the story and his character. My apologies.

There was also the question of how a colonel might be at liberty to spend time with his aunt and with new acquaintances, while the Peninsular War was at its height. He should by any normal expectation have been in Spain. I have tried to write a version of his story which respects Austen's introduction of a charming young colonel in Kent, while honouring the realities of what would have been expected of him, and what might well have befallen a colonel during these years. It would have taken a great deal for him to have been allowed to return to England, and so a great deal is what he goes through.

The letters from Fitzwilliam in Volume Three are based on the movements of the army during those dates, once Fitzwilliam had made his way to Spain and received orders. The details of the Battle of Vitoria and of the Siege of San Sebastián are based on various letters and accounts. I have drawn on the real lives of men such as General Sir Galbraith Lowry Cole, who was the second son of the Earl of Enniskillen and very troubled by a lack of money, and who was injured first at the Battle of Albuera, and more seriously at Salamanca, as well as the letters of Colonel Sir Augustus Simon Frazer, who fought in the battles of Salamanca, Vitoria and the Siege of San Sebastián. I also consulted the archive of letters from Horse Guards from the 1830s.

The story which Colonel Fitzwilliam tells the Lucas family about Mrs Fontaine, who accompanied her husband to war and searched for him on the battlefield of Salamanca, is based on the true story of Susanna Dalbiac and her husband Lieutenant-General Sir James Dalbiac.

The announcement of Fitzwilliam's injury in *The Gazette*, found by Charlotte in her father's study, is taken from the real listings of the injured and dead following the Siege of San Sebastián, in *The London Gazette* on 20 September 1813, which is available to view online.

Fordyce's sermons are, of course, mentioned in *Pride and Prejudice* and his *Sermons to Young Women*, which was wildly popular at the time and features heavily in this story, influencing Smithson's and Collins's views. The words Charlotte speaks to her husband as he is dying are from Fordyce's 'A Sermon Occasioned by the Death of Rev. Dr. Samuel Lawrence'.

Mr Collins dies from undiagnosed appendicitis, one of many afflictions which would not have been treatable at the time.

The details of the entail, discussed between Charlotte and Mr Noakes, are based on a combination of my own invention and on what Austen implies in *Pride and Prejudice*, but I thought it was important to elaborate a little, keeping closely to a legal framework that would have existed then. I wanted to be more precise because an entail in itself (and Austen mostly refers only to an 'entail') was fairly easy to bar, so it casts some doubt on Mr Bennet's character if we believe he could have in fact saved his wife and daughters from disinheritance but simply failed to do so.

A strict settlement, fixed for a certain amount of time or a certain number of generations, has precedent in the period and fits the job well of honouring Mr Bennet's character, and allowing Collins to have the ability, once the strict settlement had expired, to then bar the entail, through 'suffering a common recovery'. This is more detail than you probably need but I found it rather interesting and if you do, you might enjoy Treitel's 'Jane Austen and The Law' or Peter Appel's 'A Funhouse Mirror of Law'.

Denny, after leaving the militia, goes to work for a respectable wine merchant, Berry's. This is a real company, Britain's oldest wine and spirit merchant, founded in 1698. It holds two royal warrants, and still operates, as it did in 1813, at 3 St James's Street. It is now Berry Bros. & Rudd, but would have been known then as Berry's.

FURTHER READING

Hughes-Hallet, Penelope, *My Dear Cassandra: The Illustrated Letters of Jane Austen*, Collins & Brown, 1990

Kelly, Helena, *Jane Austen, the Secret Radical*, Icon Books, 2016

Muir, Rory, *Gentlemen of Uncertain Fortune: How Younger Sons Made their Way in Jane Austen's England*, Yale University Press, 2019

Muir, Rory, *Love and Marriage in the Age of Jane Austen*, Yale University Press, 2024

Muir, Rory, *Wellington: The Path to Victory 1769-1814*, Yale University Press, 2015

Mullan, John, *What Matters in Jane Austen? Twenty Essential Questions Answered*, Bloomsbury Publishing, 2013

ACKNOWLEDGEMENTS

This book has been a leap of faith for everyone involved, including myself. I had the rough idea for this story – a pairing of Charlotte and Fitzwilliam – a few years ago, but it would never have become this novel without the belief and support of the following people.

My first editor, Anna Mrowiec, who expected me to write a non-fiction book about Austen and instead got a surprise in our first meeting, when I pitched her a fan fiction passion project, and she backed it straight away. Thank you for your patience, your wisdom and your enthusiasm – I knew working with someone who was as much of an Austen geek as me would be a good call! Thank you for *Sir William Lucas cutting his potato into twelve equal parts*, and other gems you contributed.

My second editor, Kate Norman, who took over the book with such care and attention and who has been an insightful and supportive guiding hand on the path to publication.

And to my US editor, Gaby Mongelli, who has championed the book and lovingly prepared it for the US Austenites!

Thank you to Kallie Townsend and Helena Fouracre whose work in the PR and marketing of the novel has been brilliant and inspired. Thank you for putting so much into it! To Daisy Woods, who designed the beautiful cover which suits the book perfectly.

To Katie Lumsden, my copyeditor, who is so clever and so good at what she does; understanding the period, and Austen, so well, but leaving room for my own style and quirks. And to Joe Murray, my proofreader, who worked so hard on the final rounds!

A huge thank you to Dr Zack White. Without his incredible knowledge of the Napoleonic wars, the intricate details of every battle, of army life both on the home front and abroad, this book could not have been written. We have joked that there is now a backstory to Colonel Fitzwilliam that is so complete, sitting waiting, that we might owe him a novel of his own!

Thank you to Professor Hannah Greig for your wise counsel on subjects such as weddings, funerals, the Regency high street, manners, balls, carriage rides and all manner of small details. Thanks for reminding me that while social norms existed, so too did people's whims and desires, and will to break the rules!

To Dr David Foster, thank you for taking the time to help me understand historical inheritance law, which is somehow both more complicated and less complicated than I had been making it! Thanks to you, Charlotte got her home!

To Dr Sumita Sinha for the gruesome task of detailing what appendicitis would look like if untreated. What a lovely way to hear from an old school friend!

To Dr Rory Muir, whose books have been the bedrock of my research, particularly *Gentlemen of Uncertain Fortune*, and who was kind enough to consult with me about my plotlines and offer helpful suggestions – Denny owes you his thriving career as a wine merchant!

My husband Marcus has spent hours listening to me when I have been stuck on a storyline, chatting to me when I have been excited about a character breakthrough, and offering up ideas and inspiration to keep my engine running when it had come to a halt. This is not his favourite genre and yet he has shared it with me without reservation, and has also taken our son out for walks so I could write in peace. Thank you, I love you.

My agent, Sophie, who has always backed me to do the things I have a passion for, even if they don't really follow a straight path.

Writing a non-comedy novel wasn't a natural next step for me – it took me out of the comedy game for six months, and was a risk, and the deadline seemed totally undoable, but she said, 'if anyone can do this, you can.' She encouraged me to follow my heart and my instinct, as she always does, and I am always grateful.

To the cast of Austentatious for telling hundreds of Austen stories with me for the last fifteen years, and to the entire team behind the 1995 television production of *Pride and Prejudice*, whom I don't know but to whom I owe a debt of gratitude; it is that production (viewed so many times over the years) which made me fall in love with Austen first. I have loved Austen's novels, obviously, but it was the '95 *P&P* that lit the flame.

Lastly, of course, to Jane Austen. A woman who has shaped my career in many different ways. Her books contain so much more than country life and manners. They pose the same questions about life, love, desire, money, and choice, which we ask today. The answers are not so very different.